KATHERINE RAMSLAND

TRACK THE RIPPER

BOOK TWO OF *THE HEARTS OF DARKNESS* SERIES

For more information contact:
Riverdale Avenue Books
5676 Riverdale Avenue
Riverdale, NY 10471.

www.riverdaleavebooks.com

Design by www.formatting4U.com
Cover design by Scott Carpenter

Digital ISBN: 9781626014664
Print ISBN: 9781626014688

First Edition July 2018

What they are saying about Katherine Ramsland's books

Praise for *Confession of a Serial Killer:*

"Based on her extensive, years-long communications with Dennis Rader, Katherine Ramsland's CONFESSION OF A SERIAL KILLER not only presents a definitive portrait of one of our country's most infamous modern criminals—the self-named "BTK Killer"— but provides a uniquely illuminating look into the workings of the psychopathic mind. Among other revelations, we learn that the subject's code name for a serial killer is "Minotaur"—a peculiarly apt term, given his dark and twisted psychology. By combining Rader's autobiographical writings with her own expert commentary, Ramsland guides us through that terrifying labyrinth, shedding brilliant light on every shadowy corner along the way."
—Harold Schechter, author of *The Serial Killer Files*

"Dr. Ramsland offers us insights into the mind of a serial killer rarely seen in criminological literature. I could not put it down. I am absolutely fascinated in her ability to forge a relationship with BTK that allowed him to share the inner most secrets of his Dark Side. This is a must read book for anyone wanting to understand the fantasies, behaviors and mind-set of one of the most notorious serial sexual predators of our time."
—Eric W. Hickey, Ph.D., author of *Serial Killers and their Victims*

"Katherine Ramsland has crafted a one-of-a-kind book, one that allows the reader to journey directly into the mind of BTK, aka Dennis Rader, a serial killer who eluded authorities for over 30 years. I could ramble on effusively about what she has accomplished through her dialogue with Rader and her review of tons of prime source material, but I won't. Just know this: It's a hell of a book. Buy it. Read it. It may keep you up at night, but you won't regret it."
—Gregg McCrary, former FBI Profiler

"I wish I knew then, what I know now. Katherine Ramsland has peeled back the layers of this serial killer. Her work not only benefits the families of the victims, but also will be cathartic for our community as a whole to understand how evil exists."
—Nola Tedesco Foulston, Esq.
Former Sedgwick County District Attorney

"Ramsland's books are incisive and thorough, and demonstrate a depth of knowledge not only about criminal behavior, but about human behavior as well. She has the rare ability to explain complex phenomena in simple terms."
— Dr. Louis Schlesinger, professor of forensic psychology, John Jay College of Criminal Justice

"Dr. Ramsland has the ability to comprehend complex issues, analyze them meticulously, and express her opinions and conclusions in a completely objective manner."
— Cyril Wecht, Past President, American Academy of Forensic Sciences

Praise for *Inside the Minds of Healthcare Serial Killers*

"Timely and riveting...
— Beatrice Yorker, Dean, College of Healthcare and Human Services, Cal State, LA

Praise for *Beating the Devil's Game*

"Once again Katherine Ramsland has brilliantly captured the insights and drama of some fascinating cases."
— Dr. Henry C. Lee,

Praise for *The Real Life of a Forensic Scientist*

"... strongly recommended for every practitioner, student, and devotee of this exciting profession."
— Dr. Cyril Wecht, past president of American Academy of Forensic Sciences

"A must read for the CSI crowd."
— Dr. Michael Baden, former chief medical examiner, NYC
Praise for *Ghost: Investigating the Other Side*

"The best book of its kind I've ever read."
— Dean Koontz, *New York Times* bestselling author

"Ramsland is a master of foreboding."
— *Publishers Weekly*

Chapter One

I'd just helped save the world. I thought I deserved to get laid. But then I learned I'd made the world much more dangerous.

I'd just boarded a private jet when I heard a male TV commentator's voice. "The news is just coming in. It's a parent's worst nightmare! A security guard and four staff members were killed this morning as parents dropped off their children at Fountainbridge Daycare, near London. It seems to have been an ambush. Two teachers are in critical condition."

A female anchor with Middle Eastern features took over. "A teacher's aide was shot as she tried to protect two children, and others were rushed to a hospital with serious injuries. Witnesses described several gunmen, suggesting a terrorist act, but no one has claimed credit. We're hearing reports of at least one child carried off. Others are missing. Medical personnel are arriving. This is an ongoing situation. Stay tuned for updates. We will bring it to you as we learn more."

The camera cut to an agitated young man out of breath. "There was a lot of screaming!" he said. "I heard shooting! Kids were running. I ran outside, but I didn't know what to do! I saw a dark van speed away, going south."

Next, a middle-aged woman with red hair, being interviewed in a calmer context, explained the daycare's mission. "We strive for security and quality in our program. This is an excellent facility for young families—"

The male anchor cut in. "We're hearing now about injuries."

It felt surreal. I sat in a white leather swivel chair in a pine-scented cabin of a luxury Airbus watching this terrorist event unfold on a large-screen TV. Elegant glass plates of perfectly arranged cheese and apple slices sat on a Danish-Modern style teak table. On-screen, people sorted through chaos.

This was the youngest group of victims I'd ever seen. Kids as young as four were in critical condition. Some had been abducted.

And I knew there was far more to this story than these newscasters would ever know.

I focused on the news report to block the sense of dread that twisted my stomach. Why the hell hadn't I left this plane when I'd had the chance? Too late now. We'd taken off. My stupid romantic ideas about flying to Paris for a cup of coffee at a quiet sidewalk café with the supernatural creature I'd just seduced had evaporated. I was here; Sitri was not.

Earlier that evening, just a day after an occult group had killed my father during their murder spree, Sitri had urged me to come with him. He'd said that my life as an NYPD detective was over. I was one of the *noea*, the children of human/angel couplings, and I belonged with others like myself. He was right. I was ready. But I'd hoped for time to adjust, and to be with *him*, not be thrust into a new emergency.

The British news anchors looked alarmed as they announced another shooting at a daycare in Norway. Still no group claiming credit.

Sitri had brought me on his Ducati racing bike to a remote airstrip. I'd expected him to board the rumbling Airbus with me, but he'd stayed on the bike. "I will see you in Paris," he'd promised.

"You're not going with me?"

"I'm needed elsewhere. Get some sleep while you can."

I'd been about to say, *forget it, take me back home*, when a slender brown-skinned woman in a stylish gray Kiely dress appeared at the top of the airstairs and gestured for me to come. Her black hair was swept so perfectly into a knotted side ponytail that I'd felt ridiculous in my throw-on jeans and T-shirt under Sitri's leather jacket. He'd said he needed me, so I'd jumped on his bike. I hadn't realized I'd be on display.

"Adria is *noea*, like you." He'd gestured toward this woman. "She can show you what to do."

"But—"

He'd revved the black Ducati and was gone. I'd watched him disappear, astonished. It was as if our heated encounter had never happened. He'd quite literally left me in the dust.

2

"Come!" Adria gestured.

Self-conscious over my cuts and bruises, I'd climbed the steps. "I should get a cab and go back."

She looked surprised. "*Non*, not at all! *S'il vous plaît*. Come in!" She introduced herself. Her accent was French and her Dior perfume made me feel even plainer. "We've been waiting for you." She touched my tangled blond hair. "We can fix this in here. It is time for you to return."

"Return?"

"Come in, so I can close the door. Quick! We must be on our way."

"I don't have my passport. I can't—"

"*Ne vous inquiétez pas*. We have it. You will have everything you need."

So, that's how I was on the plane now, learning the terrible news. Adria had motioned for me to sit in this chair, so we could hear the latest. I snuck a glance around the cabin. It was so sturdy I barely heard the engine's hum. If this was Sitri's plane, he had money. A *lot* of money. I wondered what part I could possibly play. Besides some detective skills, I had no resources.

Adria gestured toward a woman with pale skin and boy-cut auburn hair on the other side of the cabin. Her back to us, she talked urgently on her phone with a refined Irish accent. Her creamy silk blouse and short black skirt showed the same slender build and height as me. "That is Leith," Adria said. "Please excuse her manner. Even at her best, she can be abrupt."

I heard her say, "How many?" and then, "He should be there by now. He'll find you."

I wondered if she meant Sitri. He could travel faster than this plane, I'd learned. Or maybe she meant the other *ma'lakh*, Pascher. He was also in this band of celestial warriors. I'd met two, but I'd seen others. My hasty lessons had been thrust at me recently, along with some hasty thrusting, and I had a thousand questions.

On the screen, news anchors seemed confused as they reviewed what little they knew. Terrorism experts were on the phones to offer their ideas and onscreen crawlers suggested hysterical feedback from social media. I looked at Adria. I didn't know if she realized that I'd just stopped a lunatic who claimed to be Jack the Ripper from

3

coordinating a world-ending catastrophe. Some of his associates were dead, but he'd escaped. "Is this about us?"

Adria nodded. "*Oui*, they had a back-up plan. They are wasting no time."

I stared at her. "We're heading into another fight?"

She touched my shoulder. "*Je suis désolé*, I'm so sorry. I know you need rest."

She was right. I'd just lost my father and had barely begun to grieve. I had injuries, too. Touching my neck, I remembered my companion from that struggle. Her injuries had been worse. If not for her, I would've died. "Do you know Charmaine?"

"*Oui*, of course. She is in back."

"She's here? Is she all right?"

"Come with me."

Adria led me down a narrow hall and opened a door to a small bedroom with dim lighting that smelled of antiseptic salve. On a double bed, under a tan blanket, lay Charmaine. Her slender Asian build hardly raised the blanket, except for over the extra padding around her injured left leg. Her almond eyes were closed and her black hair was pulled back. I flinched at her swollen face and hesitated to wake her. She probably hated me. Her condition was my fault. Just last night, before midnight, she'd begged me to kill her. The vampire who'd broken her leg and crushed her ribs had contaminated her blood. She'd said it would separate her forever from Pascher, her lover. She preferred to die.

I hadn't done it. Charmaine, who'd owed me nothing, had saved me during the fiery melee. Just in time, Pascher had arrived and carried her out. We hadn't spoken since that awful moment. I'd known her just a day, but I needed contact with something familiar, so I touched her hand. Aside from shallow breathing, she didn't stir. I looked at Adria. "Will she be okay?"

"Physically, she can heal. As for the rest…" She shrugged.

"You don't have some way to…to… cleanse her?"

"We have healers. They can tell us."

"Where's Pascher?" He and Charmaine had shown me the first bond I'd seen between a *noea* and a *ma'lakh*. I'd thought it was the stuff of ancient tales, but then I'd seen them together. Their intense heat for each other had given me some lusty ideas about Sitri. Except that he'd basically just abandoned me.

4

In the other room, Leith let out an agonized shout. "No…!"

Adria ran out. I followed.

"They took two in Oslo!" Leith said. "At least three from London."

"More than half a dozen children are confirmed missing," said the female anchor. "A search is underway. It's hoped that some children might have escaped during the commotion. All security personnel are notifying local residents to be alert. Stay tuned to this breaking story."

There was some suggestion of a well-executed plan and the perpetrators waiting inside the buildings, but witness reports were conflicting. Leith dropped onto a leather loveseat with a look of dejection. Adria stared at the screen and hugged herself.

Leith's phone made a chirping sound. She sat up to answer. "Yes," she said. She glanced at me with narrowed eyes. "We know. But it's just three, right?"

I sat down and waited. The cabin air was thick with blame. Directed at me.

Leith ended her call. She stood, crossed over to me and held out a hand. "I'm sorry. Leith. I'm afraid we're in a bit of a state here."

I nodded. "I can see that. Do you know these missing kids?"

Leith and Adria looked at each other. I felt like that girl who came to a party but doesn't really belong.

"It's all right," I said. "You don't have to tell me anything. I don't even know what I'm doing here. Once we land, maybe someone can help me get back."

Adria frowned. "Back? Sitri said you're coming with us to your—"

A sharp glance and shake of Leith's head stopped her.

I held up my hands. "Obviously, I'm not privy to anything. I've only pieced together some story from the past few days about my mother that I hardly believe and I've made a hasty decision to come that I wish I hadn't." I was referring to the tale my aunt had told me. My mother, Kaitlyn, had engaged in some crazy threesome with a *ma'lakh* and a human to produce a unique child—me. I hadn't yet absorbed it. "I don't want to interfere. I'm not—"

"Get in here!"

Charmaine's throaty command startled us all. She sounded

5

angry, but at least I knew her better than these two. We'd fought vampires together. I returned to the bedroom, followed by Adria and Leith.

"He said he was going back for you," Charmaine croaked. She meant Sitri. It took effort for her to address me.

"Yes," I said. "He came, but he …" I shrugged. "He … baited me."

Char snorted. "Get used to it." She gestured for me to sit on the bed. I did, which made her clench her swollen eyes. Then she scanned the bruises on my neck where I'd been choked. "Be patient. This is what you need to know." She coughed. "You're going home. Keep your flat in Manhattan if you want, but you own a building in St.-Germaine. Kaitlyn gave it to Alexandre. Now it's yours. It's our command center. Five of us live there."

"What?" Alexandre was my father. My recently deceased father. "I would know if he—"

"No, you would not. There's very little about you that you know." Charmaine took a labored breath. "It's been kept from you, by design, to keep you safe. But now you must be told. You've been to this building. You were born there and you lived there as a child, but you won't remember. So stop fussing." She winced. "We brought you into this because we need you. If we don't get that ring back, we're *all* dead, including you."

Adria looked shocked, as if Charmaine had just revealed a secret.

The ring had been my mother's. It contained her special blood, formed into a diamond. She'd left it in my care and I'd let it fall into the wrong hands. A man who'd introduced himself as Scott Bateman, my father's protégé, had grabbed it. He'd told me then that *he* was Jack the Ripper. He'd offered other names he'd used, identities he'd stolen, but the *noea* knew him as Miegul.

"I don't understand," I said.

"Kaitlyn's blood is in the gem," Charmaine continued. "It carries vital information about our entire network. Generations of *noea* all over the world. Miegul can pierce our shield and locate us." She gestured toward the door. "They're already finding us. That out there, that shooting. It's the fourth one in less than six hours, and one of a dozen—" She coughed hard, and Adria poured some water and handed it to her. "A dozen abductions that no one has yet linked. Our kids are at those facilities. *Noea.* That's who they're taking."

"Who's doing this?" I asked. "And why?"

"I'll tell her," Adria said to Charmaine. "You rest."

Charmaine looked to her right. "Where's Pasch?"

"With Sitri, in London."

She made a move to get up, but Adria stopped her. "Pascher insisted that you not move. You can't do anything, anyway. We are monitoring the situation."

"What did I miss?"

Adria shook her head so subtly I almost missed it, but when Leith tapped my shoulder, I knew they still had secrets. "Let me show you the plane," she said, "in case you want to catch a nap or grab some food."

Annoyed, I allowed myself to be handled. I was an NYPD detective, after all, and I'd just helped thwart an event meant to shatter the earth. I thought they should give me more credit.

But this current catastrophe was at least partly my fault. Miegul was also a hybrid offspring, one of the few males that had escaped the *ma'lakhim* purge centuries ago. As I'd heard it, the females had been allowed to live while the males were slain. In retaliation, Miegul and his ilk hated—and hunted—*noea.* I hoped they hadn't grabbed the children for something horrible.

The door closed behind me and I heard Adria speak French urgently.

I followed Leith. The TV anchor was discussing three linked shootings, in London, Oslo, and Rome. Char had mentioned a fourth. Outside, I noticed light, although I knew we couldn't yet be near the sunrise. Leith showed me an opulent galley that smelled of freshly brewed French coffee and offered me a glass of wine.

"Definitely," I said.

"*Vin Malique*, coming up." She poured a garnet-colored liquid for both of us. Considering the luxury that surrounded me, I wasn't surprised at its quality. The wine seemed to melt into my tongue.

Did the *ma'lakhim* drink wine, I wondered? I didn't know exactly what they were except that they were associated with the paintings of warrior angels that graced many museums. They certainly weren't *angels* in the sentimental sense; they burned with fire, as ready to destroy as protect. Their fatal flaw, according to the stories, was their lust for human females, especially for our blood.

Just 24 hours earlier, I'd used mine to seduce Sitri. I'd pushed it into his mouth, igniting a fire that brought us together. He'd filled me while pushing his tongue against my throat to take my blood. I'd intended to link to his mind, but he'd twisted it back on me, nearly disabling me. The sex had knocked my socks off. *What they can do*, Charmaine had warned, *you'll never give up*. I certainly wanted more. Even now, when I pressed the spot on my neck where his tongue had pierced my skin for blood, it sent an erotic wave straight to my crotch. I intended to have another go, first chance I got.

Leith watched me. Her greenish-blue eyes were large and pretty, highlighted with expertly applied plum liner, but her serious expression disturbed me. She looked at the bruise that peeked out from under the bandage on my neck, left by Miegul's hand.

"What?" I asked.

"I've heard about you. I just …wonder…."

"You have the advantage, then, as I've heard nothing about you. Not any of you."

Leith nodded. "You know we're *noea*, right? Like you, but we don't have your special parentage."

I heard a note of jealousy. "I plan to help with this pursuit, at Sitri's invitation. But don't worry. When we get my ring back, I'm going home."

She raised an eyebrow. With a mock toast, she said, "I doubt that."

I was about to retort when Adria interrupted. "Sitri says they're tracking us."

Sitri. He'd spoken with her but not me? Then I recalled: my blood had opened a connection between us, but Charmaine had made me block it.

"They've probably anticipated where we'll land," said Leith.

I felt like someone was turning me round and round, keeping me from getting my footing. "Can one of you please tell me what's going on? Who's tracking us? Who's grabbing your kids?"

Leith shrugged and looked away. Adria gestured for me to follow her. In Charmaine's room, she opened a locked cupboard and pulled out a wooden box that resembled an oversized tissue box cover

8

with an exquisitely painted glass top. She set it on the bedside table and gestured for me to sit down. Leith sat nearby. Charmaine watched me.

"I apologize for being blunt." Adria tapped the box. "Here is your father. Alexandre. His ashes."

I stared at it. My mouth went dry and my eyes welled up. I couldn't breathe. He'd died in a blazing fire in a mansion on Long Island, where'd we'd defeated Miegul's attempt to trap Sitri. I'd been there. The place had burned to the ground. I'd thought my father was gone, with no trace. A tear ran down my cheek as I touched the box. "How?"

"They can endure the heat," Adria said. She meant the *ma'lakhim*. I recalled Pascher telling me, "Our element is fire."

I looked at Char. Her eyes confirmed it. She'd been there, too. That moment flashed back when Dad had taken a bullet meant for me. I'd had just enough time to assure him I was proud of him and to kiss him good-bye before I had to flee from the fire. Everyone, including my partner on the NYPD, had thought he was a traitor, a criminal, a murderer, but he'd actually been a hero. I wiped my face and took the box in my hands.

Adria gave me a tissue. "He's revered among us. I thought you should know. He will be honored in a special place. But our immediate concern is you. You're Kaitlyn's daughter. To our enemies, you're a prize, so a lot of security surrounds this plane. But this weakens security for other *noea*, and Ignis is breaking through to grab our children."

"Ignis?"

"The *nejah* network—the males, like Miegul, and the *Ina*, which are the weakest *ma'lakhim*. They hate us. With the ring, they can locate us. We are getting our girls into safe places, but in some cases, we were too late."

I looked at my right hand. One small act of anger, yanking off my mother's ring, had caused a cataclysm. Sitri had been gracious not to blame me. He'd given no hint of the danger I'd punched into their world. *Our* world, because I was one of them. And I was on a plane that these Ignis assholes were tracking.

"Why do they want your children?" I asked.

"To recruit them," said Leith. "Or use them as bait."

"Bait?" But I already knew. Miegul had used me to lure Sitri. "Would they trade them for me?"

"No!" Charmaine shouted. "I *knew* you'd say that. Alexandre died to protect you. Don't be stupid!"

Leave it to Char to snap me back to reality.

Adria asked her to take it easy before she turned to me. "Dianysus, in your world, you were a detective. Just someone trying to do—"

"You're a *princess*!" Leith broke in. "You can't just go out and about and act on your own. They'd snap you up right off!"

I looked from one to the other. Not much was sinking in. But I knew a few things about my legendary mother, too.

I put my father's ashes on the table and sat up. "Let's get this straight. My mother took risks, right? I've heard that she was bold. She protected what she loved." I wasn't entirely sure about this, but they were listening. "I am *not* a princess. I'm the daughter of two— no *three*—warriors. You can try to stop me or you can join me. But I'll tell you this: I will be on the winning side."

Charmaine smirked. We'd already battled side-by-side. She, I knew, was with me. She looked at Adria. "Loose cannon. I told you."

"I accept the compliment." I touched Sitri's leather jacket over the inside pocket where I'd stashed my secret weapons: the *Book of Fate* and the mystical concave crystal that translated celestial codes. Napoleon had used this book. In *my* hands, it had led me to Sitri. Whatever lay ahead, I was ready. "Do we trust our pilot?"

Adria nodded. "Dorion. He's Sitri's … eh, what would you call it? Deputy?"

"Sitri's second officer, after Pascher," said Charmaine. "A *ma'lakh*."

"Then pour me another glass of that amazing wine and let's make a plan."

Chapter Two

Keys to doors to dangerous places must be deceptively simple; otherwise we wouldn't touch them.

After learning about other places we might land, I asked Adria for a private area. She showed me to a cramped cabin that looked like an office but had a bunk to sit on. I spotted my brown and gold Louis Vuitton luggage, which still bore Sitri's citrusy scent. That was comforting. Sort of.

I wasn't about to show anyone the *Book of Fate*—A.K.A, the *Oraculum*—although Adria had been curious. Sitri knew what a treasure it was. He'd saved it from the fire. I now knew it was too powerful to handle carelessly. In whatever way it worked as a reputed prognosticator, I'd seen it become a conduit. With it and the concave crystal I also carried, I could form a portal through which to lure angels, if I had the sigils that commanded them. My father, a historian with surprising resources, had acquired the crystal and *Oraculum*. People believed that both were in a museum, but they were wrong. At this moment I owned the items that an angel had secretly given to humans as a means to translate their language. Why the crystal worked with the *Oraculum*, an item that Napoleon had used to chart his battles, I didn't know. But it was easy to misuse. He'd done it, and so had I.

Yesterday, I'd forgotten a forbidden date for tapping its power, which had sparked this whole situation, but today I was safe. The device worked best with erotic energy. I'd discovered that pressing the spot where Sitri's tongue had punctured my skin just before all hell broke loose raised the heat. It hurt, but then it tickled my hungry places, opening me. I basked for a moment in the warm rush that ran to my breasts and arched my back. It was easy to recall the feeling of his muscular chest, his fingers exploring, his lips pressing, his cock

11

penetrating. His clothes had melted off him while he'd deftly removed mine. My fantasies hadn't come close to what it was like to be against him, imbibing his scent and gripping his taut buttocks.

I was breathing harder now, nearly moaning from need. But I controlled the tension to fuel the energy for this strange little book to work. I'd seen how Scott Bateman, a.k.a., Miegul, a.k.a., Jack the Ripper had tried to use it to trap Sitri. A diamond-shaped portal had emerged from the coded print on the middle set of pages. Because Miegul had blooded Sitri's sigil, Sitri had no choice. Sigils summon them. He had to come through. But he'd arrived with scorching fire, destroying the place while Miegul fled.

At the moment, I only needed the *Oraculum's* guidance. Over the past few days, it had given me warnings. I hadn't liked them but they'd been right. Tapping into my own heat, I opened it.

The pocket-size book operated as a list of questions and answers. Its limited set of questions corresponded to long lists of possible answers for each one. How they linked up to the questions depended on how I channeled the energy.

My first task was to select a question. I scanned the list. Not my love life…not my fortune…not future travel…. At the ninth question, I stopped. This was it: "Shall I be successful in my present undertaking?" I had an idea of how we could deflect our trackers, but I hoped for affirmation.

The link to an answer depended on how I drew four parallel lines of stars, allowing "the force" to use me to form the pattern. Then, I performed a set of calculations and compared my resulting pattern to those patterns on the list that corresponded to answers. I found my answer: *Success will depend much on perseverance.*

I slumped in disappointment. As usual, this response was highly interpretable. It gave me no sense of direction. Still, it was more positive than those from the past three days, about bad luck and enemies looking for me. Persevere, then. I would keep that in mind. But I needed more.

A knock on the door interrupted me. "Do you need anything?" It was Adria. She sounded impatient.

"I'm fine. I'll be out soon."

According to the rules, I couldn't ask the same question twice on the same day. I scanned the list again before I saw a question that hit home: "Will I recover my property?" I could focus on the ring. That was my ultimate mission, after all. But this was risky. If it told me no, I'd lost the race before I left the gate. Did I want to go there?

Adria was waiting. Now or never. I drew the stars and did the calculations. The answer was quick. As I read it, I let out my breath. *You will recover your property—unexpectedly.*

Whatever that meant. At least there was hope.

Still, I had no clear direction. I had to speak to Charmaine, alone. I slipped out and entered her room. Still awake, she was having trouble getting comfortable.

"I need this thing restored," I said, "my vision connection with Sitri. How do I do it?" When Sitri tasted my blood, he could see through my eyes. Charmaine had urged me to block it and shown me how. I wanted to reverse it.

Her voice was weak but firm. "No."

"Why not?"

"If they take us, our *affinité* reveals Sitri and Pascher."

Affinité. Good word. I liked it. "If they take us?"

She didn't answer. But she had this *affinité* thing with Pascher, so I persisted. "You're not connected?"

"Closed it... before... that house. Distracts them." She coughed so hard I cringed. "To reopen, he must be with you, and not blocking from his side. Can't do it alone."

"But after we blocked it, he could still see me. I wasn't invisible."

"Closed only the mind. Physical block is harder. Requires ingesting—" She coughed.

This was perplexing. Sometimes these *ma'lakhim* could see us, sometimes they couldn't. Sometimes they could actually see through our eyes. I needed to understand this thing better, but Charmaine was tired.

Frustrated, I left her. When I entered the main cabin, I heard the latest news. There'd been a fourth mass shooting in yet another country. Leith paced the length of the cabin, as if she wanted to claw her way out of the plane.

"It appears to be a coordinated assault," said the anchor. "We're trying to identify the source. No group has taken credit, but world leaders believe this is a terror attack." Several serious criminologists

13

Katherine Ramsland

and a military advisor with a deeply creased face made cryptic comments.

"They don't have a clue," said Adria.

Leith shook her head. "We don't, either. Nettaline hasn't learned anything yet."

"Nettaline?" I wondered how many more of these women there were.

"One of us," said Adria. "Her daughter, Sheine, was at Fountainbridge, one of the targeted daycares. We think they were looking for her, specifically."

"Why?"

"She has abilities they can use."

"How old?"

"Six."

"What will they do to her?"

Leith and Adria exchanged worried glances.

"It's too soon to say," Adria scolded her. "Maybe she got away. She's clever. Stop fretting till we know." To me, she said, "Do you still want to speak with Dorion?"

"Yes."

Adria showed me to the cockpit door and entered. I heard a resonant male voice, which I could now identify from its distinctly rich quality as *ma'lakh*. I was getting better at this. Adria beckoned for me to come in.

Dorion looked surprised that I wanted to confer with him, even guarded. As I sat in the co-pilot seat, he glanced at Sitri's mark on my throat, below the bandage. I assumed it gave me status.

Dorion was cute! He reminded me of an art teacher I'd had in my junior year in college. His silver hair curled loosely around his ears and he had that same flickering glow in his Persian blue eyes that I'd seen with Pascher and Sitri—like those electric candles that simulate real flames. Despite his smooth skin, I figured he was much older than he appeared.

I'd known about these creatures for just two days, but I tried to act as if discussing strategy with a *ma'lakh*, a warrior angel, was perfectly normal. It helped that he looked human. I hadn't channeled a plan from some supernatural force as I'd hoped, but I'd asked for a meeting so I devised a more human idea. I suggested skirting our

14

target runway, by twisting away at the last minute toward an airstrip further south. Deflect their expectations.

Dorion nodded. "I will ask Pascher."

I perked up. "Should I tell him? He knows me a little."

"It's done."

"Done... how?"

He pointed to his forehead. "We're efficient."

Interesting. High-speed telepathic communication.

"Did he approve?"

"Sitri did, but he directed me to a different place."

I blinked. Faster than I could think it, he'd shot a message to Pascher, who'd conveyed it to Sitri, who'd considered and revised it. Astonishing. But I felt left out. I wanted Sitri to talk to *me*. I had to remind myself that I was a newcomer. And I couldn't communicate telepathically. Still, there was something privileged about witnessing it.

As Dorion made adjustments with dials and switches, he kept glancing at me. I recalled my aunt saying that the *ma'lakhim* are fascinated with the gossipy parts of human lives. They're hooked on things that raise our emotional heat—love, anger, desperation, jealousy. "Like being addicted to reality shows," Aunt Krystal had said.

"Is there something you want to know?" I asked.

He looked forward and seemed to go still. I sensed I'd breached protocol, perhaps embarrassed him. "I don't really know how to act with... you... " I'd nearly said *your kind*, but that seemed insulting. "I mean, I don't know what I can or can't say."

He glanced at me in surprise, as if I could say anything, and why didn't I know this? Maybe I really *was* some kind of princess.

Just then, a faint yellow line along the horizon caught my attention. Sunrise. We were moving fast! "That's beautiful," I said.

Dorion pointed. "Look to the side." I briefly saw the shimmering outline of numerous faces, turned toward the sun. They flashed and vanished.

"It's quick," he said. "It's an effect from the first light."

"What was it?"

"Your escort."

I looked at him. "What?"

"They're always around you, but visible only at certain times."

I scanned the skies. They were gone. "I hate to say this," I told Dorion, "but that's kind of creepy."

He laughed. It broke the tension. "They're part of our network," he explained. "It's like a radar system. They alert Sitri if you're in danger. You see them as faces because your eyes process patterns, but they're just energy. The *diam*, we call them."

"So, they won't judge what I'm wearing behind my back?"

He smiled. "They won't give you any advice."

I liked him. Not just cute, he was easy to amuse. It gave me hope that I might soften Sitri's grim intensity. Granted, our few encounters had been in dire circumstances, but I believed that he'd have a smile as inspiring as Dorion's. I intended to find it.

"Why do I need these... *diam*?" I asked.

"For protection."

"I've done pretty well on my own."

He nodded, but his manner said there was more to the story.

"They've been around me for a while," I commented.

"Since you were born." He glanced at me. "You could see them when you were a child."

Another surprise. "You knew me then? Why don't I remember you?"

I had so many questions and now I had a *ma'lakh* who seemed willing to talk. But Adria interrupted us. She asked me to return to the main cabin.

"Later," I said to Dorion. He glanced at Adria.

When she shut the door to the cockpit, she said, "You shouldn't ask them things."

"Why not?"

"You put them on the spot. They don't want to be rude, but they answer to Sitri. He has his own timing for you. If you could please be patient—"

I stopped. "I don't get it. Why am I in the dark about all this? What can't anyone just tell me?"

Adria cocked her head. "*C'est pas... excusez-moi...*it's not that simple. You're like someone who's been asleep for 20 years. If you wake and discover everything at once, you will be overwhelmed. And we don't know how you will react."

She walked away and I followed. "It can't be that dramatic. I haven't been asleep. I've been in the world, just a different one."

"Not a different world," Adria corrected me. "This is a different universe."

"And it's one you might not like," Leith added. "You had to prove yourself as a female detective, right?"

I nodded. "Yes."

"Was it tough?"

"Yes."

"Multiply that times ten."

Chapter Three

I was relieved to finally land and prepare to leave that tense plane. I'd sensed that Adria was trying to manage me, while Leith viewed me as a tedious burden. I'd tried to spot the *diam* again, but nothing like that was visible outside.

We'd kept course for a private strip near Orly, but a quick turn to lose our tail had sent us north toward the English Channel. Unable to sleep, I'd held my father's ashes for a while and listened to the ominous news about murdered people and missing children. Leith had stayed on the phone, glancing at me several times.

The instant the door opened, Pascher entered as if he'd stepped *down* into the plane from thin air. I looked for Sitri, but Pascher was alone. Still, this gorgeous black-haired *ma'lakh*, dressed in jeans and a black shirt, reminded me of why I'd wanted to be here. Lean and graceful, he carried the sense of a serious mission.

These creatures opened up a profound new mystery about the universe. Their presence—and pleasing scent—filled the room. They all seemed to have blue eyes, in different shades. Sitri's were the darkest, with that purplish midnight cast, while Pascher's were cobalt and Dorion's a shade lighter.

Pascher strode through the cabin to the back. He emerged with Charmaine in his arms, her head pressed against his shoulder. As he passed me, he nodded acknowledgment. Although I was the reason she was hurt, I'd also saved her life.

Adria beckoned for me to follow him. I descended the stairs to a paved landing strip near a small building. The morning breeze caressed my skin and smelled of ocean, but sticky air foretold an uncomfortable day.

"Go with them," Adria said. "We'll take your luggage into the city."

Pascher and Dorion placed Charmaine into a waiting chopper, its engine running. Dorion got out, Pascher took the pilot seat on the right, and I climbed into a single fold-down seat in back, facing the bench seat on which they'd strapped Charmaine. Her petite frame just fit, with her head slightly raised.

"Sitri asks for your patience," said Pascher. "I am taking you to a *maison sécurisée*, a safe place."

I nodded. I had no context for what was happening, except that we were involved in this escalating international emergency. Sitri had given me the impression he was some kind of protector of the natural order. How could I make demands? Yet without resources, I felt off-balance. I wished I'd at least brought my gun. I was in France. I had no phone, no friends, and no weapon. Alexandre, my father, had kept the information from me that I now needed to navigate this world. Sitri had invited me here, but he'd abandoned me. I put noise-buffering headphones on Charmaine and myself before I fastened my harness-like seatbelt. Pascher took us up.

When we were in the air, I pondered what lay ahead. My father had said nothing about owning real estate in St.-Germain, not even when I'd stayed in Montmartre during a college semester abroad. I'd probably passed his building many times as I'd walked through the Latin Quarter. Why the secrecy?

We flew smoothly for ten minutes before I saw Pascher's hand tighten on the control stick. "Keep her steady," he said. I leaned forward and supported Charmaine. Pascher made a maneuver that jolted us and made Charmaine gasp. I saw flashes of light dart around us. Was this my radar shield?

I tried to hold Charmaine in place, but Pascher swung the chopper unpredictably. He dove and pulled it almost onto its right side. Char grabbed something for leverage and kept her eyes closed tight.

Something hit us. We lost altitude—and my stomach—but then leveled out. I wondered if our tail from the plane had figured out our deflection and come after us. I gripped my seat. Pascher picked up speed, grabbed something on his right, and took us higher.

I watched more flashes of green and orange light outside. The air grew colder. I pulled the leather jacket close and kept an eye on Charmaine.

19

"Up here." Pascher gestured to me.

I froze. He wanted me to co-pilot. I'd never flown a chopper. I'd been inside only three, including this one. I didn't want our safety in *my* hands. But what had I just said to Adria? I had to rise to this.

With a thumping heart, I unfastened my seatbelt and moved to the co-pilot seat to his left. I strapped myself in. Pascher showed me the collective control at my left side for going up and down, the pedals at my feet for switching direction and balancing the torque, the cyclic stick on the T-bar between us to move forward or backwards, and something about a throttle, correlator and governor. He pointed to some small metal switches overhead and glowing dials on the dashboard. While keeping control, he said something about a gauge for the rate of climb and another for engine power. I couldn't keep it straight.

He touched my hand. "This is just a precaution."

"We're going too fast. I might do something wrong!"

"You know how to do this. Focus on the controls. Think about what each one does. Forward, back, up, down, right, left, fast, slow. It's all about coordination and balance. Try it now while I'm here."

"*Here?* What?"

Something hit us again. The chopper shimmied. Charmaine gasped.

"What is it?" I asked. "Who's doing this?" My heart pounded so hard it hurt. I imagined us hurtling straight down to the ground. What did he mean, *you know how to do this*?

"Keep it steady and aim there."

I blinked at where he pointed. Past a thick bank of clouds I saw a multicolored flash.

"Be that warrior!" Charmaine shouted.

I pointed at each item and repeated what Pascher had said about its function. He corrected me twice. I took a deep breath and went through it again. I saw my hand shake when I pointed at a dial.

"The throttle is like on a motorcycle," he said, "except that it turns in the opposite direction. Remember that."

"Don't you dare jump out of here!" I warned. He'd done that in New York. But then, he'd had a real co-pilot. Would he risk Charmaine?

"Relax," he said. "It will come back."

"I've never—"

Then, it did feel ok. Not fine, but ok. When I gripped the cyclic, it felt right. I knew what to do. My feet relaxed slightly on the pedals. My leg muscles responded, as if I had body memories for this.

We veered off course, to the left, and pitched a little. I held my breath. But I focused as Pascher watched. He seemed calm, as if we were on the ground, training. He cautioned me to use a looser grip. When we veered right, I brought it under control.

I let out my breath. I shouldn't have had that extra glass of wine. But we held steady. Pascher nodded. "Like that. You have it."

"Don't go."

To my left, I saw a flash. The chopper bumped and shook. I gripped the cyclic and steadied the pedals. I was flying! I breathed in, sat back against the seat, and looked for Pascher's approval. But his seat was empty. I froze. We were now going to die!

Chapter Four

My heart thumped so hard I barely heard Charmaine say, "Don't panic! He's close."

Swallowing, I mentally checked off everything Pascher had shown me. I hoped I wouldn't steer us into something I couldn't see. At least the sun was up now. My shoulders tightened. *Balance*, he'd said. I had only to stay level and keep moving forward. Nothing tricky. Just keep us in the air. I looked for that flash of light.

"You've done it before," Charmaine said into her mic.

"I've never done this."

"You have. Sitri blacked it out, but you had lessons. It will come."

I didn't believe her. "Is Pascher coming back?"

"Just keep doing what you're doing."

Something threw us off. I gripped the controls as the chopper shuddered. A bright flash in front made me look away. I grabbed the throttle to open it, but the engine sputtered. We started to drop.

No! No! No!

"Opposite!" Char shouted. *Like a motorcycle, but the other way.*

I corrected. With a jolt, the engine caught and roared back. My heart was in my throat.

"Sorry, sorry!" I said. I swallowed and stared forward. My hands felt slippery. Why did they think I could do this? I tried to stay calm.

We veered left again and lost altitude. Char talked me through it. An intense throbbing in my ears shut out her voice. I saw a ball of light coming at us, so I turned right and took it up higher. Success! I breathed out. OK!

Then another flash.

"What do you see ahead?" Char asked.

I looked around. "Orange flashes. Is that good?"

"Take it backwards."

How? I looked for a rearview mirror where I expected one, but saw only a bar between the front windows. A small screen, like a smartphone, provided a limited view behind, as did a side mirror. What did I need? The collective. Forward, backward. I eased it and felt the momentum slow and then we moved in reverse.

We dropped. The chopper spun right. I gasped. I couldn't control it.

"Pedals!" Char yelled.

I concentrated on my feet. *Perseverance*, the *Oraculum* had said. It had promised success. Don't give up. But I wanted to.

"Push forward," said Char. "Take it down."

"What?"

"Dive. Then up, but careful. Not too fast."

Out of breath, I did what seemed right. I wiped sweat from my eyes. To my relief, my maneuvers worked. My throat was dry. This was crazy! I wasn't a pilot. My heart ached from pounding so hard and my fingers tingled. Maybe it *was* a good thing I'd had the wine. When we crashed, I wouldn't feel it as much.

I looked to my left and saw a green and blue swirl of light that expanded outward. Should I move? I was about to ask Char when I felt pressure on the T-bar and something touch my hand. I glanced right. Dorion sat in the pilot seat. *How did these guys do that?*

"I'll take it," he said. "Good work."

I heard Pascher's voice in back with Charmaine. "We'll be there soon," he told her.

I was relieved to let go. I sat back and clenched my fists to control my shaking. Beneath the jacket, my shirt felt damp. My heart still thumped and my mouth tasted like I'd been eating dust. I needed water.

"What was that?" I asked. "What just happened?"

"It was a blind attack," said Pascher. "Not targeted, so it was weak. They don't know about you yet. They were probing. It's over now. They won't follow us."

"Know about me?"

"Miegul knows we're hunting him. He doesn't yet know you're involved, but he's trying to find out. We have shields up. You're safe."

I took a breath and looked over at Dorion. "And how can you

guys just pop in and out like that? Or, is that something I already know? Like flying a helicopter?"

"Be patient," said Char. "Sitri decides."

Dorion winked at me, which helped me to relax. "Welcome to Paris," he said.

I looked outside. He was right. We were hovering over my beloved City of Light. Early morning fog blurred it, but I knew where we were.

We flew slowly over the northwest area. Below, I saw the buildings of Montmartre, "La Butte," crowded onto jumbled blocks of winding narrow streets. I knew it well. For three months, I'd lived in an apartment here with a great view of the city. I smiled. Finally, something felt familiar. If I were on the ground, I could find my way around.

I now realized there'd been a lot more to that semester than philosophy classes at the university. Apparently, I'd had helicopter lessons I couldn't recall. I suspected there was much more.

The lopsided pentagonal patch below, I knew, was *Cimetière* de *Montmartre*, a place wondrously overcrowded with aboveground vaults. I'd often sit and read among the memorialized remains of its dead artists, writers, dancers and poets. The round shape of the Sacre-Couer, about a mile east, was just as easy to pick out.

To my surprise, Dorion headed toward the cemetery. Its many narrow avenues were too crowded with fully leafed trees for a landing. But he slowed and turned in place until we faced south. Then he brought us straight down over a relatively treeless area, where the vaults were raised higher. It was far enough from the very public road that crossed the cemetery at its eastern edge that we wouldn't draw much attention. I watched boxy shapes of alternating white, pewter, steel gray and occasional rusty orange rise to meet us until Dorion hovered over a tight cluster of mausoleums. This place dated back to the early nineteenth century.

"Sitri's here," said Pascher. "We can't land, but there's no wind, so you can get down without difficulty. You can use a ladder or I can lower you with a harness. Which do you prefer?"

Chapter Five

There was absolutely nothing about this trip that resembled my idea of a good time. It was my fault. When Sitri had come for me, I'd swooned on romantic images. But this world was difficult and dangerous—no time for strolls on the beach. I kicked myself. It was the story of my life: jump, and *then* think about it.

I shrugged. "The ladder." At least, I was getting closer to Sitri. And it was morning.

Dorion nodded. "You will be safe."

Pascher slid the door open on the right. My heart thumped as I removed my headset and climbed into the back. Pascher lowered the flexible ladder. I looked down, but morning fog blocked my view of whatever lay directly below. The last time I'd been on a ladder like this, two nights ago, Miegul had nearly caught me. I blocked the image. That ladder had also been my bridge into this strange new world. I felt for the *Oraculum* in the pocket of Sitri's jacket to remind myself of my mission. *I will get the ring back.*

Pascher's firm grip steadied me as I turned so I could crawl out backwards and step carefully onto the first rung. It felt perilously narrow. But this was no time to act like a child. I took the next step down. My foot slipped. Pascher kept his hand tight on me. "You can't fall," he said.

I recalled how the ladder had detached on our last trip, with Charmaine still on it, and he'd zipped out to catch her. The image wasn't comforting. I took another step down, then another. Pascher let go but watched. A slight breeze moved me. I froze. I felt the ladder tighten below and looked down. Someone on the ground anchored the other end. Another of *them*, I suspected. I couldn't see who it was.

I was grateful that the air was relatively calm, although the humidity moistened my palms. I needed to get on solid ground. One step at a time. I held my breath and gripped each rung as I went down, exploring with my foot for the next one. At least this time I had shoes. But my progress felt ridiculously slow. I just made myself do it.

As I pushed off the bottom rung and jumped to the ground, I saw in the strangely lit denim-colored eyes of the person who'd helped that I was indeed meeting another *ma'lakh*. Number four! His chestnut hair was longer than I'd seen on the others, touching his shoulders. Orias introduced himself, but didn't say where he stood in Sitri's hierarchy.

"How many of you are there?" I asked.

"It depends on the need," he said. "But one of us is usually close."

Orias' manner was deferential, as Dorion's had been. *I'm a princess*, I thought.

The ladder went up and the chopper rose and flew off. Across the cemetery, a crow cackled, making this place feel grim and empty. I didn't know this creature, Orias. I didn't know where my building was in St.-Germain. My sole comfort was that I'd retrieved my ID and passport from Adria, so if I had to, I could find my way through the city. I'd once lived near here in Montmartre. I could figure something out.

I looked around. "I thought Sitri was here."

Orias gestured to his right. "Come with me."

The odor of decomposed foliage wafted toward us as I followed him to the front of an ornate mausoleum with stately columns and tarnished copper decor. It was taller than those around it, and broader. Like most other tombs there, a "Famille" designation was carved over the door, under a symbol. *Famille Incende.* Family of fire? I thought it must be code. Moss and damp leaves filling the wall cracks reminded me of how I'd once imagined ghosts leaving through such cracks for their nightly walks. Orias opened one of the double wooden doors and gestured for me to enter. "Quickly," he said.

The darkness made me hesitate. "Inside?"

"Underground protects us."

Underground! So, I just had to trust him, whoever he was, and let myself be led into a tomb. Taking one last breath of fresh air, I entered.

He shut and locked the door behind us. My heart beat against the cloying stale air as my eyes adjusted to the slivers of light that shone through a set of narrow glazed windows. I bumped against a large object in the middle—a tomb.

"All right?" Orias asked.

"I'm fine," I lied. I figured he smelled my sweat and heard the tremor in my voice. This was definitely creepy. The moldy odor thickened my throat and I slid my hands inside my pockets. I wondered if this place held human remains.

I knew about tunnels beneath Paris and that some entrances were in secret places in the large cemeteries. I'd seen one in Père Lachaise, several miles to the west. I figured we were about to enter another. I hoped Sitri would be at the end of this bizarre journey through the Looking Glass. I also hoped I wouldn't see any rats.

Orias moved the tomb's heavy lid with ease, as if it were on rollers. I saw the top of a set of chiseled steps, wide enough for two abreast. This wasn't a mausoleum. It wasn't even a creepy little slither spot into darkness. I sensed that this underground passage had been well used for a long time.

Orias retrieved something from a shelf and suddenly we had light. He'd switched on a bright flashlight. "For the first part," he said. He used the beam to show me each stair ahead in a staircase framed on both sides by earthy stone walls.

"Couldn't I just meet Sitri in some nice patisserie?" I asked.

"He is waiting." He moved the flashlight. "Please."

I sensed that if I refused, he'd pick me up and deliver me. After I'd taken enough steps to be clear of the top, Orias came behind and pulled the lid closed over us. My throat seemed to close with it. I wanted to run back up and get out, but I moved downward.

I pressed against the rough stone on my right. We were going deep. I didn't know how many stairs I'd have to take. All I saw was darkness. I began to worry that I'd made a terrible mistake. But surely Pascher knew Orias. He wouldn't have left me in his care if it were unsafe. I pulled Sitri's jacket close against the cooler air, breathed in its reassuring scent, and held tight to a cold metal railing. Orias shone the light ahead. There was a landing, and then more stairs.

Sitri had better be here, I thought. I was tired of having no answers. I mourned my father, but I was peeved that he hadn't prepared me for this. He'd known about it. For all I knew, he'd been down here. I wished I knew more. Ahead, it looked completely black.

Chapter Six

I'd been relieved to be safely on the ground. Now I regretted leaving the helicopter.

Below, I heard the muffled sound of a little girl yelling a name. Another one giggled. I wondered what they could possibly be doing in this damp, dark cave. Orias flashed the light on a solid steel door a few steps below, which opened into a bright room. Standing inside was another tall creature, with darker skin. Orias introduced Pehel, whose smooth hair was so black it shone blue. I offered a hand, but he bowed politely and would not touch me.

Orias stepped back as Pehel took over. His voice was quiet and smooth as he said, "Please come with me." I looked behind me, but the door was closed and Orias was gone. Pehel showed me to a spacious furnished area with ceilings at least 12 feet up and half a dozen doorways. I was surprised to see large murals of gardens painted along two walls. It hardly seemed like we were underground. The stone-grey floor felt softly resilient, like a thick layer of cork, and the air was surprisingly fresh. I breathed in relief.

A young brunette woman in jeans and a green T-shirt crossed the room, leading a gangly brown-skinned girl in a bright blue hoodie. She looked over at me. Another girl in black leggings and a purple shirt burst through a door, followed by a woman carrying a blond child in full-body pajamas. The girl hugged a stuffed rabbit. Two children in matching white jackets and rubber boots with polka dots solemnly carried bags over to a table. One had a ponytail, the other dark braids. She wore a flowered backpack bulging with stuff and chewed on a candy bar. Down a hallway, I heard giggles. This was like a daycare center.

Then I saw Sitri and a warm sensation flushed through me. Why had I had second thoughts? He sat on a padded bench across the room, still in his leathers and black T-shirt, but barefoot. My dazzling *ma'lakh* held a redheaded little girl in a denim jacket on his lap, while a brunette in bright pink hugged against him on the right and a girl kneeling on a plush rug in front of him held his attention with her excited chatter. Her hand was on his knee. They clearly adored him. He looked so different from the flaming warrior in New York and even the "private investigator" who'd first approached me.

The brunette in the green T-shirt took the girl from his lap and urged the others to come with her.

Finally. Time for *us*. Then I felt self-conscious. I probably stank from stress. I smoothed my hair as best I could. Small fingers grabbed my left hand and I looked down at a girl with ebony skin, wearing a lavender sweater over a green dress. She grinned up at me. She looked about five. I squeezed her hand.

"Hi!" I said, leaning toward her. "Who are you?"

She said something in a language I didn't know.

And then Sitri was there, his hand on her head. "This is Nwaneki," he said. He bent low to let her hug him, telling her something that she apparently understood before she ran off. When he stood up, he seemed very tall in this underground place. He nodded to Pehel, who bowed his head slightly and stepped behind me. A faint *whirr* made me turn. Pehel had vanished.

Sitri touched my arm and I looked up into his dark eyes. "Welcome to *céleste sous la terre*," he said. "Our private catacomb." Despite his friendly greeting, I sensed impatience. "I'm glad you're here. Are you hungry?"

"I'm all right, but—"

"Come with me."

It wasn't the embrace I'd expected. He seemed preoccupied. Our intimate encounter the night before last had been fast and furious, yes, but in such an amazing flow of intimate pleasure I thought he must want it again. I know *I* did. And he'd gone out of his way to invite me here. Yet now he was distant.

Then again, he was a *ma'lakh*. I had no idea what he felt. But he could have at least congratulated me on flying a helicopter.

I watched the shine on the black leather that hugged his tight butt as I followed him down a narrow corridor to another room. We entered and I saw a dozen black chairs surrounding a large wooden conference table, piled high with papers and books. Lining the walls were large framed maps, at least eight feet across, their tops touching the ceiling. Sitri spoke in French to a small elderly woman, who stepped toward me with a mug that smelled like rich French coffee. She bowed slightly when I accepted it, and left.

I snorted. "Is this your idea of a cup of coffee in Paris?"

He shrugged. "You like Montmartre."

"Not exactly this view of it. I recall some mention of a Left Bank café."

"In time."

Sitri closed the door, dimming the sounds from the other area. Despite being underground, it smelled fresh in here, as if air was pumped in. It was cool but not cold, and the coffee tasted rich and nutty, with an interesting flavor I couldn't identify.

Sitri pulled out a chair for me. "I apologize for this situation, but you do rise well to a challenge. This won't take long."

I remained standing. I sensed tension. "What's going on? Char told me about Ignis and all these kids being taken."

He nodded. "When Miegul fled from New York, he went to London. His attempt to trap me was only part of his plan. He also needed the ring, which he acquired. He brought it here and Ignis used it to locate the children—"

"But why?"

Sitri went over to a detailed map of Europe and tapped London. It lit up. "Here," he said. Then, "here," for Rome, "here" for Warsaw, and "here" for Oslo. He looked at me. "Four attacks, in quick succession."

I shrugged. I'd heard this on the news. I didn't know what he wanted me to see. I looked from one highlighted city to the other. Norway, England, Italy and Poland. North, west, south and east.

"Think in *symbols*," Sitri said.

Lines running from north to south and east to west would make a cross. But then I saw it. If one drew lines from Oslo to Warsaw to Rome to London to Oslo, they would form a diamond.

Chapter Seven

Not all diamonds glitter.

I stared at the map. "The portal! *He's* behind this? Miegul?"

"It's just the start. This part is a warning."

Now I knew why he was all business. Kids were in danger, maybe a lot of them.

He returned to me and reached into the inner pocket of the jacket I wore. Startled, I leaned away. He brushed my breast with the back of his hand as he removed the *Oraculum*. "This will interfere." He placed it on the table. From the top of a stack of books nearby, he picked up a similar pocketsize leather-bound book, thicker than the *Oraculum*, and waved it. "The ring will be where *this* has been."

I set down the mug and held out my hand. This was the main reason I'd come, to retrieve the ring that Miegul had stolen from me. The *Oraculum* had even predicted that I would—"unexpectedly." Sitri let me take it.

The book smelled slightly musty. When I opened it, I saw that some pages toward the end had been torn. The faded hand-printed letters had a delicate feminine appearance. It might have been a foreign language or a group of codes. The symbols looked like tiny figures mixed among circles and squiggly lines. They didn't resemble the celestial script that had lured me into this mess. This language was something else. But it did look vaguely familiar.

I felt Sitri watching me in the tense way he'd done in New York when he'd needed me to see for him. He was like a thoroughbred ready to run but held in check at the starting gate. So, I thought, something blocks him.

The *noea* and their male counterparts, the *nejah*, could shield themselves from the *ma'lakhim*. But they—we—were visible to each other. In New York, I'd had to show Sitri Miegul's location. I'd also

31

relayed patterns, read codes, and spotted important signals. I kind of liked having him needing me, if only briefly.

Sitri watched the map. His hands were on his hips and one finger tapped a restless beat.

"I'm trying," I said. I flipped through a couple of fragile pages. On some, the style of writing changed. Several pages bore traces of mildew and one had dark oily stains. I handled it with care. From my father, the historian, I knew the significant damage even a small rip could do.

"I don't see anything," I said. "I can't read it. Is there something I should look for?"

Sitri looked down at me. "Like that"—he gestured toward the *Oraculum*—"it's more than words. Let it show itself, where it's been."

Where it's been? He made no sense. I was tired. I'd been through a lot. I'd expected to arrive at a nice place in the heart of Paris, not some underground bunker. I'd hoped for breakfast in an outdoor café, croissants not codes.

"Where did you get this?" I thumbed another page and stared at the script. "What's it—?"

Then I remembered John Dee's crystal. It was in my pocket. He'd employed it during the 16th century to reverse the celestial symbols to make them accessible. Miegul had used it to raise a *ma'lakhim* portal from within the pages of the *Oraculum*. It might work as well with this book. I laid the book flat on the table, open in the middle. Taking the crystal from my pocket, I placed it, concave hump upward, on the pages.

Sitri glanced down and his eyes widened. "Not with that!" He reached for it.

Too late. A hot burst of light shot through the crystal, blinding me while some force zinged from my fingertips through my hands and up my arms. I jerked back, stunned. It seared into my head, like seeing a flash of bright sun during a migraine. I put my hands to my face.

"I need... I think I need... "

I stepped away from the table and rushed to the door, struggled to open it, and ran down the corridor. I made it just short of the open area before I had to stop and touch a wall to keep my balance. My sinuses throbbed and my heart pounded so hard I couldn't hear. I thought I might vomit. I needed air. Real air, from outside.

But I was underground. Trapped. I panicked. Where had that Orias creature gone? I had to get out. I put my hand to my chest and panted. My ears burned and the cut on my throat pulsed.

Sitri couldn't make me do this. Charmaine had said that. *He can't tell you what to do.* I'd barely recovered from an inferno, from being choked to within an inch of my life, from my father's devastating murder, and from one stunning discovery after another about this alternate world and my place in it. Now Sitri wanted me to revive that taxing mental state and *perform*? I leaned on the wall, sweating.

"Dianysus." His voice behind me was quiet.

"No." I shook my head and took another step. "I want to go. Show me how to get out of here." I despised him for this. He hadn't prepared me. Something had *hit* me. My legs tensed. I wanted to run. I had to get away.

Across the room I saw that child, Nwaneki. She smiled and waved at me. Weakly, I waved back. I felt Sitri behind me. I knew what was at stake. These kids. They were here for their safety. But others had been taken. They were scared, maybe hurt.

I turned slowly around, still touching the wall. "What do you want from me?"

He held out a hand. "You can find them. I will guide you."

I closed my eyes. I recalled that just a few hours before, I'd assured my sister *noea* that I could fill my mother's shoes. We would win. *Persevere!* But here I was, quaking. I was clearly not the amazing Kaitlyn. But I had to try.

Chapter Eight

I let Sitri put an arm around me to guide me back. His pleasing scent cleared my head. When he closed the door and dimmed the lights, I breathed evenly and touched the cool tabletop.

"Take off your shoes," Sitri said. "Do not touch the crystal." He moved it to the middle of the table.

I slipped my shoes off. The cushioned floor felt warm. Sitri handed me the mug. "This will help."

I took a sip and swallowed before I asked, "What *was* that? What hit me?"

"A pulse," he said. "Our language floats. It was coming to me, but the crystal pulled it to you."

"Pulled it?" I was sure I'd misheard him.

"You pulled *noea* from the dossier—" he gestured at the open book, "and ours from the air. They clash. That was my error. I should have taken the crystal from you."

I looked at the book I'd opened. I reached down and touched its edge. "What is it?"

"*Écrits*. Writings. A dossier."

"And I should see something in it?"

"*From* it. Many energies have infused it. Ignis had it."

I raised an eyebrow. Stolen intel. "It will show me where it's been?"

Sitri tapped it. "Where this has been is where they took our children. And the ring."

Our children. I didn't want to know what this might mean.

"Let it *reveal*." He picked it up, closed it, and slipped it into the jacket pocket where I'd had the *Oraculum*. His hand against my shirt felt intimate. "We have little time. You see things. I can interpret them."

"Can't you still see what I see?"

His eyes flickered as he glanced at my throat. "No."

Ah. Right. I'd blocked him. But we were here now, together. Charmaine had said that to get reconnected he had to be with me. "What should I do?"

Sitri came around behind me and brushed his fingers against the back of my neck, moving my hair. A chill raced up my back. He gripped the upper part of my arms as his mouth came close to my ear. His voice was low and breathy. "Relax." His warm hands distracted me. It seemed as if his fingers were sending currents straight to my breasts. I wanted to turn around and press against him, to arouse him.

He was waiting.

I put down the mug. The crystal lay nearby. I wished it were further away. When I touched the jacket pocket, my fingertips tingled. A current ran through my hand and up my arm. I twitched back and bumped Sitri. He held me. He was here. Close. He turned me to my right, to face the European map. I lifted my shoulders to breathe in, caught his scent, and let them go loose.

"That's it," he whispered. His breath warmed my ear. "*Abandoner*."

Surrender. In lovely French. How I wanted to, but in a bedroom, not this unter-mortem conference room.

Sitri's left hand moved under my T-shirt to frame my right breast, with his thumb resting on my breastbone. A pulse of heat raised my nipple. I gasped and stiffened, losing the effect.

"I have you," Sitri assured me. "You will feel heat. Let it build."

I leaned back against him. He pressed closer. He had to have felt my heart quicken. His warm fingertips rested on my skin, but seemed to penetrate. I put my left hand on his hip, feeling warmth under the smooth, supple leather. Against the small of my back, I felt him harden.

Good. I needed him to do this *with* me.

He whispered something. *Logaeth*, they called it. The celestial tongue. The melodic tone ignited an itch between my legs. It floated, just as he'd said. I felt it in the roots of my hair. My ears burned and a chill swept through me, raising goose bumps. I heard another male voice, distant, and then another, yet the words were not in this room. An exquisite gulp of desire shot through me. My breath came faster. I envisioned a hot embrace on the table, getting stretched and filled. I pushed it away, but it persisted. A sweet taste formed on my tongue.

Then I realized: the coffee. It was an aphrodisiac. The *Oraculum* had worked best when I was aroused. Those codes had surfed the waves of lust. Apparently, this was the same. His language *floated*. This was the communication system. Ero-telepathy. I gripped the edge of the dossier. I had to channel it.

"Shhh," said Sitri, as if to quiet my thoughts. "Let it come."

The magic words!

When I'd relaxed on the helicopter, some suppressed ability to maneuver it had flowed into my legs and hands. When I loosened up, I became a conductor. I went limp and let myself drift. Sitri tensed to hold me. His other hand moved down my belly. Two fingers pushed into my jeans. Yes, that. It felt as if warm oil radiated across my skin. I opened the button and zipper. With a light touch, he caressed me. I gasped. A finger on his other hand moved just under my right nipple. I gripped his arm. His scent grew acute. My vision blurred, then clarified. The dim lights brightened and I could make out the tiniest map details.

I saw a red flash. Then it was gone and the room darkened. In another area, I saw a second flash. This was it! The locations.

"How do I... let you in?" I whispered.

"Just point."

He kissed my neck, close to where his tongue had punctured me in New York to draw my blood. I stretched my head away to give him space and ripped off the bandage. He gripped me until it hurt. He *must* want more. I did. I wanted him in me. I grabbed his arm, but he was making me melt. I pressed my head against his chest and placed my left foot on a nearby chair, opening to him. He gently kissed the back of my head.

"I can't... I need... "

"Steady. You are the receiver. Listen!"

I heard the door open, but Sitri didn't stop. I sensed others enter. I stiffened, self-conscious, but Sitri's fingers kept working me. His cock pressed against me while his left hand ran down, then up my side to my breast. Close to my ear I heard an intake of breath that sounded like restrained pleasure. He whispered something that sounded French. A shock of sensation through my nipple arched my back. I started to rock. I needed to be filled.

36

Then a flash sparked on the map. "There!" I pointed to it. This was magical. My body itself, in heat, drew it out. Krystal had explained that information flowed best through hot blood. The dossier used these currents, showing me where it had been. It felt warm against my side.

Next to me I sensed several figures. This room felt crowded. Then empty. They were coming and going, as if arriving to get orders and moving out.

Then a sensation washed through me, like a runner's high. I was in a zone. My breathing evened out but my heart beat hard. Sitri whispered something and I began to float, moving through a dark tunnel that led to another, and then rounded a bend into another, toward a soft blue light. My fingers curled on his arm.

"There." My voice was husky. I pointed out three more areas and thought I saw the wall move, as if a large worm was working its way under the painted map from one lit area to another. It left a faint trail of light. Soon, there were several trails. I teetered on an erotic tightrope. Panting, I was nearing a climax. Energy pulsed through me. "I can't... hold it... "

Sitri's voice continued in a lyrical rhythm as if guiding me though an erotic meditation. His hands kept moving, on me, then off me, bringing me up but just short of a peak. I came close, receded, then climbed again.

"Stay with me," he said.

This was exquisite torture, so different from the crest of ordinary lust. I saw those shadowy *diam* float past, followed by streaks of blue, green, and purple lights. I smelled vanilla and my lips went numb.

Suddenly, I spoke words I didn't understand. A female voice answered me. In the air, I traced the design of the illuminated lines. Sitri went still, gripping me against him. I heard him say a single word, "No."

Then he lowered me into a chair. My hand was empty. The book was gone. The map dimmed. I had the distant impression that two males entered and spoke with Sitri in a strange language. I drifted, leaning back. I hit something unyielding and thought I might fall. A wave of dizziness like the aftermath of a drinking party brought me forward. I put my head in my hands. I had no idea what I should do. I wanted to lie down.

37

My head spun and the sweet taste turned bitter. My tongue was swollen and dry. I rubbed my left thumb and fingertip together but felt nothing. I was coming down *hard*. I leaned my face on the table and gripped the edge, breathing to keep from vomiting. I was empty. The noise blurred into a buzz and I closed my eyes, rocking myself. A trickle of blood ran from my throat down my chest. I touched it and saw red on my fingertips. I rubbed it off on Sitri's jacket.

Then he was with me, down on one knee, his hand under my chin and his thumb caressing my cheek. He said something, but I didn't understand. I felt pressure against my swollen lips before it all receded. The driving need to have him became a faint ripple, taking with it the heat. I dug my fingers into his shoulder, leaned on him and started to shake.

Chapter Nine

What looks like a haven might be just a way station.

Something bright woke me. I saw a white ceiling, high overhead, with ornate gold trim along the edges. I rolled over. I was under a blanket on a bed in a room with tall windows and antique French furniture. I sat up. The door was closed. I was alone. I wasn't in the catacomb. But my tongue was still numb.

Somehow, I'd gotten here. I vaguely recalled stairs, a car, being held, being carried. Someone had removed my jeans and I'd felt too drained to assist. I wondered how long I'd been asleep. And what had happened in the world. I had no phone to check.

I'd shown Sitri something. There'd been a map. I recalled how he'd touched me, playing me like an instrument, and his strange words. Then the flashes. Then exhaustion. And that was all.

I slumped in disappointment. *That's* why he'd brought me here. He needed me to get information. He'd *drugged* me to get it. He'd put something in the coffee. Had I aligned with the *better* angels, I wondered? I lay there, recalling Sitri's touch and how he'd worked me into a sweat, but had ultimately left me hungry. It was like watching an aroused man preparing to enter you. You're ready and he's so close, within a hair's breadth of contact, and then... nothing.

"Damn!" I said. "Why would he do that?" *Next time, we drink from the same cup or I don't drink at all.*

Maybe there wouldn't be a next time. Maybe he'd gotten what he needed. I looked around. A large vase of yellow roses offered a sweet scent. My suitcases sat across the room on a table next to a pile of plush white towels and a set of toiletries in silver and purple containers.

I sat on the edge of the bed and took mental inventory. No, I hadn't had sex. I was pretty sure. I had a slight headache and clammy skin, and I was hungry. My mouth felt like cotton.

I got up, steadied myself on the bedpost, and went over to a door that offered a glimpse of a bright, spacious en-suite. This wasn't a hotel room. I saw the large glass-enclosed double-sized shower. I nearly melted. Nothing was going to stop me from getting in. I locked the bathroom door and pulled off the rest of my clothes, as well as the remaining bandages on my cuts.

The hot water felt wonderful. I let the eight-inch square rain-style showerhead spray me with a liquid blast and breathed in the shampoo's sweet almond aroma. I didn't care where I was or who might walk in. This was heaven! The water ran over my hair, my skin, my face. I ignored the sting from my cuts but touched the place under my breast where Sitri's hand had been. It felt tender, possibly bruised. I tried to remember more. The water streamed over me but offered no revelations. Reluctantly, I shut it off.

As I dried myself with a fluffy towel, memories trickled in. I wondered how I'd even survived the past few days. Donning a plush white robe, I picked up a hairdryer and comb and started in on my thick hair. I had tried to trim away where the fire had singed it, but I'd missed some strands. The cut on my face and hand, and the bruises on my neck were still clear. The small puncture that Sitri had made when he'd taken my blood was raw. I wondered if he'd taken more. I touched it and felt a shock run to my left nipple. I tried again. Same result. He hadn't just taken blood; he'd *injected* something. This tiny red mark was like an ignition switch. With care, I applied a small bandage over it. Then I dressed my other cuts.

The routine of combing each section of my hair grounded me and helped to organize my thoughts. Three days ago, I'd been just a cop working a gruesome murder case and trying to locate my missing father. I'd learned about angel codes and ancient tales. I'd met a man who claimed to be Jack the Ripper and had seduced a creature who could transform into a wheel of fire. Then there was that FBI agent, Pierce, who'd shown me the Ripper's original letter. On it was a code begging whoever could read it to "kill us all." Commit mass murder. Burn everything, my father had said as he lay dying. His house had burned to the ground.

I had few definite answers, but I could deduce some things. Sitri, a centuries-old celestial guardian, had known my mother, whom he'd taken from me when I was four to join Mayon, my *ma'lakh* father while Alexandre, my human father, assumed my care. That much my Aunt Krystal had told me. She and Alexandre were members of a cadre of humans who assist and protect the *ma'lakhim* and their hybrid progeny, the *noea*.

I'd recently learned that I was in this category. The *noea* were female. The male hybrids, the *nejah*, had developed into monsters, insatiable vampires. So, their fathers had annihilated all except for those few who'd escaped. My "brothers" were aligned with our resentful enemies, a.k.a., Ignis, the lesser *ma'lakhim*. This magical *ma'lakhim* blood facilitated everything in our network and formed our bonds. It electrified our world like a subway train's third rail. My own gifts, which I was just discovering, came from it. And Ignis was grabbing the *noea* children to get it.

I put down the hairdryer. It sounded crazy. Yet, I'd seen things. I'd been with Sitri. *That* had not been a human male. What had he done to me last night? I'd reached an orgasmic state, without release, and had moved into some other zone, as if the lust had been a threshold to a much more powerful state. Talk about Alice in Wonderland! There was so much more to all this than I could process.

Adria was right. I had to take this one step at a time.

I'd learned about medieval angel traps used to capture a *ma'lakh*. I'd met Scott Bateman, a.k.a., Miegul, a.k.a., Jack the Ripper, who'd hoped to trap Sitri. I'd seen Sitri in action, a celestial burner who'd torched a fireproof fortress overnight into cinders and ash.

I wondered how Alexandre could have been so central to this world and told me nothing. We'd been close, but I'd been clueless. Now that I thought about it, the breadcrumbs had been there in the things he'd studied. I'd thought he was a scholar of angelic lore. Sometimes I'd even thought he was crazy. He'd hidden in plain sight the fact that he'd been my protector. Ultimately, he'd given his life for me. Tears stung my eyes at the memory of him dying, weakly reaching for Sitri's extended hand.

I took a breath, blinked hard and lifted the hairdryer.

I'd seduced Sitri that night to learn his plan, but he'd used me instead and left me behind. Not for long. I'd followed, which is how Charmaine got hurt trying to help me. I'd seen this world, the monsters and the warriors. Lastly, Sitri had invited me to be part of it.

41

I'd hoped it meant that he hungered for *me* the way I did for him, but so far he'd been aloof. My aunt had told me he'd kept his distance as I grew up. But surely that had changed now. We'd had sex. *Spectacular* sex. It had been *hot*!

But had I even made an impression? I didn't know.

I looked at my wounds. They didn't help. I turned off the dryer and went out to find some clothes. At the threshold I stopped, startled.

Chapter Ten

Even when home is sweet, it's not necessarily inviting.

A gorgeous woman sat in the chair by the window. Her mahogany hair lay in a mass of tiny ringlets along her right shoulder and down to her waist. When she rose with a smile, I saw that she dressed with exquisite style, in a tan Jenny Packham dress. She was as tall as me, and slender. She greeted me as if she knew me.

"*Bonjour*. How wonderful that you're up," she said. "*Parfait!* I'm Portia." She reached and took my hand. "*Je n'en crois pas mes yeux!* Look at you! We've seen pictures, but you're so grown up!"

I must have looked confused, because she added, "I knew you when you lived here, just a baby."

"That's not possible. You couldn't be—"

"Oh, we age well. You will, too. But we will address all of this."

"Did you know my mother?"

"Of course. For many years."

This was incomprehensible. To me, my mother was a ghost. Yet, she'd been here 27 years ago, when I was born. This had been her home.

"But how can I assist?" asked Portia. "You have missed *le déjeuner*, but we prepared coffee and refreshments. We have had the best boutiques bring in clothes, over there, in your *vestiaire*, your dressing room." She pointed. "If you dislike them, we will bring others, but do look. We tried to find things that will please. You are in Paris, in your home. Sitri brought you over this morning."

I raised an eyebrow and felt myself blush. I imagined him carrying me and placing me on this bed, maybe removing my jeans. "He's here?"

"No, no. He came an hour ago to leave this for you." She pointed to a bag next to the chair where she'd been sitting. She raised an eyebrow, as if she thought it was something sexy. Then she gestured at

43

the spacious area around us. "This was your mother's room. I think it is perfect for you. I'll leave you to dress, but this room is on the top floor of the residence. When you're ready, take the elevator just down the hall to the third floor. You will hear us. After you eat, perhaps I can give you a tour. We have a library and music room. On the ground floor, we have a café, a salon, and a dress shop. We are so glad to have you here. *Enchante*. Charmaine is especially eager to see you."

"Charmaine?"

"Yes. She is recovering, although she loathes sitting still. But you can see for yourself."

"What about the kids? Last night? What happened?"

She grabbed my hand. *"Merci beaucoup*, where are my manners? Thank you so much for your help! We can see parts of *their* network."

The map. The worm trails. The portal. "From that book?"

"Ah. *Les Écrits*. Written by *noea*. It came to us recently."

"What do you mean?"

She sighed. "It belongs to us, but it was stolen. Some of our sisters go to Ignis. They use what they know against us. That dossier was written in our original language. The codes are embedded in ancient ceremonies that few of us can decipher."

"But... we did. Right?"

"We have locations. *Et nous sont reconnaissant*, we are so grateful. Unfortunately, there were losses. We are still sorting it, but we rescued 15."

"Fifteen! They were all—?"

"Noea, yes. Ignis tried to take more, and it was well coordinated. But our defense was nearly as fast."

"Ah! Those kids under the cemetery."

"Yes, underground. Its composition protects them. It is temporary. We will explain it to you downstairs."

"What about Sheine? Did they find her?"

"Unfortunately, no. We're still getting reports. *S'il vous plait*, is there anything you need? Just let me know." She handed me a cell phone. "Use this if you need anything. It is already programmed with several numbers, including your aunt and even your partner, the detective."

"Jack?" Just saying his name made my stomach drop. What I wouldn't give to have him here right now.

44

"Sitri thought you would want it."

"And Sitri's number?" I doubted he carried a phone. He'd given me a number before that didn't even ring when called.

Portia smiled. "You can discuss this with him. *À bientôt.*"

With another squeeze of my hand, she left. I went straight to the dressing room.

It was a full room in itself, with tall windows and lined to the high ceiling with shelves and hanging bars. At least a dozen white garment bags begged to be explored. In Paris, women dressed well, whether just walking to the store or going to the opera. They were always aware of how they looked to others. I'd picked up this fashion sense. I never stood out to the Parisians, but I certainly had to my fellow cops. Jack had always made cracks and had taken some ribbing, but I think he liked that his partner—me—was a bit of arm candy.

I unzipped a bag and caught my breath at the forest green shimmer. Not a lunch dress, not at all, unless lunch was served at Versailles. Another bag produced a royal blue L. K. Bennett sleeveless dress that stopped above the knee, with a low-cut neckline and a single front pleat. Demure but flirty. It matched a pair of stiletto shoes on the wall shelf. I picked them up. Brand new, my size.

I dressed and arranged my honey blonde hair, now with full body and curl, around my neck. The dress flattered me. The events of the past few days had reduced my weight. I felt like a model. I recalled Sitri's hands on my arms in that underground room and touched my skin where his fingers had been. This would be the first time I was dressed well for an encounter with him.

I'd first met him—as "Agent Gregory Brenner"—on a humid night in my office. I'd smelled of sweat and the decomposing corpse I'd just stood over. Later, I'd been in a poorly matched disguise, with my hair stuffed into a baseball cap. Also sweaty. I'd worn a short skirt, yes, and he'd noticed, but it was not my best look. Then I'd been running through the Brooklyn streets in ripped clothing when he'd swept me onto his motorcycle. After that, I'd stood barefoot and grimy, with tangled hair, in his Upper Eastside penthouse.

None of those encounters had worked well for me. Worse, I'd grabbed leathers that didn't fit to go run after him. Then last night, I'd just thrown on some jeans and a T-shirt.

I cringed. No wonder he hadn't shown interest. But I'd change that.

For the first time, I could really look good. And I did. In the bathroom, I found a fully stocked cosmetics cabinet with expensive products, some still unopened. I worked on myself till I was satisfied. Hair, check. Eyes, check. Legs, check. My best features. I had cuts and bruises, but he knew why.

Then I remembered the bag that Sitri had left for me. I went over and put it on a chair. Inside was a large *Le 66* box, tied with a ribbon. Wrapped in white tissue, I found a softly supple light gray leather jacket. I tried it on. Perfect fit, with two deep inner pockets and light enough for a summer evening. Apparently a motorcycle was in my future. I noticed that Sitri's jacket wasn't here.

I took off the jacket and straightened my dress. I knew these women would judge everything about me. I was barging into their world, becoming their landlady. I wondered if the *noea* here worried that I'd ask them to leave. I reminded myself to be watchful. I figured I had an enemy or two under this roof. I made a note to call Krystal, although I didn't trust this phone. If I had the status that Leith had suggested, they would monitor me. A princess, she'd said.

I opened a set of glass doors on the far side of my room and discovered a balcony. I went out. The day was bright and warm. It had been years since I'd seen this beautiful city. I recognized the St. Germain area—the brainy part of Paris. Although I'd lived on La Butte when I'd studied here, I'd often walked the streets where Latin scholars, existential philosophers and literary writers had wrestled with ideas. Their contributions to the human spirit were still noted in monuments at the expansive gardens of the Luxembourg Palace, and their shabby apartments and crowded salons bore plaques among the endless array of used bookshops, bistros and brasseries. I loved the clean lines, block after block in Saint-Germain-des-Prés, of the repetitive white, six-story buildings with wrought iron window grills. Now I supposedly owned one. I was in it, looking out.

I went to the rail and gripped it, but quickly let go. I'd *been* here. I remembered this. I'd been *on* the rail, standing on it. Like I was going to jump. I pressed my brain for more context, but the sensation was gone. I'd been a child here. I wouldn't have been standing on the rail. That was crazy! Even weirder—I hadn't been afraid.

I took a deep breath, smoothed my new dress, and prepared to meet the *noea*. It was time to get some answers.

Chapter Eleven

Angel bread is a complex mix. In legend, it was the only thing an angel could eat.

As I walked out of the elevator onto the third floor, I heard violin music in one area. It sounded live. I saw a white cat run into a room. Curious, I followed it and found a large table in a spacious area around which sat several gorgeous women. One of them was Charmaine, in a reclining chair, with her leg wrapped and propped up. I nodded toward her. The color was back in her pretty Asian face, but her eyes were still puffy. I also recognized Adria and Leith, but not the woman with olive skin, bright blue eyes and straight black hair. She looked as if she'd been crying.

Portia came out from a side door with a raised platter that exuded an aroma I knew well: angel bread. My aunt had made it nearly every day. Little did I know growing up that it was for her mystical visitors. Portia greeted me and pointed. "You know Leith," she said. "Next to her is Nettaline. They're nearly inseparable, unless Dorion is here."

Nettaline rose and acknowledged me. I recalled the name: Sheine was her daughter. "You and I are related," she said. "Distantly, through your mother's sister." From her faint accent, I thought she had some Italian ancestry.

"I hope to learn more about that," I told her.

Portia interrupted us. "All right, girls. *Nous avons des affaires*. It is time for business."

Leith grabbed a chunk of angel bread before she winked at me and left the room with Nettaline. Adria lingered long enough to show her manners. "You look so beautiful in that dress. A perfect color for you."

I thanked her and waited for Portia to close the door. The emotional tone felt off. I didn't trust this situation.

"We will not be disturbed," she said. "The *ma'lakhim* respect our privacy. Even Sitri does not enter unless he must."

"And how are you?" I asked Charmaine. I took a chair close to her while Portia poured me a cup of coffee in a delicate floral china cup. The aroma spoke of the best quality.

Charmaine shrugged. "Sitri and Pasch are getting something they think will work." I knew she meant something for cleansing her blood. After the vampires had grabbed her in New York, she'd said she was now poison to Pascher. She had begged me to kill her.

"It *will* work," said Portia. "Arren is a true healer. She'll know what to do."

"She doesn't go near the *nejah* or their vampires," Charmaine snapped. "She heals wings."

Had I just heard that? I reminded myself that I was in a strange new world. New *universe*.

Portia looked annoyed. "You did not train under her. I did. You are not the first to be poisoned. She will know about this infection." She turned to me and gestured toward the food.

I hadn't eaten much since all of this began. I missed French food. It smelled of cream and warm butter. After a few bites of a moist croissant and a perfectly textured mushroom quiche, I said, "Who's going to start? May I? Because I have a *lot* of questions."

"We shall begin with the most urgent item," said Portia, "Sitri."

I glance at Charmaine, who was looking away. I sensed discord: they did not agree. "Maybe he should be here?"

"He leaves *noea* matters to us."

Noea matters. I didn't like the sound of this. It was downright tribal.

"Two days ago," Charmaine broke in, "you pushed your way into something that the *ma'lakhim* take very seriously."

I shrugged. I thought she meant how I'd tricked Sitri into taking my blood, to seduce him and prevent him from killing my father. This seemed justified to me.

She continued. "You were told about the blood ceremony, the *kaisahoni*. Sharing blood shares vision. The *affinité* is sacred. You didn't know what you were doing."

The story of my life. How many times had I heard *that* line?

"There are protocols," said Portia. "It is arranged, with

48

mentoring, but you went in blind. It was an urgent circumstance, *oui,* but this does not erase the consequences."

"Consequences?" I looked from one to the other. I sensed something dark.

"You have initiated a process that has become dangerous." Portia looked uneasy. "An *affinité* with Sitri seals you to him."

I could hardly believe this. "Are we really concerned about matchmaking at a time like this?"

"Not matchmaking." She looked at Charmaine as if she were struggling to find the right words.

Charmaine stepped in. "When you share blood, it opens a channel between you and him. You each see what the other sees. You can block it, but if Ignis catches you, they can still use the connection to find and lure him."

Ah. I'd put *him* at risk. "Wouldn't he know this? I don't see—"

"This is bigger than you," Charmaine interrupted. "It affects us all."

Portia nodded. "We can try to annul it and dissolve the seal. There is still time."

I was confused. "Annul it? Does Sitri know you're telling me this?"

"He knows we will protect our interests."

"Then why did he invite me here? Why didn't he just leave me in New York?"

Char's impatience bubbled up. "Because you have abilities that can help. But *he* didn't initiate the *affinité*, you did, to use him. It thrust you into our world before you were ready. That's not what he wants, either."

Portia seemed to want to be gentler. "We debated over bringing you into this at all and Sitri wanted you to have a full human life before you were shown who you are. Although Kaitlyn intended one of her daughters for—"

"*One* of?"

Char shook her head. "Stop interrupting. *Listen.* The point is that you used your blood to achieve a goal. You didn't know it would make you both more vulnerable. We want to block it, but you must agree."

Something in Charmaine's expression suggested she wasn't entirely on board. It was Portia's idea, and now I knew who led this coterie. I sat up straight. "Let me see if I have this right. I was born and raised to eventually be one of you. With some unique gift, I just helped to find your kids. I've started this *affinité* thing with Sitri and now you want me to erase it."

Charmaine nodded. "Yes."

I'd expected her to say the opposite, or at least stay silent.

"These liaisons are difficult," said Portia. "*Very* difficult. You must be prepared. When the time is right, you can reconsider."

I shrugged. "Liaison? How is a one-night stand a liaison?"

They looked at each other as if they were adults talking to a child.

"Look," I said. "He invited me here. I don't think a tumble in bed makes us an item, but if it's that serious, then fine. I'll back off. But I don't really believe you."

To Charmaine, I said, "What about you and Pascher? You wanted to die rather than lose your... your... *thing*. And you want me to give it up?"

She looked down, so I turned to Portia. "And have you ever been in one of these... liaisons?"

"I was with Tariel. For a long time, he was Sitri's *kunoui*, his closest one—what Pascher is now. But Tariel was caught. He has been gone for over two decades."

I'd been chastened. "Sorry. *Je suis vraiment désolé.*"

"Do not think of it. You could not know."

I closed my eyes and tried to stay calm. It seemed as if each time I stepped onto what looked like solid ground, it moved. "So, if I cut off Sitri, will it subtract me out of this world? Erase my memories? Put me back on the streets of New York?"

"You can still help us recover the ring," said Charmaine. "You're a detective. You have skills. You've blocked the *affinité* and it will fade if not renewed. Just don't let him—"

A frantic knocking interrupted us. "They're coming!" someone shouted. I thought it was Adria. Then it felt as if the building had been hit.

"It's them," said Portia. She looked flushed as she stood up. "*Excuse.*"

Chapter Twelve

I know my flaw. It's jumping in before I test the water. Or the fire.

When Portia left, I turned to Charmaine. "You don't believe this."

The building trembled again.

"That's Sitri's entourage," she said. "This room will be soon be flooded with *ma'lakhim*. But I agree with Portia. You don't know what you're doing. You have Kaitlyn's crazy courage, but you don't know enough. You're in too—"

Pascher burst in. He seemed excited. He swept past me and bent to kiss Charmaine, who allowed him only to brush his lips on her cheek. "*Nous l'avons!*" he said. "We have it." Then he sat down and whispered something I didn't hear. It made her smile and touch his face.

Orias came next, followed by the dark-skinned Pehel and two more males. I realized from their dazzling appearance they must be *ma'lakhim*. They glanced at me with curious expressions. Orias introduced Tibreth, with caramel hair and eyes like Dorion's, and Kihr, with curly hair that reminded me of rich coffee. Several cats jumped up on the table, seemingly attracted to them, and a white terrier ran in and started to bark. Their casual dress, mostly jeans and T-shirts, made me feel like I was among a rowdy group of undercover detectives.

Adria entered, grabbed a remote and turned on a large flat screen television attached to the wall. "You won't believe this," she said. "I just saw this on the Internet chatter."

I looked for Sitri, but he didn't come in. Portia was not back, either. My stomach lurched. Was she trying to separate me from Sitri so *she* could have him? Was there already something between them? Perhaps she was with him now.

I rethought my position. Maybe it *would* be best to extricate myself. I had forced my blood into Sitri's mouth, knowing it would be like crack cocaine to an addict. Maybe he didn't want this. I felt less like a princess and much more like a joke.

The news caught my attention. The *ma'lakhim* grabbed chunks of bread as they watched the screen. I heard comments among them in another language. They didn't sound surprised at what they were hearing. I recalled Sitri's comment that this thing had long been planned.

"...this group, the Black Torch, has claimed credit for the recent spate of shootings and kidnappings of children," said a uniformed man who looked official. "It's an international organization that has been in the darkest of dark zones on what they call the Winternet. At least one of their social media networks is named Wipeout, and they communicate with a string of mobile apps. Authorities have identified TEZER as one of them. It sends a coded message before it vanishes.

"Digital experts from international agencies are hard at work scanning the Net, hoping to trace the source. This group is organized, they're taking children, they're killing people, and they're threatening large-scale mass violence. One statement on their network warns that they—and we quote—'will make a mark unlike anything the world has ever seen.' So far, attacks have happened in London, Oslo, Rome and Warsaw. Early reports suggest a connection with a serial killer who committed suicide in his cell in New York last night. Among his effects were detailed plans for these incidents."

I was shocked. "New York!"

They all looked at me. I excused myself and left the room. Something big was happening in New York and I wasn't there!

I walked fast down a long hallway. I spotted Dorion in one of the rooms, holding Nettaline, as she clung to him. I realized that these two formed another liaison. He was Sheine's father.

Seeking a private area, I spotted a set of doors with glass windows. The room inside looked like an art gallery. Paintings hung from the walls and several sculptures graced the center, surrounded by padded benches. This would work. I entered and closed the door before I dug in my bag for the cell phone Portia had given me. It might be bugged, but I had to call Jack, my partner on the NYPD.

This wasn't my normal phone, so I hoped he wouldn't let my

call go to voicemail. To my relief, he picked up. I greeted him in relief.

"Hey, doll! It's about time. Couldn't reach you."

"I'm in Paris. What's going on?"

"Haven't you seen the news? It's some kind of coordinated attack in different places."

"I just heard about New York."

"Yeah, it's a mess here, and it's all connected. What'cha doin' in Paris?"

"Long story. My father had property here and—"

"Look, Deelilah, I'm about to catch a plane myself."

"You? You never travel." I started to pace.

"We have a solid lead on Nick. I'm heading to London. Thanks to your intel, we think he was a courier for the London attack. I'll be there early tomorrow, Dandeelyon."

I still seethed over how I'd missed the fact that Nick Capaldi, our colleague, was a bad cop. He'd helped Miegul to trap my father and murder his associates. Behind the scenes, he'd manipulated evidence and helped Miegul to flee.

"I'll get there," I promised. "Just let me know where you'll be."

I came around a corner and stopped short. Jack was talking but I didn't hear it. "I gotta go, Jack," I mumbled. "Text me when you get in. I'll see you in London."

I stood transfixed before a richly hued mural that took up an entire wall, up to the 12-foot ceiling and spanning at least 30 feet, like some kind of Michelangelo painting. The focal point at the bottom was a child—a blonde girl in a light gray shift, viewed from behind. She reached up a tiny bare arm, hand open, to a bright, enormous winged creature that crouched over her. I assumed this was a rendering of a *ma'lakh* in its truest form. Framed by a darkly purple background, it was mesmerizing.

Yet it was also disturbing. I had the same feeling I'd had when I'd seen Sitri emerge from a whirlwind of fire. This thing was dangerous. The huge filmy wings, layered in many shades of purple and red, stretched majestically over the *ma'lakh*'s back before arching to touch the ground behind him as he knelt to the child's level. His large eyes were dark and sad. He reached toward her extended hand, almost touching his long fingers to her tiny ones.

53

Thick blond hair tumbled over his shoulders, like in those medieval paintings I'd seen in the Met, hiding his male parts. He wore nothing to soften the luminous sheen of his smooth, muscled skin. The tones were so expertly textured I could imagine both figures breaking into motion.

Those eyes. This creature looked like Sitri, the way he'd gazed at me several times. I couldn't reconcile it. This was not the hot "Agent Brenner" who'd enticed me in New York. It wasn't even the enflamed destroyer, or the trickster who'd kissed the back of my neck in Montmartre.

I had to be mistaken. But those were his dark blue eyes, his angular face. I backed up. Portia and Charmaine were right. I had no idea what I was getting into. I'd had sex with him. But I'd been with a *man*, not.... *this*.

Heat flushed through me. I pressed a hand against my pounding heart. I couldn't imagine what it meant to be *sealed* to this creature. My mother had intended one of her daughters—me—for him? It felt more like a sacrifice to the gods than an arranged liaison.

I took another step back. I should leave, just get out. That would be the smart thing to do.

But I couldn't. I had no resources, no money. And Jack was coming.

Jack!

He'd help. I just had to get to London. Portia would probably be pleased to pay my way. I'd *give* her this place if she'd get me back to New York.

I squinted at the painting. It was so familiar. I'd seen it before. Of course I had; I'd *lived* here as a child.

Then I saw a brief flash from a feathery pattern inside the left wing. I watched, waiting, until it flashed again. A symbol. I peered more closely. The symbol had looked like what I'd briefly seen in that *noea* dossier. Then two more emerged from the same area. I thought I could see more, buried in the wing's shadow, but they were dim.

I took a tentative step toward where the wings draped along the ground. I touched the paint. It smelled dusty, and was hard and unyielding. Whatever had been there was gone.

But a memory was present, like a pod fiber floating in the air that defies capture. I recalled a soft, frothy sensation and the delicate fragrance of flowers. I could almost smell it. I'd heard a woman warn me, *"Faites attention!* Touch lightly." She was teaching me something. I strained to recall. I couldn't see her face.

Holding my breath, I traced the painted lines to try to pull out the rest of this memory. I had touched him. I recalled this creature's stillness as he let my tiny fingers explore his vulnerable spot where the wings emerged from his back. I'd been so careful. He'd smiled at me. I'd buried my hand into all that warm softness. The wings had moved, thrilling me. I'd felt enveloped in care and trust.

I pressed against the wall, both hands flat on the painting. I'd touched him. I had *touched* him. In this form.

Someone, another woman, had sounded surprised. "She can't!" They were discussing me. I'd ignored them. I hadn't been scared.

I put my face against the wall as if it would yield answers from beneath the hardened paint. The image had just elicited the special vision from my childhood that I called my probe. The memory was there. I had to invite it. Like flying the helicopter. Relax, let it come.

There. That delicious citrus fragrance. I breathed in. Then I sensed I wasn't alone.

"What do you see?"

Chapter Thirteen

Startled, I turned. Sitri stood there, arms folded, not ten feet from me. Shadowed by light from a window behind him, he watched me. Still in leather, he felt ominous. And he looked so human. My nipples tightened. There was no way I was cutting *him* off.

He gestured toward the painting. "Can you see them?"

I nodded. "These symbols. What are they?"

He glanced at the image, then back at me. "It's a test. This is where we first knew you had vision. Few can see them."

He'd confirmed my memory. I'd been here. "I don't know what they mean."

He stepped closer and swept his fingers along the arch of the wing where I'd seen the symbols glow. "It took Kaitlyn years to finish this."

"My mother painted this?"

"Yes." He pointed at the girl. "This is her. This is when we first met, what she saw."

So, it *was* him. My heart beat faster. He looked at me as if to gauge how I was processing all of this. "Does this scare you?"

The tight shake of my head gave away my lie. I wanted to say, *show me your wings*, but instead I squeaked out, "Was she?"

"Even at this age, she was fierce." His eyes narrowed. "So were you."

"What do the symbols mean?"

"They're *noea*. If you stayed here long enough, you'd see hundreds. But I need you for something else."

In his eyes I thought I saw a hint of vulnerability, like in the painting. Kaitlyn, the child, had found his sweet spot. I wanted to find it, too.

I held up a hand. "Wait! I just did something for you, something big. You owe me."

He looked amused. "Put it on your list."

"What list?"

"The things you think I owe you."

I blinked at him. "You *do* owe me. You could have left me in New York. But you brought me here. You've put me through a hell of a lot. I want to know what's going on. What was that thing you did to me last night? So I could see those flashes?"

"*Synthetry.*"

"What?"

"A plateau. The point of true intimacy, when shared. You found the balance between your passion and the dossier's energy, so you could pull the information it had absorbed. We found most of the children, but some are still missing." His eyes changed. He glanced at the mural behind me, at the child. "Our world is dangerous. When I started this"—he gestured toward it—"I made enemies. We thrive at a cost."

Started this. Another hole in my story.

I lifted my chin. "I want my memories back."

"No."

That was not the reply I'd expected. "I helped you. I *depleted* myself to help you." I tapped the wall. "I remember being here in this house, and you were here. I want more."

Sitri put a hand on my right shoulder. When I looked up I knew he could see the bandage over where he'd left his mark. I yearned to reconnect. I wanted to touch him again like I had as a child, in that soft, warm place.

"You will receive what you need," he said, "*when* you need it. Right now, Charmaine has little time."

This alarmed me. "Little time?"

"The poison is changing her blood. Yours can help her fight it."

Damn! I owed her. "I still have questions. About my mother and who I am."

I saw a subtle shift in his eyes before he said, "Later."

"And I want to go to London."

"I expected that you would."

"How do you—?" Of course. "You know where Nick is." That's how Jack got the "solid" lead.

"When you're ready, I will have someone take you."

57

I felt the pressure of Charmaine's condition, but I didn't want to leave. I handed him the phone. "Give me a number."

He pushed it away. "You don't need this with me."

Frustrated, I said, "You still owe me."

"Put it on your list."

I started to leave, but then had a thought. I turned back and said, "For future reference, for this synthetry thing, you don't have to drug me."

He looked amused. He folded his arms over his chest and said, "I didn't."

Chapter Fourteen

Sometimes you don't know the value of what you have until others show you.

With that revelation still buzzing, I sat down in front of Charmaine. The television continued to run outraged headlines, but the sound was off. Portia had cleared the room, including Pascher. She explained to me that the brew from Arren had to be activated. Arren had sent her own blood for it, since she was descended from Kaitlyn's sister, but it had failed.

I understood. "So you want some of mine."

"You don't owe me," said Charmaine.

"In fact, I do. You rescued me in New York, so if I can help you reconnect with Pascher, let's do it."

Portia raised the syringe. "I will take only what we need."

I held out my arm. Drawing half of a syringe, she squirted my blood into a cup of brownish liquid that looked like broth and smelled like black tea. Charmaine sniffed, stirred it, and drank it. She grimaced and closed her eyes. I didn't know what to expect.

"Maybe I should draw more," Portia said, "just in case. We can store it."

"No!" said Charmaine. "Not a good idea." She glanced around as if she thought someone had overheard.

Portia looked at me. "If we're the only three who know and we lock it away..."

Charmaine shook her head. "Too risky."

Portia shrugged and went into the kitchen. I followed her. I held out my arm. "I agree with you. I think you should keep some here."

"Char is right. It would be risky."

"And it might be risky *not* having it. Who knows? If you won't stick me, I will."

59

She nodded. In a drawer, she found a glass vial and bent over my arm. I tried not to flinch when the needle hit. It was hard to believe that my blood had magical qualities, but they knew better than I did. After she stoppered the vial with a purple cap, Portia grabbed a small wooden box with an ornate bronze latch from a cupboard. When she opened it, I saw a red satin cushion. "I will store it in a safe place," Portia assured me. "Locked."

"What's that painting in the gallery?" I asked. "The one with Kaitlyn and Sitri. She was a child."

She looked surprised. "You don't remember?"

"No."

"It depicts an important event for us. It is our inception. Back then, the *ma'lakhim* were wiping out their progeny. The *nejah* were devouring everything, causing starvation when crops failed and herds diminished. They started consuming the children. The *ma'lakhim* decided to stop the horror by erasing their existence among us, killing male and female. Hundreds were wiped out, maybe thousands. It was at least three generations. Sitri participated, but when he saw Kaitlyn, he could not continue. She was so bold. She walked right up to him to make him stop. And he did. Instead of killing her, he showed her how to hide. And she showed others. It changed everything for the *noea*. And for him. On this day, Sitri became our protector."

"When did all this happen?"

"Centuries ago."

I hardly knew what to say. "My mother has lived for centuries?"

Portia peered at me as if she was confused. "She has *Lumé* blood and she is fully sealed, blood to blood, to a *Ser*. Of course. She can renew."

I stared at her. I couldn't process this. It had unsettling implications for me as well.

"Kaitlyn was *la Reine*, our queen," Portia continued. "None of us would be here if not for her. Even Sitri. And *that* is quite a story."

"Maybe I already know. If I could just get my memories back."

Portia squinted at me. "It is better, I think, if you learn than remember." She held up the box. "I will put this in a safe place."

This seemed like a kind way to tell me to stop asking. But now I understood Leith's comment on the plane: You're a *princess*. It sounded like Sitri owed Kaitlyn, big time. Maybe that's why he was my guardian. Maybe he didn't want me to realize just how indebted he was. And yet, he'd wanted me here. He knew I wouldn't quit till I had what I wanted.

I went out to Charmaine. She seemed to be asleep, with her head back against the chair. I was about to leave to prepare for London when she started to talk.

"There's something you should know," she said, opening her eyes. "This is important. Just listen." She took a quick breath. "These liaisons, they're not what you think. I love Pasch deeply. But at times I've hated him, too. The *ma'lakhim* have a function. They do what they're made for, without apology. Sitri will protect you, but if your needs thwart his purpose, you lose. Period. They don't negotiate. It's... it hurts."

I sat down next to her. "Char, I don't fully grasp it. I know that. It doesn't help to have so many blanks where my memories should be. But I also know that whatever this is, it's been an important part of my life, a part that everyone I know has hidden from me. I intend to get answers, even if it pits me *against* Sitri."

"It will."

I was startled. "What does *that* mean?"

"He will protect you."

I shrugged.

"Some memories would... "

"What?"

"Some would hurt you."

I stared at her. But I couldn't argue. Something about this comment rang true. I'd pinpointed the deepest pain of my childhood to the day my mother had abandoned me, but maybe there was something else. Maybe it wasn't about her at all. Before I could press for more, Charmaine said, "Don't give him any more blood. Don't even tell him you stored some here."

Nothing got past her. "I think everyone is making too big a deal over this."

"That's because you don't know much. But you know why Miegul wants it. That should make you careful."

She was right. Miegul had wanted my blood to bait an angel trap. That much I'd seen for myself. I didn't know Portia. I didn't even know Charmaine, actually. I should be more careful. I thought about asking Portia to give back the vial of blood when Nettaline rushed in. Even in a plain white T-shirt and black jeans, with her black hair and blue eyes, she was a stunner. "We're off to Glastonbury," she said. "Dorion is preparing the helicopter."

Char raised a hand. "Wait." To me she said, "Go with them."

"No. I'm going to London."

"Glastonbury will answer some questions. Then, go to London."

"It won't take long to get there," said Nettaline.

"But Sitri—"

"He's there."

I didn't understand. "No, I just saw him down the hall. He's not in England."

"He is, and he's waiting. So, you must dress down. Quickly! Meet us on the roof. The stairway up to it is near your suite. Bring a jacket."

Chapter Fifteen

My head was spinning. I managed to change, locate the rooftop, and join them on the sporty Eurocopter in just under eight minutes, even as I stewed over what Charmaine had said. *Hurt you.* This just kept getting worse.

I'd considered jeans, but decided instead on a loose skirt and silk tank top. I knew it was hot in London today. Into a light carryall, I'd packed jeans, along with my passport. I could send for my suitcases once I got back to New York. I placed the crystal and *Oraculum* inside one that I could lock. For the chopper, I grabbed the leather jacket that Sitri had given me. I'd forgotten to thank him. Apparently, I'd see him in Glastonbury.

Maybe for the last time.

Whatever my mother had intended for me, this was *my* life. She wasn't here anymore. I hadn't been here even a day and it felt as if everyone around me knew things that *I* should know. For all their seeming friendliness, on a deeper level, they were not my friends. They were hiding things, maybe setting me up. They certainly had reason to want me out of the picture.

As I rushed to get things into my overnight bag, I noticed the *noea* dossier that I'd held in Montmartre. It lay on the table. I hesitated. If I wanted to leave this world behind, that was part of it. But the thing intrigued me. I went over and picked it up.

Nothing.

The others were waiting. I was so tempted to open it.

No time.

I slipped it into my overnight bag. I could look at it in London.

Portia met me on the roof, where the chopper was running. She handed me a small navy blue bag. "Charmaine said you should take these. The girls can show you how to use them." She grabbed my arm affectionately. *"Je vous remercie* for your assistance."

I nodded. I didn't tell her I expected to get Jack to take me home.

Nettaline sat in the co-pilot seat and Leith was in the back, behind Dorion. She handed me a headset. I clamped my hair into a tight twist before I put it on. In the bag from Portia I found a pair of soft leather slip-on flats, with moccasin-like soles. Not what I would choose. "Why these?" I asked.

Leith gestured toward her feet. She wore similar shoes. "Just try them." Nettaline turned and showed me hers.

As we lifted off, I shrugged, removed my sandals and put them on. They surprised me. I couldn't believe how well they fit, as if they'd been made for me. I felt barefoot but fully protected. I liked them.

Nettaline smiled. "We all have them. They're quiet and they leave no prints, not even in mud."

I snorted. "No prints? Are we going on some kind of caper?"

"Trust us, you will love them. When we land, we'll show you how they work."

I was feeling a little like a Manson girl, about to go on a creepy crawly mission.

"What's in Glastonbury?" I asked. I already knew one thing: it was the place, according to legend, from which my concave scrying crystal and a book of celestial codes had been exhumed centuries ago. John Dee and his partner in the occult, Edward Kelley, believed they'd found a way to use the crystal to talk with angels. They'd been given some red powder, which allegedly facilitated their magic. The story I'd read suggested that an angel had presented these items to Kelley. Since Kelley had been a con artist, I'd doubted his claims. Now I wasn't sure.

"We located a secret Ignis stronghold," said Nettaline.

"You did?" I asked. "How?"

They all looked at me. "You showed us," said Dorion. "You don't remember?"

"I recall showing Sitri some lights on some maps on a wall. He didn't tell me what it meant, but I sense that he's quite the minimalist. How about an idiot's guide to *ma'lakhology* before we get there? I'd like to know what I'm heading in to."

"I'll tell her," said Leith.

"Good." I leaned back and looked at her. "First, how do they move so fast? I was with Sitri and ten minutes later he's 200 miles away."

She laughed. Her boy-cut hair fit her assertive personality, yet her large blue-green eyes softened her look. "Yes, that's hard to grasp. They can penetrate energy fields. In some forms, physical laws don't affect them. That's what the wings are for."

"They fly?"

Dorion looked over at Nettaline with a veiled expression. It felt awkward to be talking about *ma'lakhim* with him right here. But I needed answers.

Leith seemed to consider what to say. "Not like a bird, but they push through force fields that hinder the rest of us. But, yeah, in their lightest form, which we can't see, they can be up here, outside the helicopter." She pointed out the window. "You'll get used to it. They sense something somewhere in the world that requires their attention and they just go! Zip! If Sitri called Dorion right now, he'd be gone. We'd have to take over."

"With no warning?"

"Depends on the urgency."

"What if no one else is in the chopper?"

"Then he wouldn't be, either. They only fly or drive things if we need it. Otherwise..." She gestured, letting me know they had no need of such things.

Nettaline turned around in her seat. "They can be as solid as us, like Dorion is now, or they can be *le vent*, the wind." She kissed her fingers and made a gesture as if they disappeared. "They have transitional forms, including some with full wings. Some forms are transparent, some we can't see at all. You might just see the wings briefly before they vanish. We have a chart in the library that shows them all. With *fiducie*, when they trust you, they show you more." She squeezed Dorion's arm. "I hope Sitri restores your memories. He used to take you out to the country to see them zip around in the night sky and listen to their music."

This startled me. "He did?"

"*Oui*. When you were *une petite fille*."

What could *that* have been like? "I have the impression he doesn't want me to remember."

I sensed an awkward moment, but Nettaline recovered. "At

first," she said, "they thought you should be trained right away. I don't know why they—"

Leith interrupted. "You've had some training, but not in a focused way."

"They? Who made these decisions?"

Nettaline picked it back up. "Mayon, Kaitlyn and Sitri, and other *Lumé*. Also Alexandre. Anyway, back to your question. If they're trapped in solid form like this"—she gestured toward Dorion—"they can be killed, like us. But usually, they shift too fast for someone to harm them."

I recalled how Sitri had rammed a motorcycle at high speed straight into Miegul's car in New York, but he'd walked away without a scratch.

"Miegul's gang tries to trap them while they're shifting, at the physical end," said Leith, "because it's the best way to siphon their power. They're still solid enough to be trapped, but they're also fully *ma'lakh*. They can stay trapped in that form for a long time. They can be hurt but not killed. If they reach their most ethereal form, only other *ma'lakhim* can do any damage, and it has to be at the same level or higher."

"Only a *Lumé* can kill another *Lumé*," Nettaline added.

"And what is a *Lumé*?"

"Like Sitri. The oldest ones. Chief? General?" She looked at Dorion. He glanced at me and said, "You have no word for it. He is a destroyer, but only after he can no longer protect."

"Right, he told me that. He can turn into fire. I saw that. There are others like him?"

"You saw him?" Leith asked. She looked impressed. "You could look at him?"

"Yes."

"It didn't hurt your eyes?"

"It was bright, and hot, but it didn't hurt."

She nodded. "That's a gift. Maybe you'll get to see his full expression. I've heard that's quite a sight. During a storm, he can pull down lightning."

"Leith," Dorion interrupted. "We'll be there soon." I had the impression he thought she was telling me too much. I looked out and was surprised that I could see land already. We'd traveled fast.

"OK, right," said Leith. "Here's what you need to know before we arrive. You know what Ignis is, right?"

"Sort of. The enemy."

"They want to wipe us out." She pointed at Nettaline, herself and me. "The *noea*. This all comes back to us: who wants us dead and who wants us alive?"

"Leith!"

"Nettie thinks it's so much more complicated, but it all amounts to a conflict over decisions made eons ago, and who has power and who else wants it."

Nettaline turned around again. "*Assez*! We are only just part of it. The *ma'lakhim* already had their own battles, but when Sitri saved Kaitlyn, it was divisive. It became a whole new arena. And that still affects us. You know that story, yes?"

"Portia told me the bare bones."

"Kaitlyn knew why Sitri was there, but instead of running away like she was told, she went right up to him. And that's when everything changed for us, the *noea*. Some *ma'lakhim* sided with him and some stayed loyal to the original plan. But the *nejah* were still hunted, so Ignis formed in their defense. Because we were protected, our brothers despised us."

Dorion looked at her but stayed quiet as she continued.

"Ignis is an alliance of the weakest *ma'lakhim* and the *nejah* who've escaped the various purges, but they've also recruited *noea* and some human associates, like we have. Without a *Lumé* or *Ser*, they can't do much against Sitri, so they try to hurt *us*. With Kaitlyn's ring, they've acquired a directory of our important locations. So, they can grab our children. They got over two dozen last night, but thanks to you, we rescued most of them. You showed us the hot spots."

I couldn't grasp how a ring of such importance had been given to me when I was a child. "How many *noea* are there?"

Nettaline gestured to Leith. "She knows all the numbers."

Leith shrugged. "It's hard to keep track. Around the world? There are thousands with some trace of *ma'lakhim* blood. But most don't realize it. And some want nothing to do with it. But more than 200 are specifically protected, and less than half are getting trained to participate with us." She looked squarely at me. "We have 48 full-time healers or warriors. We used to have a lot more."

67

"To the point," Nettaline continued, "we thwarted part of their assault and now the children are shielded. We will also try to get the others back."

"Can you?"

"We hope. Ignis has shields as well, which they adapt quickly. It is a constant process on both sides of acquiring and exploiting information before it changes. They once had a stronghold in Glastonbury, which we destroyed, but we think they placed another one nearby. We haven't located it yet, exactly, because it's underground. When the ground composition is just right, it becomes a shield."

"So Ignis has these places, too?"

"They are all over the world, mostly underground and in shielded buildings or caves. The ones you showed us are important, though. You saw them because they took some *noea* children there."

"I thought I saw them because of some book—that dossier."

Nettaline looked back at me. I had the impression I'd just revealed a secret. She grabbed Dorion's arm, but he shook his head.

"What dossier?" she asked.

I had to be more careful. It was a secret all right, but I wasn't sure whose. Now it was mine. I pressed my foot against the bag. "I don't know. I couldn't read it. Truthfully, I have no idea how I got the information. I was kind of in a trance."

"*C'est bien,*" Nettaline said, "we just have to be careful today. If they sense we're near where they're keeping our children, they might kill them."

"So these assaults on daycares," I said, "they're all related to this?"

"Yes."

"And what about this Black Torch group?"

"We are still puzzled over this, but it is not a human terrorist group. It's part of Miegul's operation."

"And Sheine. She's your daughter, right?"

Nettaline nodded and gestured toward Dorion. "Ours. She's six." She pulled out a phone and leaned toward me to show me a photo. Sheine was a sweet looking girl, with a round face, tiny nose, hair in loose black curls, and dark blue eyes with large irises. Her open smile, seemingly eager for affection, reached into my soul.

"She's so cute." I wanted to say I was sorry. Her abduction was the result of my act.

"She was in London for training. That made her a target. The more training they have, the more value. They know we train only the *noea* with unique abilities. Sheine can effect apports. She can move things through energy fields without touching them. It's rare. They could hurt her and use her to hurt us."

"But there's hope, right?"

Nettaline nodded as she rubbed the side of Dorion's arm. "We've had three children. Only Sheine is still alive. We know the risks of having them, but when you love a *ma'lakh*, you just want them. At least, I do."

Dorion reached over to touch her knee. I saw a tear slide down her cheek. Leith put a hand on her shoulder. "We'll find her, I'm sure of it."

"Do you think they were looking for her specifically?" I asked.

"Of those still missing," Dorion said, "we can make out at least part of their objective. We think they performed a sweep to net certain children."

"Why her?"

"She's only six, but she can read symbols like you can. She has absorbed many of the codes from Kaitlyn's paintings. They might want that information or they have some purpose we don't yet know."

"But how do they know about these kids?"

"They have spies," Leith said. "Some of the *a'ika*, maybe. A trainer. A *noea* with sympathies, or with a *nejah* lover. Or they have leverage with one of us. We had one instance where a *noea* with Ignis had her children training with ours. Her daughter provided all kinds of information to them. We lost several *ma'lakhim*."

"And they want Sheine because of her abilities?" I asked.

"She is Dorion's daughter," Nettaline said. "They know his status and they hope his concern for her will weaken Sitri's protection, or inspire betrayal."

I sensed a shift in the air. I guessed this was one of those situations to which Charmaine had referred: conflicting agendas and hurt feelings.

"I'm sure she's scared, but…"

Nettaline looked at me. "But?"

69

I shrugged. "Being *noea* seems to come with... I don't know... resilience? Bravado?"

"We're not all like Kaitlyn," Leith said.

"No, you're right." Nettaline nodded. "She's independent. And resourceful. She will understand why she was taken, and if she sees *une échappataoire*, a way to escape, she will do it. She won't freeze. Like when—"

A look from Dorion clipped her words. So much for a full lesson.

"It's difficult to conceive a child with a *ma'lakh*," Leith said, "especially a gifted child that can actually survive."

I blinked. "Survive?"

"The celestial traits can overwhelm the human part, or the human is too concentrated for the celestial to emerge. We've tried to figure out the percentages. First, it's hard to even conceive a child, and nearly two-thirds miscarry. Another ten percent die before or at birth. Quite a few don't make it past infancy. Of those that do, about one in four remain frail. Most are ordinary and never even learn that they're *noea*. The celestial blood has been so weakened by marriages with humans that we barely recognize them."

"But I—"

"You," said Leith, "are another story. You survived to adulthood, you developed your talents spontaneously, and—"

Nettaline turned around. "You should ask Charmaine or Portia. They can guide you better than we can." She gave Leith a look that suggested it was time to keep her mouth shut.

Leith looked out the window. I sat back. Clearly, there were things I should know before I committed to this world. Once I got to London, I'd get some perspective. And Jack would bring me back home. Jack. He really felt like home right now. I needed to be grounded. I wasn't cut out for this.

Chapter Sixteen

Who knew that a pair of shoes could make you smaller?

We landed on a flat piece of land hidden within a copse of leafy trees. Nettaline and Leith told me to leave my bag in the chopper for now. I wasn't keen about leaving the dossier, but I couldn't pull it out in front of them. I'd soon be on my way to London, so I figured it would be safe for now.

They led me toward a three-story cottage. I hadn't seen Dorion leave, but he suddenly just wasn't there. This gave me an opening. "So, where do these creatures, these *ma'lakhim*, come from? How do they even exist?"

"They don't tell us," said Nettaline, "not even after years of intimacy. That's a particular mystery you might never unravel, except that they *are* here, they *do* exist, and some of us are allowed to know them. If we don't probe too much, we can make it work. Charmaine and Portia are privy to more than we are."

"And you more than me," Leith said to Nettaline.

"But *what* are they? Angels? What's a *ma'lakh*?"

"They're angels, but…"

Leith leaned toward me, cupping her hand to whisper, "They're the bad boys.

"Like demons?"

Nettaline shook her head. "No. Not evil. They misbehaved… and still do, I guess, since they're with us. They protect the natural forces, but they got involved with human women, which was forbidden, and some revealed secrets, so they're kind of…" She looked at Leith.

"They're a lot of shades of gray," Leith offered. "Even the ones in Ignis." She stopped. "Wait. The shoes. Hold still."

I stopped.

"Do you sense anything?" she asked.

71

"No."

Nettaline pointed at her shoes. "It is subtle. Listen with your feet, where they contact the ground."

I stood still and closed my eyes. I sensed a slight vibration, like a flowing current, but it didn't mean anything to me. I shrugged and looked at them. Then it felt as if something moved, very deep below me, a dragon turning in its sleep. "It's strange. What is that?"

"The *ma'lakhim* taught us," said Leith. "They gave us the shoes. I don't know how they're made, but we love them. It adds a layer to your senses, and more information."

"What information?"

"Like if people are underground, or there's water or a cave, or if something's coming from a distance. You can sense it before you see or hear it."

"When the *ma'lakhim* get used to you," Nettaline added, "they will stay barefoot. That's what they prefer, and they acquire more information this way. You will think they cannot possibly walk on rough ground, but actually, a thin layer of energy shields them."

I'd already seen Sitri barefoot, twice. He'd urged me to remove my shoes in Montmartre. Was he comfortable? Or indifferent?

As we neared the cottage, which appeared to be a quaint but spacious bed-and-breakfast, I noticed three impressive Harleys parked in front. "Is there a biker convention here?" I asked.

Leith touched my leather jacket. "Good thing you wore this. It's nice, by the way. Not too heavy. Good for a bike."

I recalled the crazy ride in New York when Sitri had grabbed me on the run and then transferred me to Charmaine. That had been my abrupt and harrowing introduction to the *noea* and *ma'lakhim*.

Nettaline gestured toward the inn. "We have many places like this where we can meet. Run by human allies."

Krystal had told me the name of such people—*a'ika*. That's what Krystal was, too. And my father.

A white-haired woman who looked 60-ish opened the door. Nettaline introduced her as Ellen and gave her a false name for me. I figured they had their reasons for secrets. Ellen seemed welcoming but worried. She hugged Nettaline and tried to reassure her about Sheine. We went up some well-worn wooden steps to a wide hallway on the top floor. I smelled angel bread. It made me miss my aunt.

In a spacious room filled with chairs and a long oak table, Orias and Pascher were looking at a large computer screen on a wall to my right that showed a 3-D map. Floral scents from the *ma'lakhim* overpowered the delicate angel bread. Spread out on the table was an odd-looking topographic map with areas circled in red. Sitri was across the room, leaning on a wide windowsill. And there was Dorion, telling him something. I hoped it wasn't how I'd spilled the beans about the dossier. A lean *ma'lakh* with caramel-colored hair stood by—Tibreth, I recalled. He glanced at me and left by a door on the opposite side of the room.

Sitri invited me over. I liked when men looked at me appreciatively, but I felt absolutely naked as I passed through this room. They all watched me. I sensed these *ma'lakhim* knew a lot about me. As I approached Sitri, I glanced down his leather-clad legs to his bare feet. Now I understood.

"Orias will take you to London," he said. He eyed the leather jacket I wore with approval.

I patted it. "Thank you for this. I like it. Shall I wait downstairs?"

Pascher tapped the map on the table. "Can you confirm this first?"

I realized why it looked so strange: it wasn't topographical. Instead, it mapped underground caves and tunnels in southeastern England. I knew that many tunnels existed throughout this area, from mines and smuggling operations. I suspected that the *ma'lakhim* had their own complex subterranean world, deeper than any human could dig. Pascher pointed to the circled areas. "We located entry spots, here and here. And we know the tunnels and caves they've used in the past."

Nettaline came over to stand with me. I scanned the map. Something wasn't right.

"Why are you ignoring this area?" I asked, pointing northwest of Glastonbury. "See this here? There's a large hollow area underground. And a tunnel. A long one. I see a vague shadow of it here. Don't you?"

Pascher looked at me. I fought the urge to avert my eyes. I wondered if I'd ever get past my startle reflex to that subtle *ma'lakh* flicker.

"If it is *nejah*," said Nettaline, "it could be shielded. They cannot see."

Sitri came to the table as I traced out what I saw. I tapped it. "This is where you need to go."

Sitri seemed annoyed. He looked at Nettaline. "Do you see it?"

"*Non*," she said, "but I trust what she sees."

At the other end of the table, Leith agreed. "We should check."

This was weird. It looked perfectly clear to me. I was tempted to rub the map. How could none of them see it? "I'm sure I pointed it out on the Montmartre map." Some of what I'd experienced that morning flowed back. "This area made an impression on me, because I knew that Glastonbury was where they supposedly got—"

I stopped. I'd been about to dismiss Edward Kelley's silly claim about learning an angel language. But it hadn't been silly. This language was real and he'd actually been shown how to read the celestial script. The concave crystal—the one that had recently blasted me with energy—had let him read it backwards. And I was in a room right now with four creatures that *spoke* this language.

They all watched me, waiting.

I stretched my fingers and started over. "It made an impression, because it's related to Miegul and the mysterious red powder and his Jack the Ripper blood ceremonies, right? They used the powder back then to trap one of you." I sensed restlessness, even anger, but I continued. "And Glastonbury is associated with John Dee. At least *Miegul* thinks so, and that's the point. We have to imagine what *he* would do. So, when I saw flashes on the map right here,"—I pointed—"it made sense to me. Miegul thinks this place is important to *you*. As if it's sacred ground."

"It is," said Sitri. "They cannot penetrate there."

Pascher looked at Sitri. "Unless…" He went silent but I thought they were communicating. The air was tense. Sitri turned to Nettaline. "Do you get anything from Sheine?"

Tears wet her eyes. She shook her head.

A dark mood numbed the room. I recalled how awful it had been when I was separated from my mother when I was four. It had haunted me for years with a sharp ache of longing and loss. I thought Sheine, must be terrified no matter how smart she might be. I felt like I'd failed her.

74

"She might be here," I said. "It's not far from London. This area spoke to me, and now I can see its location clearly. You should check."

"I will go," said Dorion. He was pleading more than volunteering.

Sitri shook his head. "No." To Orias, he said, "Take Dianysus to London." Then he strode from the room.

Chapter Seventeen

I know my flaw: it's believing that I know my flaw.

I looked at Pascher. "Where's he going?"

With a sweep of his hand, Pascher gestured that I should go after him.

I left the room and raced down the stairs. No sign of him. I went outside to where the Harleys were parked. Sitri was pulling the largest one out of the line.

I ran over to him. "How will you find this place without me?"

"I know where it is."

I looked at his feet. "You're not riding barefoot."

Sitri mounted the bike and started it. I couldn't believe it. He was *leaving*. I hiked up my skirt, stepped on the peg, and scrambled on behind him.

Then I knew. He'd baited me. Again. He didn't need the bike. Not unless I was going, too.

He squeezed my bare leg, turned his head and said, "Stay close." I'd ridden with him before. I didn't need to be told twice.

After 20 minutes of racing north over small roads and around tight curves that tensed my thighs and left me breathless, we arrived in a forested area of the countryside, next to a crumbling old cemetery. Hills kept me from judging its size. I pushed off, relieved, and brushed dead bugs off my legs. Sitri parked off the road, behind an untrimmed hedge. As he walked back, I asked, "Do you ever drive safely?"

He looked puzzled. "You're unharmed. Would I risk you?"

"Hmm. Let me think. In the five days that I've known you, have I ever been at risk?"

He tilted his head. "What percentage was from *your* decisions?"

He was right. I'd repeatedly ignored his attempts to protect me.

Sitri gave me a small flashlight before he dug into his jacket pocket and produced a gun. "You can't carry this in London, but you should have it here."

It was a Glock 43, small and single stack but easy to carry. He handed me an extra 9mm magazine before he tugged on the jacket. "This has a gun pocket inside."

I took the gun. "Thank you." It felt good to be armed again. "This shortens my list of things you owe me." I held out my hand. "Keys, please, or fob, or whatever starts the bike. So you won't leave me stranded." I was sure he knew I'd been a motorcycle cop once and could handle a bike.

"You don't trust me?"

"You're unpredictable."

He handed over the fob. "Don't go off on your own."

"You don't trust *me*?"

"*You* are predictable."

I opened my mouth in surprise. "I am *not*! I didn't go to London, did I?"

"Which proves it."

Before I could retort, he turned, gestured for me to follow, and entered the cemetery.

"Wait!"

He stopped and looked back.

"Someone's here." Oddly enough, I felt it first in my feet. "I think it's kids." I felt something faint, like a breath. It wasn't a vibration, more like a sense of heat. There was something distinctly female about it. "She *was* here." It was an odd sensation, but I did "get" something about this girl whose picture I'd just seen. "I can—" I stopped. "Someone's... aware of me."

Sitri watched me. Then he came over, took my right hand and placed his left foot over my right foot. He gently pressed. I wanted to put my face against his chest and bathe in that scent, but I made myself concentrate.

At first, nothing happened. Then I felt hot darts shoot through the sole of my foot. I tried to pull away, but Sitri's pressure kept me planted. He gripped my hand. I glanced at his foot. He kissed my forehead and touched his mark on my throat, which swept through me in a flush of heat. I looked up, into those flames in his dark blue eyes.

77

I considered offering him a way to see for himself. I wanted to reconnect, but he removed his foot, turned his head, and seemed to be listening. I heard an engine in the distance,

"Something has happened," he said. He brought my hands together and pressed them between his, watching me. "What did you sense?"

"Kids. Girls. Five or six, I think. But two were... " I shook my head. I couldn't say it.

Sitri nodded. "There's death here. It's bad. Do you see the ring?"

This surprised me. "Is it here?"

"It might have been. This is where we made it. Do you see Miegul?"

I shook my head.

"If he's close, you will know. If he did come here, it was to use the ring to locate its source. He probably thinks Sheine can show him."

"Can she?"

Sitri gave me a strange look. "I don't know. You girls often surprise us." He turned toward the cemetery and took my arm. "Be careful of the thorns."

We walked past the first cluster of weathered headstones. Untended weeds proved a challenge for my bare legs, but I managed to keep up, still simmering with questions. Sitri had just given me new information.

"I thought the gem was made from my mother's blood," I said. \

"Partly." He guided me around a dark area that turned out to be a large hole. "She's from our line, the *Lumé*. It was her idea to make the powder, for us. For healing. We all contributed. From it, we made the gem. There *is* more here, but only a *Lumé* can approach it."

"How did Edward Kelley find it? How did he know?"

"One of us gave it to him, to use him."

"Is he part of Ignis, then?"

Sitri didn't answer. He stopped and looked to his right. I saw movement across the cemetery. It was difficult to see in the shadowy dusk, but something was there. Sitri went still, watching.

From behind a tall, chipped stone with a rounded top, about ten yards away, a fox jumped out. I was relieved until I saw it come straight at us. I reached for my gun, but Sitri stopped me. To my surprise, he crouched and held out a hand. The fox came up to him.

I wanted to shout, "He could be rabid!" I kept my hand near my gun pocket.

The creature made a little yap as Sitri lifted it to his chest. I stepped back. Then I recalled how the cats had followed the *ma'lakhim* into the dining room when they'd arrived. Sitri seemed to be listening.

"You used to like foxes," he said.

I put out my hand tentatively, afraid it would bite. I scratched it a little. It made a giggly sound. I recalled doing this before. With Sitri. He was right. I used to adore foxes.

"From her," he said, "we can learn things. She's been in a cooler place, underground. Do you feel it?"

I nodded. Her fur held heavier cold air.

"She's not hungry," Sitri continued, "and there's an odor on her breath."

I wasn't sure where he was going with this. He put the fox down and she scampered away, toward the west.

"We follow her," he said. "She has been near the bodies."

Chapter Eighteen

A cemetery always has secrets. This one had some shockers. Blood from the *ma'lakhim* elite was stored here. And somewhere nearby were bodies, other than those already in the ground.

As we stepped among crowded mossy stones, Sitri said, "Humans were here, and possibly *nejah*, but I sense no life now. If *you* do, tell me, especially if you think Miegul is here. He is tracking you."

I looked around, chilled. I didn't like the sound of that. "What should I expect?"

"If it feels like you're looking at something but the perspective is off, then he's trying to see what you see. This would show him your location. But you can also see what he sees, and where he is. If that happens, signal to me. Don't shut it off. We want to follow him."

"What if I'm looking at you?"

"He can watch, but he can't get close. We must learn his movements."

Sitri stopped again and stood still. I waited. Then I felt it, too. Under my feet, I sensed a hollowness.

"It's here," he said.

"Under the cemetery?"

"The caves were here first. But we sealed them, to prevent access. Recently, they have been opened." He began walking again. The purpose in his stride suggested he knew where to find what he was looking for. I kept an eye open for movement. I didn't like that Miegul could learn where I was. I felt for the gun to reassure myself.

We walked to the edge of the cemetery where the fox had gone and approached a drop-off. I didn't see an opening until we were nearly on top of it. Cool air wafted up. I saw large pieces of rock that had been blasted out. The damp smell from inside carried something else that made me queasy.

Sitri stood still, as if assessing the situation.

"Is this what we're looking for?" I asked.

"Inside. This opening is recent. It should not be here."

He took my hand to help me scramble over the rocks and get into the cave. The shoes were remarkable in the way they gripped the unstable surfaces. Once we'd climbed down, the tunnel was large with a high curved ceiling and a flat floor. I turned on the flashlight but figured Sitri could see in the dark.

"Let the girls lead you," he said. "If they're alive, you will know where they are."

I didn't like the sound of that. I'd seen dead kids as a detective. It's not something you forget. "Why wouldn't they be alive?" I asked.

"Ignis takes only those of value to them."

"You've seen this before?"

"Too many times. But I sense something different about this. They should not have gotten in here."

We heard movement. Sitri told me to wait, then vanished into the darkness. I wasn't sure what to do. I didn't like just standing there alone. The others were coming, I knew, but I wasn't sure when. There was no way I was going to wait. I didn't want to use the light until I was well away from the mouth of the cave. I reached to my right to locate a wall. The cool surface was smoother than I expected. Once I was oriented, I kept going. I didn't relish staying behind alone after what he'd just revealed. Miegul could be anywhere.

I stubbed my toe more than once trying to feel my way, but after I was about 30 feet in, the ground grew even. Sensing that the ceiling overhead was fairly high. I pulled out the flashlight and turned it on. I saw intricate work on the walls, as if there'd once been a veritable city down here. This world just kept getting larger. This wasn't just a cave.

I kept moving. The shoes were amazing. They made no sound and buffered me from feeling the rough terrain. Yet, like the girls had said, I could feel things through the soles.

I came into an open area with a domed ceiling, much grander than the map had suggested. The place was damp and smelled musty, but the odor of death was thicker. Recent death. My heart sank. I trained the light toward a dark area on the ground that felt ominous. I could barely process what I was seeing.

Then Sitri was next to me. "Did I not ask you to wait?"

"No. You *told* me to wait. And I decided not to. I'm skilled at this. If we're partners—"

"Partners trust each other."

That was a tough one. "Since you know me so well, Sitri, tell me. Do I trust you?"

"You once did."

Hmm. I was at a loss.

Sitri took my right hand. He gripped it so that my ring finger and little finger were free, but the other two fingers curled inward. He positioned my hand over my left breast. "This is the signal you made up. Two fingers over your heart. This was *our* signal. Trust."

We'd been through something together in New York. He'd had my back, just as I'd tried to have his. "Okay. But just don't keep me in a corner."

He held out his hand to let me lead the way.

On the floor were several shapes that I thought must be bodies. I went closer, shone my flashlight, and counted three. Sitri walked among them, looking from one to another. "From the daycare center," he said. "Teachers." He knelt and touched one, turning it. "Poisoned."

I put my hand over my nose and stepped over an adult male, expecting him to rise up and shout, "Surprise! We got you." But the silent corpses remained still. Cave sweat had settled on this one's face, making him look clammy. One had released noxious excrement.

Sitri pointed. "Shine the light on that wall."

I did so. It was filled with carved symbols. "What are they?"

"*Noea*. Or *nejah*. They have the same origin."

"Can you read it?"

Instead of answering, he went over to the wall and knelt. I followed with the light. I was shocked to see two small girls, posed, leaning against each other. Sitri picked one up. He held her close. I realized this was one of the kidnapped *noea* kids. I didn't know what to say. I sensed we were not alone. I turned with the light, and barely saw the dark-skinned Pehel step from the shadows. Orias followed. It was like watching them emerge from behind a dark waterfall, at first blurred and then solid.

Sitri said something I didn't understand, angry, abrupt. Orias picked up the other dead child and carried her out. Pehel took the one from Sitri. To my right, Dorion appeared and went over to the wall.

"Wait!" I said. "You can't just remove them. We need to call someone, the police. This is a crime scene!"

Dorion looked at me. "We police our world. We know who did it."

This silenced me. I truly was in a different universe. I sensed someone next to me. The light showed me Nettaline's stricken face. Leith stood with her, holding her hand.

"Are they *noea*?" I asked.

Nettaline nodded. "I know them. They were with Sheine at Fountainbridge."

I searched for something to say. "What was she wearing?" I asked. "Was it a yellow dress and purple sweater?"

Nettaline looked surprised. "Yes."

"She was here."

"How do you know? Do you see her now?"

"I sensed her when we first arrived. I think we should keep looking."

"Do you have any idea where?" Leith asked. "Down here or above ground?"

I didn't know. I realized I should have said nothing. I'd given them hope, with nothing to support it.

Sitri backed up and the wall where the bodies had been was suddenly illuminated. For a moment, I had to look away. Sitri and Dorion stood silent as they studied it. The symbols stretched out on both sides. Pascher stepped out from the darkness to stand nearby. I sensed they were communicating.

"Do you know what they're saying?" I asked Leith.

"When they do it like that, we can't penetrate it. But even when they talk, it's layered. Lots of it is hidden."

"They're worried," Nettaline said. "That much I understand."

"Do they ever just say, 'Oh shit!'?" I whispered.

"I think that's what they *are* saying," said Leith. "Whatever they see here, it's not good."

Sitri bent and placed his hand on the lower part of the wall, between where the two girls had been posed. I couldn't see what he was touching. Dorion and Pascher watched, their forms utterly still.

I looked at the bodies on the floor. Poison. Murder/suicide? We needed to check for footprints, items left by the bodies, a note. When

I looked back at the wall, three symbols illuminated. I caught my breath. Sitri glanced at me. "Which ones?"

I went closer and pointed. Sitri looked at Pascher.

"What are they?" I asked. "What do they mean?"

I felt a tug on my arm. Nettaline stood next to me. "Come," she said. "I want to show you something."

"No, no, I need to see this."

"Now!"

Once again, I was being handled. I followed her over to the three bodies.

"What are they?" I asked. "Those are *noea* symbols, aren't they?"

"Most are."

"How can the *ma'lakhim* see them?"

"They're carved into the wall. They can see that they're on the wall but cannot read them."

Leith came up beside us. She pointed her flashlight down. "Look"

A boot print in the fine dust next to one of the adult corpses distracted me. A large one, like a motorcycle boot. No one here was wearing boots. For that matter, no one here was leaving prints. I flashed my own light at the feet of the deceased male. No boots.

"Someone else was here," I said. "Or *is* here."

Chapter Nineteen

I studied the boot print's direction and shone my light along the floor. I kept walking. I was at the other side of the cave before I spotted another one. I looked back and saw from flashlight beams that Leith and Nettaline were searching close to the bodies. The *ma'lakhim* were dark forms now, but another bright flash of light at the wall made me turn away.

I found the opening of another tunnel. Whoever belonged to that boot print might have Sheine and any other surviving girls. I looked for any sign of tracks, but realized that if the *noea* girls wore shoes like mine, they weren't leaving any.

What about something else? I knew what an apport was. From supernatural lore, I'd heard that it was a physical object that appears at a séance, as if transported from the other side by the spirits. Sheine could "effect apports," they'd said. So, her "Dorion side" allowed her to use his *ma'lakh* ability to move things through physical dimensions. It was like how the traits I'd inherited from my *ma'lakhim* genetics had made me a conduit. I swept the floor with my flashlight beam, looking for anything that Sheine might have dropped to signal that she was still alive.

I saw light ahead, so I strode toward it. Soon, I stood under a shaft of light that revealed another way in. A wooden ladder rose up about 15 feet toward fresh air. I reached for it, but my toe hit something soft in the shadows. I recoiled. A moan told me we had a survivor.

I reached for my gun and knelt down. It was a man. I smelled blood.

"Who are you?" I asked.

"No! Leave..." he choked out.

"Who did this?" I saw a wound to his right side, a bad one. "Who shot you?"

85

"I didn't... " He coughed on blood. "They made us."

I pulled him into a sitting position against the wall. "Who? Who made you kill them?" I hit his face with a beam of light. He looked no older than 20. "Did you kill the girls?"

But he stared past me, terrified. I gripped the Glock and spun, holding it ready and raised my flashlight. I didn't need it. Sitri's skin shone with an eerie illumination. He put his hand on the Glock and forced it down.

The man tried to crawl under the ladder. He coughed up more blood.

"Go," Sitri told me.

"No! He's—" The intense flame that leapt into Sitri's eyes scared me. I stepped over to the ladder and went up but not fast enough to escape the piercing scream and stench of something burning. Outside, I put my hands to my ears. That man deserved to suffer if he'd murdered the others, but I didn't want to hear it. I'd seen Sitri's "vengeance is mine" side before. I'd nearly been annihilated by it. Rattled, I hugged myself.

In the evening air, things were quiet. It was just past the peak of twilight. I tried to figure out where we'd entered the cave. I didn't know how to get a fox to show me. I knew it was near the cemetery, so I started walking. I put my gun away but remained vigilant.

Within minutes, I spotted a wood frame building. It seemed abandoned, but something about it made me pause. I listened. I knew I shouldn't do this alone, but it wasn't as if I had a partner like Jack among these *ma'lakhim*. They kept secrets; he didn't. They felt dangerous; he felt safe. They wanted me to stumble my way through; Jack was a mentor.

What was I doing here? I should have let Orias take me to London.

With tentative steps, I moved closer to the building. I heard a quick rustle. I drew my gun and held it ready, my finger near the trigger. The windows were small, but I didn't think I'd need the flashlight. It was still light enough out to illuminate the interior. I located a side door. It was unlocked, so I opened it and stepped inside. I blinked hard to clear my sight. I thought I saw movement.

"Stop!" I ordered. I was in England. I had no authority here. But I wasn't about to let a potential source of information—or another killer—get away. My heart raced, but I held my hand steady. I moved silently across the room to a closed door. Reaching for the knob, I waited. I heard scuttling, like an animal, but I couldn't be sure. I tried the knob. It was locked.

A door slammed. Out a window, I saw a tall male figure dressed in black, with black hair like Miegul's. He sprinted toward a thick tree. I ran to a back door and opened it, but he'd been fast. I peered through the shadows and stayed near cover, gun raised.

I loved and hated this part. It made me alert, alive, vigilant. Not knowing what danger lay out there made my heart pound and my hands tremble. Where was Sitri, anyway? Weren't my *diam* alerting him? I breathed, steadied myself and prepared to slip out. I heard the sound of running, so I moved out into the yard. I got to the tree without being shot and found that he was gone. I took a breath. He couldn't be far. Just beyond was a hedgerow.

"We've got your back!"

I looked behind me. Nettaline and Leith stood outside the doorway from which I'd just emerged. Both had guns like mine. I guess I did have partners.

I crept around the tall hedge, trying to stay in the shadows, expecting at any minute to hear a shot. I thought I saw the figure move again, away from me. A flash made me duck. But it hadn't been a shot. I kept my gun ready and continued to move.

"We're right behind you," said Leith. "But I think he ran."

I moved quickly to the edge of the woods. Still no shot. Maybe he wasn't armed, but I was taking no chances. I passed through the tree line and came into a clearing. I heard Nettaline gasp. She rushed forward before I could stop her. Something on the ground had caught her attention. She picked it up. It was a shoe, like the ones we wore, but smaller. She sniffed it and declared, "It's Sheine's."

"Are you sure?" I asked. "These shoes look alike to me."

"I know her scent. It's her. But there's another scent, too. She didn't leave it for us, they did."

I looked on the ground where she'd found the shoe. I saw a familiar flash. It was a symbol, written large, seemingly splashed onto the ground with paint. It barely registered before it faded. I didn't recognize it, but I tried to memorize it to look up later.

"Did either of you see that?" I asked.

Nettaline nodded. "Briefly. It's from their syllabary. The *ma'lakhim*."

"Why is it out here?"

"Because of what just happened here," said Leith. "They killed the girls who had diluted blood and took the gifted ones. Then they left their mark."

I'd entered a war zone, a game of "Tag, you're dead."

"I'll tell Dorion," Nettaline said. "He will tell Sitri. Maybe they can interpret it."

The ground shook so hard I nearly lost my footing. "What's that? An explosion?"

"Sitri wants to seal this place again."

"With the bodies inside?"

"They are being moved."

Another one shook us. "But we need to investigate! Maybe the kids are still in the cave. Why is he doing this?"

Nettaline put a hand on my arm. "This is not your world, Dianysus. They understand Ignis."

"How can he collapse a cave that size?" I asked.

"He is *Lumé*. He can pull fire from underground."

I recalled my aunt telling me that a handful of these creatures could collapse the earth in a matter of days. Who *was* this guy?

Leith gestured toward the house I'd just been in. "Let's look around. The *ma'lakhim* don't see everything."

Chapter Twenty

The door I'd run through was still open. As Leith moved toward it, I yelled, "Wait! Let me clear it."

She stepped aside, her hand open. I sensed she was humoring me. Biting back a retort, I entered. My stomach flipped when I saw a scrap of cream-colored paper on the floor. I picked it up. Along one edge, it looked torn. On its face, in scribbly black ink, I saw half a dozen strange symbols.

I held it up. "Anyone recognize these?"

They leaned in. Leith shrugged, but Nettaline said. "*Noea*. But I can't make sense of it. We need more."

Another scrap lay along a wall, and a third one further in. They led like breadcrumbs toward the locked room. I picked them up. "Someone's been here. They left these when we were outside, or I'd have seen them."

"We came this way," said Nettaline. "We saw no one." She looked at Leith. "You were behind me. Did you notice?"

Leith shook her head.

I strode to the closed door and tried the knob. Still locked. A faint odor alerted me. "You didn't go in here."

They looked at each other. I recalled how Charmaine had easily opened a locked door on Long Island. She'd hinted that locks don't hinder *noea*.

"All right, whatever." I threw up my hands. "You can go through locked doors. *Did* you?"

Nettaline came over. "We did not, but I can show you. Watch for the resonance, then envision it expanding. Pull its vibration toward you."

I stared at her. "*Pull* its vibration?"

She tapped her head. "You see the lock as a hindrance, so *vous*

89

résistez, you tighten and block it. You must change *tes pensées,* how you think." With her fingers, she gestured that I should invite it to me. "*Invitez.*"

"Like with the shoes," said Leith. "You receive."

Skeptical, I gripped the knob, planted my feet, breathed in and waited. I imagined some invisible force flowing toward me. I tried the knob. It resisted. This was bad. How could they do this simple thing, but I couldn't? I tried again, turning harder. It didn't budge. Tempted to shoot it open, I stepped back. "Will one of you please do it?"

Nettaline reached over and caressed the knob. It turned and she pushed the door open. "Later, we can show—"

Her stunned face made me whip out the Glock. But I didn't need it. Everyone inside was already subdued. The stench made me step back. We had another room full of stiffened corpses, baked from the heat. What in the hell was going on?

I counted eight, mostly lying face up, their lifeless eyes open. Four males and four females. No children here, but the victims were college-age. They all wore the same outfit: black T-shirts and black pants. The T-shirts bore a flaming torch insignia on the left breast. Like those in the cave, they were recently dead, but rigor was present. I saw no blood or obvious wounds, but they looked posed. It was as if they had all ingested poison before lying down in their assigned area. Sick!

Holding a hand over my nose and mouth, I stepped in to investigate. They'd been here several hours, but not a full day. The odors were from body fluids. Some had died in agony. One, who had twisted around, had her face in her own dried and bloody vomit. The pattern they made was obvious.

"*La portail*," said Nettaline. The portal.

The females formed a diamond, with two heads meeting at the top and two heads meeting at the bottom. They lay at angles, the feet from the top two meeting the feet from the bottom two at the diamond's widest part. The males lay alongside each female, as if to reinforce the design. Leith seemed entranced, but Nettaline turned away, her face a mask of disgust. "All human. And this place stinks, *ça pue!*"

"It seems to be a cult," I observed. "They're radicalized. I've seen this before, where a leader commands followers to dress identically and assures them they'll be spiritually transformed."

Leith bent down and poked at the insignia. "I wonder what this means."

"More *essential*," said Nettaline, "why are they here, are they connected to *les cadavres* in the cave, and where are the children? Where is Sheine?"

From under a foot near the diamond's peak, Leith extracted a fourth scrap of paper.

I held out my hand. "May I see it?"

She handed it over. "More *noea* script. It must be for us, because the *ma'lakhim* can't read it."

I crouched down to lay this piece with the other three. They all appeared to be from a single page. The handwriting looked the same. "I think some are missing," I said. "Do you see any more?" These symbols looked similar to those from the wall, but I hadn't examined them long enough in the cave to be certain. On my right, Nettaline bent over me.

One symbol seemed to rise up from the page. I leaned back and cocked my head for a better perspective. "Do you see that?" I asked her.

She shook her head. "*Je n'ai pas…* I don't see like you."

A second one moved. I was sure it matched one from the cave. I expected another, but the papers ignited. I jumped to my feet. "What the hell?" I tried to stamp out the flames before they damaged the contents, but in seconds, the papers were white ash. I waved away the smoke and glanced at Nettaline. She was looking past me to the door. I gripped my gun and turned.

Pascher came through, his face intense.

"What's going on?" I asked. "I had something. I was about to read it. These bodies are a message, like the others."

Pascher stepped aside for Sitri, who ducked to avoid a threshold too low for him. "We're aware of that," he said. Their scent pushed back the stench. Sitri glanced at a dead girl without surprise. He stopped and put his hands on his slender hips to study the room, ceiling to floor. I tried not to stare at the tight leather near his fingertips. I pointed to the ashes. "Someone just now burned these."

He looked at me. "Yes."

I blinked. "*You?* Why?"

Sitri glanced at Nettaline and she made a quick gesture to Leith. "We'll be outside." They slipped out.

Sitri tapped our trust gesture against his chest. "Your protection."

Lost, I looked from him to Pascher. "How does reading these scraps—which could have helped us!—put me at risk?"

"Ignis is trying to reach you," said Sitri. "I suspected it this morning." He gestured toward the ashes. "This confirms it. They're using these symbols to try to connect."

This disturbed me. I pointed to the burned papers. "So this is a message? You know who wrote it?"

He just looked at me. Pascher glanced at him and left. This felt ominous. Alone with the dead. Sitri seemed so tall, even intimidating. I wondered if I'd done something wrong.

"Sitri?" A chill ran up my back. "Who wrote it?"

A tense moment passed before he told me, "You did."

Chapter Twenty-One

The ashes just inches from my feet might have revealed a lot; I wasn't ready.

I swallowed hard. I wanted to deny it, say I couldn't have, I don't know how to write *noea*. I just stared at the floor. Sitri knew more about my black holes than I did. I shook my head. "How is that possible?"

"It's from the dossier. It was Kaitlyn's. Each of her sisters and daughters wrote in it. Including you. You copied symbols from the painting you saw today."

I flashed on the dossier and nearly choked. I'd been careless. My heart beat fast. Where had I left it? I looked up. "And?"

"At the time, we were not aware that you are a conduit, a receiver. But someone knew. While you were drawing, Ignis used those symbols to push a communication to you. When you focused on it, they erased your protection."

My stomach tightened. Something dark was creeping toward me. I took a step back.

"They took you," he said. "And the dossier."

I felt lightheaded. "No." I couldn't breathe. "How could they? I don't... How did they get past you?"

His eyes changed. I saw pain. I recalled what Portia had said: *two decades ago*... "Is that how you lost Tariel?"

Sitri's eyes crimped, as if displeased that I knew this name. He held out his hands. "You were a child. You did not understand. And *we* didn't know until too late."

"Sitri—"

"You must block them. If you see those symbols again—any one of those three that came at you today—I want you to tell me at once. They're trying to get to you."

"How did they know I'd be here, that I'd see that wall?"

"You're tracking Miegul. He was here. But we would probably find them in other places as well, anywhere they anticipate you might go."

I wanted to ask, *what did they do to me?* But my throat tightened. That was a locked door. Beyond my ability to open.

Sitri stepped to the bodies and looked from one to another. "We have pressing matters tonight. Someone has notified the police. They will come soon. Please go outside. I must burn this place so no one connects these"—he gestured toward the bodies—"to the others."

"Others? The ones in the cave?"

"Mass suicides have happened elsewhere, in exactly this form."

"What?"

"This is the second phase of this assault. We cannot let anyone find these here."

I breathed out. I didn't like this. He was manipulating a crime scene.

As if reading my thoughts, Sitri said, "We have a reason. When Orias returns, he will take you to London. Please... outside."

I looked at the cluster of corpses again. Orchestrated mass suicides. What could it mean? I moved toward the door. Sitri caught me by the arm. He looked at me with that glow in the back of his eyes. I couldn't hold his gaze. I didn't want him to know that he'd just twisted my world into something dark and terrible. Or to guess that I'd left the dossier unsecured. I nodded, pulled away and left.

I chose a door I hoped would give me space and went outside. I wanted to be alone.

It was darker now. Mass murders. Mass suicides. It was all connected with some awful thing from my childhood. I'd been *taken*, like Sheine, because of something I could do. For how long? What had they done to me? What had happened to Tariel? And why must Sitri so dramatically manipulate this scene?

Something was here. They had secrets.

A bursting window startled me. Gray smoke rolled out, bringing a shock of heat. I moved away.

Nothing was turning out right. Less than 24 hours ago, I'd boarded a plane with a goal: to avenge my murdered father and then pursue a romantic relationship with this intriguing creature who could

94

orchestrate magic in bed. But I'd wanted Agent Gregory Brenner, with benefits, not this avenging angel who erupted in flames. I'd wanted to be his lover, not the daughter of some warrior queen who made me look pathetic.

But I hadn't known then who *I* was. I still didn't. I had sisters. Where were they? I needed my backstory. Sitri blocked it.

Did the others know? Of course they did. They'd made those cryptic comments about the dossier. I was the kid who'd opened the door to the bad guys. I'd lost my mother's ring to Miegul and put their daughters in danger. Portia had lost her beloved *ma'lakh* because of me. Nettaline had lost her daughter. And something had caused my mother to leave. *I was poison!* I couldn't be in this world. My efforts to help were just intrusions. They must all despise me.

I took a deep breath. I knew where I belonged. I'd definitely ask Jack to get me to New York. How could I be among these women? Or with Sitri? I must remind him of the loss of his right-hand man. My aunt should have warned me. Instead, she'd urged me to go with him and not look back. It had seemed like such a grand idea. Now I wanted to go home.

Feeling sweaty, I climbed a hill and sat down. The building was dissolving. As I watched the first orange and yellow flames emerge, I tried to breathe evenly. The east side of the roof caved in. Then a door shriveled and collapsed inward. I could imagine the bodies boiling and shriveling. Panic gripped my throat. I felt trapped. I pulled at my shirt. My skin prickled.

Those people inside. Whatever statement they'd hoped to make, for whatever pathetic reason, it was lost to the fire. Their lives were smoke. A wooden window frame burst into a brilliant white illumination, forcing me farther away. I'd seen arson demos, but this felt more sweeping. I was sweating. I pushed the leather jacket off my shoulders.

Most of my life, I'd hated fire. As a child I'd needed therapy, because I'd been so certain a fire would ignite in my closet and burn me alive. At times, my bedroom had felt like a closed box from which I couldn't escape. I was beginning to suspect that my phobia was related to all of this.

But I *had* the fire, Charmaine had said. In New York, I'd been able to look directly at Sitri's flaming form. It had surprised her. Even now, I could bear the heat better than I expected.

Still, on this hill, my chest constricted and my heart felt like it might explode. I wanted to get up and run. I felt as if I could reach and touch the hot sides of a box closing in. A scream started to form. I put my hand over my hair to keep sparks from landing in it. My left foot beat a hard rhythm as I fought to stay in control.

A hand on my shoulder made me jump.

Chapter Twenty-Two

Nettaline sat down next to me. I hadn't noticed her approach. *"Combien?"* she asked. "Are you okay?"

I swallowed and nodded. She was the last person I wanted to see.

"You saw Sitri burn like this in New York, no?"

"Yes. I guess. It was all so fast."

Another eruption inside made me jump. An outside wall cracked, and part of it collapsed. It felt as if it had fallen on top of me. I heard an echo in my head.

"This doesn't..." I didn't even know what to ask. "Doesn't it hurt them?"

Nettaline rubbed my arm. *"C'est bien.* He's ok."

I knew that. I'd seen him stride from a column of fire, his skin and hair aflame. He was in his element. I looked back at the building. The roof was gone and one wall had become standing ash. I could see indigo flames now. "Why are they moving bodies?"

"Something here, I think, that they must protect. The dead will be placed elsewhere."

More mysteries. "Where?"

"It depends on Sitri's message to Ignis. It is a game of wit, *jeu mental.* I don't try to understand anymore. These angel wars wear me out. When you're with a *ma'lakh*, you have two choices: you can join him as a *guerrior*—a warrior—or you can sit and wait, frightened of what might happen to him. I have done both. I would rather be with him."

I glanced at the slender woman next to me. She was tougher than I'd first thought. "Do you know what's located here?" I thought of the red powder.

Nettaline shook her head.

"Dorion won't tell you?"

"You learn what you can ask and what you cannot. They keep their secrets. Whatever is here is important."

A crashing noise inside the building drew our attention. Violet and white flames shot up. Ash hit the ground near us. I pulled in my legs.

"Leith is at the Jeep," Nettaline said. "She will take the children to their mothers. It's near London. She could take you, if you want to go with her."

"You're not?"

Nettaline dug into a pocket and opened her hand. I saw a tiny post earring with a clear gem. Its facets caught the blazing fire. "Sheine is here. She sent me this. It belongs to her."

"Sent you? Now? Tonight?"

"Yes. She can do this. She is alive. She won't, eh... *connecter avec*, connect with me, because it is dangerous, but she wants to show me she is near."

"Does Sitri know?"

"We cannot interrupt when he is *dans le feu*." She nodded toward the burning building. "Dorion will tell him."

I felt a rush of remorse. I put my hand to my mouth. "Nettaline, I'm so sorry. I didn't realize what all of this was, or how I..." I curled my hands into fists but couldn't stop my eyes from welling up.

"No, no." She reached over me to hug me. "*Nes pas désolé*. I don't blame you. *We* do not blame you. It is not your fault. You're our sister. We're glad you came home. I just want you to know that she's somewhere near, so I will stay. Dorion will be back soon and we can search."

I nodded. "I'll help, too."

"I'll tell Leith to leave, then. But one thing to watch for. Sheine has a sigil. It is a spiral, with radiating rays." She drew a quick spiral in the air. "The sun. For her name, Sheine. She picked it from one of Kaitlyn's manuscripts."

As Nettaline made her way down the slope, giving the burning building a wide berth, I watched the hungry blaze. Its heat penetrated my clothes. I breathed it in. I thought I could hear a conversation in a language that I didn't know, but it was lyrical and caressing. This was no ordinary fire. It was a purifier. Sitri was not working alone.

The earth rumbled. I looked around. Aside from the crackling fire, it seemed like the whole place had gone still. Dark clouds gathered overhead. Then the building collapsed as a geyser of white flames erupted from the ground to devour it. A wall of heat rolled up and smacked me. I jumped up and stepped further up the hill.

On my feet, I felt more in charge. I moved close to a sapling. Gripping its smooth trunk grounded me. Less afraid, I saw beauty in the crackling white and blue flames as they obliterated the remains of this building. Long grass shivered in the smoky breeze, which went east, away from me.

I recalled Nettaline's direction for loosening a lock: *pull the vibration toward you.* Would it work for the lock on my mind? Sitri blocked me, but maybe if I knew more, I'd figure out what they'd done with these kids. If Ignis had taken me when I was young, I probably knew things that could help us now.

I closed my eyes and imagined drawing this fire close. Imagined being enveloped but being okay. I felt my throat tighten and an urge to vomit, but I forced myself to focus. If I were part *Lumé*, I had fire, too. So, what did I fear? I didn't know. I wasn't sure if I wanted to open a door, or close one. My actions had caused a lot of grief. I needed to change that. I needed to do something *right*.

Then my perspective shifted. Although my eyes were closed, I saw the burning building from a different angle, and felt annoyance. I opened my eyes and blinked. It was still there. I looked around. How could I see this?

Then I remembered what Sitri had said.

Miegul. The Ripper. He'd tracked me. He was here.

Chapter Twenty-Three

Sitri had said this is how I'd know. I'd see it through his eyes. He was here; he'd brought Sheine here. She was with him.

But I wanted him dead. I wanted to shoot him myself. Just days ago, he'd caused my father's death. I stood still and scanned the area. The flickering shadows played tricks, but I thought I saw a figure down the hill to my right, near some trees. A male. He stood about 40 yards away. A prickly sensation along my arms suggested he was watching me. If I could see through his eyes, he could see through mine and would know I'd spotted him. I pressed my left arm against the pocket with the gun.

He moved.

I watched him stride away, through shadows. I set out after him. I lost sight of him, so I stepped up my pace, skirting the burning building and alert to a potential trap. Soon, I saw a low stone wall. I thought it was the boundary of the cemetery I'd crossed with Sitri to get to the cave. I pressed the gun, ready to use it. I knew Miegul might be trying to lure me to a vulnerable spot. I also knew that Sheine's life might depend on me finding her *tonight*. And Miegul had the ring. If I could get that back, we'd have advantages. Maybe we'd bring this all to an end. I couldn't stop and weigh options.

Weeds whipped my bare legs as I strode through the scattered tombstones. I cursed my decision that day to wear a skirt. London! That seemed so far away now. But I had to stay focused. Then I remembered. I was a *receiver*, Sitri had said. I needed to use that. Against the thrust of my desire for vengeance, I had to relax.

I stopped, closed my eyes, and put my hands together to focus. Miegul was here. I was sure of it. I'd seen the fire from his perspective; I'd felt his annoyance. He'd forced his blood into my mouth back in Brooklyn, and I could still see through his eyes. It was faint, sporadic. But it might just be enough for me to locate our lost girl.

I felt something through my feet. A vibration. Someone running. I opened my eyes. Not ten feet from me was a fox. I thought it was the same one that had come to Sitri. She watched me, as if waiting to be noticed. Then she turned her head and stretched her nose east. I looked that way. Across the cemetery, I saw a figure in motion.

"Thanks, sweetie," I whispered.

I couldn't believe it. I'd done it! I'd drawn the energy to me. I wasn't sure how, or whether I could repeat it, but I'd used "the force." I took off, avoiding holes and probably startling a few ghosts. But before I reached the other side, I heard an engine.

No! If he got in a car, I'd never catch up.

Then I remembered the bike. I had the key. I fished it from my pocket. Smart move. I listened to the noise of a vehicle leaving and noted the direction. I looked for the Harley. A glint of light off the fender showed me the way. Ignoring the sting of thorns on my legs, I jumped on, starting it in place, and pushed off. If Miegul had that ring, I was going to get it. I'd put an end to this horrible situation.

"Here I come, Ripper! I'm on your ass!"

I'd trained as a motorcycle cop, so I knew what I was doing, even with an unfamiliar bike on unfamiliar roads. I revved the engine to catch up. I now understood why Sitri had incinerated that man in the cave. Rage! Miegul was responsible for my father's death. He was going to pay! I'd kill him right now if he were standing in front of me!

Trees blocked my view as I drove around several tight curves, but finally I saw the taillights of a small car. He was going east. Back to London, I guessed.

I reminded myself to stay vigilant. I was certain he wasn't alone out here. I couldn't let myself get caught. If I could just get close enough to pull up beside him, I'd shoot him through the window. He'd told me a bullet wouldn't kill him, but it might disable him. Maybe he'd crash and burn.

Easy, easy, I thought. Get him to lead me to Sheine first.

I kept the bike at a steady pace. I could see the road from his perspective, so I knew it was Miegul. And he knew it was me, because he'd taken my blood, too. I wondered if he could *feel* what I was feeling and whether he was nervous or pleased. The car suddenly sped up and I lost it.

I tried to push faster, but the road was tricky. It wouldn't do to wipe out. I had to get in range again, to see Miegul's car. There weren't many side roads, but if he took one while I couldn't see him, my chase was hopeless. I came around a sharp curve and nearly crashed into a large object on the side of the road. I steered around it, drove down the road and turned around to stop and look back. It was a car. The right size. I heard no motor above my own engine, so I rode over to it and revved down to listen. A pinging sound suggested it had just been driven. Bringing the bike to a halt, I balanced it and kicked down the stand.

Before I got off, I put my foot on the road and made myself wait. I was learning. I had to listen. Sitri would be pleased, except that he *wouldn't* be pleased about my running off on my own. Exactly as he'd predicted.

I looked at the dark green Jaguar sports car. I had no idea if Miegul was still in it, aiming for me. I had no cover, no backup. But the message through my feet was that someone was moving in the woods, away. I trusted this sensation and got off the bike. Then I saw him.

Thirty yards away, a figure vanished into a copse of trees. I waited, my heart pounding. I felt some drops of rain. Damn! It would ruin my new jacket, but I needed it. I patted the gun and moved toward the retreating figure. These shoes were perfect; they made no noise, even when I picked up speed.

I followed and listened. I felt someone walking. I moved. The further I went, the darker it got. I felt for the flashlight, but I didn't want to use it yet. I stopped again. Hearing the sound of boots, I remembered the boot print from the cave. Had Miegul been there before us? I recalled how I'd seen him running along the rooftops back in Brooklyn, so I looked up in the trees. It was too dark to see anything.

To my left, I heard a branch break. I pushed my way through some bushes, scratching my legs again, and came to an opening. I worried about poison ivy, snakes and holes that could break my ankle. I took out the flashlight Sitri had given me. Shielding it, I turned it on. From what I could tell, I was on a narrow path. I decided to stay on it.

In the sky, through trees, I saw a flash. Lightning?

A noise to my right made me stop. Everything seemed still except the slight patter of rain. I walked faster, then broke into a trot. The jacket grew too warm, but I needed to move. My hair fell loose and I reached for the clip. I'd lost it. I turned around to look for it, but couldn't find it. It was so dark now that I could no longer see where I'd come from. But using the flashlight was risky. I stood still, torn between continuing and giving up.

I tried getting some sense of Miegul. Heavier drops pummeled the leaves, but the trees still protected me.

In front of me, I saw a burst of light. I ducked away, behind a tree. If Miegul was part of Ignis, he had protection. Were they watching me as I tracked him? Where were these *diam* when I needed them? Weren't they relaying my situation back to Sitri? But he was busy. *Dans en feu*, Nettie had said. Maybe they couldn't penetrate his focus.

I breathed out. This was futile. I needed to go back. I hated that I'd gotten this close to Miegul and missed. I did wonder why he wasn't coming for me. In New York, I'd been his big prize. He'd sped recklessly through Brooklyn to grab me. He had the advantage now and yet he was moving away.

Suddenly I saw something. It was from that weird perspective that wasn't mine. Then I knew. Miegul was looking at a helicopter. I could just make it out. Ours? My heart leapt into my throat. The dossier! He was going to grab it, too. I'd been stupid to leave it.

But no. This chopper was a different model. He moved closer to it.

I listened. Hearing the *whump, whump* of blades starting up, I looked around for a way to get over there. I felt trapped. Next time, no skirts! I had to be ready for any change in plans. I'd handicapped myself. I had to get smarter.

I crashed blindly through the underbrush. In minutes, I came into a clearing. Rain hit my face. I took out the Glock. The chopper was still on the ground, but the blades were moving. From the illumination of an internal light, I saw two people inside. I aimed, but it was too far and too dark to shoot, especially with the rain. I'd achieve nothing more than to show my hand. Not wise. I had no idea what kind of weapons they might have.

I lowered the Glock and felt something sharp press into my left palm. I laid my gun on the ground and got out the flashlight. To my surprise, it was an earring. I looked closer. It was a match to the one Nettaline had shown me. For an instant, I saw an illuminated swirl on the palm of my hand that had crenelated edges. Sheine!

I looked up. That was amazing! She'd sent it. Somehow, she'd tuned in to me. She knew I was like her. She was in the chopper.

I was relieved I hadn't tried to shoot. I could have hit her! To keep the earring safe, I removed one of mine and replaced it with Sheine's.

But I hadn't rescued her. I'd gotten close, but I'd failed. The chopper lifted off and I looked up in helpless rage. I felt sick. I wanted to jump out there and shout at the top of my lungs, "Give her back!" But they hovered only briefly before flying eastward.

As rain pelted my face, I stood and watched. I couldn't believe I'd been this close. If only I'd run faster. I figured that Miegul had ignored me, with my weapon, because he'd had her. He could have used her as a shield. And he'd wanted me to know. He'd let me follow him. He'd led me here. They'd wanted me to see their advantage.

Chapter Twenty-Four

I listened to the fading engine noise and watched until the chopper disappeared in a bank of dark clouds. Then I looked behind me at the woods.

I had to find my way back to the bike. I needed to tell Sitri. But I didn't have a clue where to go. I'd been so intent on following Miegul I hadn't noticed how I'd gotten here. No breadcrumbs. And it was really starting to rain.

I went to the edge of the woods. It was darker than I'd anticipated. I tried using the flashlight, but it was too small to show much except whatever was directly in front of me. I was lost. I was wet. I tried to "listen" with my feet, but the rain distracted me. I felt stupid. I should have gone to London, my original plan. I'd be there right now. I'd done pretty much nothing this evening but get in the way. Maybe worse. Maybe I'd inadvertently drawn attention to Sitri. Miegul had watched the building burn.

I couldn't face Sitri. I wondered if there was enough gas in the Harley to get to London. It was about three hours from here, tops, as I recalled. Jack would be there soon. He'd get me back to New York.

"Dianysus."

I turned around. A tall figure shimmered nearby. I blinked. Orias. Whew! The *diam* had come through after all. Of course!

"What are you doing here?" He looked at my right leg.

I followed his gaze and realized I was bleeding from a bad scratch. I reached down to wipe the blood away. Then I flashed on an idea. "Orias, I need Sitri. Now! Do your mind thing. Just... just *get* him here."

He looked confused, so I tried again. "I know where Sheine is. I tracked her here, but I can't follow her. We have to hurry. This is important! Tell Sitri to come."

"He hasn't cooled down. He can't—"

"Just *tell* him. We have a chance to end this thing, but he has to—"

A blinding light rose up behind Orias and embraced us with a blast of heat. I held up my hands protectively. I remembered Sitri in New York as a tall, illuminated figure burning his way through a supposedly fireproof mansion. I made a move toward him, but Orias stepped in my way. "Don't get close," he said. "Tell me what you need."

But I had to get close. *Very* close. I skirted Orias, who tried again to block me. He grabbed the back of my jacket, but I slipped out of it and ran toward the light. I expected another *ma'lakh* to jump in front of me, but I forged on. I had to get to Sitri.

The sheen from his skin dimmed as I approached, but the heat took my breath. I made myself bear it. I shouted, "Miegul was here! I could see him, but it's fading. He's not far. He's got Sheine! He's getting away. Go after him. Take my blood, so you can see him!"

I blinked hard and held my hand up to block the intense light, but caught a glimpse Sitri's blazing eyes and the mist that rose from sizzling raindrops that hit him. Like a swimmer who takes a gulp of air to dive deep, I closed my eyes and opened them. This scared the crap out of me. Maybe this was how Kaitlyn had felt as a small girl approaching a winged *ma'lakh* intent on killing her. Maybe she'd been scared, too. But she'd known what she had to do. And he'd responded.

I threw myself at him. "Do this!" I reached to my throat to scratch open his puncture, but Sitri grabbed my hand. His touch was searing. I raised my arms to pull him to me and used my clingy wet shirt to entice him. It got hot fast, but there was no moving back. *You have the fire,* Charmaine had said. I was sure that some part of me could bear it. I *had* to.

I threaded my fingers through Sitri's hair to urge him toward his own mark. Then his mouth was at the base of my throat, his hand around the back of my neck, and his tongue stinging me. I gasped. My blood responded and I lost my ground as our vision merged.

It was fast, but I understood. He could now see what I saw, especially as he closed in on Miegul.

I reached around him and felt his hot skin. Sitri was naked. He

106

pressed against me, aroused. His fingers slipped up my leg, under my skirt, to move my panties and feel for the place to connect. I lifted my left leg and wrapped it around him, opening to him as he came down on one knee for leverage. He balanced me and I moved against him. I felt his thumb at my most sensitive spot, pressing, which sent a hot sensation into my breasts and to the side of my throat. I arched my back, feeling his hard organ nudge against me.

But he didn't thrust. He actually moved me so he couldn't.

I gripped him. His heat grew distracting, then painful. I was scared, but I knew once he saw Miegul for himself, he'd disconnect. I inhaled his steamy scent and rubbed my hips against him. Complete this thing. *Fill me!* He must know what I craved.

I wiped blood off the scratch on my leg and ran my fingers over Sitri's lips and into his mouth. My breasts tingled and a pulse of heat from between my legs shot me straight to my peak, making me yell. Ripples of pleasure became waves. Sitri took the hot blood that now flowed to him. Still, we didn't fully connect.

Then I began to slip into darkness. This was ending. I gripped him and tried to stay aware, but I faded. I reached around Sitri to hold him. My fingers brushed against something firm but soft. I gasped. A wing! He was changing, right there, with me this close. He was becoming a *ma'lakh*! His hair came down over his chest as he pulled away.

I slipped down onto the wet grass and heard that flutter that signaled his ethereal movement. Leith had said this was how they propelled through energy fields. A bright flash made me flinch.

He was gone.

I knelt there, wet and cold, and looked into the sky. Raindrops smacked my face. I touched my throat and felt sticky blood. The wound stung.

I'd accomplished my goal. That was good. But now I was alone, in wet weeds. Empty. The warmth had vanished, and the light. I smelled something burnt. I looked around but saw no illuminated creatures. The magic was gone. I'd fallen to the earth, hard.

Rain pelted me. I looked for my jacket but didn't see it. My arms went limp and I slumped to the ground. What was wrong with me? I was a crazy woman. Why did I do these things? I lay down, turned over and looked up to see a bolt of lightning snake straight across the sky before branching into three parts. I blinked. Had it hit him? Or was it part of him? I shivered, closed my eyes and let the rain drench me. I should get up. I couldn't move.

I heard an engine, and tensed. Someone was near. I heard voices. They were approaching. I stared into darkness. I had to get up. Now. Get up! Then someone reached around me and lifted. It smelled like a *ma'lakh*. Someone touched my face. "She's so cold." Nettaline. They'd come for me. Relieved, I tried to say something, but I passed out.

How long I was out, I didn't know, but I woke and felt a vibration from a firmly padded surface under me. Something stuffed into my ears buffered the noise. A helicopter. I was on a cramped seat, under a blanket, with my head on someone's lap. I tried to rise, but felt a hand press me down. I thought I heard a woman say, "Sleep."

At some later point, I opened my eyes. My head was now on a pillow. I saw Nettaline in the co-pilot seat. She looked back at me with a worried expression. I wanted to ask about Sitri. Had it worked? Did he find Sheine? He must have. He hadn't been far behind Miegul. Surely he moved faster than a helicopter. A dizzy surge made me brace myself against the urge to vomit. My tongue was thick and dry, and I ached all over. My shirt felt stiff and smelled awful. Where was my jacket? I closed my eyes and pulled the blanket close.

But then I remembered. I reached for my earlobe. It was still there. I managed to work it out. I tried to say Nettaline's name but could only mumble, "nmlnen." She looked back. I held out my hand. She let me drop the earring into hers.

"From her," I whispered.

Nettaline looked into her hand, showed it to whoever was in the pilot seat, and started to cry. I collapsed inside. I knew what it meant. The plan had failed. If they'd found Sheine, she wouldn't be crying. She wouldn't be here. Sheine was still lost.

Chapter Twenty-Five

There's a world aboveground and a world belowground. That sounds like the ground in the middle is stable. It isn't.

Someone shook my shoulder. I lifted my head and felt soreness in my neck.

"Hard night?"

I jerked awake. Sun streamed through white lace curtains on a ten-foot window. I pushed my tangled hair from my eyes. "What—?"

"Looks like you had a hell of a time."

I sat up. "Char!"

The slender Asian *noea* stood with her hands on her waist, dressed in designer jeans and a royal blue silk blouse. "Brought you clothes. Leith said you'd need them." She grabbed my tank top from the chair and held it up before turning it toward me. I saw the burn marks. "Impressive! When you play with fire... Or, should I say, *lay* with fire?"

I looked down. I wore an unfamiliar white T-shirt. I had a faint recollection of being helped into bed, but nothing between the helicopter and this room. I ached all over as I sat on the edge of the bed. "How does this happen? How do I end up some place I don't remember going to?"

Charmaine shrugged. "He takes your juice, *épuisé.*"

"What?"

"We can show you how to prevent it."

I glanced around. "This isn't Paris."

"Belgravia."

Belgravia! I was in London. And Charmaine was in my room.

"But what are *you* doing here? And how—?" I gestured at her. "You're walking!"

"Still limping, but angel blood's amazing."

109

I caught my breath. "It worked? That stuff they gave you worked? No more poison? You're back with Pascher?"

Her broad smile made her dark eyes disappear.

Despite my aches, I jumped up to hug her. "I'm so glad! That's fantastic!"

Charmaine flinched and pushed me away. "You smell awful."

I went over to a mirror. "Oh, God!" My hair was ratted, my eye make-up was smeared, an earring was missing, and gray smoke had smudged my left cheek. I looked down at bandages on my legs.

"Had to put salve on your scratches," Charmaine said. "Go shower. I ordered breakfast."

I looked at her. "Are we in a hurry?"

"Your friend arrived."

"My friend?"

"That detective."

Jack. "Oh, right." That was a lifetime ago. "Where's my phone? He probably texted me."

"Told him you're here. We invited him to come when he's done with the DCI and their international protocols."

"Here?"

"Our building."

Of course they had a building in a ritzy part of London. I suspected the *ma'lakhim* had well-guarded buildings in every major city. "Is that wise? He'll sniff around. He's a good detective."

"That's why we chose him for you."

Chose? I looked at her. This had never occurred to me. But no point in asking. I was beginning to grasp that my life had been minutely choreographed. I just hoped Jack hadn't been forced to partner with me. "So, why invite him here?"

"Shower." She pointed.

I closed the door and scanned my image again in the mirror. I heard Charmaine on the phone, speaking urgently in clipped French. So much had changed between New York and Paris, and between Paris and London. I was *different*. Would Jack notice? Of course he would. Did I still want to go back to New York? Yes. No. Yes. I didn't know. I thought of Sitri.

And what did *he* think of me now? I'd thrown myself at him twice. The second time, he'd resisted. Why? I'd been totally ready, open, hungry. Nothing was working out like I'd hoped. I was making the worst possible impression.

I stretched my neck to examine it. The bruises from the New York ordeal were faint, but Sitri's mark was fresh—and more pronounced. I recalled the exquisite sensation of that sting from his tongue and my blood waking to him. It tightened my nipples and weakened my legs. I wondered if he was upset with my impetuous dash toward him when he was still burning. But surely I'd been right. It was for *his* enterprise. For Sheine and for the ring.

He'd let me touch his wing!

I closed my eyes to restore that sensation. Firm and strong, warm, alive, but so different from anything human. It had been intimate. He'd let me. He'd shifted while I was right there, touching him.

Gingerly, I removed the bandages. I had a lot of scratches, including a deep one on the front of my left leg that stung. Standing straight, I saw red marks on my body but no actual burns. Another mystery. How had I endured that heat?

I showered, threw on a robe, grabbed the hair dryer and returned to the bedroom. Char handed me coffee, took the hair dryer, and started to work. "Eat," she said. I understood. She was being a sister, maybe thanking me.

I was getting to like these *noea* girls. I'd never had a sister. And Charmaine was different today, not so reserved. Something had changed.

"I want to know everything," I said. The crusted berry muffin was spectacular. Still warm and fragrant, it brought sensation back to my tongue. I gulped down the strong French coffee. I needed it.

"You first," she said.

"Huh uh. You're bursting to tell me."

She separated an area of my hair to work on and looked at me in the mirror. "I was nervous," she admitted. "After I drank that stuff, I felt the same. But I was healing. My bones were cracked, not broken, so it worked fast. When Pasch came to test it, I said no. He insisted." She stopped for a moment and her pretty dark eyes grew pensive. "He said he'd rather risk poison than be apart."

I smiled. "That's sweet."

"I poked my finger and let him taste. It was fine. Then he gave me some of his, and then more, with the music, and so I'm walking." She combed through my hair, pressing the dryer close. Its warmth made my scalp tingle.

"With the music?"

"Certain types resonate with physical properties. It affects them, even changes them, so we heal faster. Kaitlyn learned this from the *ma'lakhim*."

My aunt had mentioned forbidden knowledge offered to *noea*. "What does it sound like?"

She shrugged. "Hard to describe. More a feeling."

"So with my blood, you can see what I see?"

She nodded. "Not vivid, not like the *ma'lakhim* can, but I can figure it out."

"Can Pascher?"

"Transfers to one person removed from you." She glanced at me in the mirror and added, "Pascher said you gave Sitri your blood again."

I shrugged. "No lectures! My connection to Miegul was fading. I wanted Sitri to see where he went."

"If he sees Miegul through you, Miegul will see *him*."

I'd forgotten. I felt stupid. "Isn't Sitri stronger?"

"Miegul has guardians, too."

"Sitri must know that," I said. "I didn't force him."

"Hmm. Pascher has a different story."

"He wasn't there."

"They're connected. There's no privacy with them."

I blushed. I hadn't realized. "They *all* know?"

"Sitri can block them, but you rushed him."

Double blush. "Okay, okay, I won't do it again."

Charmaine raised a skeptical eyebrow.

"Sitri could have stopped me."

"Of course. He will refuse the thing he most craves, shoved at him. It's not the blood, but what's *in* the blood, the life force. The trigger for connection. You offer, they take. They won't hold back. So you must learn *imperia*—how to control it. Take charge. Keep them hungry."

I held out my hands in surrender. "I wanted to rescue Sheine."

Charmaine gave me a look. "We have rules."

112

"Rules? Like what?"

"Ready to commit?" Her expression grew serious. I suspected she knew I meant to ask Jack to take me back to New York. I changed my question. "Why rules?"

She worked on my hair. I waited. She looked at me in the mirror. "The *ma'lakhim* are fire," she said. "Fire destroys, unless you make it useful. How?"

I shrugged. "Contain it."

"So, we have rules."

I snorted. "I've seen what they can do. Why would they obey?"

Charmaine raised her chin. "To have *us*. If they want you, they accept the parameters. So, you make them want you. But they *will* trick you."

I recalled how Sitri had baited me. "He's got me figured out."

Charmaine set down the dryer and leaned on the table. "He's watched you your whole life. He knows what leads you. When you're on a track, you don't stop. If someone tries to block you, you look for a way around them. Easy to predict, easy to bait."

"Hmmm." I nodded. "That's my weakness, I guess."

Charmaine ran her fingers through my thick hair and pulled it into a quick, elegant twist. "Flaw or strength, depends on the context. We'll teach you how to handle the *ma'lakhim*."

That was intriguing. "Did Sitri find Miegul?"

"Knows where he is."

I did a double take. "So, can't we just go attack him?"

"That is how battles are lost. You don't strike his shield, you wait for a weak spot. Sitri thinks along parallel lines, with multiple goals. You have to trust."

I recalled the mysteries at the crime scene. "What's over there in Glastonbury?"

Char yanked on my hair. "If you're still with us at the end of the day, I'll tell you."

I breathed out, frustrated. "Are Leith and Nettaline okay?"

"Nettie was grateful to get the earring. That's a good sign. Sheine is alert to opportunities."

"And she's alive."

"That can be worse. She's Dorion's girl, with unique abilities. They will use her."

Then I remembered. The dossier! I looked around. "I left a bag on the chopper. Did someone bring it in?"

Charmaine gestured toward a chair. I hoped no one had gone through it. But I had to wait until I was alone. I turned around and asked, "Are any of these missing kids yours?"

She shook her head. "We stopped having them. Ours were killed or taken." She said nothing for a moment. "At a young age, they can be retrained. The *nejah* do this. Later, they're used for reproduction."

I gasped. "Reproduction! There are more *nejah* than Miegul?"

Chapter Twenty-Six

I don't know why I kept thinking I had a grasp of things.

"There are," Charmaine said. "We don't know how many. Some have existed a long time. Some are deranged, even feral."

I didn't like the sound of that. Miegul, as the "Mage," Jack the Ripper, the leader of a death cult, was bad enough.

"Pasch and I have had four children," Charmaine continued. "One died young and one is alive, but we don't see her. When Pasch became Sitri's *kunoui*, we agreed to stop. He won't risk his standing." She looked at me. "You see Dorion. With Sheine gone, he's almost useless. Pasch won't do that. He's intensely loyal. And... it's too difficult to lose them." She seemed to be thinking. "Jhaneen, was 13 when they took her. When we finally rescued her, she was five months pregnant. She knew what it meant." Her voice thickened. "She poisoned herself. She died painfully, in my arms."

I went cold. "I'm so sorry. That's horrible!" I was beginning to get it. Being with a *ma'lakh* was high risk. This wasn't proms and weddings and happily ever after. That's why the *noea* had warned me. I wondered what Ignis had done to me.

"Are any of these kids—?"

She yanked on my hair. "That's Sitri's story. *If* he'll tell you." Charmaine looked square at me. "He won't show us, but he grieves. Deeply. In a way, the *noea* are his, all of us, because we descend from that first group that he saved from massacre."

I nodded. "Should I cut him off again, the way you showed me?"

Charmaine put her hand on my shoulder. "Leave it for now."

"Is that risky? Won't Miegul know what we discover?"

"Everything we do is risky. Miegul already knows you're with us. Right now, he has an advantage."

"Sorry. I thought I was helping."

"No time for that. We move on. Battle means shifting with conditions."

It seemed like each choice I made was wrong. I meant well. Maybe that's why Sitri remained detached. I just wasn't warrior material, not like my mother. Obviously, *she* had impressed him. I got up, picked up my ruined tank top and examined the scorch marks.

"See?" said Charmaine, "You have the fire. You got close when he was still burning."

"Why would he let me?"

"He knows what you can tolerate."

Another surprise. I looked at her. "How?"

She went silent. When she answered, she skirted my question. "That's your *Lumé* side, from Kaitlyn. They're the burners. You might need that."

"And what are the *Ser*?"

"Reflectors. They guide and channel the fire."

I put my hand to my body as if I could somehow connect with these foreign elements. I looked at Charmaine and raised an eyebrow. "It *was* pretty hot."

She pointed at the make-up bag. "Get busy."

I sorted through the various eyeliners and lipsticks. "So I'm an experiment. You're all watching to see how it's working."

Charmaine stood behind me, put her hands on either side of my head and turned my face firmly toward the mirror. "You are the *successful* result of a series of experiments. You're the lucky one. You didn't die or go crazy. You have gifts!" She let go. "But you can close it off and walk away."

Did she guess my plans? "Even if Sitri took my blood again?"

"It complicates things, but the connection will fade. If you stay, you must retrieve your power. Make him know he owes you. He does. You give him eyes where he can't see."

Put it on your list, Sitri had said. Maybe I *should* make a list.

Char had laid out several outfits. She made suggestions while I applied make-up. I was barely awake, still jetlagged. *You have the fire*. It felt more like a sputtering spark.

"Back to Jack. Why is he coming here? I can go meet him. I know this city."

"We need him. And he needs us. You must decide your allegiance. You know things that could help him, but you can't tell him."

"Can't tell him?"

"He will get what he needs."

Yes, I'd heard that one already. *You will get what you need when you need it.*

Charmaine crossed over to a set of French doors and pulled them open. The fresh breeze felt hopeful. I went over to look out on London. We were four stories up from clean streets lined with trees and brilliant white buildings. Columns below guarded prestigious entrances into what I knew were grand lobbies. This was one of the wealthiest neighborhoods in the world, where royalty from many countries owned residences. What should have felt regal and commanding seemed fragile.

As we stood there, I asked, "So, I have a choice. Will I be the Keeper of Great Secrets or a loyal partner?"

Charmaine was shorter than me by a good six inches, but when she spoke she felt much taller. "It depends on who you think your partner is. Are you *noea*, or will you be merely human? What you say and do—or don't do—today will show us. But walk away and you lose Sitri."

I watched the traffic below. "It's not like I have him."

"Give it time." After a moment, Charmaine added, "They have no biological drive to mate, like human males, but we can attract them."

I snorted. "By being pretty?"

She leaned in and whispered, "*Dangeroux*. That's why they loved Kaitlyn."

"My mother was stunning."

"And dangerous. Very. Her beauty would not have been enough. They want heat, friction. She had that. We can teach you. But now we must hurry. A lot happened last night. The press is just now reporting, but there were several other mass suicides like the one you saw."

Sitri had mentioned this. "How many?"

"Five more. Like Glastonbury, each had a pattern. And collectively they *made* a pattern."

"A message. What was it?"

She slipped back into the room. I followed. "Char…"

"You'll hear more at the meeting." She pointed to her throat. "Hide this." She meant Sitri's puncture. Then she was gone.

117

Chapter Twenty-Seven

When there are too many things to consider, it's best to take them one at a time.

I went straight to my overnight bag and opened it. Others had carried this. Had they sensed what was inside? I pulled out nearly every item, beginning to panic, before I saw the leather cover. I grabbed the dossier and breathed out.

I could hardly believe I was touching something of my mother's. My sisters had written in it, sisters I didn't know. Even I had written in it, although Sitri had incinerated those pages. I started to open it before I recalled the pulse of energy that had nearly knocked me off my feet underneath Montmartre. I pressed the leather cover. Later, when I had time. I wrapped it and placed it back inside the bag, then stashed the bag under the bed.

Next: Jack. I had to get dressed.

From the outfits Charmaine had brought, I chose a short, sleeveless ivory knit dress with a soft turtleneck that would cover my bruises and Sitri's mark. It was a snug fit. I pulled on a pair of opaque hose to hide the scratches on my legs. Over the dress, I put on a lightweight suede blazer. After I touched up my make-up and selected an exquisite pair of heeled sandals, I was ready. I sent Jack a text and he responded that he was close.

My heart thumped. I was excited to see him but nervous. I also wanted to see Sitri. I wondered if he was upset with me. I'd taken some risks last night. Why had I been so certain I should? Or could? Now, it just seemed crazy.

I met Jack in the building's sumptuous foyer. He looked up at the high ornate ceilings, impressed. Leather chairs sat next to glistening wooden tables that caught beams of silvery light from the tall windows. The royal blue carpeting silenced my tread.

I gave Jack a fierce hug.

"Well, well, DeejaVu," he said. His silly nicknames grounded me again. "Aren't you a sight! I expected you to be laid up for a week after what happened in New York, yet here you are. Looks like you been shopping."

"You as well. I didn't know you even owned a suit."

"Gotta make an impression on the DCI," he said. "But just so you know, I don't trust this situation. Feels like a set-up."

I shrugged.

Charmaine had directed me to take Jack into a conference room, where we'd all soon meet. I'd already peeked in and seen another 15-foot ceiling in a stark white room, with stunning tapestried drapes and ornate vases filled with red and white roses. An enormous multi-partitioned screen took up one wall, parallel to a long teak table surrounded by padded leather swivel chairs. It felt corporate. Near a windowed alcove decorated with expensive paintings was a sitting area where we could talk. A silver coffee urn was ready, with fresh biscotti and croissants. Jack and I were both out of place here, but he went straight for the pastries.

"I met your new boss," he said. "That guy's got connections. And money."

"New boss? When did I get kicked off the NYPD?"

"You deny that Brenner's made you an offer?" Jack stuffed a mini cinnamon croissant into his mouth.

I tried to mask my surprise. Of course Jack did not know what I knew. It seemed so long ago that I'd met Sitri as "Agent Brenner." Back when I'd thought he was just a hot guy. "No one's made me an offer," I said. "I was invited to help with the investigation into my father's murder. I want to find this guy as much as they do, and they seem to have solid resources."

"Ya know, DanDeelyon—emphasis on *lie*—I looked into this so-called international security agency. Got nothin'. Had my best team on it. How'd they convince you to come aboard? You're more careful than that. You bangin' him?"

Whew! A direct hit. Thinking fast, I threw up my hands. "You got me, Jack. Just can't get anything past your amazing powers of detection."

He smirked and nodded. "I know a deflection when I hear it. I

119

like that secretary who covered for you. Good choice. She sounds smart."

He meant Charmaine. "She's an agent, not a secretary. What did Brenner tell you?" I couldn't believe Sitri had gone to meet him.

"Nick's here. They tracked him."

I had my out! "Did it occur to you that if he was talking with you in New York, he wasn't here banging me?"

"Maybe not *last* night." He got up to pour more coffee into his porcelain cup. He held it up. "This group's a bit too genteel for me. But let's start with New York. You first. Let's hear it. What happened?"

I shrugged. "You had an idea and you were right. When we investigated Dr. Martin's murder, you suspected a student of crime history who knew my father. Good guess. He introduced himself as Scott Bateman and said he was working with my father and the historians who'd been killed."

"And when was that?"

"After you left me in front of the Met. He said he was worried for his own safety, which made sense. He'd contacted me on my aunt's computer and asked me to keep it secret, so the killer wouldn't find him. He also said he could take me to my father. As you know, Special Agent Pierce was following me, too, hoping to find my father, and so was Brenner. It was pretty dicey."

"How'd you figure you could trust him?" Jack asked.

"It wasn't about trust; it was about finding Dad. They all wanted the same thing, a document he had that was used in 19th-century immortality rituals."

"What?" Jack's eyes popped open. "And you didn't tell me?"

"I didn't know much. And I couldn't figure out Pierce's angle, or Brenner's. But Brenner knew about Bateman. He rescued me from Bateman. When the knives come out, it's not hard to see who's your friend." Bateman had, in fact, cut me.

Jack shook his head. "Back up. What's with the rituals?"

"It was an idea, described in an old journal. Bateman persuaded Nick to help him on the inside. Before he became a cop, Nick studied to be a priest, so it was easy to manipulate him with supernatural notions. After the fire at that mansion where you found me, they left the country together. If Brenner told you they came here, I guess they did."

I brushed a hand over my hair. I could hardly believe this had all happened in the space of five days. "When Pierce questioned me, he showed me an original letter supposedly written by Jack the Ripper. He'd taken it from my father's office. But it was actually penned by members of this immortality cult in 1888. *They* wrote it. But the point is, Pierce thought my father had other items that were part of those rituals. He wanted them. *He* believed they had power. Yes, Pierce the FBI agent. Apparently all his work in ritual abuse brought him in contact with people who showed him this stuff."

Jack nodded. "He was exploiting government resources."

"That's my guess. And if Brenner hadn't come along, Pierce might have forced me to give him the items."

"You had them?"

"I did."

Jack's eyes narrowed. "So why'd you trust Brenner? Wasn't he after the same thing?"

I couldn't tell Jack, 'well, because I had the most unbelievable sex of my life.' In fact, I still *didn't* know if I trusted him. "Everything happened fast. And I had nothing to give him, because Bateman grabbed it all. I knew where Bateman was going, so that's how I ended up in that mansion on Long Island."

"By yourself? Without back-up?"

Back-up. I had incredible back-up. "Let's not forget, I was officially off the case. And I did call you. Just... I couldn't wait. My father was in danger. Nothing else mattered."

"And where was Brenner?"

The image surfaced of the tornado of fire that he'd become, of how he'd ripped through the mansion to incinerate it.

"He left me with one of his agents and I got away. I wasn't under arrest. They couldn't hold me."

Jack shook his head. "Not buyin' it, Deelilah. One of my associates over here knows Brenner. Says he's got top-notch resources. You'd've been followed. And he wouldn't't've let Capaldi and Bateman slip away."

He had me cornered. I had similar questions, especially after what Charmaine had just revealed. I shrugged. "I can't answer that." Then I had an idea. "I think there's something bigger at stake. Brenner's team was watching Bateman for some time. Brenner wasn't sure what my father was up to, but he knew from Bateman's activities—this Winternet thing—that there was potential for a massive disaster. Which is exactly what we're looking at. My father thwarted part of their plan, but they came over here to regroup. Remember your suicidal suspect?"

"Yup."

"He's part of it. Nick killed him, but he was a willing sacrifice. This is a true believer cult. A death cult. The Winternet is their medium for spreading their message. The members think their deaths will ignite a massive upheaval that will end humanity but make *them* immortal. Maybe Brenner thinks Bateman will lead to bigger fish."

"And Bateman has the items?"

"I think so."

"What were they?"

"Documents. Things historians drool over. They think these documents offer secrets for how to achieve their goals. One of them was used during the Ripper murders."

Jack tilted his head, thinking. "And why does Brenner want them?"

I was *burning* to find out what Sitri had said to Jack. I could just imagine them face-to-face. Sitri had *picked* Jack for me. Why? "You think I have an inside track, but I assure you, Jack, he's told me very little. I've barely seen the guy since I got here. I feel pretty useless."

I suddenly realized the room could be bugged. Of course it was. I had to wise up.

Jack gave me a look. He didn't believe me.

"So," I continued, "Bateman got what he came for, Nick is in it with him, Brenner has intel on them, and I've got nothing but questions. Your turn. Tell me what *you* know."

"Hang on," said Jack. He got up to pour yet a third cup of coffee. "What about all those symbols you showed me? How does that fit?"

This was tricky, and now I *really* hoped no one was listening. I could imagine Charmaine's tense posture as she waited for a single slip-up. Jack was uncomfortably close to the mystery that had unveiled the *ma'lakhim*. The symbols had been from their alphabet. It contained the sigil combinations that could lure them into traps.

"They were from one of the sets of symbols that this group believes hold magic," I explained. "An ancient alphabet. Throughout the ages groups like this have tried using them to syphon power from supernatural forces."

Jack nodded. He'd seen some things, too. I tried to think of a lie that could deflect his nose.

To my relief, Charmaine and Leith came in. I believed they *had* been listening. I hoped I'd passed the test.

Chapter Twenty-Eight

I'd been to meetings all my life, but I'd never before seen how the strings were pulled. It was disconcerting but strangely exciting.

Identically dressed in medium gray Michael Kors sleeveless knit sheath dresses with draped necklines, the *noea* seemed to be in uniform. The form-fitting outfits showed off their figures, emphasized by hair drawn neatly into twists, like mine. *They've played this charade before*, I thought. Well done. Charmaine was walking better now, with only a slight limp. She led the dance. Despite her diminutive size, her authority filled the room.

"Good afternoon, Detective Nolan," she said, extending her hand. "I spoke with you on the phone. I'm Agent Amy Chauffé. We're ready to begin."

Jack stood to shake hands, while I hid my amused reaction to her suggestive name—"am hot." Charmaine invited us to the conference table, where we could see the computer screen. Jack kept his eyes on her as she showed him to a specific chair.

"Let me begin with our organization," she said. "We are entirely covert, a shadow operation. In simple terms, we're scouts. Trackers. We watch for dangerous hot spots—what you call cells—and send information to appropriate enforcement agencies. At times, we assist."

"No offense," said Jack, "but we have plenty of terrorism spotters."

"We cover much more. And no offense intended to you, but your country is young, with relatively recent concerns."

Jack held up a hand, acknowledging her point.

"You'll be told only what's necessary to work with us," Charmaine continued, "and we hope you will respect our need for discretion and confidentiality."

"Of course." Jack glanced at me. He was listening, but his face was tense.

"Our goals complement yours and you're here because you, your partner"—she gestured toward me—"and another of your detectives were involved in an operation in New York that launched our current threats. That detective, Nicholas Capaldi, is on the run, in the company of a highly dangerous individual who has links with secret networks and uses many aliases. We believe you have information that can assist us to locate their OMD, their organization of mass destruction. In return, we will help you to close your case and apprehend the offenders. We will answer questions but will not discuss our management or sources."

Jack nodded. "I guess I'll need to hear the details." He held out his hands, palms outward. "Need a confidentiality agreement? Because I also brought mine."

Leith stepped forward with a folder and placed it in front of him. "If you wouldn't mind," she said. Her elegant Irish accent must have stroked Jack's thighs. When she leaned toward him, exposing cleavage, he fumbled with the papers. She had to slide them out for him. Standing close—and I'm sure she wore a provocative perfume—she guided him through the process, her manicured fingertips lightly caressing the pages. She kept up a silky patter close to his ear. It had its effect. Charmaine winked at me. I noticed that Jack forgot his own papers. Clever.

Orias entered through another door. He wore a suit that nearly matched the color of the dresses, with a subtle gray and red tie. His chestnut hair was nicely groomed. "Agent Jean Tempete," he said to Jack. "I hope you had a good flight." Another name that played off fire. Good thing Jack didn't know French. Orias gave me a polite nod. I squirmed a little, recalling the night before.

Following him in was Pehel. It was strange to see them so formal after their relaxed style just hours ago. Pehel gave a false name, shook hands with Jack, greeted me, and sat next to Orias. Tibreth, close behind, did so as well. I thought he gave the name "Faisceau," which referred to beams of light.

I realized they had to present a front, but this formidable show had nearly convinced *me* that they were an international security organization. Maybe they were. The watchernet. But where was Sitri?

125

"Please excuse our haste," Charmaine said to Jack, "but we believe there will be more disturbances and we must get resources in place."

"I agree," he said.

We sat on one side of a long oval table, so we all could see the large screen on the opposite wall. The *ma'lakhim* were on Jack's left, with the *noea* next to them on the far curve of the oval, and across from me. I was on Jack's right. I could tell from his tapping fingers that he felt wary. It didn't help that he was stoked on caffeine. I put my hand on his arm to reassure him I was still his partner, a New Yorker in London, just like him. He gave a curt nod.

"As you already know," Orias said to Jack, "after Bateman and Capaldi left New York, they flew by private jet to London. Here, they met with others." Orias' voice was smooth and firm. Jack's fingers stopped tapping. "We believe they have separated, and Capaldi is still in London. We have a good idea where and we have surveillance, coordinated with the local police. The network we're watching operates through several channels, but the one that most concerns us is associated with a serial killer in New York, Andrew Roy Engleman, who calls himself Angel Ray Ender."

"What?" I interrupted. "That's his *name*?"

"Yeah," Jack muttered. "Our other suicide, the one yesterday."

I looked at him, surprised, but he waved a dismissive hand. The killer's image appeared on the screen. He looked like a cross between Ted Bundy and Jeffrey Dahmer: sandy-haired innocence and schoolboy charm. Except that his blue eyes looked cunning and predatory.

"For the past two years," Orias continued, "Ender had sent coded letters to numerous disciples. His notoriety, coupled with the covert nature of the Winternet and their layered apps, grew his network into critical mass, especially among young people. Some apps opened to a hidden interface, and some had duress pins set to destroy data. Our digital staff identified them without triggering them. The codes were instructions, such as for the coordinated incidents of mass suicide that took place last night. We think Bateman sent out something to this group that launched it."

A hot flush zipped through my cheeks. I figured he meant Miegul's declaration of acquiring my ring. I was glad Jack was looking at Orias, not me.

As Orias dotted the map with the locations of mass shootings and mass suicides, I noticed he'd pushed the one from last night to the south of Glastonbury, away from where it actually had been.

"None of these are contagion incidents?" Jack asked. "You're convinced they were coordinated?"

"We believe so. All sites were arranged and incinerated in the same manner, which took planning and associates. But we expect that contagion events might now occur. That's why we must interpret the context."

I recalled Sitri saying, "Something has happened" just before we entered the cave. He'd mentioned the mass suicides, but I still wasn't prepared. This thing had taken enormous form. Seven countries were involved so far. The four mass shooting sites forming the portal, a suicide in New York, and now six mass suicide sites. I looked at my ring finger and felt a chill. I'd been carrying all that power since I was a child, oblivious. I might have removed it at any point, even laid it carelessly aside, or lost it.

But maybe not. There'd been a moment at my aunt's house last week when something had entered the room during the night and tried to take it. I'd heard a sharp command and this rush of sound. Of course. Sitri, my guardian, had been watching.

So, where had he been when I finally did remove it? How could Bateman have grabbed it? Something didn't add up.

Orias pointed a thin red laser beam on a town in western France. He was about to say something when the double doors to my right swung open and Sitri entered. He filled the room. I hoped Jack wasn't watching me because I couldn't mask my astonishment. "Agent Brenner" wore a dark gray silk-and-wool Brioni suit. I didn't have to look closely to know it was hand-stitched, or to touch it to know how luxurious the fabric was—although I wanted to! A powder blue and black print Italian silk tie over a white shirt added the perfect professional touch. And he wore *shoes*. Testoni, I thought. Expensive.

Pascher, suited in dark brown, followed him and took a position near the door. Now we had four of Sitri's consociates, or aides, or whatever.

Jack stood and Sitri went behind me to extend his hand. "Please excuse my delay," Sitri said. "Thank you for coming over here."

Jack's jaw was tight. "You have quite a set-up."

127

"We try to keep up."

Sitri lightly touched my left shoulder, leaving a warm sensation that made me close my legs tight. He sat in a chair to my right that angled away on the curve of the oval. This put him next to me but able to interact with me. I tried to act like we hadn't just been in the most heated embrace, that I hadn't just touched his emerging wing. I wasn't good at living double. He nodded to me and said, "I hope you're rested. I trust that my staff has addressed your needs."

I blinked and fought a rush of warmth. Had he just make a *joke*? "I'm rested, thank you," I said, as evenly as I could, "but I still have questions."

The micro-lift at the corner of his mouth told me he got my innuendo. "We will do our best to satisfy. *Je suis à votre service.*" I was glad that only a *noea* could see the burn in his eyes. I couldn't even look at Charmaine. Or Jack.

I hoped this was going over Jack's head. Sitri had left me drained just hours ago—*épuisé*—and had used my "gift" in some mysterious way. How much *more* I wanted to say! And *see*! So *much* had happened last night. I had to learn this telepathy they all used. I sensed covert conversations going on. In fact, just after Sitri came in, Tibreth excused himself and exited.

Sitri looked around the room, his authority clear. "The group we have identified has a network in place, ready to act," he said. "We must isolate their weakness quickly. Let us lay this out."

Chapter Twenty-Nine

It's not always good to uncover what's hidden.

As Orias gave a quick summary, Jack's fingers drummed the table. He raised an eyebrow at me. I was acutely aware that I sat between him and Sitri, a buffer between my partners, between my former and current worlds. Tiny beads of sweat formed on my lip. I leaned into my hands.

Orias correlated the images of locations with what he described. I looked hard at the screen but saw nothing unusual. Some live images opened on screens at the sides of the main screen that appeared to be from drone cameras. I wondered if they were *diam* projections.

"The Black Torch, Ender's network, has claimed credit for the shootings and kidnappings," Orias said. "They created a social media site called Wipeout and several mobile apps that send vanishing codes, which they believe are untraceable. The suicide groups are related to the shootings. Some of the kidnapped children are among the dead, so we know that the appearance of voluntary mass suicide is staged. Not all of the missing have been located. This group now threatens an act of mass destruction, but the date and location remain unknown."

"Check the codes," said Sitri. "We just need to decipher them."

Jack perked up. "Excuse me. Did I just hear a suggestion that you can catch and trace the vanishing messages?"

I looked at him but felt Sitri on my other side. Jack wanted answers, Sitri had them. Only part of this story could be revealed. I took my hand away from my mouth, knowing Jack would read that as a "leak." I was on the edge of betraying him.

"Yes," said Orias. "We know who sends them and what they say."

"And this is legal?"

"In some countries. We have infiltrated the Black Torch, so we know its intent. They used a hidden app inside the Wipeout app, called *Flatline,* to launch the suicides. Another one, *LightsOut,* will signal the final event. We haven't yet learned the intent of *Bloodshot,* but it's related to the recent attacks."

Jack looked around. "Have you offered honeypots?" He meant decoys online, things that would draw the bad guys into tampering with them.

"We have," said Orias, "but they spot them quickly. We have some clandestine operations that cost them time, but these are temporary diversions. They're preparing for an attack, but we haven't yet defined the attack space."

Jack backed off. He seemed impressed.

Sitri told Orias to enhance one of the maps. I fought the urge to reach over and finger his suit. Under the table, his leg pressed against mine, as if he'd read my thoughts. I let out a breath as heat zinged up my thigh. *His staff... my needs.* I wanted to slip off my sandal and slide my foot over his. I cleared my throat and pulled my blazer close. Ivory was a poor choice for hiding arousal. I was glad I'd added the blazer. I saw Charmaine smirk and Leith glance at her. Something covert was going on.

Orias pointed the laser at a spot and tapped open a real-time image. "We think there's something important here."

If Jack weren't in the room, ready to pounce, I would have said, "Not there. You're off." I thought I saw where the true danger was. I knew Sitri could feel my concern. I rubbed my thumb and finger over my throat, as if thinking, and tapped my neck. Pehel noticed. His eyes changed. I hoped they knew I was referring to angel traps, those awful collars that the *nejah* used to capture them. Orias turned toward Pehel, then looked at me, so I figured my message had been networked.

"Let's simplify this," I said. "Can you show us just the patterns of the assaults and then just the pattern of the suicides?"

Orias tapped a few times to shift the map.

Sitri had taken my blood. The vision bond was active. He could see what I saw. His attention was on the map, but he was attuned to me. Ah! Now I realized. He'd touched me under the table to arouse me. That's why I'd spotted something.

"Give us perspective," said Sitri. "Pan back."

Now we had the U. S, with Europe and Asia. The shootings formed the diamond pattern.

"Looks like some kind of circle," said Jack. "If you eliminate the New York connection."

"There was no shooting there," I reminded him.

I could now see the lines that linked these sites. My "probe," as I called my hyper-vision, was working.

On my right, I felt Sitri's tension. For the *ma'lakhim*, these portals were used to ambush them.

"Now reverse it," said Charmaine. "Put up just the mass suicides."

Chapter Thirty

I had to stop thinking I had things figured out; this tale was a layered app.

When the six sites were clear, something flashed at me from the map. Sitri's leg moved, warming mine. I could see something forming. A symbol. It stayed briefly in place, running through these incidents to connect them before vanishing. An 'L' shape, with a slash near the top across the vertical leg. To the right was a diagonal row of three dots.

I knew little about the symbols in the *ma'lakhim* alphabet, except that when three were brought together in a certain way, face-up, they formed a sigil that called to a powerful *ma'lakh*. I'd seen Sitri's in New York when Bateman, a.k.a., Miegul, was trying to trap him. This one was not his. Nor was it one of the symbols I'd seen in the cave. But Sitri pulled two fingers under his thumb. He was tense. Charmaine's eyes were wide. She looked from the screen to Pascher. I thought Pascher's posture grew more rigid as well.

I asked for a laser pointer. Orias handed me his. I held it up to the map. "Something here," I said. Before I could finish, the laser blew out. I looked at it, confused. I pressed the button, but it wouldn't work.

Orias took it from me. "The battery died."

I got it. No one wanted me to draw even one part of this sigil. Sitri had stopped it. He watched the map without expression, but I sensed turmoil.

"If I don't miss my guess," Jack said to Sitri, "I'd say you've got a good idea of what's going on. Care to share?"

This wasn't going well. Jack thought they were holding back. Worse, I sensed he believed I was siding with them. I slid down, hoping to seem inconspicuous.

132

Sitri looked at him. "Before Ender killed himself, he left a note. We'd like to see the original."

"My people are standing by," said Jack. "Use the contact info I gave you to get them on the screen. But we've had our people all over it. There's not much there. Seems pretty obvious to us."

I was curious. It was clear that Jack and Sitri had made an arrangement. Jack hadn't told me. He, too, was holding back. My guilt evaporated.

Orias hooked in to a live feed and a uniformed man came on the screen. I didn't know him, but he was part of the NYPD.

"You done with your break, Fish?" Jack asked.

"Hey, it's damn early over here, Nolan!"

"This is Captain Jeremy Fisher," Jack told us, "who will show you the note." To the screen, Jack said, "Hold on a minute, Fish. Let me bring us all up to speed on Ender." He looked around. "So, this asshole—excuse my French." He looked at Charmaine. "Uh, sorry. No offense to anyone here." I thought Leith nearly cracked a smile. "Engleman, a.k.a., Ender, was arrested eight years ago for the brutal double homicide of woman and her daughter."

I knew some vague details about this case from Jack's files, but I wondered if Ender had been *nejah*. Like Miegul, perhaps he'd had an abiding hatred for *noea* and had been a hunter.

"He strangled them," Jack continued, "and burned them while they were dying. Sometimes he ate pieces of them. His flack—excuse me—his attorney, tried to go with an insanity defense, citing delusions about some bizarre mission to cleanse the world. Ender crashed the plan and got convicted. A couple of years later, he published a book that alluded to other murders and referred to himself as 'the Torch.' His book sold well, so that name became his handle, made him famous. Our guys have linked him to at least a dozen unsolved homicides, but no evidence. Our hands were tied. There were also two copycat murders by exuberant fans, who were convicted."

Jack took a moment to gather himself. "Ender developed a network and wrote a second book. It's like a bible. He got followers. Hence, we have the Black Torch, the dark tribe of the Torch. One of them created the Winternet, *Wipeout*, and its vanishing apps. Over the past three years, Ender's been sending coded directives to prepare key

133

people for launching a worldwide massacre. Apparently, his suicide was the trigger. And now, we have numerous deaths with his incineration signature. Ender's victim type was exclusively female, sometimes children. So, there you have it."

"We've collected some of his letters," said Charmaine. Orias opened a screen to show one and I drew in a quick breath.

Jack looked at me. "Out with it," he said. "You saw things in Francis Martin's apartment after he was killed. You manage to see things no one else does."

Sitri watched me as well, waiting, although I knew he'd seen it, too. I had to be careful. Even if I wanted to side with Jack, I couldn't reveal the full story.

"I told you, Jack," I said. "It was all in the context. Martin was looking at an alphabet that was then carved *on* him. You would've seen it, too. And let's not forget that Nick did see it but pretended he didn't. He was there to cover up."

Jack raised an eyebrow. "What do you see *here*?"

Chapter Thirty-One

Traps can bind you; they can also protect you.

I glanced at Sitri. This was my moment, my step onto the tightrope. To whom would I be loyal? Sitri intense blue eyes seemed to undress me. *My staff... your needs.*

I pushed away from the table, got up and went over to the screen. I was acutely aware of two stories forming. I had to keep them from touching. Sitri aimed to use Jack, and Jack was trying to penetrate Sitri's secrets. Both expected my allegiance, but I could commit to only one. Charmaine's words flashed in my mind: *You walk away, you lose Sitri.* Yet she'd also advised me to do exactly that.

I pointed to a word in the third line. "See here? The word, 'burn'? It's repeated here, here, here, here and here." I pointed them out. Then I turned to Orias. "Can you highlight each of these?"

He placed a transparent yellow line over each word. I stepped away and looked at Jack, although I wanted to see Sitri's reaction. "They form the same symbol that was carved on Francis Martin's stomach—our original murder victim." I didn't add that it was the symbol for an angel trap. "So, this links the murders of the historians with Ender. Either he orchestrated them or he approved them. And the guys who committed them—including Nick—came to England, where we have two of these extreme incidents. That's not a coincidence."

"I'll be damned," Jack said. He rubbed his chin.

What I did not say was that I'd seen three other symbols as well—triangles that formed Miegul's coded message to my father: *tautriadelta*. He'd also used it for his Ripper identity. This meant one thing: Ender knew him.

Finally, I looked at Sitri. He nodded, his left eyebrow slightly raised, and said, "We should look at the suicide note."

Orias rejoined Captain Fisher's screen. Fisher had the note laid out. Orias took a quick screen shot. I spotted an illuminated symbol, but I remained silent. Pehel got up and left. I looked at Sitri's long fingers as he rubbed the table and stared at the screen.

"Anyone see anything?" Jack asked. "Looks like more of his bullshit to me."

He was right. The note contained just a few lines, which sounded dramatically preachy, with predictions for catastrophe and a shocking surprise.

Sitri got up and went to the screen. He was killing me. He looked stunning in that suit, with his graceful movements, long waist, and tight muscular ass. It fit him perfectly. I looked for some indication on his back of where his wings would emerge and rubbed my fingers to bring back the sensation. He was working me, so I'd use the erotic currents. I doubt that any ordinary code master had ever hidden messages in such energy forms. But these pulsing communications came from extraordinary code masters. Did Charmaine, with my blood, sense what I was feeling?

"You can see the date here," said Sitri, pointing. "As you might expect, he viewed himself as an antichrist, so he follows a predictable pattern. Three days from his death, he tells his disciples, he will become immortal."

I knew what this meant: Ender had expected to merge with the *ma'lakh* that would be summoned with this sigil, obliterating the creature to absorb its energy. I wondered which one.

"How do you figure?" Jack asked. "I don't see it."

Sitri pointed a slender finger to the image near the signature. "Here, in the flames. He's the Torch. He uses the lines of the flames to form the phrase, 3-D-A-Z. Three days. But what looks like a solid black core at the heart of the flame is another image. Enlarge the signature, please."

As Sitri gestured, I could see inside the dark area the image of a bird, its beak pointing straight up.

"I see it now," said Jack. "What? A dove? A phoenix?"

"A peacock," said Sitri. "The ancient Greeks and some early Christian groups believed that after death, peacocks retained their form. You see them in illuminated manuscripts made by monks. So, this peacock with flames for a tail is the secret symbol of this group, the Black Torch. We've seen it in several letters. 'Kill the light' is their motto. And you can detect it inside other phrases in this note."

He looked at Orias. "Turn the signature over."

Orias complied.

"If you look closely, you can see the promise of return to life, but it's in a language no longer in use."

"But *you* happen to know it?" Jack was still suspicious.

Sitri looked at him. "It can be located if you know what you're looking for. We've studied Ender's letters since he started his campaign. He used a dead language to create his death message. But we have sophisticated code breakers. We quickly spotted his goal."

He told Orias to enhance the image. This magnified the paper on which the note was written. Sitri pointed to a shadowed watermark. "When you identify his symbology, the rest falls into place. The first mass suicide last night occurred near Glastonbury, where myths place Jesus during his childhood. Chalice Well there is reputed to have water mixed with his blood. The final mass suicide and end point location"—he pointed to the map—"was Turin, Italy, where the alleged shroud of Christ is housed in a cathedral. It adds up. Ender—which alludes to end times—selected locations to correspond with his ideology. His ideas reverberate with religions around the world. It's no surprise that he has attracted ardent followers willing to kill others for the cause and even end their own lives."

I was impressed. It was a tight rendering without a single reference to what was happening in our parallel world.

Jack was aware that suicide cults often formed around charismatic leaders who aligned themselves with a simplistic spiritual vision. This one wasn't far-fetched. But I knew there was more to the story. I wondered what the other symbol was. It had jumped out like the one I'd seen in the Ripper letter just days ago. Ender was connected to Miegul and Ignis. He had to be *nejah*. Who else could have injected the note with a spiritual energy that would reveal itself to a *noea*?

Then I spotted something else. I pointed. "Look at the R's in Ender's name. I see two of them. They're made from Ps, but the back leg is different. Can you enhance it?"

Once the Rs were enlarged, it was easy to see. "I think we can assume the 'P' is for peacock, and the leg that makes the 'P' into an 'R' is a knife blade. It's curved like a knife and has a red edge along the underside."

No one spoke for a minute, but I felt an ominous prickling. Ignis

137

planned to pose Jack the Ripper as a Christ figure, an immortal. I felt ill.

"He didn't get paper like that from the prison commissary," Jack observed.

Sitri nodded. "That's why we looked at the original. It confirms that someone on the inside worked with him."

"And his goal?"

"Have you read both of his books?"

I tensed. Jack was on the spot. But he surprised me.

"I read the first one multiple times because he described one of my investigations." Jack shrugged. "The second book, just once." His face changed and his eyes narrowed. "You think he didn't write that one, the second one." It took just two seconds for the pieces to fall into place. "So this network. It's bigger than him. He's a pawn. They used Ender to attract a following?"

"It's an idea." Sitri went back to his chair. He was guiding Jack. I was beginning to understand why he'd invited Jack into this meeting. He could have examined the original note himself. He wanted Jack to be part of it.

Jack nodded. "Ha! Like our other so-called suicide. I said it back then—Ender didn't write the second book. But no one listened. They thought I was nuts. Where was this group when I needed you?"

He leaned forward, his suspicions forgotten. "But you're suggesting an elaborate plan. Someone had to be writing letters for several years, supposedly coming from him." He put a hand to his mouth. "That's interesting. Guards can be bribed. Maybe one was part of this network, like Capaldi. Hmm. Definitely interesting. I see Ender going for it. Nothin' to lose, plenty to gain. Probably didn't know the suicide part till too late. Let me tell you, I interviewed him several times. He wasn't the brightest bulb. I don't see him knowing some dead language and he had no access to the 'net. I'm guessing your team has done a content analysis. Am I right?"

"We have."

"And your opinion is?"

Chapter Thirty-Two

You don't really know a plant until you've seen its roots.

"I can tell you what we found," said Orias. "The author of the second book was careful. He or they used phrases similar to the first book."

When Jack looked to his left to listen to Orias, I glanced at Sitri. I was startled to see him watching me. Those indigo eyes nailed me. I wondered if he felt my annoyance at the way he was maneuvering Jack. I narrowed my eyes. He tapped his ring finger as if to remind me of the stakes. Charmaine watched me, too. I turned to Orias.

"It's as if they expected a linguistic analysis," he was saying, "so we added qualitative dimensions they did not anticipate. We do find similarities between the second book and many of the letters that were sent, allegedly from Ender. Some were sent just before its publication and many after. We find differences between the first and second book, as well as between his early and later correspondence. However, there are strong similarities between the later letters and the second book. He even changed his name just before the second book was published, claiming a religious conversion."

Jack held up his hands. "You got this figured out. Someone else took over!"

"It's speculative," said Sitri. "We have watched this for a while. It's consistent with your current investigation."

I knew Jack hated to board a moving train, but this was a train he couldn't have started. Better to board than be left behind. He looked at me. "Did you say this Bateman is educated?"

I nodded. "He knows a lot about these cults. He was looking for something locked in a code."

"Shall we sketch it out?" Jack asked.

Sitri gestured, Orias responded, and part of the screen gave way to a white board.

Jack got up, grabbed a black marker and drew a stick man scenario. "So, this past week, we have four dead historians and a suspect meant to deflect us, who supposedly offs himself." He tapped the board, making small black dots. He drew a line over each "dead" figure. "He's presumably in this Black Torch network, which our DGs—the historians—must have discovered. So, that made them dangerous to this network." He pointed to me. "We have a witness to Bateman and Capaldi admitting to murder."

"And committing it," I added. Everyone looked at me. "I saw them kill the third historian during a botched experiment, and one of them killed my father." I shot Sitri a look. It had nearly been *him* who'd killed Alexandre. "Nick also killed Francis Martin. And we can add attempted murder—me." I pointed to the bruises on my throat. "Here's proof." I glanced at Charmaine. She'd nearly died there, too.

"Got any samples of Bateman's writing?" Jack asked.

I nearly said, "Yes, I have a journal" before Charmaine's expression warned me. This was my moment. It was time to decide. I could either reveal or conceal the Ripper journal from my father's stash. I stopped myself from touching my face, which Jack would read as deception. Looking directly at him, I truthfully said, "He wrote some computer notes. Not enough to analyze."

There it was! I'd kept the secret. I'd sided with the angels. I sensed a current move from one to the other. Orias looked at me. My stomach flipped. I kept my eyes on Jack but felt the intense psychic attunement. Charmaine gave me a curt nod. Leith tapped her pen.

"All right," said Jack, "so Nick's a follower. He's the grunt man. Bateman enlisted him. Ender, too, is a dupe. That leaves Bateman as the likely connection with Ender, starting at least four years ago. They must have an elaborate plan with a slow burn. So who the hell is he?" Jack drew some lines from one circle to another. When his back was turned, I snuck a glance at Sitri. He touched two fingers to his left arm—the trust gesture.

Jack turned to us. "For the sake of a narrative, this Black Torch saw an opportunity to use Ender's groupies to network its message worldwide. They made him the front man."

"I've read the documents they wanted," I said, trying to sound even, "so let me add something. Their goal has two prongs:

destruction and immortality. It's a self-sacrificing religion. They used Ender as the public face for our current mass disaster, because his MO complements their ideas. They killed the historians, because my father and his friends had discovered what this group was up to. Bateman is part of it, but it's bigger than just a few fanatics." I'd seen the vampiric monsters he'd created. I'd killed one.

"Right," said Jack. "Ender, the Torch, is a vehicle. But to his groupies, he's the head cheese. He's their focus. We gotta handle this carefully."

"Speaking of handling," Charmaine interrupted, "do you have security on Ender's corpse?"

Jack paused. "Good question. I'll check on that. We don't want him rising from the dead." He took out his phone and thumbed in a text.

"I suspect that it's already gone," said Sitri.

Jack looked up. I sensed him bristling. "You're talking a big conspiracy."

"It would involve two corrupt people, at most three, and bribe money or some other gain. Capaldi was susceptible."

Jack put his hands on his hips, still holding his phone. "Got names?"

"Start with the guard who found him," Charmaine said. Good strategy. Jack liked the women. He turned toward her, and she added, "And an accomplice in the prison morgue."

Jack appeared to be thinking. "A guard grabbed stuff from his cell and put it on the Internet. We've already suspended him, but we can bring him in."

"What items?" Leith asked.

"Pens, paper, envelopes—"

"This." Orias had already found the site. He put an image on the screen. The items had been removed, but he'd found a cached area that still showed them. I leaned in. One item looked familiar to me. I couldn't place it, but I'd seen it before. It was a small gold locket with the image of wings engraved along the sides, as if to embrace what it contained. The price was $250. I hugged myself and tried to remember. I realized that Sitri and Charmaine both felt my intense focus and knew that I'd seen something important. I avoided looking at them.

Jack had not noticed. "I'll find out what I can," he was saying, "but with Ender as a dupe, what's the big event? Any ideas? Blow up the Vatican? That's where this is heading."

"That we don't yet know," said Sitri.

"Ain't much time. He died yesterday, so we have, what…two days? Let's get on it. What's their motto? Kill the light. So, what's 'light'?"

"Paris," I blurted out. "The city of light."

"So…" Jack continued. "What's religious there? Notre Dame?"

"There are several important cathedrals in Paris," Leith told him.

I sensed that Sitri wanted to divert this discussion away from Paris, so I said, "This is Ripper stuff, so it must be London. That Ripper symbol, fused with Christ, must mean something."

Jack looked at me. "Maybe it's a deflection. Didn't you say this all started in France with that autopsy society?"

The Society of Mutual Autopsy. Miegul, a.k.a., Bateman, a.k.a., Jack the Ripper, had been part of the special operations team known as the Cerebro—the brain snatchers who'd also trapped angels to create rampaging vampires. I just shrugged.

Charmaine rescued me. "The Ripper suspect that interests Bateman studied in Paris with a spiritualist, Eliphas Levi, who came to London to spread his philosophy. It's related. He believed that true magicians must attain immortality. He inspired that London cult that Aleister Crowley founded in 1888, the Order of the Golden Dawn. And they supposedly knew the Ripper."

I had believed this was a coincidence. Maybe it wasn't. The Ripper journal in my father's collection had mentioned the "Mage" demonstrating angel traps. He'd come from France. So had Napoleon's *Oraculum*, which Miegul had used to lure Sitri. Without saying much, Charmaine was telling me that this Levi character was probably a member of Ignis, perhaps a *nejah* or a human helper who wanted to try the risky business of merging with a *ma'lakh*.

Jack's eyes narrowed. "Are you saying more than one person perpetrated the Ripper murders? It was a cult?"

"We look at all angles," Charmaine told him. "Bateman's suspect is a common link among occult practitioners in both cities. But Capaldi is in London, so we must focus on him. In truth, there are too many potential locations to narrow down to just one."

Jack was not deterred. "What about timing, then? The day after tomorrow? Is there some religious day? With all this planning, why would they choose this particular three-day period?"

Good question. Sitri looked as if he knew, but I sensed he wanted Jack to brainstorm it.

"We need a calendar," Orias said. I thought Sitri had telepathed this to him. Oddly, he placed a celestial calendar on the screen, showing planetary phases. Jack jumped up. "Look there! A solar eclipse! Kill the *light!* That's gotta be it. Wasn't there a blackout of some kind when Christ died? They want to mirror it! That's their MO. It should help us figure out the location."

Sitri stared at the suicide note on the other screen before he nodded at Jack. "It's time to join the surveillance. Capaldi might offer another piece."

Jack smacked the table. "That's what I'm here for!"

Leith rose. "I'll arrange it." She left the room.

Jack looked at his phone. "Holy hell!" he exclaimed. "You were right! The body has vanished. How in the…?"

We sat in silence as Jack frantically texted something back to New York, but I was certain the *ma'lakhim* were not surprised. I wondered what else they knew. Sitri was up to something. Straddling two worlds was getting tricky.

Charmaine stood. "Let us get on the same page." She glanced at her notes. "In the past 36 hours, there were four mass shootings and six mass suicides. We believe the Black Torch triggered them on the Winternet, starting with the apparent suicide of Angel Ray Ender. We suspect they will make it appear that he rose from the dead to cause an international upheaval. Bateman is facilitating it. In two days, a catastrophic event will occur to coincide with the solar eclipse." She looked up. "Our goal is to prevent it."

Sitri rose. "Everyone, please be watchful. This is a suicide cult. They have nothing to lose. No one should take unnecessary risks." He glanced at me.

Charmaine looked at her phone. To Jack she said, "Your limo is here."

Jack rose. He shook hands with Sitri again before Charmaine went to his side to escort him from the room. I joined them and told her, "I'll take him." She raised an eyebrow but stepped away to talk to Pascher.

143

When we were alone in the hall, Jack grabbed my arm. "You're holdin' back, DeeVa."

"I promise you, Jack, I have no job offer."

"He'll make one. Count on it. You think like him. He'd be stupid not to get you on board, and he don't strike me as stupid."

I shrugged. "Let's focus on Nick. We have to make him talk. He'll know how they got Ender's body out. Maybe he knows what they're planning. It's all so creepy!"

"You coming with me?" He raised an eyebrow. "Or has he got you *on* something else?"

I didn't play. "I'll change into jeans and meet you. Just tell me where."

"Where else?" he said. "The wicked quarter mile."

Chapter Thirty-Three

The Wicked Quarter Mile, from Commercial Road on the south and Spitalfields Market on the north, was where the Ripper murders took place. It has been studied backwards and forwards for over a century. Yet few know its deepest secrets. I'd been there twice, with no awareness then of the things I'd learned about immortality cults from the Ripper journal.

As I approached the elevator, Orias emerged from the conference room. I felt awkward. "Sorry about last—"

He held up a hand. "Not necessary." He looked me over as if evaluating how I'd survived that simmering embrace. "Sitri wants you."

I entered the conference room and heard a news announcer curtly describe the worldwide chaos. He sounded nervous. Sitri and Pascher stood in front of the screen. Sitri, his tie pulled loose, gestured that I should join them. His eyes swept over me, so I arched my back.

"I'm meeting Jack," I said, "as soon as I change."

"Pascher will take you."

"I really don't need—"

His stern expression stopped me. Sitri pointed to the screen. The announcer stopped mid-sentence and melted into the map. I saw the symbol that I'd tried to trace, boldly illuminated. A bright yellow L-shaped line ran from Oxford south to Bordeaux, in France, and east through France to Turin, Italy. Starting north of Glastonbury and crossing over the L's vertical shaft was a diagonal line of three dots. The other two landed on Paris and Geneva.

I shrugged. "Is it a sigil?"

"Part of one," said Sitri.

I peered at it. "But nothing happened in Paris."

"Something did. We haven't identified where. The third part will be there."

I had a sudden chill. I hoped we wouldn't find a diamond pattern made of murdered *noea* children. "So the event *will* happen in Paris?"

"Paris is a center. Eliphas Levi once set traps there for us."

"Why did you deflect Jack, then?"

"I need him here."

I wanted to ask about Sheine, why hadn't they found her? But a heavy sense of dread said that something more was at stake. I looked up at Sitri. "It's not your sigil. They're not targeting you."

His eyes burned. "I'd prefer that. This one shifts the game considerably. They have a deadly advantage."

Pascher watched me with an uneasy expression. I crossed my arms. Sitri gestured toward the screen. "I thought this was a *nejah* assault, just another attempt to grab our children. It's worse. Part of this sigil was in Glastonbury, where our shield should have blocked them."

I recalled the *"oh shit"* moment. *Putain.*

"Here is the second part. They have gained a powerful ally."

"Who?"

"A *Lumé*. Raydn. We had imprisoned him, but they freed him. That locket from Ender's cell was his challenge to us."

"What is it?"

"It contains a strand of hair—ours! It is priceless."

"We should get it!"

"Already gone," said Pascher.

Sitri pointed to the screen. "I see his plan. He's allowing the Black Torch cult to think he's their champion, but he's using them. This sigil is for Mayon, your father."

My mouth went dry. I looked at the screen and back at Sitri. "Why?"

His jaw tensed. "Raydn wants Kaitlyn. The eclipse falls on the date of their *kaisahoni*. In two days, he expects to trap Mayon."

The idea that my mother was this half-human *noea* who'd joined with a *ma'lakh* still jolted me. A *kaisahoni* was their wedding. I didn't know what to say.

Sitri gripped my shoulder. "If he violates the *affinité* while Mayon is alive, the penalty is death. So, he has tried several times to kill Mayon. Each time, we stopped him. I wanted to terminate him, but my brothers prevented it. I predicted that he would be back. Ignis freed him for their purposes, but he will use their resources to trap Mayon."

I was still confused. "Raydn thinks if he kills Mayon, my mother will want him?"

"Without Mayon, she will be vulnerable. If she refuses him, he has the means to destroy the entire *noea* network."

"But he'd have to get past you." Then I caught my breath. "Ohhh. He already can." They had Sitri's sigil. Miegul had reeled him in three days ago to trap him, but had underestimated him and failed. Miegul wouldn't be as clumsy again. And with the ring I'd lost to him, he had the *Lumé* blood necessary to try again. "But didn't you say that if Miegul successfully fuses a *ma'lakh* with a human, our planet would implode?" Sitri had shown me this image in New York. "Why would they do it?"

"They think they are immune." Sitri took my hands. His were warm. "I want you there when they question Capaldi. Pascher will be with you."

"No! You need him."

"I need him with *you*. I must collect our resources."

I gripped Sitri's fingers. "I have a mission, too. I lost the ring to them. Even if they pretend that Ender can rise from the dead—"

"Ender is alive."

"What?" This was a stunner.

"It's a trick."

Chapter Thirty-Four

I let go and stepped back. "You know this? You didn't tell Jack?"

"Nolan is chasing the story we need him to chase." He looked at Pascher. "Are the others in place?"

Pascher nodded.

I hated this. "You used me to dupe him? Why was he even here? You could have seen that note without him. You probably did."

Sitri leaned toward me. "*This* is why you need Pascher. You react. Be patient. Jack Nolan has a place. He was here for a reason."

He gestured toward the screen and it went dark. Then I saw two parallel lines forming, one black and one red. Sitri pointed to the black one.

"Watch and remember. You are in two worlds, with enemies in both. The Black Torch—the *nejah* network—is in the human world. The red one is ours." An area from the red line erupted and bled into the black one. "Raydn exploits the *nejah*. He offers Mayon to them." He pointed to the red line. "But he has his own purpose, aimed at us."

I looked at the screen. "So all these events, these murders and suicides, they're just a distraction."

"They make news, which spreads the network."

I pointed at the black line. "Here, Jack thinks Ender's body was snatched to make the world believe that Jack the Ripper will rise from the dead."

"Yes."

"There's already an app for it," Pascher added.

I looked at him. "An app? Like a Smartphone app?"

He showed me the image of a yellow triangle with a red spiral inside. "R-I-P-T. Ripped. It predicts the spread of a crippling digital virus. It has gone across the Winternet and bled into the Web."

"It's not just digital," Sitri added. "This is the important part,

148

and this is where you come in. RIPT *infects* people. It targets a neurotransmitter in the brain. Recipients feel enhanced and euphoric—fertile ground for this new religion."

A chill swept through me. "Like Nick Capaldi."

Sitri nodded. "Yes. He was infected."

I recalled his intensity. "Can you stop it?"

Sitri pointed to the black line. "Here. If we prevent Ignis from trapping Mayon, their plan will collapse and the euphoria will dissipate. Nolan can then prove that Ender's suicide was faked."

I nodded. "And with no immortal leader, the cult will dissolve. So... how do you block the big event?"

"We must identify its location. I need something from you. Raydn knows that you are a conduit and that you are Mayon's daughter. He could use you to lay the trap. Mayon would respond. They are looking for you. I would like you to be more careful. Let us guide you."

I pondered this. "Why didn't they grab me last night? I was alone."

"Miegul knows I have eyes, through you. I can find them."

"But I had blocked you until after he was in the chopper."

"He doesn't know that. They will try to lure you into their arena. If they get you inside their shield, they can block me. But they will do this strategically, when they have an advantage."

"So, put a GPS on me."

"I prefer that you stay out of their hands. There are too many unknowns."

I had another thought. "If they can use me, so can you."

Sitri eyes narrowed. He glanced at Pascher.

"You've used me as a receiver. So, reverse it. Plant something." I gestured to the screen. "Show me London."

The lines faded into a city map. "Whitechapel," I said. In a second, I saw the distinctive horizontal V of the main Whitechapel streets. I gestured for a closer view.

"Let's say Capaldi is here." I stepped to the map and pointed to a neighborhood where I knew a Ripper murder had occurred. "Maybe other Black Torchers, too. No matter what you think about Paris, if they expect to present Ender as the risen immortal Ripper, I think they'd do it here, the center of the Ripper mystique. Doesn't that make sense?"

I turned around. Pascher was gone. Sitri watched me, his arms crossed. I raised an eyebrow. "Is this the part where your staff meets my needs?"

He smiled. He *had* made a joke! "If you require assistance...." He let this hang in the air.

"Well, I'm not sure *your* staff is up for it."

He leaned toward me. "When you're all in, I'm all in."

I stepped back. "All in? I risked being horribly scalded so you could find Sheine. I'd say I'm all in."

He reached up and placed his right thumb against my throat, pressing on the puncture. I gasped at the heat that flowed through me. With his mouth close to my ear, bathing me in his fragrance, Sitri whispered, "I will know when you are." He let go and stood back. "Tell me your proposal."

I wanted him to say something more, just to ask if I was all right. Maybe thank me. Instead, he doubted me. I was farther from him, not closer. I would change that. I took a breath and gathered myself. "Teach me something from your language. I'll send a signal, like how Miegul signaled to me in New York. I'll make this Raydn think the *nejah* have gone rogue. Or make him think I'm in some specific location, lure him there for you."

Sitri showed no reaction to what I thought was brilliant. He shook his head. "Miegul sent no signal. You saw the portal because your blood was attuned."

How well I remembered. I'd been in a room full of lights and had just discovered that Agent Brenner, the man at the center of my ardent fantasies, was this *ma'lakh*, Sitri. He'd walked in, barefoot, in tight leather, stunningly sexy. He'd watched me with those dark blue eyes. I'd wanted him, then and there, in the middle of all those glimmering lights. And then I'd seen the portal emanate from Long Island. Tel-erotics. My lust had formed the connection.

"There must be something I can do," I said. "I remember this thing from my childhood. I'd spot patterns, messages. I saw the code in the Ripper letter that my fa—... that Alexandre showed me. There's something about this ability that *embraces* the symbols and makes them pop."

Sitri regarded me. "Raydn would expect me to use you, but I can't confront him. In a fight, we are equal."

"You have another plan?"

"We must surprise him. I'm working on that. I want you to join Nolan. When you see Capaldi, you will show him a code that will neutralize the app's viral effect. Pascher will give it to you, but only when you're close, as it will suspend your protection. You will have 30 seconds. Capaldi will give you, and only you, the information we need. Then you step away, at once."

"Thirty seconds?"

"It's enough."

"What if I can't get close?"

"Pascher will get you close."

"This is frustrating, Sitri! It's like I'm sitting on a bike, the motor is running, but I can't get it moving. Maybe if I could remember. You said I was taken. Maybe I know something."

His expression hardened.

"You have these *diam* protecting me. I'll be safe."

"That is an alert system. It protects you only if we're close. When you run off, like you did last night, our shield can be blocked. Miegul did it. He made a hole and you jumped in."

I blinked. He was right. But I had a response. "So, you should tell me this stuff. Give me a way to defend myself. At least give me my memories from before, when I was a child. I know I was around all of you. Show me!"

Sitri peered at me as if considering. I wanted to touch his back, feel if it was different from a human. Then he said, "I want something."

I stepped back. "You're bargaining?"

"I've asked, I've suggested, I've ordered. You ignore me. So, I'm bargaining."

"And the price?"

"You obey. No deviation."

I snorted. "I can't promise that. I can't predict—" Then I recalled Charmaine's words. *Make him know he owes you.* I rubbed a finger across the base of my throat. "You already owe me. Pay up. Give me some memories."

I saw the flicker in his eyes, like an expanding flame. He put his hand on his belt buckle, one finger pointing downward, suggesting that he also had a bargaining chip. There was *that*. But I knew he could smell blood in the wound just under my collar. *What he most craved*, Char had said. I tapped a finger near my throat.

Sitri leaned toward me. "Stay focused. Let Pascher direct you. Manage this one thing—" he tapped his belt—"and I will give you some memories."

My heart raced, but I tipped my chin up. "You owe me big time, top-of-my-list-big-time. You had your chance. When *you're* all in, I'm all in."

I turned and walked away. I didn't look back. I wanted him to watch my butt moving beneath tight ivory knit. *Make them want you*, Charmaine had advised. I was sure he did. Now, I needed to bring him closer.

I had to get dangerous.

Chapter Thirty-Nine

As I changed, I considered what I knew about Nick. If Sitri's plan failed, I wanted a fallback. Supposedly, RIPT had infected Nick and turned him. He was Ender's disciple. How much of *him* was still there? I gambled that he'd show something. I knew his tells. When he was scared, he blustered but his right eyelid twitched. When angry, his head went back, as if a snake preparing to strike. Keeping secrets, his lips tightened. Lying, he curled his left thumb and forefinger into an "O." Clenched nostrils showed his disdain. I suspected I'd see that today. But what made Sitri think Nick would tell me something important? I didn't know what I'd ask, assuming the cops here would even let me. On top of that, I'd have a severely limited timeframe. Thirty seconds! Too many things could go wrong.

But I couldn't think of a better plan. I trusted it would come to me. I had to. Time was running out. I looked longingly at the gun I couldn't bring, placed it in my bag on top of the dossier, and went downstairs.

Pascher and Charmaine stood in the foyer, their heads close together as if sharing a secret. Char glanced at me and they pulled apart. Like me, both were dressed down now, in jeans and polo shirts, ready for action. Charmaine handed me something that looked like a granola bar but smelled more enticing. "Eat this," she said. "No time for a meal."

Outside, the humid air raised a fine sheen of sweat on my face. I saw a black limo and walked toward it, but Charmaine took my arm and redirected me.

"That's our deflection," she said. "That's the car they'd expect, not this one." She pointed to an early model, faded blue Toyota Rav-4.

"You're kidding." I couldn't believe they had such a car in their stable.

"Someone's getting spoiled," she said. "I'll drive."

Pascher shook his head. "You will not." He opened the passenger side door for her.

She pouted. "It's 15 minutes."

"You can drive it back here."

"I'm staying with you."

"One of you at a time is enough for me."

She got in and I climbed in back. Pascher got into the driver's seat. I watched the limo pull away and took a bite from the bar Charmaine had given me. It tasted like almonds, honey and berries, but it melted on my tongue like angel bread. Pascher waited until the limo was two blocks ahead before he pulled out.

"I don't need an escort," I said. "I'll be with Jack."

He looked at me in the mirror. "Must I remind you about the last time you told me to ignore Sitri's directive?"

"But we—"

He shook his head.

I remembered New York. I'd entered a very bad place that had nearly gotten Charmaine and me killed. I sat back. "Where did Sitri go?"

"To get reinforcement," Charmaine said. She turned in her seat to look at me. Her eyes were bright. "If this were just *nejah*, he could handle it. But a *Lumé* is directing this."

"He told me. Someone named Raydn. What does it mean?"

"On the hierarchy, *Lumé* are the oldest and most powerful. They've been battling since the angel wars."

Pascher glanced at her.

Charmaine shrugged. "*They* don't call it that. We do. Once there were hundreds of *Lumé*, but now they're scarce. That's why they wouldn't let Sitri kill Raydn years ago. He's rotten but still a *Lumé*."

I saw Pascher's jaw tighten. He didn't like this.

"They're like generals. And scary. They protect the planet, but when all is lost from the mess we've made, they'll torch it. Fast. Mayon is a *Ser*. They reflect the fire, to make it hotter. Then there are bands of *Ora*, *Ina* and *diam* for other stuff." She gestured toward Pascher. "He's *Ora*. So are the others in the cohort. Ignis has mostly *Ina*, the weakest."

"So Sitri's enlisting other *Lumé*?" I asked.

154

"If he gets past—"

Pascher grabbed Charmaine's arm. "Don't scare her."

I held up my hands. "Please don't tell me he sent you with me when you should be with him."

"Dianysus," said Pascher, his eyes in the mirror. "You are important to him."

"And isn't this how he lost Tariel? Leaving him in charge of me?"

The air went tense. Charmaine leaned into her seat and looked at me with narrowed eyes. "Who told you that?"

"I figured it out. And I don't want to be responsible—"

"It's not your call."

"If Sitri's so worried about me, why did he leave that book with me? Doesn't that open a hole?"

Charmaine's face turned serious. "What book?"

"That *noea* book. The dossier."

Pascher's eyes in the mirror looked confused. "He didn't. He *wouldn't* have."

"He did."

Pascher and Charmaine exchanged quick glances before she said, "He gave it to Portia."

"Then Portia gave it to me, because it was in my room in Paris." I recalled that she'd been there when I'd emerged from the shower. "Is there a problem?"

"Did you open it?" Pascher asked.

A loud noise ahead of us swallowed my response, and several cars braked. A black SUV crashed into the side of a car that had twisted away from something I couldn't see. At the next corner, Pascher steered sharply right and zoomed off, finding space to pass cars illegally. I held my breath and gripped the seat.

"Get down," Charmaine ordered me. "As far down as you can."

"What's happening?"

"They're coming. When they spot the ruse, they'll be on us."

I ducked down and tried to keep steady as Pascher raced through the streets. I saw the tops of buildings and braced myself to get rammed.

"Chopper over there!" Charmaine said. "Stop speeding. We should blend in."

Pascher slowed the car.

"Maybe we should turn back," I suggested.

"Stay down," said Charmaine. "Can you still see Miegul?"

"No. It was fading last night. Now it's gone."

"Good. Then he can't see you, either."

I held onto the armrest and tried not to flinch each time Pascher applied the brakes or made a quick turn. He made several in the wrong direction and I lost my bearings. Pascher hit the brakes. A car behind us squealed. I flinched.

"You two go," he ordered. "Tibreth is out there."

Charmaine opened her door and shouted, "We'll get the Tube."

Chapter Thirty-Six

I sprang out and followed her. "I need a travel card."

"I'll get you through."

We disappeared into the underground, shielded now from the helicopter. True to her word, Char got us both through the turnstile without being stopped. It was like New York, when she'd easily opened a locked door.

We ran down the steps to the District line. I saw pain in Charmaine's face and knew this was bad for her leg. We made it to the platform as a train approached. Charmaine kept looking over her shoulder. She put her hand on my arm as if nervous about losing me. I smelled Pascher's scent on her.

"You think someone saw us?" I asked.

"We had a tail. It was gaining."

"Will Pascher be okay?"

She looked at me as if surprised that I didn't know. "They evaporate. Pasch was gone as soon as he parked."

I'd seen them seem to appear from out of nowhere, but I still didn't grasp it. "What about their clothes?"

Charmaine snapped her fingers. "Goes with them, like an apport. Quick change. They leave in a suit, return in jeans."

Ah! In New York, when I'd seduced Sitri, he'd shed his clothes without touching them. They'd seemed to melt off him.

"But I wore Sitri's jacket."

"It was real. They can dissolve their clothes or leave them behind."

"So, they have some extra-dimensional closet?"

Charmaine shook her head. "They create what they wear."

The train screeched to a stop and we boarded. I breathed out as we sat down. "How?"

"How what?"

"How do they create their clothes?"

Charmaine shot me a look. "We're in trouble and you're worried about clothes?"

I shrugged. "It matters to me."

"They study us. They know what we like."

This nearly knocked me out. No wonder Sitri always seemed so sexy!

"Pascher dresses for you?"

Her head snapped toward me. "Of course. Why wouldn't he? They *like* clothes. They like the feel of certain fabrics."

"Except shoes."

"Shoes distort their attunement, but they can make footwear that works. Not Sitri. The *Lumé* must have raw contact."

The train jostled us. I had to process this new information. I was going to pay more attention. It felt intimate and a little disturbing. Sitri *studied* me. He knew how much I loved clothes. He knew what I like on men. On *him*. I flashed through what I'd seen him wearing—leathers, tight jeans, an expensive tailored suit—and smiled. This was exciting.

"Know where we're going?" Charmaine asked.

"Jack sent the address. It's east of Brick Lane."

"Listen. When you're there, Pasch will stay close, but he might go invisible. If he needs to coach you, he'll put it on your mobile, so turn off alert sounds but keep checking. Be careful. Capaldi might be bait."

"Bait?"

"For you. If the dossier was in your room, we have a hole or a mole. Did you open it?"

"When I was with Sitri—"

"In your room. Alone."

"No. But he said it was taken when I was. How did he get it back?"

Charmaine put a finger to her lips.

I wasn't deterred. "So what just happened out there?"

"They thought you were in the limo. They tried to grab you."

"Sitri said they wouldn't—"

"He's gone. They will exploit it. We'll get off at Aldgate East. Busy there. Can move with the crowd."

158

It was difficult to talk with the noise of a crowded train, but I had to ask. "Why is it dangerous for Sitri to go get another *Lumé*?" I now regretted my flirty back talk.

"They're territorial. Very testy. But he has alliances."

"These angel wars. They were about us, right? The *noea*."

"Don't say that here."

Her dark eyes widened as she watched a man push his way through the car from the far end. Her body went tense. "Be ready to move," she ordered. "Keep your eyes down."

I did as she said, but I hated being protected. I glanced up once and saw from the side the fierce expression on Charmaine's face. Then she tapped my knee. "OK," she said. "He went the other way."

"Who was he?"

"Human, but aligned with *nejah*. Just a scout. He'll tell them."

"How would they know where we're getting off?"

"Nolan's associate here. He's with us, but Ignis has infiltrated his staff."

The train slowed down. We were still several stops from Aldgate East. "Should we get off?" I asked. I felt someone sit down close on my left. My stomach lurched before I realized it was Pascher.

He leaned over me to Charmaine and told her to go back. She made a face and shook her head. I sensed tension before she got up as the train screeched to a stop and shuffled out with those who disembarked. At the door, she gave Pascher a look of affectionate annoyance. "Be careful," she mouthed.

I spotted Kihr at the door on the far end and Tibreth at the other one. They were taller than anyone in the car. These *ma'lakhim* weren't taking any chances. It felt distinctly weird to be the focus of Sitri's exotic crew.

"We must get off at the next one," Pascher said.

I nodded. The train started to move. "Is Sitri tuned in?"

"No."

Pascher's expression was grim. He seemed worried.

Chapter Thirty-Seven

Pascher made me uneasy, but I saw a chance to learn. "Can I ask you something?"

He down looked at me. I couldn't tell if he was surprised or wary. He seemed to be waiting, so I forged ahead. "What does it mean to be Sitri's...uh...assistant?"

He glanced around before he said, "We call it *kunoui*, the closest one. I watch for danger so he can focus."

"A bodyguard?"

"At times. A messenger. A scout. A confidante. An advisor. Whatever he needs, I'm the first to know. He trusts me to do what he requires, at once. Without question."

I thought he was referring to my defiance. "Like protecting me."

"Especially that. If you get hurt or go missing on my watch..." He didn't finish.

I thought about Tariel. "He can't hold you responsible for what I do. Was he angry about flying me to Long Island? I mean, I insisted. You had no choice."

"You are a challenge. Today, I must get you to Whitechapel and back. It would help if you accepted my guidance."

I softened. "Now that's how to do it. Ask nicely. Sitri could take a lesson from you."

Pascher glanced at me from the corner of his eye. "As could you. Pleasing him has its benefits."

Charmaine had said that Pascher fervently embraced being Sitri's right-hand. What were *his* benefits?

I saw Kihr tense. He glanced at Pascher.

"When we arrive," Pascher said, "hold on to me. Let no one try to get your attention or pull you away. Take my arm, clamp your hands together, and keep your eyes down. Stay focused. We're going deeper underground, and it will be dark, so don't be alarmed."

160

I nodded. Sitri would love this. I was being obedient.

The train slowed as it came into Blackfriar's. We let people move out before we got up. As we disembarked, I sensed someone close, so I moved against Pascher and took his arm. Like Sitri, he was warm and had a distinctly pleasant smell, but more like hawthorn. Tibreth came up on my other side. I felt ridiculous, but I understood: my gift could be a potent weapon, as well as a trap. I should act like I was carrying a bag full of rare diamonds.

We went through a door marked "No Entry" and stopped on a landing with a metal railing. One dim overhead bulb barely illuminated grimy walls on both sides. The place smelled stale. I pulled my jacket closed against damp air. I didn't feel it when Pascher assured me I was safe. I let go of his arm.

"Follow me," he directed. "Be careful going down." I descended a long set of metal stairs, guided by a cold railing, and soon it was too dark to see. The hair on my neck raised, so when we came to a landing, I stopped and turned around. "Someone's behind us."

Pascher touched my arm. "They can't get close. One more flight." As we neared the bottom step, I felt a quick hit of warm air and Pascher's hand on my arm, drawing me into a black hole. I had to trust that he could see. I was unnerved.

But then I saw light. We came into a wide ventilated area with a rounded bricked ceiling, a string of lights, and a flat stone floor. I took a breath but then felt compression on my chest as Tibreth emerged from the dark. I turned to my right, where I sensed movement. Kihr walked toward us pushing a motorcycle. I saw "Kawasaki" on its side and suspected it was the speedy Ninja.

Pascher got on and gestured for me to get behind him.

"In case you drive like Sitri," I said. "Don't forget that you need to get me back safely."

"Just hold on. It will be dark, but I can see."

Chapter Thirty-Eight

We came up into a derelict building in Whitechapel, not far from the Royal London Hospital. I was relieved to be aboveground again, as hot as it was. We'd zipped through the tunnels, winding around a bit, but the floor had been smooth. I'd finally relaxed. Because it was dark, I'd leaned into Pascher and trusted that he knew what he was doing.

"You guys have a lot of underground places," I observed.

Pascher nodded. "It's protected, and fast."

"Why didn't we just go underground in Belgravia?"

"We have nothing direct from there."

I shrugged. "At least I didn't have to fly a helicopter." I pulled out my phone. "Let me see what Jack knows."

There were several messages. One, from Char, said that she'd retrieved the car and arrived in Belgravia. I conveyed this to Pascher and he nodded. He already knew. Of course. Their *affinité*. Jack said there was no sign of Nick, but several people had come and gone in the building they were watching. I let him know I was near. I wished I had a gun.

I heard another bike outside. "Dorion," said Pascher. "He'll take you from here. I will go ahead to see if it's clear."

"Clear?"

He seemed to realize I'd had little tutoring, so he explained. "Ignis lays traps. We clear them or find a way around them. They have pockets of protection that we cannot penetrate, as do we. So within ours, we can map a safe path and keep it clear."

"That sounds like a minefield."

"It can be like that. *You* can't see where the danger is, but we can."

I shrugged. "OK. Just get me there." I walked outside. I'd been in this area before. I'd seen the London Hospital's museum in an underground crypt with a small exhibit for Jack the Ripper. It had featured the Catherine Eddowes murder, with a map, copies of supposed Ripper letters, a newspaper article from 1888, and some drawings of the mutilated body.

Now knowing more from my father's notes and the Ripper journal, this place looked different. Hardly anything existed as it had in 1888, due to bombing during World War II and modern rebuilding, but it was still seedy. Streets and buildings were poorly marked.

It had probably been as hot then as it was right now. August 1888. Middle-aged poverty-stricken women were doing whatever they could to earn a little money. I'd been to each of the murder sites. Eddowes had been the start of all this for me. Symbols cut into her cheeks and face were from the celestial script, which had led me to Sitri. I suspected that the most ravaged victim, Mary Kelly, had been *noea*. She'd been ripped apart. That fate possibly lay in store for me if the Black Torch grabbed me. That's what Miegul had very nearly done to me in New York.

Not far away were the twisty back streets where other Ripper victims, Polly Nichols and Annie Chapman, had been killed. If we went west a few blocks, we could turn up Goulston Street, where Eddowes' ripped and bloody apron was found. This would get us close to Mitre Square, her death site.

Milling around were groups of people who looked like students. They studied maps, checked phones, and talked among themselves with such intensity I thought they might be part of the Black Torch, awaiting their hero. I suspected they had some augmented reality apps. I wondered if they knew that something was going to happen. By now, the world had news of the incinerated mass suicides. I guessed the lead-up to Ender's "resurrection" could be Ripper-like murders in this area.

I was happy to see Dorion's cute face, Persian blue eyes and silvery hair. Of Sitri's crew, he seemed the sweetest. I knew he was hurting over his missing child, but he didn't seem to blame me.

I got into position to climb aboard his black Ducati XDiavel when I felt something under my feet. I stood still, signaling to cut the engine. He did so and watched me. I looked down at the special shoes.

"I don't know," I said. "I just had this impression. Like someone wants my attention." I didn't want to say it felt like a child and give him false hope. "It's nearby."

He wore boots, but they looked like the same material as my shoes. I pointed at them. "You don't sense anything?"

"We're near the surveillance area," he said. "It's half a mile north."

"This is closer, but over that way." I pointed left.

"If Ignis shields them, I can't penetrate it."

I had a thought. "When Miegul's cult was doing this Ripper stuff back in 1888, did they have a secret place?"

"It's gone."

"All of it? Was any of it underground? Maybe sealed off? Any secret rooms? Even just the façade of a building? Can we check?"

This request deviated from the plan, but the raw sensation in my feet felt urgent. Why did I have these shoes if I couldn't respond?

Dorion looked uncertain.

"Hang on," I said. "I'll ask Char if it's ok."

He held up a hand. "Get on. You can show me where to stop."

"Should we tell Pascher?"

"I did."

Then I thought of something. "Do you have a weapon?"

"I'm equipped."

I sensed that if he saw someone holding his daughter, that person would regret it.

I got on behind him. We rode slowly for two blocks before I tapped him to pull over. I'd seen a street sign that seemed familiar.

Pascher was there before I was off the bike. He looked like he wanted to strangle me. "This thing you do! Going your own way. This is what concerns us."

I raised my chin. "I'm a detective. I follow my leads and this one is strong. You can come with me or you can stay here."

"Or you can come with me."

I shook my head. "I know you're worried about Sitri's orders, but it's my choice."

"And he authorized me to throw you over my shoulder if you get... *difficult*."

Pascher was serious. His eyes begged me to be reasonable. He can't have been happy about this assignment.

I held up my hands. "What's the problem? It's a temporary diversion."

"When you set a plan, we move ahead and clear it. If you

change, we're not where we need to be." He pointed to his chest. "In this form, we are limited. That sliver of *disiono* is all they need to cut you away from us. We're fast, but so are they."

I stared at him. "*Disiono*? Is that a word?"

He struggled to translate. "Not together, not coordinated… disconnected. If you pass beyond the boundary of our shield, even for a few seconds, you are exposed."

"What about the *diam*?"

"You lose them!"

Dorion leaned toward me. "Crossing an Ignis threshold scrapes them off. Ignis watches for those opportunities."

Ah. That's why Sitri was trying to keep me corralled. I hadn't realized what an elaborate operation surrounded me. Or how permeable it was.

"Won't I know?"

"Not before Ignis does. They watch their borders as closely as we do."

"I'm sorry, but—"

"Sitri cares about you," Pascher continued.

"About my ability, you mean."

He looked puzzled, but Dorion said, "It's not separate. It's—"

Pascher broke in. "He expects us to protect you. We must be able to anticipate and be where you are."

I shrugged. "But I don't know where I'm going. I'm responding to something that's trying to get my attention. What if it's a signal from those kids? What if they're around here? Shouldn't we at least check? We can do it quickly. If it's nothing, I'll go with you." I glanced over at Dorion. "What if it's Sheine?" I looked back at Pascher. Would he really deprive Dorion this chance?

They looked at each other. They were communicating.

"Ok, just stop!" I cut my hand through the air between them. "I'm part of this planning committee. An *equal* part. No secrets. Talk *to* me."

They looked startled.

"This is what we're doing," I continued. "I will respond to this thing, and you will support me. When we know what we're dealing with, we'll make another plan. So, if you think you need to sling me over your shoulder, Pascher, do it. Otherwise, let's get on with this so I can get to Jack!"

Pascher placed his hand, curled up, to his mouth and Dorion turned away.

They were *amused!* I put my hands on my hips and said, "I'm serious!"

"I'm know," Pascher said. "But that's what Kaitlyn would have said."

Dorion grinned at me. "And *how* she would say it."

I considered this. "Did you respect her?"

He nodded. "Yes, we did."

"Here's an idea. Pascher, are you tuned in to Char?"

"Yes."

"She can sense what I'm experiencing. So use her to confirm what I hear or see. Let's just try it."

"And if she warns you to stay away from something, will you listen?"

I had to think about this. "Yes, all right, it's a deal."

I felt someone behind me. I turned. Orias was there. This was damn sexy! Three of these gorgeous creatures, ready to do what I said. Pehel appeared a few yards away.

"Well, guys, let's *do* this."

I texted Jack, *Close but delayed.*

Operation moved, he sent back. *Potential hostg sit. Wait for details.*

I conveyed this to Pascher.

"Who could the hostage be?" asked Orias.

I believed they were thinking what I was thinking: the kids. Pascher sent Pehel to find out.

"Here's the plan," I said. "I'm going to walk along this street until something pops. You three can travel however you like, but stick close."

I recognized the name of this street from my research. The Ripper suspect whose identity Miegul had stolen had lodged here in 1888—or Miegul had. If Miegul, then the Ripper journal he'd said was his had described an underground room. I told them the address.

"It's here," I said. "There's a room somewhere, underground, where they once trapped a *ma'lakh* inside a murdered man." I pointed at my feet. "Under us."

Chapter Thirty-Nine

I glanced around at the dull brick buildings. The busy street felt claustrophobic from the awkward hodgepodge of architectural styles, attractive only for pubs, boutique businesses, or people seeking basic apartments. Most of the doors were dirty white or drab gray, with peeling paint that suggested indifference. Adjacent to squat old buildings, modern ones soared a dizzying dozen stories up.

I needed "assistance," as Sitri had put it. I placed two fingers under my shirt collar to find the ignition—his puncture.

Pascher pulled on my arm. "Not here. This is *nejah* territory."

Suddenly, I knew their plan. I felt a twist in my gut. "They're going to burn them," I whispered. "Alive! They're going to burn this whole place."

I stepped away from Pascher and pressed on the spot where Sitri had connected before I glanced around. Three buildings away, I saw what I was looking for: an illuminated upside down triangle. A century ago, D'Onston/Miegul had drawn it invisibly on the exterior. He'd told an associate that it warded off evil. In truth, it drew power. It was the bottom half of a celestial portal. I pointed. "That building? Can you get me inside?"

Pascher told Orias to get the helicopter, in case they found more girls. He went with me to a door that was set back into an arched frame, and listened. "It's abandoned," he said. "No one lives here." I heard a click and knew he'd opened whatever lock barred our access. A tattered sign suggested a business had used the place as a mail drop. I opened the door and went in.

The dark hallway stank of stale urine, dirt and rotting food. Squatters. I put my hand over my mouth and nose.

Dorion appeared next to me. "You can't get below from here."

"I'm looking for a secret room." I recalled what I'd read in the

Ripper journal—how the "Mage" had led a ceremony that had merged a trapped *ma'lakh* with a recently murdered man to create a creature with enormous blood lust. Mentally, I panned away to try to glean details of the location. I felt the tug of something, as if someone was aware of me. I stayed still, trying to "pull" some details. I saw a tunnel—

Pascher grabbed my arm and pushed me out to the street.

"I nearly had something," I protested.

"They nearly had *you*," he said. "We can't do it this way."

Dorion looked up. So did Pascher.

"What?" I glanced at the top of the six-story building across the street. A flash of light made me blink. I refocused. Then I gasped. A set of wings with multiple shades of blue opened and spread out before disappearing.

I stared "What is it?" But Pascher was gone. Dorion seemed agitated. He shook his head and looked up again. "*Lumé*."

He urged me into the protective arch of the doorway. "It's Teios. He once protected Raydn."

Raydn! The one that Sitri was worried about. I turned to go back inside, but he stopped me. "Wait. Pascher is with him."

"If he's an enemy—"

"Teios mediates. He's not a friend or an enemy."

"Those wings! That was amazing."

Dorion nodded. "Yes, the wings of a *Lumé* are spectacular, even to us. He is absorbing information, checking the area, checking you."

I smelled smoke and took a deeper breath. "Do you smell that? It's fire. They've started." I ran through the door and looked for a way to get to the cellar. The participants in the Mage's ceremony had been ordinary men. They couldn't go through solid walls. They'd been here, in some underground area, so there had to be a way to find it.

Dorion stepped from thin air to block me.

"Look for a way down!" I told him. "They're here. We have to find them."

"It's not safe in here. Wait for Pascher."

The smell was stronger now. "I'm not leaving! We get them first!"

A child screamed. It was distant but distinctly a girl. I remembered—I'd been trapped like that. "We need to find them!" I skirted Dorion and ran toward the sound. "We're coming!" I yelled. I tried a door, but it was locked. I went to another, and another. All locked.

"Open these!" I shouted. "Now!"

One knob turned in my hand and I opened a door to stairs that descended into darkness. Smoke wafted up. I pulled my shirt over my nose. Another frightened girl's voice joined the first. Fighting panic, I found a light switch and started down. "We're here!"

I felt the fire's heat. Then I saw flames. This wasn't a burning building, it was a large ring of fire on the floor, thriving on some mysterious fuel. In the middle was a wooden box with a lid. It resembled a coffin. I made out three distinct voices, begging for us to hurry. I looked for a way to get to them, but there were no breaks in the fire. I crouched to jump over it, but I was jerked back.

"It's a trap!" Pascher yelled.

From inside a little girl screamed. Or maybe it was me. I struggled, but Pascher would not let go. "Char can see it." He pulled me toward the stairs, grabbed me by the shoulders, and made me look straight at him. "It's an illusion. She says they're trying to lure you into something."

I looked around him back to the fire. He was right. There were no flames or any evidence that they'd been there. Why had it seemed so real?

Dorion stood next to the box. He lifted the lid and shook his head. "Empty."

"I heard them!" I insisted.

Then another figure emerged from the dark, a tall figure with short brunette hair and light brown skin. Close to him, a *ma'lakh* with shoulder-length white hair appeared. Both wore dark clothing, but their skin shone bright. The white-haired one regarded me with a curious expression, while the dark-haired creature gestured for me to approach. Pascher exchanged words with him that I couldn't understand, but I heard Sitri's name. Pascher let go of me. I looked at him and he nodded that I should go over.

I squeezed my hands together to calm myself. My cellphone vibrated. Jack! But this was no time to answer. I was meeting another *Lumé*, Teios.

When I was close, I noticed he smelled like Sitri and had the

169

same dark blue irises. He looked me over. I figured he knew who I was. He must have thought the same about me, because without introductions he launched right in, his voice deep and imposing. "An Ignis tunnel is near us. There might be an entrance. Look for a sign."

The *ma'lakhim* watched me. I looked around the cellar room. Three bare bulbs did little to illuminate the 20 x 30 room, but I shouldn't need more light. No matter the conditions, these symbols jumped out. Faded white walls, plastered over, gave up no clues. I scoured the ceiling and the floor. I even looked behind an old cabinet and went partly up the steps. I expected my probe to flash something at me, but nothing happened.

They were waiting. Jack was waiting. I couldn't come through.

Pascher came up to me and touched my shoulder. "Char says you're blocking. Relax."

I nodded and took a breath. I concentrated on the shoes. The sensations were faint but still there. I shrugged and pointed to the box. "It was there. Maybe it's empty, but something came from there."

I went over and lifted the lid myself. To my surprise, there it was. The faint outline of a portal. This box had no bottom. The three-by-four-foot portal was etched into the concrete floor, centered inside the box frame. I looked at Dorion. "You didn't see this?"

He came next to me. "What?"

Teios was close as well, watching.

I leaned in and used my finger to show them. "A portal. Right here. Not a hole, but an outline."

Teios looked to Pascher, who said, "Char confirms it."

I realized that I was the only one in the room who could see a *nejah*-created signal. I pressed on the cold concrete at the portal's center. "They're under here." To get a better look, I stepped into the box.

The floor collapsed. I fell through a hole. I gasped and choked on dust.

Then it felt like I was floating. I landed easily on a solid surface amid the rubble. Dorion appeared beside me, supporting me. I looked up. The hole I'd made overhead was 12 feet up.

To my right, a glow came off Pascher, allowing me to see. A girl shouted his name. He turned around. Three young girls sat on a mattress on the floor along a wall. One launched herself at Pascher. He knelt down and caught her in a hug. The other two jumped up, their arms outstretched, and Dorion went to them. A redhead child started to cry.

Then I heard the distinct *click* of a semi-auto slide. I ducked and spun. Three bullets hit the wall near Dorion. Two figures fled through a doorway, but I knew one of them. There was no mistaking that belly.

"Nick!"

I followed him into a dark tunnel.

Chapter Forty

Nick and his associate had flashlights. One pulled ahead. I was sure it wasn't Nick. He'd never been in shape for police work, let alone running through a tunnel. I was grateful for my silent shoes, which buffered my feet from the rough surface.

This hadn't been the plan. I was supposed to see him in an interrogation room, safe and well-lit.

Suddenly, one light beam stopped, turned, and came toward me. Nick was on me before I could turn round.

"You bitch!" he yelled. "We had it! You ruined it! But we'll win this round." As he reached for my throat, I tried to duck, but he caught me. Then he went over backwards as if he'd been hit. I heard his head crack against the ground. He lay there, stunned from the impact. I couldn't see Pascher, but I knew his smell.

I crouched down and grabbed Nick's flashlight and weapon. I shone the beam in his face. "You can't touch me and you know why. Sit up!"

Groaning, he shoved himself back toward the wall. Sensations in my feet told me that his friend had doubled back. I put the muzzle to Nick's head. "Call him off. If he gets close, I'll shoot him." Nick's nostrils clenched. He dug for his phone and started to thumb in a text. I set down the flashlight, grabbed the phone, and used a thumb to erase his plea for help. I then texted, "Run!"

He forced a laugh. "This is so much bigger than you. There's nothing you or your friends"—he gestured in the air—"can do to stop it." He lunged but was once more pushed back.

I looked at the app icons on his phone. The yellow RIPT triangle stood out. It felt alive. It seemed aware of me. I felt nudged from behind just as my own phone grew hot. Thirty seconds. I'd just wasted ten.

I pocketed Nick's phone and got mine out. I saw Jack's text. *Nic gone. BOLO.*

No kidding! I entered my security code. An unfamiliar app glowed red. This was it. I was stepping, naked, into the supernatural arena, where apps could infect the human brain. I sensed Pascher close on my right. I heard the *whirr* of wings, felt a shift, and thought another *ma'lakh* had arrived. I turned my head just enough to see the white hair from the corner of my eye. Teios' *kunoui*. Teios must be close. A glow behind me illuminated the tunnel.

I turned my phone to show Nick the app. He looked confused. His right eyelid twitched. Ten seconds. He breathed hard. I felt a force move through me. Nick looked over my head and his expression changed to shock. His eyes watered. He placed his hands on the ground at his sides as if he wanted to push himself back through the wall. I kept the phone steady.

Then he lunged at me and grabbed the front of my shirt, shouting, "Lights out!" He tried to take the phone. I set down the gun to keep control. Nick reached for it. I grabbed the barrel but he had the grip. He jerked it downward, hard, forcing me to let go. I'd made a deadly mistake.

I raised my hand over my face and looked away, flinching at the loud retort. Warm liquid spattered on my palm and jacket. I wasn't hit. Ears ringing, I lowered my hand, but Pascher pulled me away. I saw the top of Nick's head, the skull open and bloody.

I stumbled onto one knee. Pascher caught me and put his arm around me. I was shaking. I could barely move.

"In here." Pascher guided me into the room where the girls had been. It was empty. He opened a door to a stone staircase and urged me to go.

"But Nick…"

"They will come for him."

I turned and looked at him. "Did you do that?"

"Go up."

"We didn't get anything. He didn't say anything."

On my right, I felt tugging on my arm. Orias was just above me.

"Wait! Wait." I looked back at Pascher. "I have to tell Jack."

"He should not hear it from you."

"But he's waiting for me. He texted—"

173

Pascher stayed firm. "Dianysus. Please leave this building. Immediately."

Then he was gone, back inside. Orias led me up. The door opened and Leith was there. She guided me into the street.

I blinked in the sunlight, feeling sick.

Leith pulled a package of moist wipes from her bag and cleaned me off. She grimaced. "Good thing Sitri put a seal on this jacket. This stuff comes right off. What the hell happened down there?"

I shook my head. I had to tell Jack. I searched for my phone, but it was gone. I must have dropped mine when Nick shot himself. It had happened so fast. I told Orias to relay this to Pascher. Whatever was on that phone, I didn't want it in the wrong hands. Nick's associate might have come back and found it... and him. The image of his shattered head made the gorge rise in my throat. I knew this was a suicide cult, but I'd thought the app would dissolve the virus. Instead, Nick had made a vile threat.

Orias helped me to sit against a ledge. "We need to go. Can you walk?"

"Did the kids get out?"

"Yes. They're safe."

"Sheine?"

He shook his head.

I nodded. "OK, I just need to collect myself." I felt in my pockets and realized that I also didn't have Nick's phone. I'd put it in my pocket, but it was gone.

"I'll take her over," Leith said.

Orias looked to his right, up the street. Then he said, "Quickly."

My eyes burned from all the dust. I closed them. Nick was dead. Whatever he knew that could have helped stop this madness was gone. I'd let Sitri down.

Leith snapped her fingers in my face. "Let's go." She pointed to the high-rise building up the street. "The helicopter is coming. Follow me."

Leith ran in front of a car, oblivious to the horn from an angry driver. I followed. She shot through a revolving glass door and ran across a wide foyer. Holding the elevator door, she urged me to hurry. I pushed myself. When the door closed, I doubled over and breathed out. Leith smirked the way she had when we'd first met. "You sure

174

know how to ruffle feathers, so to speak. You're here just two days and you've made all kinds of trouble."

I stared at her. "I just found three kids!"

"And broke holes in our defense."

"What?"

"Ours *and* theirs. They're mobilizing fast." Leith used her T-shirt to wipe her sweaty face. "Ignis throws this stuff out there like breadcrumbs. They hooked you, and they know it."

"What do you mean?"

"Kids trapped in a fire? That doesn't sound familiar?"

My stomach twisted. My response came out as a whisper. "No."

She nodded. "So, they haven't told you yet. Ask Portia. She knows the whole story."

"You tell me."

"It's not my place. But I can see what they're trying to do."

I shrugged. "Got a better plan?"

"Do what you said on the plane. *Lead*. Be a warrior. Don't follow *their* trail; make them follow *you*. You're Kaitlyn's daughter. Surprise them."

We stared at each other as the elevator moved upward. I should have seen that. It irked me that she'd spotted it. I recalled my proposal to Sitri and asked, "Is it possible to infiltrate?"

She raised an eyebrow. "*Now* you sound like Kaitlyn."

I shook my head. "I don't have her courage."

"Not courage, skill. She learned their secrets and used it. She was extraordinarily sensual. She knew how to walk through a room and leave every male there, human or otherwise, as hard as marble. She weakened them, then manipulated them."

We passed the twelfth floor. There wasn't much time. "I don't have that ability."

"Use your own gifts. This is how it works. The *diam* surround you, like a network, and give off danger signals if an enemy approaches. For that to be effective, a *ma'lakh* must be near. If you pass through an Ignis threshold, you lose your protection."

"Okay, I know that."

"Here's the important part. Once you're out of their range, you can use Varian or another herb to go invisible. They can't track you. You know about this, right?"

"I've heard. Even the *diam* can't sense me?"

"Correct."

"So, assuming we get desperate, how would I do it?"

We reached the top floor and the doors opened.

"Not here," she said. "They're too close. And I have to talk to Nettie. She makes it. Find me later."

"Sitri won't like it."

She shrugged. "He's *ma'lakh*, you're *noea*. Decide for yourself. For us. *That's* what Kaitlyn would do."

We emerged on the roof. Near a two-foot wall at the far end, I saw Dorion and Pehel with Teios and his *kunoui*. They watched something to the northeast—smoke. A building was burning just across Whitechapel High Street. I heard sirens. When I reached the wall next to Dorion, a geyser of flame shot up not far away.

"Where is that?" I asked him.

He put a hand on my shoulder to gently push me to safer ground. "Angel Alley."

"What? Is this Angel Ray Ender's coming-out party?"

"It might be the pre-show."

I peered out at the flames. They seemed more robust than an ordinary fire, even one with accelerant. I felt the heat from here. I stared for a moment, mesmerized, until I saw something odd. "Hey, what's that?"

Teios came over. "What do you see?"

I pointed. "It comes and goes, but I think I see signals."

I heard a helicopter coming in behind us, but I ignored it to focus. A figure floated in the flames, rippling, like what I'd seen under Montmartre. Before I could describe it, I felt hands on both of my arms, turning me away.

"You need to leave!" It was Teios.

"What?" I looked at the helicopter. Pascher was there, beckoning.

Teios stepped between me and the fire, blocking my view. "Now!"

"Okay." I went toward the chopper, but took a quick look back. To my shock, Teios stepped onto the wall and launched into the air. His *kunoui* followed, with light gray wings growing out of his back. A flash of orange to my left transformed Pehel as he leapt over and

176

melted into the air. Dorion went in a burst of aquamarine. It reminded me of a video I'd seen of a sea sapphire. In a flash, it had evolved through red, blue, and gold into a transparent form before vanishing.

Spectacular! I'd just seen the *ma'lakhim* change. They'd let me. I was part of this crew. They trusted me.

Leith pulled my arm and urged me to go. As I ran to the chopper, I saw smoke rising from the building where the girls had been trapped. Another fire. But I knew that wasn't why Teios had ordered me to leave. He'd seen the danger. Not two blocks away, Sitri's foe was trying to connect. Raydn was here. *He* was the geyser of flame.

Chapter Forty-One

When I climbed into the chopper, Charmaine was twisted around in the pilot's seat toward Pascher as he leaned in through the open back door. When she stretched her neck, I saw where he'd recently connected. I blushed, as if I'd seen them naked. He kissed her, nodded to me and banged the door shut.

I felt it. Settling into a seat, I put on a headset. "I wasn't that bad."

Charmaine glanced sideways at me.

I shrugged. "It all worked out. He's not coming with us?"

"Sitri's back."

I breathed out. Sitri! I hadn't exactly earned some memories. I'd gone off the plan and I'd failed with Nick. But we'd saved three girls before the building went up in flames. That had to count.

"Are the girls okay?"

Charmaine nodded. "Dehydrated and scared, not harmed."

"Sheine?"

"No. Three still missing." She glanced at me. "Each has abilities that can be used against us."

I sat back, disappointed. I was certain I'd checked off one of my goals today. Strapping in, I asked, "Are we safe in this?"

Charmaine gestured outside. "Kihr and Tibreth are close." She started to lift us when I remembered. "Wait! Ask Pascher if he found my phone. I have to call Jack."

"He's gone."

"Can't you just—?" I swirled my finger near my head.

"Not now."

I slumped. I had to believe that he wouldn't just leave it with Nick's body, not after they were so careful last night. But I wanted to see that disinfecting app. I wanted to know why Sitri had thought it

178

would work. He'd seemed certain, but I felt like I'd sent us down a steep incline toward a cliff.

Charmaine removed a phone from her pocket. "Nolan knows about Capaldi."

"He knows?"

"Let him tell you. Act surprised."

I grabbed the phone and texted a message with the number to call. It rang right away.

"Jack! Everything all right?"

"Hardly. This place is burning! Three different spots. These people are pathological arsonists."

This gave me a cover. "I know. We had to get out. I lost my phone and couldn't go back."

"Yeah, three buildings gone. Black Torch claimed credit. We got more suicides, including Nick. Offed himself where Brenner told us. Was there the whole time."

"That's not—" I glanced at Char. "Oh! Wow. He must have felt cornered. And the hostages?"

"Gone, or he punked us."

"What about Ender?"

"No trace. We ID'ed the insider. He's gone, too. Led some kind of suicide circle in New York. Eight more dead."

Ech! My city was now infected. I shifted in my seat, uneasy with the lies. "Are you heading back?"

"Nope, staying here, on Brenner's dime. Got multiple investigations if you want in."

"I'm on one, thanks."

"I don't doubt it, Dee*Lay*. Emphasis on 'lay.' Anything on Project Eclipse?"

"Just that we're running out of time."

"You on a chopper?"

"Yes, and nearly out of range. Glad you're safe. I'll be in touch."

I ended the call before he could ask where I was going and returned Charmaine's phone. "They already moved Nick's body?"

"They work fast. Feel bad?"

"I didn't like him. Did Pascher kill him? Or did the app pull the trigger?"

"Does it matter?"

179

"Nick was supposed to tell us something and now he can't." I felt my jacket pockets again to be sure I had no phones. "I think a *ma'lakh* picked my pocket."

Charmaine snorted. "They're good at that."

"I've seen that RIPT app before. Not in the news, but somewhere else." I strained to pinpoint the memory. "It seemed...*aware* of me."

"You shouldn't have looked."

I shrugged. "Pascher was there, and that other one, Teios' guy. His *kuoni*."

"*Kunoui*. That's Handre. Vigilant. Protective."

I recalled Nick being slung hard to the ground. Had it been Handre? "Sitri knows I failed, doesn't he?"

Charmaine glanced around before she responded. "Did you not feel something when you confronted Capaldi? I did."

I remembered. A sense of something flowing through me. "Yes, but all he said was 'lights out.' Like a battle cry. I thought the counter-app was supposed to kill the virus."

"It did. Teios was behind you, full *Lumé*. When the virus dissolved, Capaldi saw a real *ma'lakh*. With *you*. I think it deflated him."

I considered this. "But he's a believer. He should have redeemed himself. He could have told us the location of this big event."

"Maybe didn't know." Charmaine made a maneuver that angled us and changed our direction. "Something went through you. Two seconds later, Sitri wanted us in Paris. He has a plan."

I stared at her. Maybe I *did* have a shot at some "memories." I'd found Nick, even if not quite the way he'd expected.

Charmaine pulled something from her pocket and handed it to me. "Eat this."

I was hungry, but for real food not another biscuit. I chewed fast and nearly swallowed it whole. "What's in these?"

"A barrier."

I sat up straight. "Barrier?"

"To block *épuisé*. Until you know how."

I rolled my tongue around my mouth and envisioned another round with Sitri—one where I didn't black out. "Can Sitri still see what I see?"

"No. And *they* can't use you to locate him."

Ah. That's why she'd given this to me in the car. "Am I invisible to him?" My heart stopped. "Or poison?"

Charmaine shook her head. "Different process." She glanced at me. "This one keeps you alert, just in case." She moved the collective, taking us higher, before she said, "Sitri doesn't have to see what you see. If you stay inside the shields, he knows where you are." She gestured in the air, which I assumed was a signal for our guardians.

I looked over at her. "So when he's blocked, he can lose me? Maybe I should give him some advantage..."

Charmaine shook her head.

"Okay, okay. How's your leg?"

"Good enough. Can run if I have to."

"Do you know what's going on in Whitechapel? Any news reports?"

"We think they're creating a spectacle, maybe deflecting the press from other activities. Media speculation is all over the place."

"Jack said there were more suicides."

"Disciples. Lots of press about warning signs and offers of suicide assistance. Plenty of frustrated experts discussing the threat. They don't know the timing or how to find a Black Torch member, or how to decipher the Winternet. They're seeking disaffected members. Won't happen. So the focus is on the fire in Whitechapel. No mention yet of Ender's Ripper connection or his disappearance. We think they're pacing it."

"Raydn was back there, right? He was close."

She nodded. "Teios blocked him."

"Dorion said Teios doesn't take sides."

"He protects the *Lumé*, mostly from each other. He will prevent Sitri from killing Raydn if he finds him."

"So, he takes Raydn's side."

Charmaine shook her head. "He will protect either one. That's his function."

I took a breath, knowing my next question would annoy her. "Doesn't your thing with Pascher make Sitri vulnerable?" She glanced at me, her almond eyes narrowed. I persisted. "If I were Raydn, I'd grab you and make Pascher choose."

181

Charmaine worked the controls to move us forward. "He knows it wouldn't work. Their duty to their *Lumé* is first."

"I've seen Pascher with you. I think he'd do whatever it took to save you."

She shook her head. "He wouldn't. Sitri knows he wouldn't."

"So he lets you be together."

She moved the cyclic, jolting me. "*Lets* us? Sitri arranged it."

I stared at her. I'd been wrong. Again.

Charmaine adjusted her earphones. "Kaitlyn initiated the liaisons to get the *ma'lakhim* invested in us. Sitri knows we can do things that they cannot. So, he allows it. But with his cohort, he comes first. They're tested before they're trusted."

"That doesn't bother you?"

She pushed us slightly left and forward. "Accept it or leave them. I tried. Three times."

This surprised me. "You broke up?"

"Yes. And that was before Pasch was Sitri's *kunoui*. I wish he wasn't. It's the most dangerous spot."

Our speed increased and we whizzed past green, blue, and white lights that came up on both sides before Charmaine said, "We train. We commit. Strength, speed, language, weapons, how to fly these…" she gestured around us. "Use camouflage, leap from heights, detect threats. If you want to be fully *with* them, you prepare and prove yourself. Pasch was my mentor first. Kaitlyn and Sitri directed our *affinité*. They did this with any *noea* who wanted to be involved with Sitri's cohort. The matches serve the community. Otherwise, they do not happen."

I hadn't imagined this degree of organization. "Have they ever… mismatched?"

Her hand tightened on the cyclic. I'd hit a nerve. Finally, she said, "There has been treachery. We pared down. Only the most loyal. We're the best. Ignis knows of us, but the residence is under shield. When you leave it, you must be vigilant. We tried with Marie."

"Marie?"

"Mary. Mary Kelly."

Chapter Forty-Two

We were back in Ripper territory. Officially, Mary Kelly was the Ripper's last murder victim. According to the Ripper journal my father had, one of Miegul's monsters had torn her apart. Missing from this horrendous gore-fest was her heart, which had been ripped from her body.

"Mary Kelly?" I asked. "The Ripper's victim?"

"We warned her."

"She was *noea*?" I'd suspected it.

The chopper took a hit, jarring us both. I grabbed my seat and held my breath as Charmaine fought to keep us steady. We spun to the left before we dropped down so fast I felt my stomach. Charmaine's face gave no sign of her thoughts. "Take the controls!" She removed her headset and climbed into the cramped area in back and opened the door. Cool air rushed in.

My heart pounding, I put my feet to the pedals and tried to remember what Pascher had told me about the various sticks, buttons, dials and handles. We listed to the side and started to dive before I pulled it up. But I'd lost speed. *Don't panic!* I forced myself to breathe evenly and think about what I was doing. I grabbed the throttle. *Not like a motorcycle*, I remembered.

Something that glowed orange in the distance was coming straight at me. I looked out the open door and saw no sign of Charmaine. I prayed I hadn't shaken her off. "Char!" But her discarded headset reminded me that she couldn't hear.

The idea that I might be in this chopper alone, a target, made my grip weak. I pulled up on the collective at my left and the orange thing went under me. The chopper shook, as if I'd hit a rippling wake. I pushed on the cyclic in front of me. Too hard. I jerked the chopper. *Easy, easy.* I maneuvered sideways and then pitched forward.

Wiping sweat off my face, I tried again. *Relax*. I managed to balance it but felt something bang against my side of the chopper. I didn't look. I maintained control. Charmaine came back to her seat and put on her headset. I breathed in relief and dried my hand on my jeans.

She took over, but her next words were not reassuring. "A rip in the shield. The hits are strong. They're putting a lot of force against us. Probably angry."

I felt the chopper slow down. "Can they repair it?"

"Better to jump."

My heart stopped. "What?"

"We're over land now. They can consolidate our shield if we get out. We'll be all right."

"I thought you said we were safe!"

She looked at me. "We were. Now we're not."

"What about your injuries?" I glanced over my shoulder. "And where are the parachutes?"

"Don't need them. You follow me."

"Charmaine! I'm not jumping! Are you crazy?"

She brought the chopper into a hover position and leaned toward me. "You fell through a floor today. Right?'

"Yes."

"Were you hurt?"

"Twelve feet is not—"

"It is. When you were three, you would jump off the top balcony. Six stories! You loved it."

The experience came back. It was a game I'd played. I'd push myself off, giggling, and float to the ground. Just like in that house today. I remembered Sitri there, and a copper-haired *ma'lakh* I didn't know.

Kihr entered, his curly hair in tangles. He crouched in back. "It's time."

Char tossed her headset. She beckoned for me to follow. Kihr gave her a hand as she moved to the back. With no hesitation, she launched herself out the door.

I panted, not quite believing this. We were really jumping! I looked outside to see how far it was. I couldn't even see the ground. This didn't seem possible. But Charmaine was gone.

Kihr gestured, his face encouraging. My turn. I remembered the incident in New York when the ladder had let go, Charmaine with it. Moments later, Pascher had her with him in his seat. Right now, two *ma'lakhim* were watching. They wouldn't let me fall. Of course they wouldn't. I could do this.

My mouth went dry. I tried to unfasten my seatbelt but couldn't unlatch it. My fingers weren't working right. Feeling helpless, I looked at Kihr. He understood. It came loose. I removed my headset and pushed off the seat. My heart beat so hard it hurt.

I saw my overnight bag. The dossier. "Wait!" I unzipped the bag and felt for the leather-bound book. It was there, under my gun. Stuffing both into my two inside pockets, I zipped up and let Kihr help me to the edge. "You will be fine," he promised. "I will make it as soft as possible."

I saw Tibreth take over the controls. It felt warm in here. I wanted to stay inside. Maybe the attack was over.

Kihr tapped my arm. "Now."

I swallowed. I waited a beat. Then two. I jumped.

The cold air punched me in the stomach and face, as if I'd dove too flat into a pool. I couldn't breathe. But then I slowed down and felt warmer. Sounds sharpened and I started to glide. I saw land coming at me, so I closed my eyes. *I'm not going to die!* I felt like I was in a dream. I remembered this sensation from my childhood. Then my feet came under me and I landed like a gymnast, soft and balanced. Score! I was alive. It felt amazing. I looked up. I wanted to try that again.

But then my stomach caught up. I thought I would vomit. I held my gut and stood up straight, but nearly fell. I sat down on the hard pebbles of a dirt road. Rocking to keep from retching, I looked around. The place was spinning. I felt a rain drop. Then several. Great!

I had no idea how far away Charmaine might be. I didn't know which direction to take. The dossier felt hot in my jacket. I pulled it out. Laying my hand on the cover, I hesitated. If I opened it, I might draw some force right here where I was, without defenses. Sitri was cut off, but surely Kihr or one of the others was nearby. My fingers explored the cover and I pushed into the pages. Just one glimpse and I'd close it fast. But isn't that what Pandora had believed? I swallowed and looked up. I saw no flash of light that might identify a *ma'lakh*. But then again, they might stop me from looking. Char had said that Sitri did not want me to have this book.

I shoved my finger in a little further but pressed on the cover, as if opening it fully might spring the lock on a cage for some creature inside.

"It's just language," I whispered. This book had shocked me before, but only because I'd used the crystal with it. After that, it had shown me what we needed. Holding it, with Sitri aroused and pressing against me, I'd pulled symbols that offered significant information.

As I sat there, I put some pieces together. A *Lumé* had once given that very crystal and some powdered *Lumé* blood to John Dee and Edward Kelley so they could decipher celestial language and learn forbidden secrets. The *Lumé* had to be Raydn. He'd lusted for my mother and kidnapped me to lure her to him. Sitri had tried to kill him, Teios had intervened, and they'd ultimately imprisoned the renegade. But someone from Ignis had recently freed him. I suspected that he now had the ring with my mother's blood. He was using Ignis' Black Torch network to lure Mayon for elimination.

That image jarred me. I stood. Through my feet, I sensed a car coming. I put the dossier back in my pocket and looked for a place to hide. Then I heard an engine. The car was coming fast. Had I drawn it? I ran to a thick tree to hide.

Chapter Forty-Three

A dark SUV came barreling down the road. I tried to keep the tree between it and me, but as it drew even with the tree it skidded to a stop. The window came down.

"Get in!" It was Charmaine.

When I strapped in, she said, "Two more seconds in the chopper and you'd have been caught. When I say move, you have to move!" She looked over at me as she pulled out.

"How did you find me?"

"I watched where you came down." She pointed to her eyes. "I can also still see what you see. And Tibreth sent a flare."

"Whose car is this?" I recalled how Charmaine had "found" a motorcycle on Long Island.

She shrugged. "Someone who won't be around to miss it if we don't accomplish our mission."

I nodded. Point taken. "How was that free fall even possible?"

"Our *ma'lakh* blood. They use it to support us."

"What kind do you have?"

"A mix. A little *Lumé*, some *Ora*. More human than you."

"How much am I?"

"About one-third, with Alexandre's contribution. One-third of each, human, *Ser* and *Lumé*."

This rattled me. I'd had no sense that I wasn't even half human.

Despite the winding road and the rain now pelting the windshield, Charmaine sped up. When she nearly left the road, I tightened my seatbelt. Maybe I could jump from a chopper unscathed, but a rollover could probably do some damage. We traveled for a few minutes in silence before she said, "Don't open the dossier on your own."

I looked at her. She must have sensed what I'd been thinking. "Why not?"

187

"Ignis had it for years. You don't know what they put into it."

"How did we get it back?"

She shrugged. "Portia gave it to Sitri."

Portia! I felt a twinge of jealousy again. And suspicion. "Maybe there's something in it we can use."

Charmaine went quiet. Then she said, "You were good today. You think for you, and for us." She looked out the window to her left. "Hold on." She accelerated so fast I gripped the seat. When she slowed, she said, "The *Lumé* have several protected spots. One is near Glastonbury."

I held my breath. She was opening a door. She'd promised that she would.

"That story is true about Dee and Kelley receiving the crystal and red powder there. But it was a betrayal. Those items belonged to the *Lumé*. The crystal was formed with water from the lake."

"Lake?"

"Underground. The synthemanteum. The *Lumé* immerse in it. Their wings are full of sensors. The water cleans and sharpens them." She glanced at me. "That's what you smell. Like flowers. Brugmansia, or angel trumpets. Kind of citrusy. It's the water. Otherwise they wouldn't smell like anything because they don't sweat."

Synthemanteum. I sensed something that made my heart race, but it remained elusive.

"Sitri blocks your memories, but the *noea* think you should know."

I held still, as if a single shallow breath could change her mind. My mouth tasted like stale coffee.

She made a sharp turn that pushed me hard against the door. I saw her glance in the rearview mirror as if nervous about a tail. Then she told me something that changed everything. "Before you, Kaitlyn had another daughter, Asha."

"What?"

"Just listen. Over the years, Kaitlyn had several daughters. She wanted Sitri to have a part of her. But things went wrong. Some miscarried. Two died young. One was too frail. Although Asha was strong, Sitri rejected her immediately, before she was born. He said she would develop the same savage hunger that infected the males."

I started to ask a question, but Charmaine shushed me. "You must hear this. So Kaitlyn tried the experiment with Alexandre, to anchor a daughter more firmly in the human world, with less risk of *ma'lakh* infection." She pointed. "You."

"So she gave me to Sitri?"

"She only set up a possibility." She pointed to herself and me. "*We* direct our liaisons. But stop interrupting. There's more at stake right now."

"Ok, go ahead. So, Kaitlyn tried this experiment."

"Asha was 12 when you were born. Sitri was intrigued and his attention to you made her angry. She tried to hurt you several times, and when you were four, she helped Raydn grab you."

Charmaine looked at me. I shrugged and shook my head. It was hard to learn I had a sister—one who hated me. But despite a bad taste in my mouth and a tightening gut, this tale felt like watching a movie. "I don't remember any of it."

"I'm not restoring your emotional memories. Just explaining. For a reason. When you disappeared, Sitri and Mayon launched an assault on Raydn. They caught him, clipped his wings, and made him reveal where you were. But Asha had locked you into a closet and set the building on fire…"

I felt a chill from head to toe. My childhood terrors… a burning closet…

"They found you, but you were badly burned, nearly dead—"

I swallowed hard. My thighs clenched. "How is that—?" I rubbed the back of my hand. I knew what fire-damaged skin looked like. Mine showed no sign.

Her expression stopped me. My heart thumped. I couldn't breathe.

"Now *listen*. This is important. Sitri took you to their lake and immersed you, to heal you. And it changed you. You could bear heat. *Intense* heat."

I looked straight ahead, unable to move. I recalled what she'd said to me in New York. *You have the fire*. That's why I was able to embrace Sitri last night—why he'd known I could.

I hugged myself, feeling ill. The water might have healed my skin, but it had not healed my mind. My night terrors about fire had defied a dozen therapists, even meds. I gripped my arms and stared ahead. I had the fire, but fire scared me. "And after that, my mother left."

"To protect you. She knew that she'd attract our enemies over and over, especially if Asha was with them. You'd never be safe. So, she took you to New York to hide you with Alexandre and Krystal, as a normal child. It worked."

Charmaine reached over to touch me. I nodded. "It explains a lot." My walk through fire where my father had died. My experience with Sitri below Montmartre. I didn't have to try to be dangerous. I *was* dangerous. More than a conduit, I could be a weapon. For either side. And *against* either side. Sitri *needed* my commitment. I could do a lot of damage. And now, cut off, he could not tell what I was thinking or anticipate what I might do.

I sensed Charmaine watching me. Had she felt that shift in my thoughts?

"One more thing," Charmaine said. "You've been in the water and you have Kaitlyn's *Lumé* blood. Possibly, Sitri gave you his, too. We don't know, but... "

I sat back, surprised. "Doesn't that...?"

"Seal you. Yes, when you gave him your blood in New York, it did. But not a full seal, because you didn't have full knowledge. You can still retract. But the point right now is this: you can do things."

I rubbed my skin and gave her a sharp look. "Things?"

She slowed to make another turn, ignoring a stop sign. "Recall what you saw on the vampire's neck in New York?"

"An angel trap. Miegul had one for Sitri."

Charmaine nodded. "You can remove them."

"What?"

"You can touch it without being burned."

I wasn't sure where she was going with this. "Can't any of us?"

"No."

"Why me?"

"Because Kaitlyn made them."

Chapter Forty-Four

The shocks kept coming. I'd wanted answers. Now I wasn't so sure. "My mother made angel traps?"

"To survive. Sitri had let her live, but she was on her own. A *ma'lakh* could show up any second and wipe her out. So, she hid and she studied them and devised traps that they could not remove. She was ten when she caught her first one."

I realized I was rocking. I gripped my legs and took a breath. This was all so bizarre, but then it dawned on me what Charmaine had in mind. "You think Tariel's alive. That he's trapped and I can free him." I couldn't tell from my pounding heart whether I was scared or excited.

Charmaine shrugged. "It will benefit us to have skills that Ignis won't expect." She looked at me. "I've seen what happens. Once trapped, a *ma'lakh* often dissolves or explodes. We call it *saeclia*. Or they surrender and stay trapped. Some have been trapped for years."

"If Kaitlyn made the traps, how does Ignis have them?"

"Theft and replication, but no imitation works like hers."

"Wouldn't Sitri know if Tariel is alive?"

"There is a ..." she struggled for a word as she gestured toward her chest. "A tether. *Laisse*. A coded connection. Only the *kunoui* knows the code. If caught, they go dark. No link. Erased. It's hard to know if they're gone or still trapped."

Got it. This wasn't about Tariel. It was about Pascher. She needed to know that he could be rescued. Her clipped manner made sense. She kept a lid on her panic.

"Wouldn't Sitri keep looking?"

"He looks. It's dangerous. He seeks holes in their shield, but holes are often traps."

I stared out the window. Each new revelation pinged in my brain like the lightning that cut through the sky. I had two fathers and a fearless hybrid mother. I'd been burned and baptized in magic water, maybe sealed with blood into a bond I hadn't chosen. Now I had powers. I could see mysterious symbols and absorb a floating language. And as we faced a world catastrophe, I'd have to act on behalf of this fuzzy alternate reality. I thought about what Leith had said. *Kaitlyn would take charge.*

I knew what I had to do. I had to find the ring myself. Alone. I had to learn how to become invisible. Charmaine knew, but she was linked to Pascher, who would pass this information to Sitri. I'd heard that during primitive times a rogue angel had shown the *noea* how to become invisible. I wondered if this was part of the forbidden information that John Dee had acquired. I pressed the dossier. I needed Dee's concave crystal, but it was in my room in Paris.

"What was the trap?" I asked. "For Tariel. How did they fool him?"

"A process," Charmaine continued. "One day, you told Sitri a name that you said you heard in your head. You pointed to your throat. You were too young to understand, but Sitri knew it was a missing *kunoui*. With your information, Sitri located him. But it was the first piece of bait, to draw him away. Ignis sent another name. Sitri told Tariel to stay with you while he searched. The trap was set."

"By whom?"

"Asha. She had spotted your conduit ability when she watched you draw the figures from the painting. She was already toying with going over to Ignis, so she sent symbols that erased your security."

I caught my breath. "They trapped Tariel *through* me?"

Charmaine nodded. "Asha did. As Sitri had predicted."

I cringed. I must remind him of his own missing *kunoui*. "Did he kill her?"

Charmaine seemed startled. "No. She's Kaitlyn's daughter. Only *noea* can make that decision."

I looked at her. "So she's alive?"

"We think she might be. Possibly, she helped Ignis to locate Raydn."

I stared out the window. Raydn had been close to me today. Maybe my sister had been there. Would she know me? "Sitri knows that you're telling me this, right?"

"He asked us to wait, but it's time."

Charmaine slammed on the brakes. In the gathering darkness, I barely made out something large blocking our way. A black Bentley stretch limo.

Chapter Forty-Five

What new adventure lay before us? Charmaine jumped out and gestured for me to follow. The rain had let up but still glanced off my jacket. The driver's door of the Bentley opened and a tall man with a slender frame and long black hair like Pascher's emerged. He opened the back door. Charmaine kept moving, but I approached with caution.

A large dark-skinned male dressed entirely in black got out. Charmaine stopped in her tracks. "He sent *you*? I'm impressed."

The man held out his arms. "I insisted."

Charmaine ran up and hugged him. Then she turned to me and said, "This is Bodin. Sitri's ally. He will get us to Paris."

Charmaine got into the limo. Bodin bowed toward me. "I could not resist seeing Kaitlyn's daughter again." He boldly looked me over. "Dianysus. So pleased to see you."

He spoke in a clipped but refined manner, as if he rarely used English. He had a *Lume's* indigo eyes, but he was stockier than Sitri, and more effusive. He seemed vaguely familiar, so I figured I'd known him as a child. He introduced the driver, Larrent, whom I assumed was his *kunoui*, and invited me into the car. He followed me, and the door closed.

The customized interior smelled so citrusy I could almost taste a fresh orange. Charmaine had said they bathed in this lake. *That* image was hot. A steamy underground lake of crystalline water, and these naked warrior males. I envisioned one emerging and expanding his wings to shake off water drops.

On a softly lit bar along the side, I saw bottles of wine, plates of cheese and fruit, and slices from French baguettes. Bodin urged us to eat. He didn't have to ask twice. It was the same wine from the plane and I was more than ready. He poured me a glass and lifted his own. "We shall drink to reunions."

"On the darkest of nights," Charmaine added, "as usual."

"What is this wine?" I asked.

Charmaine smiled. "*Vin Malique*, we call it. From a special place, very pure. It's the only thing they can drink"—she gestured toward Bodin—"besides pure water."

I looked at him. "Why?"

"No digestion, no excretion. We can only absorb."

"You don't eat?"

"Only what can dissolve into us." He patted his torso.

Charmaine smiled toward me. "There are advantages to that." Growing serious, she said, "If something happens to Sitri, Bodin becomes your guardian."

This alarmed me. "Happens to Sitri! What do you mean?"

"It's a battle. There will be losses."

I shook my head as if I could somehow erase this. "Surely not one of…"

Bodin touched my hand. "He will have my support. If we disable Raydn, the danger is less."

I forced a smile. Bodin nodded. "You were always Sitri's girl. I'm pleased to see this has not changed."

This comment intrigued me. I wanted to ask what he meant, but the car suddenly went down a steep incline and entered a tunnel. Then we accelerated.

"Taking the short cut," said Charmaine. "Be there in half the time." She looked at Bodin and asked, "Did you find it?"

"We identified four probable locations."

Charmaine held her wine glass toward me. "I told you it worked with Capaldi."

"What are you talking about? Find what?"

"The heart. Mary Kelly's heart. If we retrieve it, we can disrupt their trap."

I put down my glass. "Back up. You started this story before we jumped. What does Mary Kelly have to do with this?"

"She was *Ser* lineage. That's rare. *Ser* are easier to trap than *Lumé* but are just as elite." Bodin gave her a doubtful look, which she acknowledged. "Excluding present company. So, occultists like Levi aimed for trapping a *Ser*. He learned about Marie—that's what we called her—and when she came to Paris, she was abducted. Levi experimented with her. We rescued her and urged her to stay. But something scared her. Something she saw. She left us and went back to London."

Where she had died. Horribly, her flesh, skin and guts spread all over the room. But that had been in 1888. Charmaine was truly a mystery.

"What did she see?"

Charmaine shrugged and nibbled on a chunk of white cheese. "Maybe a ceremony. Maybe discovered how they intended to use her as bait to summon a *Ser*. Maybe saw a *ma'lakh* go down. That's..." Her voice trailed off. She exchanged glances with Bodin.

He picked up the story. "They preserved her heart. We believe they will use it tonight to trap Mayon."

From the Ripper journal I'd learned that the "Mage" had come to London from Paris to teach the Whitechapel cult about trapping *ma'lakhim*. Clearly, Levi had trained this man in the ceremony for merging *ma'lakhim* with humans. They'd launched the Ripper spree. Now, thanks to a piece of his final victim, Jack the Ripper as a Christ figure would be "raised" from the dead and immortalized. Angel Ray Ender.

But this story had a hole. "They must have failed back then. Why didn't they keep trying? In all these years..."

Charmaine glanced at me. "They need fresh blood. When they first tried, a *Ser* came and they got a trap on him, but he went into *saeclia*. That's what they do. Having bait doesn't ensure success."

My heart picked up speed. In New York, Miegul had had Sitri's sigil. He'd also had Kaitlyn's ring with *Lumé* blood, and he'd cut me. But Sitri had attacked and all Hell broke loose. "So, they know Mayon's sigil. They have Mary Kelly's heart—"

"And they have Sheine. She is a small fraction *Ser*. Her blood injected into the heart could be sufficient."

"Don't they have Asha? She's half *Ser*, right?"

"We don't know if she's there. But her blood is infected. It would repel, not attract."

Bodin added the rest. "To achieve what they need, they might kill Sheine."

My hope to infiltrate had just crashed. I couldn't add more risk. With me, a daughter of Mayon, they could force him into their trap without the heart. I turned to Bodin. "You know where this heart is? You can at least thwart this?"

"We have coordinates."

The limo made a wide turn. I grabbed my wine glass.

"From Capaldi," Charmaine added.

Bodin nodded. "When you dissolved the virus, he opened up. We pulled from him where he has been. All are places where Levi did rituals."

Charmaine held up her fingers to count them off. "St. Sulpice, obviously. Whitechapel, Choisy and Montmartre."

"Sacré-Cœur?" I asked. Then it struck me. "Church of the Sacred Heart!"

Chapter Forty-Six

From the broad terrace of the Basilique du Sacré-Cœur, I'd had striking views of Paris. I'd walked among the endless lines of tourists and devotees who'd come to see the church's white triple-arched Byzantine portico. The spot had once attracted pagan worship. I understood how an occultist like Levi would exploit its potential for luring a *ma'lakh*. It was creepy to think that Mary Kelly's preserved heart might be there now.

"We've checked there before," Charmaine said to Bodin. "Thoroughly."

"They brought it recently. Capaldi's mobile phone confirms it. Sitri is there now."

Charmaine's eyes widened. "It's tonight! Before the eclipse tomorrow? If they succeed, it's over." She glanced at me.

Time to mobilize. *It's over* meant over for us and for all of humanity.

Bodin set down his glass. "Not over for the *nejah*, not according to their belief. For them, the *ma'limersion* is only part of a larger plan."

"I hope the ratters are out," Charmaine said.

"Ratters?" I knew only of tough little dogs by that name that killed rats.

"What we call them. *Ora* that excel at tracking and killing Ignis elements outside their shields. Gives us cover."

Bodin reached for a small wooden box. I heard a sharp click, as if it had been locked, and he opened it. Inside, cradled in dark blue fabric, was my concave crystal.

I looked at him in surprise. He seemed to read my thoughts. "There are others. This one is pure. It has never been in human or *nejah* hands. Please, pick it up." He held the box toward me. "We must prepare."

I looked at Charmaine and she nodded. Still, I hesitated. "I don't know if I—"

Bodin gave Charmaine a questioning look.

She touched my hand. "You've been in the water. It will respond to you."

From behind a seat, Bodin pulled out a bag. I recognized it. The overnight bag I'd left on the chopper. My items were safe! He placed it near me. "Will you please retrieve the book?"

He meant the dossier. I placed my hand over my jacket pocket. "It's here." I took it out. "But Sitri warned me not to use it with the crystal."

"It will be safe. These codes are locked through layers. The third element is absent."

I peered at him, confused.

"Sitri. And, of course…" He pulled his hand up in a gesture that felt as if he'd caressed me. I blushed. He meant the erotic part. He continued. "Kaitlyn preferred the islands of Paris, but Mayon favored the higher ground of Montmartre. In both areas they created underground spaces for protection, but when she lost this book, Ignis used it to locate and inhabit Mayon's area. The heart could be there. We must narrow down to a location."

"How?"

"This book. Kaitlyn used *noea* symbols, and Mayon and Sitri both added their energies." He looked at Charmaine. "You can read *noea*." To me, he said, "You are the conduit for *Ser* and *Lumé* energy, which I will translate. Together we can decipher coordinates."

He gave Charmaine a pen and tablet to keep track. The dossier felt hot. Bodin opened a tray table and gestured for me to lay the book on it. "It will be in the early pages," he said, "when they were here together."

It felt strange to envision my mother and a father I didn't know exploring this place together, centuries ago, as lovers. I held my breath and opened the dossier. I watched it and waited. Nothing came out of it, no floating symbols, no forceful push. The car hit a bump, which made me jump. But it was just an ordinary incident. I tried again.

Charmaine watched as I carefully turned the fragile pages. She pointed to a drawing that resembled a map. "The islands. Île de la

Cité." She urged me to turn the page. I saw another crudely drawn map but nothing stood out. I went through four more pages before she held up her hand for me to stop. "Go back."

I turned back three pages until she said, "Try this. I recognized Kaitlyn's mark for Mayon, but I can't read the other one. It could be *Ser*." She gestured toward the crystal. "We need to see that symbol reversed."

I looked at Bodin. "Can't you read it?"

"I do not look in this book. I will read it from the air when you see it."

The car began to ascend. I flattened the book so Bodin could place the crystal on the page. "Please sit back," he told me. "You are too close."

I did so. He gestured for me to hold the crystal over the page with its rounded part facing upward. "This draws on only the documents. The other way brings a stronger force." I recalled that this was how Dee and Kelley had used it to reverse symbols to communicate with angels, because direct contact would overwhelm them. Bodin gestured for me to look. The symbols reversed, but they looked ordinary. I shook my head.

Bodin watched. "Wait a moment."

Sitri's mark started to itch. I rubbed my thumb and forefinger together to keep from touching it.

Charmaine passed the tablet and pen to me. "Let it come through you. Don't think about it."

"What if—?"

"They will not reach you down here."

I felt nauseous. The car bumped again. I pulled my feet together and rocked a little. Closing my eyes, I picked up the pen, held it over the tablet, and let my hand move on its own. As with the *Oraculum*, I sensed I was drawing symbols. Then it stopped. My stomach settled. I felt the tablet slide away from me, so I opened my eyes.

Charmaine looked at the results and nodded. "This is deep but not far below the lowest level of the church. But this is not a defined location."

I couldn't figure out how she knew. I watched her pull out her phone and tap in a text. "What are you doing?"

"Portia has another piece of this puzzle."

I looked at the symbols I'd drawn. I wished I'd memorized some of the celestial alphabet. I couldn't make any sense of the items on the tablet. I touched them but felt nothing. Suddenly the car slowed and stopped. Bodin opened the door. "I will see you inside." He stepped out, transforming in front of me. Two feet of his wing, in vivid shades of gray, black and red, swept across my right hand before he vanished. My mouth must have been open, because Charmaine put her hand under my chin to shut it.

"You're going to see a lot of that tonight. You can't gawk."

I shook my head. "That was amazing!" My skin was still warm from the contact. The door closed and the car continued to ascend. I wanted to see that again. "What did I miss?" I looked at the tablet but nothing made sense. "Why did he leave?"

"They're gathering. We must work fast."

Chapter Forty-Seven

You can fully appreciate a security breach only from the inside, often too late.

I looked down. The crystal was still here. I placed it in a free pocket, apart from the dossier, while Charmaine read the return text. Her face hardened. "She knows where it is. This is bad."

"I thought that's what we wanted."

Charmaine shook her head. "Kaitlyn's map and Portia's calculations place the heart in a *nejah* tunnel. We can enter, but the *ma'lakhim* cannot pass their shields. No protection."

I sat up. "Have you ever done it?"

"With Kaitlyn."

I shrugged. "Sorry, I'm not her, but we don't have options."

"The *ma'lakhim* can draw them away, maybe." She looked at me. "Not you. You should go back to the residence."

I blinked. "What?"

"Can't risk you."

"Didn't you just hear Bodin? He expects me. I'm not leaving." I patted my gun.

"Can't kill *nejah* that easily."

"Maybe not, but it'll hurt."

"Sitri should decide."

I was all for getting close to Sitri. I wanted to see him in the light of what I now knew. Kaitlyn might have "set up a possibility," but Charmaine hadn't said what Sitri thought. Maybe he wasn't all in. Yet she'd said that *we* direct the "liaisons." Maybe he awaited my move. And I had some moves I wanted to make.

Glancing out, I saw light as a door ahead of us slid upward. We emerged onto a street I knew, close to the basilica. I wondered how many secret doorways into tunnels I'd missed when I'd lived on Montmartre.

We pulled up on the expansive front terrace of Sacré-Cœur. To my surprise, it was empty. It felt desolate in the evening's dimming light. Spare glimmers of light in the city below suggested the odds were against us. Even the Eiffel Tower was uncharacteristically dark.

When we emerged from the car into the moist pre-storm air, I noticed that our driver was gone. Portia stood on the stairs near the church door, beckoning for us to hurry. A stab of anger shot through me. She must have come with Sitri. But *I* was Sitri's girl.

"They've cleared the place," she said. Portia led the way to a side door, which got us into the inner sanctum. I looked up at the massive carved sculpture of a white angel in the back niche, wings up. He pressed a long staff into a writhing dragon at his feet. Before, I'd viewed this as some sculptor's idea of a mythical creature. How different it looked to me now!

Portia leaned close. "Don't be dazzled. *Soit ferme*. Keep your ground."

Charmaine pulled on her arm. "Dianysus should not be here. Larrent can take her over the river."

"Sitri thinks that with three *Lumé* here, the *nejah* will be enticed away long enough for us to get in and out. We should be safe. Three of us is better than two."

"Where's Leith?"

"Not here yet. We cannot wait. Everything is in motion *now*."

Satisfied that I was staying, I drew my jacket close as we entered the dark, cavernous church. Sitri was here somewhere. I wanted to see him. With all its shadowed arches and domes overhead, the place felt immense. I noticed Orias along the far side, seeming to stand guard, along with Pehel, whose dark skin blended into the shadows. Nearby were Handre, the white-haired *ma'lakh* who'd been with Teios, and a golden-haired creature I'd never seen before. In winged form, their bodies were bright. I looked up to the ceiling murals with their spiritual figures and thought I saw the movement of wings. I kept watching behind us.

Near the front, below the massive mural of Christ that curved to follow the rounded dome, I saw Bodin with Teios. They wore sleeveless garments that covered them to their knees. Portia quickened her stride, so I trotted to catch up. Suddenly, she stopped and turned to her right. Up front, the *Lumé* watched in the same direction. A swish of wings and shifts in the air made me turn around. Three more *ma'lakhim* had appeared, including Tibreth. Then another stepped from the shadows. Soon I counted a dozen. But I didn't see Sitri.

Portia grabbed my arm and urged me to stay close. Bodin suddenly stepped out of a portal in front of us. I caught a glimpse of his red and black wings before they vanished into his solid form. The gauzy mantle transformed into dark clothing.

"Where is Sitri?" Portia asked him. "He said he'd be here."

"Up top. He thinks Raydn will come."

"We need the distraction down *here*."

A loud noise in the back, where we'd entered, made us all look. Bodin came even with me, his arm outstretched to protect. I gasped. He was taller now by a foot, brighter and *different*. His wings emerged and arched high, spreading behind him. Portia pulled me back. I saw Teios on my other side, blue wings up, similarly alert. Their bodies were too bright to look at but I saw how their hair flowed thick and long to their waist. The Renaissance painters had gotten these details right. Teios' wings made a quick lift, throwing off bright blue sparks. Then he vanished.

I felt for my gun. "What's happening?"

"We must go," Portia said. "They are creating a buffer."

Portia grabbed my arm and started to guide me, but I saw Teios ten yards to my right in solid form, gripping something at his throat. He went to his knees. His gorgeous blue wings thrashed as if he were making a desperate attempt to get leverage. A ball of fire rolled near him along the floor. Then I knew. He was trapped! Any second, he might self-destruct.

I ripped away from Portia and ran to him, oblivious to her shouts for me to stop. "Cover me!" I yelled.

I reached Teios as he fell to the stone floor, choking, struggling to tear the thing off. Nearby, I heard a horrible shrieking sound that reverberated through the nave. To my shock, a *ma'lakh* on my right went up in flames. The burst of light illuminated Teios' distress. *There will be losses*. I hadn't expected *this*. I couldn't let Teios go dark.

Dropping to my knees, I put my hand on the angel trap at his throat. It was three inches wide and felt like a blend of leather, fibers, and metal. It soon burned my fingers, but I kept them in place. Teios stopped moving, as if to assist me. But I didn't know what to do. Charmaine had said I could remove this thing, but she hadn't said how. Would knowledge just come, like in the helicopter? Or was it like the locks that challenged me to "pull" something? I searched for whatever held the trap in place. Teios was suffocating.

"Char!" I yelled. Where was she?

Handre bent over me and pulled on my arm. I shook him off, but he came again. He didn't understand. I pushed my weight against him and shook my head. His eyes looked desperate. Teios placed his hand over mine and glared at Handre. I sensed communication before Handre pulled back. He turned away. To my horror, he ignited. I couldn't move. This beautiful creature was going up in flames! Green sparks shot out twenty feet as he cried in distress. The stench filled my nostrils. In seconds, he was gone. And it looked as if Teios had reached his limit, too.

Chapter Forty-Eight

Teios kicked hard, just missing me but tearing through his left wing. His wide blue eyes pushed words at me that felt like a warning. He was going to pull the pin. I shook my head. I sensed others nearby. My fingers burned. I couldn't hold this much longer.

Something over me dimmed the light, like a blanket coming down. I crouched defensively but kept exploring the tight band for a way to remove it. I prayed that something would shoot forth and free this *Lumé*. I felt a body against me and an arm go tight around my waist as a male hand with long fingers pressed on mine. I jerked back, but couldn't move.

"Take a breath; hold it." Sitri!

A lock of blond hair fell over my shoulder. I gripped it with my free hand while I took a deep breath. Wings folded me into a warm pocket as a blast of heat shot down my arm and through my hand. A vibrating buzz at my fingertips startled me, but I held still. Then a wave of need rippled through me, arching my back. My nipples hardened and I rubbed against Sitri's erection. Letting out my breath, I gasped at the urgent need that gripped me as another shot of fire passed through my arm. I gulped down a deep breath and held still. Sitri nudged me where I craved it. I gripped his hair. A contraction signaled a climax building. I needed him to thrust! He moved his hand to my crotch to massage me. I couldn't hold it. I let out my breath as spasms of pleasure swept through me.

My hand seemed to melt through the trap. The stench of something burning made me retch. I wanted to pull away, but I remained enveloped in this citrusy womb. As my vision cleared, I saw dark bare feet. Bodin was there.

Teios gasped and rolled to his side, leaving behind a charred, broken ring on the floor. It had worked! The trap was off.

But *I* craved more. I grabbed Sitri's arm to keep him close. He caressed my hair but pulled me to my feet. His wings opened to give me space. The air cooled around me, bringing down my own heat. I saw him now as a *ma'lakh*, a *Lumé*—tall, bright, with long hair, like in Kaitlyn's painting. He gave me a look of appreciation before he ordered, "Stay back."

Unsteady but elated, I backed away, staring at the magenta and red sheen of his wings as they draped to the floor. I sensed someone close to my left side and turned to see Pascher, also winged. He gestured that I should move further away. I did so, bumping into Charmaine on my right side. She looked stunned, but her eyes said *I told you*. I knew she was thinking that what happened to Handre could have been Pascher's fate. *Kunoui* was indeed a dangerous position.

My left hand tingled. When I made a fist, my skin felt hot. I was surprised to see what looked like a nasty sunburn on my skin from my wrist to my fingertips.

I sensed the *ma'lakhim* gathering. Teios lay still. Portia had her hand to her mouth as if she couldn't bear the sight. This crisis was clearly not over. I saw the burn mark on the floor that had once been Handre and looked away. I couldn't believe that one of these stunning creatures could be so quickly snuffed. Two, in fact, had gone down.

Some of the *ma'lakhim* gathered near us and formed a ring, their wings arched to add protection. Sitri knelt and placed his hands on the bottom of Teios feet, while Bodin went to one knee at his head. The blast of fire Sitri sent into Teios nearly knocked me over. I backed up again.

Teios' arm moved. Flames snaked around him, spreading over his wings. Portia took a step closer, but Sitri waved her back.

"His wing needs repair," she said.

"Wait!"

A second shot of heat, like a defibrillator, caused Teios to arch his back. I prayed for it to work.

In the back of the church, I heard growling. I peered through the darkness to see half a dozen large shadowy figures coming toward us. Charmaine grabbed me. "Vampires!" she hissed. "Go!"

Chapter Forty-Nine

I heard a *whirrr* as Orias emerged near us, his silvery wings out like a shield. I'd seen these vampires before, in New York, when they'd attacked Charmaine and me. They were mutant hybrid humans, merged via angel traps with the lowest functioning *ma'lakhim*. They had a raging bloodlust. I suspected they'd been launched as the second wave, to exploit this *Lumé* vulnerability and assault the *noea*—us. Sitri, still on his knees, rolled a four-foot ball of flames toward them, igniting several wooden pews. It sent one creature shrieking back against another, and both went to the floor. Smoke rose from them.

I turned and ran. I looked back to see Sitri on his feet, his enormous wings spreading wide just as he disappeared into a column of flame. Orias rushed me through a door and slammed it shut. Portia was down a dark hallway, where she gestured for us to come.

"Move!" she shouted. "This way!" She turned to run, but a vampire jumped out from the shadows and caught her in its grip. She screamed. Charmaine ran straight at them, and I followed. I knew from my prior encounter that a throat puncture would free the trapped *ma'lakh* and kill the vampire, but I had no knife. Charmaine launched herself at the creature while I looked for something sharp. The vampire knocked Charmaine away and pulled Portia up to its mouth. I removed my Glock and steadied my sights, but they were moving too much. A shot could hit Portia. She pummeled it with her fists, yelling and trying to keep its teeth off her, but she was no match for this thing.

I saw what I needed. A fireplace. Next to it were tools. I knocked aside the coal shovel and grabbed the poker. Charmaine was on her feet. She launched herself at the creature's legs, kicking hard, which forced him off balance. Portia used her weight to topple him. Charmaine pulled his head back by the hair. As I ran up, I saw the angel trap. I aimed for the vulnerable spot below, but he pulled away and my blow glanced off his jaw. Portia scrambled away and the vampire leapt to his feet to come at me. I turned to run, but he caught up and pushed me hard to the ground. I dropped the poker. He dragged me, scraping my hands on the stone floor.

Portia grabbed the poker. She swung it hard at his head, making him drop me. He went at her, pinning her to a wall, but Charmaine leapt onto his back. On my feet, I grabbed the poker. I looked for a spot on his neck to stick it, but I risked hitting Portia.

"Do it!" she shouted.

I felt pressure on the poker, as if someone was grabbing it from me. I turned toward this new threat. But it was Dorion. I released the poker to him. Tibreth emerged on the other side, hovering over the vampire, beige wings spread. Charmaine scrambled out of the way as the *ma'lakhim* flung the vampire to the ground. Their rage at this perverse creature came at me in waves of heat.

Tibreth pressed his foot on the vampire's head to expose the throat. Dorion pushed the poker in hard, then stepped back. Black blood gushed forth onto the floor. Portia jumped out of the way. The vampire shrieked in agony, but he was defeated. I felt the force of the trapped *ma'lakh* leave him. Dorion said some strange words that seemed to send it away. Its human host quickly expired.

Portia limped over to Charmaine, rubbing her throat. Charmaine examined it. I recalled how a vampire's bite had poisoned Char in New York.

Dorion reduced into his human form before he asked, "Are you all right?"

Charmaine nodded. To Portia she said, "We can't do this with no protection."

Portia looked at Dorion. "What's the scope of this? How many?"

"This was the first wave. Four invisible *nejah* came in with traps, but only two succeeded." He glanced at me as if he didn't believe what he'd seen me do. "The vampires they sent have died or retreated."

"Handre…?" I asked.

"Gone. And another from Teios' cohort."

"What about Teios?" Portia asked. "His wing was ripped."

"Alive. Bodin took him to Arren. Sitri thinks they assaulted Teios to remove the buffer between him and Raydn."

Everyone had to be thinking it: *these two could now fight to the death.*

Chapter Fifty

Dorion went still. He seemed to be listening.

"What is it?" I asked.

He looked stricken. "Sheine. She's here. I sense her." He pointed at his feet. "Below."

Portia crossed her arms. "Then we were right about the location. The heart will be here, too. We must find her. We had these tunnels long before they did. I can find my way. Tell Sitri to summon Bodin back so they can draw the *nejah* into the church. We need a significant distraction. And the ratters must be ready."

Tibreth disappeared but Dorion remained. "I should go with you."

"You will not get two steps past their shield. Sitri needs you. Leave this to us. We can be in and out before they realize."

"Dianysus should stay up here."

Portia disagreed. "We need her. Sheine can connect to her. We must be quick. Go!"

When he left, I looked at Portia. "How can *we* pass their shield?"

"If they believe they can trap a *Lumé*—especially if Raydn thinks he can disable Sitri—they will send their best hunters into the church. The ratters will pick off some of them. Down below, I can dismantle their electronics. They will sense a disturbance, but if we work fast, they will not know where we are."

She strode away. I sensed that Charmaine was not on board, but there was no time to argue. Sitri was supporting us, so we had to support him. I recalled that sense of him pressing on me, embracing me, giving me fire. We'd been a team. I followed Portia.

We left the building, jogging into a narrow alley until we came to a locked door. Portia pushed it open and led us down a steep circular stair with gray stone on both sides. It smelled of disuse but my feet felt the worn treads. Portia seemed to know this place. She touched a wire, which lit up a string of small lights high on the walls. They did little to illuminate our path ahead. I grabbed a metal rail. I figured that we were entering *nejah* territory, but I also knew that my parents had created this entry into the underground. They'd been here first.

We had to be very close to the spacious crypt under the basilica that supposedly contained the heart of Christ, but we seemed to be going deeper. A door opened into a darker tunnel. It was cool in here but clammy. I heard Portia whisper to Charmaine. To me she said, "Stay close." We entered a tunnel. I couldn't see well but it felt narrow. I saw images on the wall and figured my mother had made them.

I had a sudden flash that Portia intended to deliver me to Ignis. That's why she'd insisted I come. What a perfect way for her to clear the way to Sitri. I looked back toward the stairs. But even if I ran, I had no idea what I was up against. I couldn't fight one of these monstrous vampires alone. If only I'd gone with Dorion.

I followed Portia and Charmaine into what felt like an underground room. Portia stopped and whispered, "This is where Kaitlyn indicated in the book. I've been here with her. We're close." I followed them under an arch into a small room with an ethereal light. In the center on a raised podium was an ornate box. Portia went up to it and I heard a metal lock release. This was too easy. Something was wrong.

"Don't open it!" I backed away.

Portia looked around. "It's electrified. I can defuse it."

I wasn't backing down. "We need to get out." My hammering heart and a cold sweat affirmed my alarm.

Portia glanced at Charmaine and shrugged. "We can't leave it. Even if we don't find Sheine, she won't be as useful without this."

I moved away. "There's something wrong here. They're expecting us." I strode back in the direction of the stairs. Behind me, I heard steps. I looked back. Lights illuminated the area near the podium. Three males stood there, holding impressive weapons. Desert Eagles, I thought, with a .50-caliber punch. All were dressed in black, prepared for battle. One looked familiar. I searched my memory. Then I knew.

Angel Ray Ender, in the flesh. He certainly was not dead.

Chapter Fifty-One

They *had* been waiting. Praying they hadn't seen me, I moved silently into the shadows and removed my own weapon. Ender took a step toward Portia.

"Are you here for my rebirthday party?" he asked. "Because we'd love to have some *noea* to rip. What a perfect touch. Thank you so much for coming. Surely you don't intend to steal my favorite gift."

We were no match for these three. Whatever ratters were out tonight, they wouldn't get inside here. I calculated my chances of getting up the steps to find the *ma'lakhim*. They had to know we were in trouble. Except that we'd moved outside our shield.

"Go ahead," said Ender. "Pick up the box. I'd love to see your face when you open it."

The taller of his companions looked around, his weapon ready, as if he sensed me. Thankfully, he had no night-vision enhancers.

"Make her go in," Ender said. The short man pushed Charmaine away and grabbed Portia. He put the gun to her head and forced her backwards toward the podium. "How easy it was to get you here! The queen bitches! We set this up just for you. Consider it payback for our man in London. Nasty work! And just so you know, we've trapped your guardians as well. They won't be coming to help. End of the line for you."

My heart sank. He had to be lying. But I'd seen how fast they'd gotten the trap on Teios. I couldn't imagine one on Sitri. I knew that Charmaine could still sense things that I experienced so I tried to convey a plan of action. If she could take the short guy, I could shoot at least one of the other two, hopefully Ender. I waited a beat and raised my gun to get Ender in my sights.

He looked directly at me just as Charmaine rushed the guy with

211

Portia and pushed him hard against the podium. He got off a shot, but Portia leapt out of the way and a current of electricity sizzled through the air. The guy screamed as the jolt lit him up, popped a mass of blisters on his skin and fried him. He went into a seizure, his eyes wide open in surprised agony, and fell on the podium, crushing it and spilling the ornamental box to the floor.

Ender's surprise was my opportunity. I pulled the trigger, but he stepped forward and I missed. It gave away my position. I ducked, but his return fire tore a hole in the sleeve of my jacket. The third guy shot toward me as well, but the darkness was my advantage. Ender ducked back into an alcove and I found a new position. I went to one knee for better leverage. When the tall guy peeked around the doorframe, I got him. This left Ender alone. We had to leave before he gained more resources.

Portia grabbed the box and ran past me toward the stairs. Charmaine had her weapon out and she backed away, prepared to shoot. She came even with me and said, "Go!"

This was no time to argue. Ender got off two more shots, which sounded like a cannon firing, but they ricocheted off the wall. My ears ringing, I took the steps two at a time, hoping Charmaine was close behind. Another shot below me said she was still in the room. But Ender had not returned fire.

Out of breath, I climbed the steps. This had been stupid; of course, they'd been ready. They had resources like ours. They could tap in, just like we could. What had Portia been thinking? My heart pounded. I imagined Ender killing Charmaine and reaching me. I picked up my pace. I heard steps behind me, but saw light at the top. I came out, relieved to be on the street. But there was no sign of Portia. My chest hurt. I leaned on the wall in the alley to catch my breath. Where had she gone?

Again, I wondered if she'd gone rogue. But no, she'd nearly touched the box. She'd have died. But maybe that was a ruse. Maybe she'd have stopped and come up with some reason why I should do it. She'd said she could defuse it, but perhaps she'd lied. The image of that guy getting zapped, shrieking and twitching, turned my stomach.

Charmaine raced out, also laboring to breathe, and slammed the door. I heard several locks click into place.

"Did you get him?" I asked.

"Went out… other side."

"Did you recognize him?"

She put her hands to her hips, leaned forward, and nodded. "Ender." When she had her breath, she said, "Good plan."

"Just lucky. Do you have any sense of Pascher?"

"Blocked."

"Then they might be—"

"Let's go." She took off toward the church. I followed her and we went in together. To my surprise, the place was empty. Where were all the *ma'lakhim* I'd seen earlier? Ender had said he'd trapped our guardians. I looked up to the dome center and around the walls. No wings, no sparks. In the center aisle, several dark clumps suggested that the vampires had lost. But so had we, in a way. I thought of Handre.

"Here!" To our right, Portia stepped from behind a column. She had one arm around the box. I followed Charmaine over to her. "It's in here," she said. "We have it."

"Then let's leave now!"

At the far end, Orias emerged from the shadows. I was relieved. Not all of our guardians were trapped. Striding to him, I asked, "Where's Sitri? We just saw Ender. He's here in Paris."

"Raydn might be as well. Sitri is trying to pick up his track."

"So, he's not…he's okay?"

"Yes. Sheine was not there?"

I shook my head. "Sorry, no. Ender was waiting. We didn't get very far."

"We got this." Portia held up the box. "They can't complete without it."

Orias glanced at it. "They have retreated for now. You should go to the cemetery."

"Too close." Portia tapped the box. "We must get this into protection. Away from here."

"Go under, then. We have no extra coverage for you. We lost two more."

Charmaine looked alarmed. "Who?"

"Jariscal, from Bodin's group. And Kihr."

"No!" This shook me to my bones. I'd just seen him on the chopper. He'd handled me with kindness.

"We're going now," said Portia. "You be careful." To us, she said, "We should split up. I left a bike in the tunnel. I will take the box."

Charmaine nodded. "We can find a bike."

As we parted from Portia, a bolt of lightning illuminated the wet streets. I recalled how it had rained in New York in exactly the spots where Sitri had started fires. "Do they control the weather?"

"Not control, but they can manipulate it. Sitri can shoot energy into clouds and get lightning to slide down its path."

Charmaine looked through the array of parked motorcycles. Lots of people used them in Paris to get around on the narrow streets, so it was easy to find a long row of designated parking for them. Charmaine selected a black BMW with no luggage packs. She hopped on, started it and checked the gas before gesturing for me to mount behind her.

We'd planned to return to where we could enter the tunnel, but we heard a car racing on a nearby street. Someone was coming!

Chapter Fifty-Two

Charmaine took off through a small cemetery before emerging on the Rue Norvins and turning left. She seemed to have an instinct for which roads would have little traffic and she didn't hesitate to drive onto a sidewalk if necessary. I recognized the Rue Gabrielle as we entered a sharp curve, but then she made turns that suggested deflection. We picked up speed. Charmaine headed straight for a double door. I tensed and braced for impact, but the doors swung inward and put us on a downward trajectory into a dark tunnel. My heart pounding, I breathed out. I grabbed the saddle as we raced through darkness. Only the sound of our engine echoed in the cool corridor.

I knew that by normal routes St.-Germain was about 20 minutes away. At our clip underground, we cut that time in half and emerged through another set of doors onto a wet street. Light rain tapped my jacket. We were at the Pont de la Concorde on the Right Bank near the river, so we still had to cross a bridge. I looked around, but saw no one following. Despite the summer evening, only two cars were present. I figured the news had scared people.

We crossed the Seine and headed up the Quay d'Orsay toward the Boulevard St.-Germain. Just a few blocks more. We were home free.

But then we weren't. A black Renault SUV crossed in front of us and screeched to a stop. Charmaine went into a skid, which dumped us both and slammed the bike against the Renault. I hit the ground and rolled, skinning my left hand. Charmaine jumped to her feet as a back door opened on the SUV.

A man emerged and came straight toward me. Miegul! My father's murderer. I got up and grabbed my Glock. Charmaine blocked me. I heard a loud pop to my right and saw a bright flash hit

215

the street a block away. It skittered up the wet pavement, raising sizzling brown steam as it raced toward the Renault. Doors opened and the occupants emerged. The bolt went under their car and flung it into the air. It rolled onto its side. Another bolt hit it from above us. The engine ignited, filling the air with the smell of hot metal.

I looked up and saw flashes of red. Bodin, I guessed. On the top of a building down the street were dark magenta shimmers. Sitri. Lightning branched across the sky, aimed to hit him. I gasped but then saw an electrical charge frame Sitri's outstretched wings before racing down to skate along the wet boulevard toward us. On impulse, I stepped out and held up my hands, palms outward. A hot force ricocheted off them and hit a runner. He screamed and lit up.

"Now!" Charmaine ordered. I followed her, leaping over chunks of broken pavement.

A man shouted and chased after us, but he went down, shrieking. I looked back and saw a shadowy winged creature, too thin to be *Lumé*, float down to the street, followed by another. I wondered if these were the ratters. Further away, a male scream told me another "rat" was caught. I wanted to get at least one shot at Miegul but couldn't see him.

Charmaine made a sharp turn and went down a set of stairs. We entered a cellar room and got into an elevator. As it rose, I slumped against the wall, hurting. My hands stung. I saw that Char had a few nasty scrapes. Through panting, I managed to ask, "Are you okay?"

"Have to be."

"Did you see Sitri? That was amazing!"

"What were *you* doing?"

"I don't know. I just did it." I still felt the buzz.

She grabbed my right hand and looked at the palm, then my left. "Instinct. Your *Ser* blood. They're the fire handlers. They refract *Lumé* fire, to intensify it. Sheine can do that."

I shrugged. "I'm afraid of fire."

"Only your human part. The rest *is* fire. You weren't burnt, but we should put honey here. It heals." She indicated where my skin was red from sending fire to the trap on Teios. "I knew you could do it."

"I didn't. If Sitri hadn't…"

"He gave you a surge. *You* did it. The maker is also the breaker. You have Kaitlyn's blood."

216

I rubbed the back of my left hand. "How did you know the *Lumé* were up there?"

"Pasch."

"And were those other things—?"

"Ratters."

"Are they on our side?"

"The *Lumé* can direct them, but stay clear of them. Feral, like the *ma'lakhim* in the vampires."

"Where do *they* go when they're cut loose?"

"Suspended in a poison lake. Same water we use to make our invisibility powders. It immobilizes them."

"And that's where Raydn was?"

"Same treatment, different place. Next time, Sitri will kill him." As the elevator stopped on the third floor, Charmaine said, "You cannot react to Miegul like that."

I nodded. "I know. I'll be more careful."

She pressed the "close door" button. "I mean, don't shoot him. We need him alive."

"Why?"

"He can show us where the girls are." She opened the doors and urged me to go out.

Adria met us with hot towels. I saw activity down the hall and looked for Sitri, but saw none of his cohort.

"Oh, your hand!" Adria exclaimed.

I held it up in. "I think it's okay." I flexed my fingers, which felt swollen.

"Is Arren here?" Charmaine asked.

"*Oui*, working on Teios in the *salle de guérison*. Portia just came in."

"With the box?"

"She is putting it in a safe place. She will join Arren."

Charmaine nudged me. "You should see this."

Chapter Fifty-Three

Before we entered, I heard an unusual type of music and a female voice, very pure, singing in a melodic foreign language. Charmaine had mentioned music that healed. This certainly sounded healing. It was almost Celtic, with classical overtones. We went through a silky white curtain into a spacious room that was bright and warm. The harmonies seemed to increase, although I saw only two people in the room.

Teios lay on his stomach on a thick mattress on a raised platform the size of a queen bed, his face turned away. His black hair was tangled and dusty. A broad wooden stool sat by the platform. At each end, tall rails going up at least ten feet supported what looked like weaver's frames. From them hung braided fabric slings. Teios' blue wings were fully spread across the mattress, passing beyond the edges three feet on both sides. He wore nothing, but his brown skin was bright, not like human skin. I saw the dark area on the back of his neck where the trap had dug in.

I breathed in the citrus fragrance and nodded to Nettaline, who sat on a stool at the other side of the platform. She played an instrument I hadn't seen before, although it sounded vaguely familiar. She held it like a violin, but used her fingers to make a pure, light sound similar to a flute. Around the room on light blue walls were charts and full-color illustrations. I realized from those that showed wings that they depicted various parts of a *ma'lakh* body. Some wings were folded, some stretched out; some showed the external side, which looked like a raptor's wing, while some revealed the under-layers. Most were white or light gray at the top, spreading gradually into colors, which were most vivid at the tips. This was an infirmary for injured angels.

A tall woman bent over Teios' damaged left wing. Her belted black sleeveless shift emphasized her remarkably slender form. The

218

rich, crystalline voice was hers. Intent on her work, she didn't look up, but a slight shift in her posture said she knew we had entered. Her dark brown hair, entwined with red leather thongs, was pulled into a thick, waist-length ponytail that came over her shoulder. Her bare hands and lower arms were stained with droplets of bright red blood, too close to magenta to be human.

I knew her. The memory came at once. This was Arren. The healer. I'd met her as a child. She was distinct, with large dark blue eyes and the most remarkable arched eyebrows. She'd once shown me how to handle the wings, carefully, sensually, with a touch so light it barely made contact. Except that I recalled how soft and firm the feathers were, how vibrantly beautiful the colors had been, and how good they'd smelled. I'd touched them. The memory was clear.

Arren stopped singing and looked at us. "Let me finish this before I speak with you. Char, can you bring fresh water? This wing is bleeding still."

Portia came in through another door. "I can help."

Arren nodded. "Please. This injury must be closed quickly. I need more voice."

Nettaline never missed a beat, as if she'd played this music many times. I removed my jacket. Its scuffs and stains—and bullet hole—showed me a record of the most intense day I'd ever had. I hung it over a chair where I could see it and pulled up a tall wooden stool. Portia glanced at me. "Are you all right?"

I shrugged. "Aside from a close encounter with some pavement and a bolt of lightning, I'm fine."

Charmaine set a bowl of water next to Arren, adding, "It worked. Very strategic. Wasn't sure they had our backs."

Portia joined the song, followed by Charmaine. The harmonic beauty of the three distinct female voices, low to high, gave me the first sense of peace I'd had since I arrived in Paris. An unusual echo made it seem as if a choir had joined from some distant place. Whatever thoughts I'd had of leaving, they dissolved. I wanted to learn this intimate art of touching and healing these intriguing creatures. This was my birthright.

Adria came in with plates of quiche and a carafe of strong French coffee. I accepted a cup. I needed a boost. I was exhausted, but there was no way I was going to miss this.

219

Adria saw where I'd skinned my hand. "You're hurt. I will get some honey."

"Charmaine is, too. She hit the pavement pretty hard."

Arren looked up at me. "Dianysus, I am happy to have you with us. Do you remember how to do this?" Her eyes had a sad, compassionate expression.

"I remember you, but I don't recall details."

"You were young. If you want to learn, go to the other side, with Char. She can show you how to check that wing."

This made me nervous. "Are you sure?" Somehow this seemed even more precarious than flying a helicopter. I could hurt more than help.

"We need to work quickly. There are more injured ones."

Char went alert. "Who?"

Arren stated names I didn't know. Portia looked surprised. "Denloran? He is Teios' second. All three of his were hit? This was strategic."

I went over to Char's side, near Teios' right wing. I'd just joined a *ma'lakhim* MASH unit. This was no time to worry over my abilities.

Charmaine showed me how to run my fingers carefully across the feathers in a specific direction while looking for holes. "The outer feathers, the dense ones, are tough," she said, "but underneath they have these." She lifted the top layer and ran her fingertips over some fragile shafts with tiny barbs at the ends. "They use these sensors to read the energies. We must repair them." She had me touch another area. "You will come across old scars like this. Not important. I need to see the areas that feel thin. Just show me. I will do the repair."

"When their wings are damaged," Arren added, "they cannot shift into other forms. Once we close the holes, Teios can move to a more secure place."

"Is he unconscious?"

"He is in a state of stillness, alert but controlled. We call it *somnotique*. This procedure is sensitive, and any wrong move from him can undo what we have done."

Charmaine set water next to me. Adria treated our injuries with a warm cotton pad that apparently had a mix of honey and some other healing substances. My abrasions hurt, but the honey concoction felt soothing. Charmaine had a rip in her jeans that showed a serious scrape on her leg. She tried to wave Adria away, but Adria ignored her and treated the injury. While she worked, she joined in with the singing.

I bent over Teios' wing. Up close, the various shades of blue, layered like a raptor's wing, were vibrant. I could also see from his leg and foot that what had looked like skin was actually a layer of luminous pliable substance, similar to a sculpting fondant. Unlike the multiple Renaissance paintings of angels in flowing robes, they apparently wore nothing when winged or simple sleeveless mantles. This full-wings form, while solid, was definitely not human.

Arren glanced at me. "Touch it."

Chapter Fifty-Four

This seemed too intimate. I looked at her and she urged me to go ahead. "This is a transitional shield against the heat as they shift forms, to cool them before they take human form. The luminosity helps them to absorb information."

I lightly touched the firm calf muscle. It reminded me of the feel of a flower petal but tough, not fragile. The coating seemed to thin out near the bottom of his feet, which looked more like human skin. I rubbed my finger against my thumb, producing a strong citrus fragrance. I nodded gratefully to Arren for the lesson and prepared for business.

"He is very light right now," Arren said. "When we're finished, he will push into the energy field and disappear. So, if his wings move, stand back."

This did nothing to calm my nerves. I carefully touched a feather. It shimmered, startling me. But Teios remained still. I had to stay controlled. The singing continued and I could hardly bear the ethereal beauty. Memories flooded in of handling *ma'lakhim* wings. This was okay. I'd done this. I patted an area as lightly as I could, moving in a circular pattern, and identified a spot I thought was damaged. Charmaine checked it. "Good. That's what it feels like." She showed me how to lift the layers to look underneath.

"Is it painful for them?"

"If you do it too fast or in the wrong direction."

"What about his neck?" I asked. "Was that damaged?"

Arren looked at me. "The *Lumé* will check. That was brave. If you had not acted, we would have lost him."

"I thought the traps were for... well, trapping them. He was suffocating."

"It was tight, but this keeps them from shifting. In this form, they are as vulnerable as humans."

"But why did Handre... what was that word?" I looked at Char. She frowned. "*Saeclia?*"

"Yes, when they self-destruct. He wasn't trapped. Did Teios order him to...do it?"

"It is part of the *kunoui's* duty," Arren said. "If the tether is compromised, he must go dark. Sometimes, completely. The *nejah* were coordinated. They broke through at once."

I couldn't even look at Charmaine. She'd said she hated that Pascher was in such a position. Now I understood. Despite their power, these creatures had serious weaknesses. Their enemies knew them well. But I'd seen Teios' expression when he'd looked at Handre. Something had happened that struck me as unusual.

Arren asked Charmaine to check the arch of Teios' wing where it met his back. She nodded and went there to explore. As she ran her fingers over the dip between his back and the wing's upward arch, blue sparks crackled like static electricity. "Feels tender," she said, "not broken."

"Their wings can break?" This surprised me.

"Break, yes," said Arren, "or be ripped off."

I cringed. As Charmaine and Portia sang, Arren raised an eyebrow at me. "I will tell you a little secret about these wings." I saw Nettaline smile as Arren continued. "They have an erotic place. If you want to bring a *ma'lakh* to his knees, you lightly rub." Her hands were busy, but she gestured with her chin. "Where Charmaine is touching, along the arch. The patagial foreskin. This is the most intimate you can be with them. If they let you touch there, they completely trust you. When they are in human form, you would caress their back along the line where their wings would be. It will make them quite hard. Also, roll a layer of warm air over the bottom of their feet. With this skill, you will always bring them back to you."

I looked at the back of Teios' head. "Can he hear us?"

"Oh, they are not self-conscious about this. The sensual is what lures them into human form. And to us."

Portia nodded. She stopped singing to add her own comment. "Tariel loved being touched there. He could not get enough."

I felt a pang of sadness for her. Tariel was gone because of me. I moved to another area of Teios' wing, felt it for a thin spot and then asked, "What was he like?"

223

Her smile told me she was pleased that I'd asked. "I met him when I was young, about 13. There was a hot spot simmering near our village, so in human form, the *ma'lakhim* wandered among us to locate it. They spotted my ability to manipulate electricity. I knew nothing about being *noea*, but Tariel kept returning to speak with my parents. They were *a'ika*, raising me as their daughter. My real mother was dead."

"What did he look like?" I asked.

"My first impression was of his face. It was kind and sweet, like Dorion, but he had dark copper hair, thick and wavy. Cobalt eyes like Pascher's. You already know that they watch for *noea* with useful talents, so Tariel explained what I could be. Finally I accepted the training. I met Sitri and others like me." She gestured toward Charmaine.

"Tariel had his eye on her," Arren said. "But he had to wait. *We* initiate." She looked at Portia. "I had to nudge you."

"*Oui*, I did not know he was so entranced. But I liked when he came around. Eventually we became lovers."

I'd misjudged her. She was not going for Sitri. She still loved Tariel.

"Be careful around Arren," Charmaine warned. "She's a vigilant matchmaker."

Arren smiled. "Love is the greatest healer."

I envisioned Sitri coming to me in this form, with his blond hair long, like at the basilica. He would bow his head and let me touch the vulnerable arch of his wing. The foreskin. I would watch him swell with each caress. His indigo eyes would glaze with lust. I'd stroke the curve again and explore his *ma'lakh* skin, tracing his chest and stomach muscles with my finger. He'd reach for me, but I'd hold back.

I suddenly realized I was breathing hard. I swallowed. I noticed Arren watching me. She nodded and I blushed.

Leith walked in. "It looks like a war zone outside. Who slammed our street?"

Charmaine looked up. "Our side. Any news?"

"Whitechapel burns out of control, and we now have suicide portals in a dozen countries and more Black Torch threats. Lots of social media chatter. The news is out that Ender, the deceased cult leader, is missing. Some cult member has announced that Ender will rise from the dead. So, their passion play is on. The media experts can barely function. No one knows what to do." She glanced at Charmaine and me. "Looks like I missed the party here." She picked up my rain-stained jacket and examined the scuffs and holes. "Just two days and you've put *this* to the test." She placed it over the chair and grabbed a sponge to wipe off the remaining blood spatters from Nick's suicide. I tensed. My gun and the dossier were still in the pockets.

"Here." Charmaine drew my attention to a hole on Teios' wing that needed repair. "This is a good example."

I could see how the sensors were torn loose or missing. Under Charmaine's direction, I used a damp cloth to dab at the dried blood. I tried to avoid applying pressure, cringing when I thought I'd hurt Teios. His stillness didn't reassure me. When the spot seemed clean, I sensed Charmaine going alert. The air had grown warmer. I looked up. Sitri was standing at Teios' head, Pascher with him.

Chapter Fifty-Five

I sat up to watch. Arren did as well but continued to sing. Pascher glanced at Charmaine and she looked as if she were making a supreme effort not to run to him and hug him.

Sitri was in human form now, in black jeans and a wine-colored shirt. I could see the fabric's quality from across the room. He leaned down toward Teios' head. I sensed anger and caught something from him about Raydn. He ran his hand under Teios' hair over the back of his neck as if feeling for damage. He kept it there for at least five seconds before moving down his back, between his wings. Pascher watched closely, his face guarded. I hoped there was no serious internal injury. Maybe I hadn't moved fast enough. Maybe one second sooner would have made all the difference.

Sitri glanced at Arren. "He's fading."

"We are working as quickly as we can."

I swallowed hard, stunned that we might still lose him.

Sitri came around to Teios' right side, his eyes fixed on the white upper part of his wing, seeming to carefully check every square inch. His mood felt ominous. Charmaine took a step back. At one spot toward the middle of the wing, Sitri pushed his hand deep under a row of feathers. He seemed to be listening.

"I checked that wing myself," Arren said. She pointed at the left wing in her own hands. "This one needs your attention."

Sitri remained focused on the right wing. He pushed his hand in again, going deeper, exploring. In a moment, he drew out a tiny dark object the size of a fly. It broke loose and rose upward, like a miniature drone, but he caught and crushed it. A whiff of smoke rose from his fist. "This is how they targeted him so fast. This was attuned to him."

"Who would do this?" Portia asked.

"Only his cohort can be inside his resonance."

Charmaine shook her head. "Not Handre! I would never believe that."

Sitri remained impassive. "There have been worse betrayals."

I recalled Handre trying to pull me away. I wondered if I should mention it.

"Raydn would also know the resonance," Portia pointed out. "If he wants to kill you, he would eliminate Teios."

Sitri glanced at her. "It was not Raydn."

He came around Charmaine, moving his hand along the wing, exploring two more spots, until he was close to me. I prepared to step away. Without looking up, Sitri said, "Our Nisi is full of surprises today."

I looked around, confused. Arren winked at me. I realized that Sitri had just primed my memory. I had a flash of running toward him as a child, crossing an expanse of rain-flecked grass. He'd picked me up. He'd called me Nisi.

Sitri gestured for me to come close, on his left. "Put your hand here." He slid his right hand into the feathers. I stepped in and did the same, going under the stiff layers, near his. I flinched at the sparks but thrilled at the prickly texture of the sensors. Sitri's fingers found mine, moving me through the fragrant softness to a thin spot. His left hand went to my waist, feeling warm through my shirt. I was self-conscious about how I must look and smell after my long day in dust and dirt. He urged me to lean closer.

Deep inside Teios' wing, my fingertips vibrated as if I were touching the strings of the instrument that Nettaline played. I felt the sensors respond the way a flower might turn toward the sun. The music flowed to me, through my fingers! The thin area thickened and the hole began to close. I was healing it! This was exciting. And I knew I'd done this before. My mother had shown me. I closed my eyes and moved against Sitri. I could almost smell Kaitlyn's rose perfume as she'd hovered over me. The memory made me smile.

Sitri caressed my back, eliciting a chill, before he moved around me to my left side. He stepped up onto the mattress, barefoot, and balanced on the edge. I suspected that he was literally as light as a feather. He reached down and lifted Teios' left wing, making sparks. Several fell on me, fading like dying fireworks. As Sitri spread the wing upward, I noticed how the shades of blue blended through shimmery layers. The tip reached past his six-foot-six height and I clearly saw the foot-long tear near the center. Teios' foot had made it as he'd thrashed around.

When Sitri ran two fingers over its raw edges, I cringed. That *had* to hurt. I saw a burst of flames as he sealed the area, like using a blowtorch on metal. I expected to smell scorched feathers, but instead the citrus scent thickened. *Our essence is fire*, Pascher had told me. As Sitri focused on this delicate task, I explored the beauty of his angular face. A stray lock of ash blond hair came forward from behind his ear and I wanted to touch it, smooth it back into place. Run my fingers over his shoulder to his back. *We* initiate, Arren had said. I had to get him alone. He knew now that I was aware of my ties to him.

Teios' right wing twitched. I backed away. But then it went still.

Chapter Fifty-Six

The room grew tense. Sitri looked concerned. My stomach twisted. Sitri took a step and turned his back to me. I didn't mind the view. The shirt hugged his perfectly curved back from his shoulders to his narrow waist. The muscles of his ass looked toned. Under other circumstances, I would have been all over him. I wished I could see his naked back through his shirt. When the time was right...

Charmaine crossed her arms and glanced at Pascher. She looked unhappy. Portia watched Sitri, one hand raised, as if she expected instructions. Arren rubbed the bottom of Teios' feet with a soft *trrrillll*.

Sitri looked around. His glance fell on me. He pulled down the overhead sling and strapped the wing into it. Then he moved to the left side of the wing and gestured to me. "Come up." I went over to the wooden stool on the right side of the platform.

"Shoes off," Charmaine told me.

I removed them and stepped up onto the firm mattress. Charmaine moved the right wing so I could step over it. I hoped Sitri didn't intend to arouse my erotic energy. I didn't relish getting hot and bothered in front of these women. It wouldn't take much. Just getting close to him again had me flustered. I breathed in his scent, with full awareness now of what it was—he *bathed* in a lake that smelled like this. I could envision him, wings spread out, emerging onto stone steps with a glistening naked body.

When he raised an eyebrow at me, I wondered if Charmaine had actually cut me off. Maybe he *did* know my thoughts. I got into position where he indicated, and Teios' wing partially blocked my view of him.

Portia climbed up on the mattress and stood behind me, as if she knew what was coming.

Sitri noticed the redness on the back of my left hand. He took my hand in his and saw the abrasion where I'd skinned it on the street. "Does this hurt?"

I nodded. "A little."

"We put honey on it," Arren said.

He placed both of his hands over my burn. The sting receded into a pleasantly warm sensation. Sitri looked at me as if searching for information. He needed to know where I stood. In his world, I was an unstable element. Despite those gorgeous dark eyes probing mine, I didn't really know. Not exactly *all in*. But then I sensed that he wasn't seeking information; he was *sending* it. I focused. He wanted me to know something, but I couldn't quite grasp it.

"Your other hand," he said. I held it up. He inspected it, touched each of my fingertips, and nodded. "Use this one."

Portia positioned me closer to Teios' wing. She placed my right hand, open palm, against the damaged part. It felt as if Sitri had coated my fingertips with something that magnified the sensations. "Keep it there," Portia instructed. "You can reflect his fire."

Alarmed, I looked at Sitri. My heart rapped in my chest. Despite what I'd learned and even what I'd done with the lightning, this terror still gripped me. Noise in my ears drowned out the music. I balled my left hand into a fist.

On the other side of the wing, Sitri made the trust sign. "Be still. Keep your eyes on me. You will feel heat, but no flame will touch you. Imagine your palm as a mirror. Push back, reflect, like you just did outside. We must do this now."

I nodded but felt no degree of confidence that I could perform. Under the wing, Sitri's bare foot touched mine. I caught my breath at the feel of his warm skin. The sensation climbed up my leg to my crotch. A faint twist at the corner of Sitri's mouth told me he knew its effect.

Portia raised her hands behind me, shoulder-height, as if to catch me. Sitri touched the tear in the wing. The scent grew so intense I had to breathe through my mouth. I heard a sizzling sound. The heat vibrated from my fingertips down my fingers and into my palm. At first, it was pleasant, but soon it grew uncomfortable. My heart thumped. I swallowed and drew in a breath. I reminded myself that a bolt of fire had gone through my arm earlier that evening and I hadn't been hurt. I tried to remain still.

Nettaline changed the tune, and the singing shifted with it. I felt musical vibrations flow into the wound's edges as Sitri slowly ran his fingers over the damaged area. The wing brightened, its sparks startling me. It trembled. I saw the tear slowly draw together. Portia supported my arm. Sitri glanced at me and I nodded that I was okay.

The healed wing suddenly arched high, leaving the sling. Teios' right wing rose behind us. Portia crouched down and Sitri pulled me against him. A hot *whoosh* of air took my breath as I leaned into his firm chest. I saw Teios' wings draw up, like a hawk preparing to fly. He rose to his hands and knees. As he straightened up, he pushed with his wings, and slipped through a portal that closed behind him. He was gone.

Nettaline jumped up and shouted, *"Oui!"* while Portia stood and clapped. Sitri squeezed my arm and stepped away as he turned to follow Teios. His clothes dissolved into those reddish-purple wings. One slid softly across my breast, raising my nipples, before he vanished. I crossed my arms and stepped back.

Whatever we'd just done had worked. Teios had pushed into some other dimension. And Sitri had granted me intimate entre into their world—seeing, learning, healing.

Arren reached up to assist me to step down. "Well done, Nisi." Into my ear, she whispered, "I think he just flirted a little."

I blushed. I wished I'd understood what he'd silently conveyed.

Nettaline rushed over to hug me, and Charmaine smiled for the first time since we'd entered the room. Despite everything we faced, we'd saved Teios. I felt like I was part of something significant.

Leith came up with my jacket and shoes. "We have a long night ahead. Time for a hot shower." She winked. "Or maybe a cold one." Putting an arm around my shoulder, she guided me into the hall. Before we reached the elevator, Leith said, "What you asked for is in your pocket. Keep it to yourself."

I entered the elevator and pressed the button for the top floor, expecting her to join me and explain, but she stepped away and winked again before the doors closed.

Suddenly, I was alone. Confused. The elevator rose. Images of this strange day passed through my mind, especially my contact with Sitri. He'd shot flames through my arm and embraced me in his wings. He'd sent me lightning and shown me how to heal with music. What had he been trying to tell me?

231

I thought Leith had been strange. She'd practically pushed me out of the healing room. She wanted me to keep something secret. Unsure about surveillance, I waited until I was on my own floor before I put my hand in my jacket pocket. I pulled out a hard, round tablet the size and thickness of an aspirin. It smelled like almonds and resembled dark chocolate. I wasn't sure what to do with it.

Then I remembered: *What you asked for*. I'd asked her how to make myself invisible to the *ma'lakhim*. Here it was. My ultimate test. With this, I could slip out, unnoticed. I'd started this ball rolling. But would I—*could* I—live up to my mother's legacy? That bold claim I'd made on the plane seemed so distant now—and riskier. I put the tablet back in my pocket.

Chapter Fifty-Seven

Each time I entered a different place, my world shifted. I barely had my footing in one when I'd land in another. I needed a game plan to ground me. I knew enough now to form one. Sitri had just treated me as a partner. I'd shifted from "predictable" to "full of surprises." In the cemetery, he'd admitted that they never knew which abilities the *ma'lakhim*-human connection would yield in their offspring. Since mine had been suppressed most of my life, he might be learning them pretty much when I was.

I undressed and stepped into the shower. I touched my breast where Sitri's wing had brushed it. The delicate sensation lingered. As hot water ran over me, I fervently wished for him to appear. There was room in here, even for his wings. I imagined him holding me as water ran over us. He would take my blood, his mouth on my throat, as he grew aroused. I'd slip my hands up his back to feel along the emergence of his wings while his erection grew firm against me. *Bring him to his knees!*

But he wasn't coming. He had more urgent matters. And so did I.

I lifted my face to the water. I had to wash off this day: Nick's suicide, my failure to rescue Sheine, my lies to Jack, my sister's betrayal, the burning of Whitechapel, and watching the horrible blazing death of a *ma'lakh*. On the other side was the rescue of three girls, saving Teios, my deepening link to Sitri, jumping from a helicopter, and my surprising gifts. What had the Oraculum said? *I will acquire my property, unexpectedly.* I was certainly on *that* road.

Except that I still did not have the ring. We'd thwarted tonight's ceremony to lure Mayon, but we had to wait until they tried again. And we still hadn't learned the location of Ignis' world-crushing event.

I got out and dried my hair enough to pull it into the French twist Charmaine had given me earlier. That meeting now seemed ages ago.

In my room, I picked up and fingered the brown tablet that could turn me invisible… and make me poison to Sitri. Varian, they called it. Charmaine said it was made from poisoned water where renegade *ma'lakhim* were suspended. I recalled the tragic story of how a nasty *ma'lakh* named Taym had first given this water to a *noea*, who'd accidentally killed her lover.

So, I could become invisible. Yet even if I could slip out undetected, there was a problem. My *Ser* blood could help Miegul and Ender lure Mayon. That wasn't good. On the other hand, it might save Sheine. She was more vulnerable. By all accounts, my father was a powerful *ma'lakh*. Surely if they did use me, he couldn't be defeated so easily. Miegul had failed with Sitri. Yet the attack in Sacré-Cœur showed how quickly they could pull down a *Lumé* if they got a trap on. We'd nearly lost Teios.

Still, I didn't know where to go. Paris was a big city. I knew nothing about the underground tunnels. I needed guidance. But from whom? I had no phone.

I removed the dossier and crystal from my jacket, retrieved my other crystal and the *Oraculum*, and set them all near me on the gold brocade settee. Would Sitri know if I opened the dossier? I'd seen things in its pages that I wanted to look at again. I fingered the cracked leather. Someone had left this book in my room. Portia? Sitri? Or someone else?

The *Oraculum* had answers to such questions. It relied on inducing a full erotic trance, but Sitri's mark, with its zinging heat, could shortcut the process. I could work up something just from the memory of his fingers on mine as he'd guided me into Teios' wing. *That* had been hot!

I picked it up and scanned the list of questions. None seemed to address this difficult situation. I decided on the one I'd asked on the plane. "Shall I have success in my undertaking?"

Next, I had to decide on my "undertaking." Undercover among the *nejah* was too broad. I already knew I would recover the ring. What about the dossier? Could I use it to advance my goal?

Sitri's wing feather sliding over my nipple, and his suggestive words—*"My staff… your needs"*—were sufficient to get me going. His fingers… the arch of his wings… that lock of hair that I wanted to touch…

I sat up. The painting in the gallery downstairs. *That* would work!

Chapter Fifty-Eight

I pulled on a clean pair of jeans and a black sleeveless blouse. The collar covered Sitri's mark. Aiming to rejoin the team once I had an answer, I grabbed my jacket. Despite its battered condition, it was versatile. I put a full magazine in the Glock, placed my items in the various pockets, hid Bodin's crystal under my pillow and took the elevator to the third floor.

The hallway was dim. The place felt deserted. I slipped into the gallery.

So much had happened since I'd first seen the painting of Kaitlyn and Sitri. A soft light played on it now, making the reds and purples on his translucent wings shimmer with fire. The image took my breath. Kaitlyn had hidden his naked form behind long locks of blond hair, but I knew he had working male parts. A hot flush went through me at the memory of our heated sex in New York and the embrace where I'd felt his wing emerge.

I sat on the bench in front of the painting, took off my jacket and removed the items I'd need from the pockets. I figured Sitri's *diam* network was informing him. I wondered how specific they'd get. Hopefully he was busy. I laid out the tablet and sat up straight to focus on Sitri's image.

Something tickled my brain. Fleeting. Yes. I had touched that hair as a child, dug my fingers into it like I owned it. I recalled the silky sensation. I closed my eyes and brought back its pleasing scent. I'd pulled on it and played with it. I'd braided it, but it wouldn't stay, so I'd tried again and again, making him laugh.

I ran a fingertip over his puncture on my throat to trigger that hot pulse. It grew intense, fast. I unbuttoned my shirt and lightly caressed my left nipple. I envisioned Sitri in New York, in leather, suggestively swollen. I'd pushed my blood into his mouth and felt that smooth tongue. He'd responded, his dark eyes enflamed as he entered me and put his mouth on my throat. I imagined his fragrant wings emerging to envelop me.

Against my leg, the dossier gave off some heat. The symbols that were hidden in the patterns of Sitri's wings began to animate.

Yeah, this worked. I wanted him here, right now. I envisioned the intimacy under Montmartre cemetery, him standing behind me, pressing his hard cock against me. He'd put his hand under my breast and squeezed to enhance the sensations. He understood a woman's body. He went for the sweet spot. I leaned back, applied my fingers and opened my legs.

On the painting, the symbols came alive in different sizes and colors. I made out what sounded like words, which had a musical tone. *His* language. I wanted Sitri there, to place his mouth on my throat, to make that quick puncture and lick blood off my neck. I needed him to push into me.

I rocked a little and watched his image. The eyes, lit with fire, looked not at the little girl with her raised hand but at me. I breathed. *Find the balance.* I'd done this before. I could almost hear him whisper, "Look into the eyes. It will come to you."

Flames ran through his wings as if lightning illuminated them. The blue eyes brightened and I felt something warm move through me, followed by chills. Synesthesia, the merging of senses. Synfluence. Synthetry.

"Listen." The word was as clear as if someone was there. I held still, then heard another one, in a different language. I remembered. Sitri had told it to me once: "This is my name, in our language." I remained perfectly still. His name. His real name, in a form that couldn't cross my physical tongue. I sat up and caught it as it floated to me. I felt the chill of a caress across my throat and down my back. Symbols brightened on the painting. I wanted to touch myself, scratch my itch, but I had to *use* this, not end it. I was an opening through which invisible forces moved. I felt my climactic spasms begin, begging for friction from an equally hungry cock, but I evened my breathing, holding…holding…

Everything went still. Desire lingered but faded. The spell was over. I looked up at the painting of that red-winged warrior angel and said, "One day, I'm going to have you in *that* form! *All* in!"

I looked down at the tablet. The parallel lines of stars were already drawn.

I didn't remember even touching the pencil. This had happened before, when I'd dreamed erotically of Sitri and discovered the finished equation. He'd used the *Oraculum* to guide me. I picked up the tablet, made the calculations, and ran my fingers down the page of answers to locate the corresponding item. As usual, I didn't like it.

"Beware—an enemy is endeavoring to bring you to strife and misfortune."

I sat back and put my hand on my chest. This seemed jarringly clear. Whoever had left the dossier for me intended me harm. There was power in these pages. Apparently, Ignis could locate me through them. I touched the book and felt heat. I thought I sensed a mild buzz, like it was searching for connection.

I swallowed hard. My human father, Alexandre, had drilled me to always look beyond the obvious. I was skimming the surface. I had to think more deeply. What if my enemy was Charmaine, who'd given me things to eat that blocked Sitri? Maybe she'd told me an elaborate lie to prime me. Or, maybe it was Leith, only pretending to help.

Then I had a stunning thought. What if my enemy was *Sitri*?

Chapter Fifty-Nine

That I couldn't bear. But I made myself consider the evidence, see him in a different light. Sitri had first shown me the dossier. Maybe he hadn't given it to Portia. Maybe that, too, was a lie. I didn't really know him. Maybe I'd landed on the wrong side. I thought again about the ring. How had he *not* known it was vulnerable to *nejah* theft when I'd removed it? He'd had so much energy surrounding me and he'd known that Miegul was close. He'd been protecting me—and the ring—for years.

Or so he'd said. Maybe he'd been *waiting* for me to take it off. He'd retrieved the *Oraculum* from the fire in New York and the ring had been with it. But, no, Miegul had put the ring in his pocket and Miegul was shielded.

At this moment, *anyone* could be my enemy.

I hesitated. I caressed the dossier cover. Maybe the answer I sought was inside. Just a peek? I picked up the concave crystal to examine it. This had come from the *Lumé* water, the lake where they bathed to cleanse and sharpen their sensors. I'd used it once with the dossier successfully, but under Bodin's guidance.

What would Kaitlyn do?

She'd been bold. She'd have explored. I took a breath. If I made the wrong move, I could make everything worse. But I had resources. I placed the crystal down and tapped the leather. One look. What could it hurt? I'd do it fast.

I brushed my thumb against the edge of the fragile pages. I'd opened it before. Just one quick glance. I was curious how many pages had been removed. I'd like to see what else I might have scribbled.

I pushed my left thumb between two pages. I waited for a second for ominous vibrations.

Nothing.

I held my breath. Slowly, I opened it. Nothing. I thumbed through a few pages. Still nothing that set this dossier apart from any other book. Then something made me pause. I opened it fully and saw a detailed drawing, probably my mother's. I knew that image. Ender's locket! It was a pencil sketch, but it was exactly the locket we'd seen among Ender's effects—the items on the website. Sitri had said it held a strand of *Lumé* hair.

I peered more closely at the sketched lines that formed wings along the locket's edge. Protection. How had Ender gotten it? And how had his network missed its importance? *Or had they?* I grabbed the concave crystal and held it over the image, which reversed it. *Now* I felt something. The *Lumé* language floated. Yes, there was a force here. I tried to pull it, like with the music. I heard the faint tone of my mother's voice. She was telling me about the locket. I sensed she was giving it to me. Was it mine?

I sat up. Of course! They'd grabbed me. If I'd been wearing this locket, they'd have taken it. Maybe they'd put it online in a fake auction to signal to me.

I turned the page. I saw symbols and scribbles I didn't understand. Some looked like recipes. The crystal reversed them but failed to help. Then on a page toward the middle, I saw something familiar. I laid the crystal on it and was shocked to see it take a new form: the triangle icon with the interior spiral that Ignis used for the RIPT virus. It was from the *noea,* specifically, my mother. As if *she* was its origin.

My heart racing, I searched through what I knew: centuries ago, a rogue *Lumé* had given this concave crystal to John Dee and Edward Kelley, with powdered blood from the stash my mother had prepared that was also the source of the gem on the ring I'd lost. They'd used the crystal and powder to create a portal inside my *Oraculum* for luring angels.

I had it! The RIPT virus that had turned Nick and others into mindless, suicidal disciples derived from the *Lumé* essence. *Devotion,* not despair, inspired these mass suicides. This virus was a perversion. It was the *Lumé* essence, reversed and made into a vehicle for destruction.

Or was it?

Kaitlyn had recorded all of this in her dossier. The RIPT triangle was here. This dossier had been in Ignis hands over the past two decades, thanks to my sister. They'd used it to create the contagion. Somehow, the dossier had come back to Sitri's side. *That* mystery suddenly seemed key. Who had sent it back, and why?

I flipped through more pages and saw the handwriting change. It was a dossier—a collection of writings. My sisters had recorded things, and I'd written in it. I saw the RIPT symbol again, further back, in a distinctly different form of handwriting. I guessed it was Asha's. The author had used black traced over in red, so that the black lines seemed to glow with fire along both sides. Then the words, *Tuer la lumiére*. Kill the light. That was the Black Torch motto. Yes, this had to be Asha. She was part of this Black Torch network.

The maker is also the breaker. Kaitlyn had made the viral force. Asha or I could use it. Either of us could break it.

My ears were ringing and there was pressure in my head. Panicked, I slammed the dossier closed. I felt dizzy. I stilled my mind and sensed a presence near me. In the painting, several symbols illuminated. I looked away. This was how Raydn had dismantled my security before. He was trying again to reach me. I couldn't let him in.

I stood up. I had to get my feet on the ground. I needed answers. What was Sitri withholding?

I checked the time. Nearly 11:00 p.m. I put the crystal in my outside left pocket, and the Varian went into my jeans pocket for quick access. In the right pocket, I stuffed the dossier, and inside on the left was my weapon. The *Oraculum* would stay behind. I needed to hide it.

Chapter Sixty

Down the hall, I passed the open double doors to another room that sparked a memory: leather-bound books. The library. Good hiding place. As I stepped inside, I spotted a wall of painted *ma'lakhim* figures. It was a series of seven depictions of how these creatures shifted from human form to a nearly invisible flash of light. Only three forms were clearly male, and two of these had wings. Under them, colored bands represented the five types, and a chart showing shades of blue corresponded to each. The darkest blue was *Lumé*, so I assumed the chart was for eye color. *Ser* had a bright Azure color, like mine. But this was no time for study.

Across the room to my right, a circular staircase snaked up to an opening in the floor overhead. From being sneaky as a child, I knew that it went to a loft. I'd been forbidden to climb these steps but I'd done it, anyway, coming upon my mother, with her stunning platinum hair, gilding oils with flakes of gold. She'd yelled at me, but I'd seen her handiwork before a nanny took me away. Later, when she wasn't there, I'd crept up again to stare at the ornamented images that drew her attention more than me. Even as a child I'd understood that her art was her ruling passion.

I pushed aside a tall ladder that stood against the highest stacks and drew the eye to images of angels in winged warrior mode on the ceilings. On a lower shelf, I slid the *Oraculum* deep into a spot between two aged Latin tomes, one of which had a metal band around it that locked. This would help me to locate it later. When I replaced the ladder, ready to leave, I saw symbols pop from within gold-framed illuminated manuscript pages on the wall.

I stopped, surprised. In the crowded montage of images and words I spotted a peacock. Its beak pointed upward at an uncomfortable angle—exactly like the one in Ender's signature.

This couldn't be a coincidence. Ender was *nejah*. He wasn't a dopy dupe, as per Jack's theory, but a full partner in this apocalypse. He might be as old as Miegul. Maybe he was one of the original *Lumé* sons that had escaped the purge.

The dossier grew warm in my pocket. It was time to rejoin the *noea*.

I stepped around a bookcase and froze. At a long conference table across the room, I saw a plump, fortyish man. Glasses perched on his nose as he tapped on a keyboard. Behind him on the wall was an enormous screen, alive with blinking digital maps, charts, diagrams, and geographical images. More laptops and tablets littered the table, along with paper maps, three piles of books, and several stacks of papers. He picked up a cellphone. It resembled the one I'd taken from Nick.

I strode toward him. "Where did you get that?"

Startled, the man looked up. His eyes opened wide. "*Puis-je vous aider?*" He removed his glasses to peer at me. He wasn't a *ma'lakh*.

On the table was another phone I recognized. I pointed. "That's mine. Who gave it to you?"

"And you are… oh!" He jumped to his feet. "How did I not see it? *Pardon*. I'm so sorry. Wow!" He gave an awkward bow. "You're obviously… oh, sorry, I don't know quite how to address you. I mean, I never met you, but I know about you. Detective Brentano?"

"Please answer my question."

"They gave it…Orias…he wanted me to… I…I'm Jason Biegel. I'm the IT guy, for lack of a better word. Call me Jason. Forgive me, I've been at this all evening, trying to figure this out. I knew you were here, I just didn't know if I'd meet you, and oh, your father was so proud of you. I'm sorry about Alexandre, truly. He was such a genius, really, a… Oh, sorry, I shouldn't talk about him, I guess, I—" He picked up my phone and waved it. "We need to know about this. It's so puzzling—" He pointed the screen toward me.

I saw a bright image. "Stop!" I held out my hand. He gave me the cellphone. I looked at the screen. Among the half a dozen icons I'd seen before was an unfamiliar one that blinked a bright gold. I pointed at it. "What's this?"

He shrugged and shook his head. "I thought you'd know. I can't get it open. It's not in the settings anywhere, not even hidden ones."

I looked closely. It was a simple gold circle, like a wedding ring, but with a red inner lining. Something shadowy in the middle was too small to see. "I didn't load anything onto this phone," I said, "and it wasn't there the last time I saw it, in London. Pascher retrieved it. Did you ask him?"

His green eyes widened. "Pascher? I don't... I'm not allowed..."

"Orias gave it to you. What did he tell you?"

"He doesn't know, either. I've hacked into this other phone"— he gestured toward Nick's cellphone—"but nothing on it tells us much. He'd barely used it. Just a burner phone. It had their virus and some coded texts, mostly about you. We checked the Winternet for matching images, but this isn't there."

Nick had grabbed my phone and shouted something—"lights out"—just before he'd killed himself. Could he have pushed the icon onto my phone with some *nejah* trick? I had no clue what it meant.

I looked at Jason. "You're American."

"Canadian, actually, but, yeah, I lived in Chicago for years. Been here five years. Oh. You don't know me. I'm part of the group, the *a'ika*, like your father and Krystal. A mere mortal, but a guardian, too. We have to pass tests of perception and dedication. It took me years. I track tech trends, build models, find ancient maps, interpret codes, network with support, whatever they need...but, oh, sorry, I'm supposed to get this information down to Orias. You should come with me."

He spoke so fast I could hardly keep up. He kept looking at the door as if he expected to be caught doing something he shouldn't be.

"So you know Sitri?"

Jason's eyes widened. "Hardly! I've seen him from a distance a couple of times since I've been here. A glimpse of any *Lumé* is something we live for, but he's scary, too. One wrong word... I'm sure he'd just blot me out."

"He would?"

"You're new. You don't know the stories. But, yeah, he won't hesitate to throw a few flames."

He was right. I'd seen it.

Jason peered at me. "But you've seen him, haven't you? I've heard about New York." He waited, perhaps hoping for a crumb of gossip.

"Another time," I said.

"Oh, sure, of course. Hemfidelity and all. I shouldn't have asked."

"*Hem*fidelity?"

"The blood bond. Loyalty, protection. Death to violators."

"What?"

Jason shifted his weight from foot to foot. "Maybe we should go downstairs? Orias is waiting." He grabbed the cellphones before taking me to a tall bookcase that opened to reveal a hidden elevator. He pressed the button. As we entered, he continued. "Our caretaking preserves their secrecy. We assist with human networks, like law enforcement, accountants, lawyers, service people. The closest I get is Orias, which in itself is breathtaking. And I married a *noea*."

"You did?"

"Don't ask me why she wanted me, but she did. Our daughter, Melanie, is seven. She's missing. She'll watch out for Sheine, if they're together. They're best friends." His eyes welled up. I realized that he was barely keeping it together.

"Does Melanie have a gift?"

"She sees words, like if my wife and I are trying to communicate just with looks, she can see words passing between us. She's best with *noea* words. Makes it difficult to keep secrets."

I put my hands on my hips. "Jason, we'll find her. How does the Ignis network stack up against ours?"

"It's hard to say, but they're all over the world, like us. The *nejah* have their allies, their humans, and some *ma'lakhim*. Sometimes, like now, they attract a *Lumé*."

"Do they have a name for us?"

"I don't know. *Nejah* caught outside a shield are obliterated."

I remembered Sitri cremating the man in the cave. "The *disiono*?"

"Yeah, no-man's-land. There are zones. Like, this building is safe, but at the edges, security thins out, and then there are holes. That's how you—"

The doors opened to cooler air. I was shocked to see a huge underground area that looked like a grand drawing room, without windows. Bright lamps on gray stone walls illuminated murals depicting angelic activity with lightning and fire. Four solid red doors along one wall suggested deeper mysteries.

Chapter Sixty-One

Jason led me to set of pocket doors that opened when we came within four feet. He ushered me into another space that resembled the conference room in London, only twice the size. On the other side, I saw Arren with Bodin—or at least, his black and red wings. He braced himself against a wooden beam that ran waist-high along the wall, his back to us, wings spread out behind him. As Arren examined the feathers, clusters of red sparks jumped out. I had the impression from the way she spoke that they knew each other intimately. This was another liaison. Bodin and the wing healer.

Next to me, Jason stood transfixed. "That's a *Lumé*!" he whispered. "I've never been this close to one. Look at those wings! I know *you've* seen them, but—" As he turned toward me, he jumped back, wide-eyed. Then he bowed, stuttering, "Excuse me, sir, I'm just, I'm on my way, I'm looking for, I know that I should…I'm looking for Orias."

Pascher was behind me on my right, his eyes intense. "In the map room, waiting for you."

"Oh, you know who I… yes, of course, sir. Right away, sir. I'll just… get out of…" Jason bumped into a table as he turned to go. Seeing Bodin in that direction, he changed course, bowed again, and fled.

I looked at Pascher. "You just made his day. I hope you gave Char some time and made *her* day."

"Sitri sent her to St. Sulpice."

I raised an eyebrow. "He sent her… Wait! I'm *missing* something?"

"The heart they brought from Sacré-Cœur was a fake."

"Fake! But we found it with the—"

"It *was* there, to bait you. We think they switched it before you entered the tunnel. Portia and Char went back out."

245

I caught my breath. "Ignis still has Mary Kelly's heart?"

"We believe so."

This was serious. I zipped up my jacket. "It's not far. How should I get there?"

"You will stay here."

"But—"

"Please come with me."

I slowly unzipped and looked for Bodin, but he and Arren were gone. Had they all left without me? Didn't they realize I was an asset? I hated being held back. This "princess" role did not suit me. Walking with Pascher, I asked, "Are they on their own?"

"They have resources."

"Can't you take me over there? I can stay on the sidelines."

His raised eyebrow said he knew better. We stopped outside a closed door and Pascher cocked his head. "Shall I tell Sitri to wait until you're back?"

"He's here?"

This changed everything. The door slid open, showing me a long lamp-lit room. Sitri was at the other end, watching a live screen. I stepped inside and the door closed behind me.

Chapter Sixty-Three

Sudden silence told me this room was sealed. We were alone. Finally! My heart quickened.

I glanced at the long padded couch aimed toward three large screens on the wall to my right. I could imagine doing things with him on that. Plenty of room.

But Sitri didn't greet me. His attention was on the screen. He looked so different to me now. We were more connected than any fling would have achieved. Hemfidelity. I wondered how he viewed me. Did he *want* me to initiate something? This looked like the perfect set-up.

I slipped out of my jacket and tossed it onto the couch. *Be dangerous*, Char had said. No more waiting. I would *make* our moment. If I could shed my clothes as easily as he could, I'd have done it. I breathed in his scent.

Charmaine's voice came from one side of the four-by-six-foot split screen on which Sitri focused. From blurred images in motion, I realized she wore a body cam. She spoke in French, but I easily translated: "We've checked this place. Empty."

Portia's voice cut in from the other screen. "We see no evidence of preparation. It will not be here. At least, not soon."

Sitri crossed his arms. "You went all the way down?"

"Going there now."

I came up next to him and watched until the images went dark before I said, "But you already knew that, right?"

He turned toward me and looked down, making me wish I'd worn heels. I stood as straight as possible and pointed to the screen. "You sent away the two who keep us disconnected."

He glanced at the screen before he said, "I sent our best trackers."

I shrugged. "Yeah, okay." I touched his mark on my throat. "So, you wouldn't take this."

Sitri narrowed his eyes, but I saw the twin flames ignite in them. "They protect your interests. Yes, I disagree. I want to be able to track you. But I accept their decision."

I folded my arms. "It's *my* decision." Another flash lit his eyes as I continued. "I don't know whose advice is best, but *my* instincts aren't bad. We wouldn't have even seen Nick if I hadn't found those girls. He wasn't where anyone thought. And he wasn't exactly cooperative. But I stayed with it. I think I've shown you that I'm all in. Right?"

Sitri put a hand on my left shoulder. "It is not an action, Dianysus, no matter how selfless. Commitment is a perspective. You will *see* differently."

I raised my chin. Another lock that resisted me. "But you've given me memories. You must think—"

"You're closer." He held out his right hand, palm up. "Let me see your arm."

I offered the arm through which he'd shot fire. The redness had faded, but my hand was still slightly swollen. "It's better."

He placed his other hand lightly on top of mine. "Squeeze your fingers together."

I managed it without flinching. He peered at me. "You're brave but reckless. If Teios had erupted, you would have been caught in it."

I pulled my hand away. "I was hoping for something more like, 'thank you.' Maybe I should put it on my list. Will Teios recover?"

Sitri put his hands on his hips. "He will. How did you know you could remove a trap?"

"I didn't."

"Then why did you try?"

I hesitated. Charmaine had revealed stuff in confidence. He was right. I wasn't all in. Caught between his question and *noea* loyalty, I blocked him. "Would my mother have answered that?"

Sitri's eyebrows drew together as a brief flare of anger lit his eyes. "If she thought I should know."

I flashed the trust signal with my two fingers. "Then all you need to know is that it wasn't some crazy impulse. If you ever need it, you'd better hope I won't stand around over-thinking!"

He looked amused. "*You* over-thinking. I can't even envision that."

"So, what were you trying to tell me?"

"This." He went over to the middle screen and gestured for me to join him.

Damn! This was no way to seduce him. I had to turn this around. It was still disconcerting to be this close. His direct gaze, with those burning midnight blue eyes, lit my own fire. *We initiate*, Arren had said. I wanted to take that one short step into his arms, make him kiss me, guide his mouth to penetrate and take my blood. But his next words shifted everything.

"Sheine might have sent you something. I need to know what it is."

Ah! That's why I was in here. He thought I knew something. "How? What?"

Sitri illuminated the screen. He guided me to his right. I flinched. It was the scene in the Whitechapel tunnel. Someone had recorded it! Nick was there, alive, leaning against the wall after he'd been slammed to the ground. I was crouched down, correcting the text to his buddy on his phone.

My ears burned from a sudden flush of heat. "How did you get this?"

"Teios." Sitri reached around me to grip my right shoulder. He was close to his puncture on my throat, but my collar blocked him. The citrus fragrance was intense. "I apologize, but I need you to look closely."

I nodded. Teios had been behind me. I swallowed hard and kept watching. I knew what was coming and didn't want to see Nick's horrible suicide. I leaned into Sitri's arm. He'd sent me there to get something, so that brief time before Nick's death was clearly important.

I hugged myself and held my breath as I watched Nick grab my phone and shout, "Lights out!" His last words. Lights out for *him*. When I saw him reach toward my gun, I jerked back and averted my eyes, but I heard nothing. I looked up. Sitri had stalled the recording. I breathed out and felt myself trembling as if I were still in that tunnel. He rubbed my right arm.

"Here." Sitri's quiet voice as he bent near my ear sent a chill up my back. Without touching anything, he reversed the video to the point just before Nick had grabbed my phone. "When you showed him the icon that erased the virus in his brain, it opened him. Dorion used this channel to search for Sheine. Before it closed, we knew she was in Paris. And something came back. It came to you."

I shook my head, attuned to his hand. "I don't know. Everything happened fast. Maybe I dropped it."

"A communication. A message, or directions."

"Why to me? Why not Dorion?"

"When I know what it is, I can answer that."

The site of his puncture throbbed, as if my blood called to him. I touched it, making it sting, and felt something wet. I saw a small smear of red on my fingertip. He had to smell it.

Sitri leaned close to whisper, "Focus."

I took a breath and looked at the screen. "I remember only that Nick shot himself, and I couldn't hear anything, and Pascher grabbed me and made me go up to the street. It was all a rush. I was looking for—"

"What you received is still with you. Let it come."

The scene ran again, but slowly. I felt Sitri's warmth behind me, along my back, as I watched. When I'd flashed the icon at Nick, he'd looked at my phone. The recording stopped.

"Look at his eyes." Sitri moved several frames.

Nick's eyes shifted. The pupils dilated. A micro-expression showed his surprise, then relief and submission. In that moment, he'd become a conduit. His grab for my phone was not aggressive. He's been a puppet. His fingers went around the phone and Sitri froze the frame.

I nodded. "I see it." A thin shimmer outlined Nick's hand.

"Concentrate."

I took a breath and waited. Then I realized. Jason had shown me. "On my phone... that new icon... it must have come through him, through his hand."

"What do you see *here*?"

I heard his frustration. He wanted to see for himself. I wanted it, too. I watched, hoping for something to jump out. The shimmer briefly brightened but then faded with each new frame. Sitri stopped it just as Nick reached for the gun. I shook my head.

He pointed. "The light was Dorion's message going through. Something came back, directly afterward. It shifted the color."

I slumped, helpless. I saw nothing. But below Montmartre, after Sitri's erotic boost, I'd seen messages. Maybe that's what I needed. Maybe that's why the puncture he'd made on my throat was bleeding.

This was it. My moment. *He'll take whatever you give.* I unfastened a button on my blouse and opened my collar.

Chapter Sixty-Three

I waited a beat. Then another. I felt his tension. He knew. Would he defy the *noea*? Sitri ran two fingers down the side of my neck.

I reached back to touch the firm muscle of his thigh, and squeezed. His hand tightened on my shoulder. I wanted it to slide down to my breast. I stretched my neck, ready to turn and push my hands up his shirt, to touch his back and ignite him the way Arren had told me—*where the wings would be*. I wanted those wings wrapped around me again, while I received ecstasy from his mouth and tongue. *Take it!*

Charmaine's voice barked from the other screen. "Something's here, Sitri! Look!"

The moment collapsed. Sitri let go and stepped away. My breath went out of my body. They'd blocked me again. Frustrated, I crossed my arms and watched the other screen.

Charmaine's light picked up a shimmer from what looked like spider webs. "New tunnel below the church," she said. "Looks like the other cables. Can you see them?"

"Get out now," Sitri said. "Both of you."

Portia broke in. "I should try to rebuild this."

"Not yet. Send the coordinates and images to Orias, and come back."

They acknowledged his order and the screen went dark. I stared at it. "Cables? They're going to blow up the church from down below?"

Sitri looked at me. "Not just a church. The heart of Paris. If they take down a major international hub and threaten others, they command the world's attention."

My little patch of solid ground slipped away. "So even if we block this thing with Mayon, they could still destroy the city!"

252

Sitri studied the screen on which Nick's image was frozen as if considering his next move. I looked again but still saw nothing. Then Sitri said, "Come with me."

He turned to his right, but I stepped in front of him. "Sitri!" I raised my chin. We were *not* finished!

He looked down at my open shirt. Then he placed his left hand along my jaw to cradle my face. Glancing first at his blood mark on my throat, he looked into my eyes. I thought he would kiss me now, finally, but instead I felt something warm on my tongue that tasted delicately sweet—and familiar. A memory. I touched his hand and closed my eyes. I'd been in water. I'd been terrified. He'd pushed a finger into my mouth and I'd tasted this. Soon, I'd felt safe. Char had guessed right. He'd given me his blood. I opened my eyes.

Sitri tapped over his heart with our trust signal. "Do you understand?"

I blinked. I didn't know what to say. I think I nodded.

He cocked his head. "I was hoping for something more like, 'thank you'."

I opened my mouth in surprise. *Touché!* "I... don't... ok, no more list. I think you just erased it."

"Keep your list. I like to owe you." He ran a finger down my throat and across his mark, which flushed me with erotic heat. Then he leaned in to kiss me. I reached for him to prolong it but he pulled away and said, "Keep this simmering. The answers will come."

A door slid open, bringing a rush of noise from an adjacent room.

Chapter Sixty-Four

Sitri strode through, so I buttoned up, grabbed my jacket, and followed. I could barely process what had just happened. We were connected. He'd kissed me! But I still didn't see anything differently. And I didn't know what Sheine might have sent.

Sitri crossed to where Bodin and Nettaline were looking down at a large table a foot thick. Jason glanced at me from a computer, his eyes nearly popping from his head. I knew he was thinking, *two of them in the same room*! Not to mention Pascher and Tibreth appearing, and Orias already here, along with several winged *ma'lakhim* I didn't know. Leith leaned over Jason, reading a digital tablet. This had to be his idea of heaven.

Bodin held out a hand to me. When I was close, he gave me a shoulder hug. "I'm happy to see you have recovered," he said. "Teios will thank you when he can."

I looked down. Under a glass cover I saw a 3-D map of Paris and outlying regions. Beneath the streets and buildings were many long snake-like shadows, inter-connected. Some were gray and some nearly black. Bodin pointed. "Our tunnels, and theirs."

I could hardly believe it. "Paris sits on top of all this?"

"They are too deep to affect the city, unless they collapse. Some were in place before humans came."

Nettaline looked at me. "We can move fast when we use them. Ignis tends to place theirs—the black ones—near ours, and *avoir accès*—get access. Sometimes they do."

I saw orange, yellow, and green marks in various places. "What do these markers mean?"

"By elimination," Bodin explained, "we identified the most obvious locations for Ignis to act tonight, and selected alternatives. We drove them from Montmartre, but they will make a second attempt, maybe a third. This is an important night for them. It will come in waves until they succeed."

I knew we were dealing with two lines of attack: the *nejah's* intent to trap Mayon to immortalize Ender, and Raydn's plan to exploit this event to grab my mother. I'd recently lost my human father. This was a lot to process. I pointed at a blinking green light on the Right Bank, near the Louvre. "What's that?"

Bodin crossed his arms. "Where Kihr was last above ground."

"Kihr! You tracked him? How?"

"He volunteered to be caught. He sent signals when he could."

I looked at Pascher, but his face revealed nothing. I guessed they accepted self-sacrifice as part of their job. How did these *Lumé* command such intense devotion?

"So, you can find him?"

"We hope to. He is behind their shield now."

Sitri gestured toward Orias, who nudged Jason. He rose to his feet, looking like a pup resigned to a bath. He seemed truly frightened. Leith locked her arm in his to assist him across the room.

"Jason has developed a network of cataphiles," Sitri said. He looked at Jason. "Can you explain to Dianysus?"

Jason whispered to Leith and she guided him toward me, on the side away from Bodin. He reached for the edge of the table as Leith stepped to his other side. I winked at him and smiled. Trembling, he kept his eyes on me. I rubbed his arm. "Cataphiles? Those people who love it underground?"

His face relaxed. I'd hit the right button. "Yeah, yeah, some of them are *a'ika*. They're allowed into our...*their*... tunnels." He glanced nervously around me at Bodin. "We have regular meetings, so they were ready. When they spotted cables in a tunnel under the Louvre two days ago, they alerted us. Er, I mean..." He gestured with his chin toward Sitri.

"And what were the cables?"

"For explosives, but they're not electrical, they're not really cables, they're very thin, almost invisible, and made of something unique—"

"They're coated with pieces of us," Sitri said. "Our skin, our wings, our hair. From the trapped ones. The relays and currents use our energy."

I swallowed. I envisioned Kihr getting skinned or plucked. This was ugly.

Jason continued. "Yes, I wasn't going to, I mean... but yes, that's what it is." He'd started to tremble again. "So, the cables are difficult to see. But cataphiles know every inch of their territory. They notice the slightest changes. They're proud of being protectors. One of them, Blackbird, she spotted the first webs. She told the others and they started looking. We've found them in six tunnels so far."

I could imagine these human moles moving around in the dark with penlights on their caps, mapping the ethereal wires. I was touched.

Jason tapped the glass. "The orange lines are where we've mapped them. The new one would go here." He traced a line to St. Sulpice. "We'll plant interrupters at strategic spots."

"You've blocked them?"

"Not yet." Jason looked at Sitri as if unsure what he should say. I recalled his terror of being blotted out. Leith took over. "If we place them now, they'll know we've seen them."

"Why are we waiting?"

"Because of Sheine," Nettaline said. "We have to get her and the others out of the way. Because we are not just *blocking* the conduction."

Chapter Sixty-Five

Sitri went to the side of the map across from me. "Wherever they have Sheine, they have others who matter to us." He pointed across the room at a *ma'lakh* I didn't know. "His daughter is still missing." He looked at Jason. "And his daughter, Melanie. We must rescue them before Ignis sets off the explosives, because our blocks will redirect the force to their center." His eyes were ablaze as he looked at me. "We will tear out *their* heart."

Jason took a step back, hiding behind me. A pulse pumped in my throat. This was intense. The timing would be tricky. It was clever, but damage to the enemy at the wrong time meant significant losses for us. I sensed an urgent communication between Sitri and Bodin, too fast for me to decipher aside from a reference to "her."

Nettaline came to me. Her fear for her daughter was palpable. "Do you see anything?"

I shook my head. "Nothing unusual."

"Are you sure?"

I looked at Sitri, wishing we'd connected and he'd gotten what he needed. He watched me as well. I felt blind. I focused on the map, expecting something to jump out the way the symbols had danced in the painting upstairs. But nothing happened. Sitri had told me to keep my hunger simmering, but that wasn't easy with everyone watching me, expecting something.

I looked at the orange lines for a pattern. They were present on both banks, going up into every *arrondissement,* including Montmartre. They were thickest under the Eiffel Tower, the Arc de Triumph, the Jardin des Tuilleries, the Louvre, the Bourse, the Invalides, St. Sulpice, and even our own building. It was horrifying to imagine so much destruction. Talk about killing the light!

I shrugged. "Any hints?"

"It might be related to the icon on your phone," Jason offered.

"Didn't you bring it down here?"

A screen lit up on the wall and there it was: my phone screen with the mysterious icon. A ring with a red interior. Enlarged, I noticed something else. It wasn't a smooth ring. It looked like it had spikes on the outside edges. But this clarified nothing. The image inside it was still blurred.

I held up my hands. "It's just a circle. I mean, it could be anything." Once more I felt that forlorn sense that I'd failed. Everything had been in place. Maybe even Sheine had done her part. We'd found the right city for this impending event, and now I couldn't provide the last, most vital piece of the puzzle.

Orias came over with a piece of paper in his hand. "Maybe we can find something in this." He placed it on the glass. I recognized it. Ender's suicide note. I looked more closely. It wasn't a copy. "How did you get this?"

His expression said what I already knew: they have resources.

I leaned in. Something about the handwriting was familiar. I read it again. It was mostly blather about world domination and rising from flames, but again I spotted the way the strategically placed use of the word, "burn," formed the angel trap. Just before the peacock signature was the motto, "kill the light." I already knew this was related to my sister.

"Do you have the crystal?" Bodin asked.

I picked up my jacket and took it from the pocket. Glancing at Sitri, I saw no sign that he was concerned. I offered it to Orias, but he shook his head and leaned away.

"Oh, sorry." It was *Lumé*. He couldn't touch it.

"Remember, keep the rounded side up," said Bodin. "Otherwise it will draw energy from us instead of the letter."

I nodded and held it over the note.

"Don't let it touch the paper," Orias warned.

I moved it over the angel trap pattern first, but got nothing. I felt a shift in the air and looked up to see more *ma'lakhim* in the room. Most had wings, but primarily in muted colors or shade of gray. They seemed to be waiting.

When I hovered over the motto, I saw a flash of light. Over the peacock signature—the immortality code—the crystal magnified the image. I leaned in. There was something bright red on the chest. I wondered if it was some of the red powder given with this crystal to Kelley and Dee. Both items had *Lumé* origins. I felt a light vibration. The red spot grew bright and seemed to flood into the crystal. I had to look away. When I did, a red shape popped on the map. I blinked, trying to see it more clearly. It came into focus. The peacock. At the same time in my head, I heard a female voice: "I have what you seek. Come alone."

Chapter Sixty-Six

I nearly froze but pretended I hadn't heard it. I kept my eyes moving, searching, hoping to seem clueless. I didn't dare look at Sitri. If he knew what I'd seen, he'd lock me in my room. As a cop, I'd always advised people against going alone, too, but these were dire circumstances. It might be the only way to get the ring, or rescue Sheine, or whatever this messenger meant. But who was she and how did she know what I was looking for?

"Can I see the actual phone?" I asked.

Pascher brought it over. I felt all eyes on me as I placed it next to the note. Holding the crystal over the circular icon, I watched the red interior shimmer. The dark image inside was now clear. A peacock, its beak pointed upward. Again, the crystal flooded with crimson light. "Whoever wrote the suicide note planted this icon," I said. "I think he might have access to your blood stash. They're all related." I didn't add that I'd seen the same peacock in my mother's art and the RIPT icon in the dossier.

The dossier! That was it. I'd seen phrases in it that sounded like this note. Someone associated with that book had contacted Ender. I scanned the note again, trying to memorize its features.

Placing the crystal aside, I touched the gold ring on the phone screen. To my surprise, a spiked gold circle appeared on the map. Nettaline gasped.

Leith leaned in. "Sainte-Chapelle! That makes sense. Light's out! That place is full of stained glass windows. It's all about light!"

"And there are no cables under the Île de la Cité." Nettaline reached over the map and tapped the glass.

Bodin nodded. "It's not a target. They want to use it. They might already be there." He and Sitri exchanged glances.

Orias returned to the computer, tapped a few times, and brought up vivid images of Sainte-Chapelle. I recalled my own visit to the cavernous upstairs room. It was an ethereal place, with light coming in from fifteen different tall and ornate stained glass windows, under an intricately arched ceiling. The windows showed hundreds of biblical scenes, but what had enchanted me was the interplay of soft red, blue and yellow light. It was simultaneously warm and cold, the perfect place for a *ma'limersion*, as Bodin had called it. It would accommodate a creature with enormous wings—like Mayon.

"Kaitlyn loved the place," Nettaline observed. "She worked on the window design, and it was built for religious relics, like the true cross and the crown of thorns. That would fit with Glastonbury and Turin. If Ender wants to make a biblical splash, it works."

"That's it!" I said. "That's what the spikes on the icon are. The crown of thorns. And his peacock on the suicide note is inside this icon"—I pointed to the phone screen.

I was deflecting. This was *not* the spot I'd seen when I heard the message. My target was on the Left Bank. I hadn't forgotten what the *Oraculum* had told me before I'd understood what we faced: *You will recover your property—unexpectedly.* My path was set. I scanned the map. I already knew what stood there. I looked up into Sitri's narrowed eyes. He was watching me.

A shift in the air made me look over my shoulder. The *ma'lakhim* were still, as if collectively attuned to something.

Chapter Sixty-Seven

Several *ma'lakhim* vanished. The air seemed to close around them as they moved into it. I stole another glance at Sitri, but he was looking at Bodin. I caught a fleeting impression of a plan to attack Raydn.

I grabbed my jacket and heard the fluttering sound of the *ma'lakhim* pushing off. In seconds, the room was nearly empty.

Jason stood frozen and wide-eyed. Leith nudged him. "Go contact Blackbird and make sure they see nothing in the tunnels under Sainte-Chapelle. We must be certain." When he was gone, she looked at me. "What now?"

I grabbed Ender's suicide note. It bore a speck of *Lumé* blood. I now suspected he hadn't written it. I folded it and put it into an inside pocket.

Nettaline touched my shoulder. "You saw something."

"I need to go."

"You think Sheine sent—"

"It's too sophisticated, Nettie. Whoever is behind this has access to *Lumé* blood, the pure stuff, not from one of us."

Leith nodded. "Raydn."

Nettaline looked alarmed. "*Tu ne peux pas y aller*… You can't go to *him*!"

Leith shook her head. "It can't be his, or Sitri and Bodin would have seen it."

"Maybe they did," Nettaline responded. "Maybe that's why they left."

"I have to go." I turned and strode to the elevator. My destination was not that far. While the others headed for Sainte-Chapelle, where Miegul and Ender would try again to lure and trap Mayon, I could follow my own lead to Ignis. They had something I wanted.

And I had another advantage. The *Oraculum*. With the crystal and *my* blood, I could set up a portal and use Mayon's sigil to draw him to another spot. I'd seen Miegul set his trap for Sitri in New York: the sigil, the crystal, the portal, and *Lumé* blood. If I could draw Mayon first, we'd thwart Miegul's effort. Then Ender couldn't fuse with a *ma'lakh* and couldn't present himself as immortal. This seemed like such an obvious countermeasure I wondered why Sitri hadn't suggested it. The dossier burned in my pocket. *Beware—an enemy is endeavoring to bring you to strife and misfortune.*

I ran to the library. The place was dark now, but I recalled the spot where I'd placed the *Oraculum*. I shoved aside the book with the iron lock, but the *Oraculum* wasn't there. My heart raced. I moved several other books and scanned the shelves. I couldn't believe it. The *Oraculum* was gone!

"He made me take it."

I turned to find Jason behind me.

"Who?"

"Orias. He told me to go get it. I didn't know it was yours. When they tell you to do something, you do it!"

"Why did he want it?"

His eyes went wide. "I don't ask."

"Where is it? I need it."

Jason looked terrified.

I touched his shoulder. "Calm down. I don't breathe fire. Just show me where you put it."

"Orias has it."

I exhaled. So, Sitri had it. Plan A was done. I had to regroup. "Show me how to get to the tunnels."

"To Sainte-Chapelle?"

That would do. "Yes."

"I can set up a bike for you."

On the elevator, Jason told me that Blackbird had assured him there were no lines to explosives beneath the Île de la Cité. He also said that Charmaine and Portia had gone over to Sainte-Chapelle.

"Good. I'll see them there." I'd keep up the pretense until I was clear. *Come alone.*

We entered what looked like a large garage that held different types of vehicles. Jason led the way down another set of steps. To my dismay, Charmaine and Portia were there, dressed in leather and leaning on their bikes.

Chapter Sixty-Eight

Jason stuttered a few words before he fled back up the steps. I approached Charmaine, who looked displeased. "Pascher says you saw something on the map. From Sheine?"

"No." That was honest. But now I knew that Sitri suspected I was holding back.

"Sitri sent us to bring you over," Portia said. "Ready?"

"I'm going alone." I hoped they'd get the message. I couldn't be certain how much Charmaine might convey to Pascher.

Portia shook her head. "We don't let our sisters go solo."

Charmaine stepped closer and peered at me. "You know something."

I stood my ground.

She nodded. "I should leave. If I don't, Pascher will sense something." To Portia, she said, "She's all yours." Getting on her bike, she revved it and took off.

I had not looked for a showdown with Portia, but here it was.

"Let's not waste time," I said. "I'm not going with you and you're not coming with me."

"You will defy Sitri?"

I had a thought. "What did he tell you, exactly?"

"To come here and bring you there."

I was amused. This had happened in New York. Once again, the master of ambiguity had left himself wide open. "He didn't say when."

Portia looked doubtful. "You know what he meant."

"This is *noea* business."

She eyed me, uncertain.

"Would you stand in my mother's way?"

"Kaitlyn was—" Portia paused and narrowed her eyes. Then she

264

went to her saddlebag and took something out. Holding out her hand, she asked, "Can you see these?"

On her palm were three red capsules. I nodded. "They're not invisible."

"In fact, they are, to all but *noea*. This is Disparin. It's stronger than the Varian that Leith gave you. Varian makes you invisible only to *ma'lakhim*, not *nejah*, but Disparin covers both. Use them sparingly. They wear off in 30 minutes. We used them in St. Sulpice. This is what I have left. I think you will need them. But also take the Varian. If something goes wrong, at least your toxic blood will thwart them." She removed something from her pocket. Another Varian tablet. "If you see Sheine, give her one, too. They might already have taken her blood, but if she's still alive, this could protect her."

I accepted. Portia slipped a thin leather knife sheath from under her waistband. "This, too." She touched her throat. "For vampires. I have another." She gave me a hard look before she got on her bike. "Be careful."

I wondered if she trusted me or just wanted me to die. I looked for a way out to the street. I had to hoof it, but my destination wasn't more than half a mile from here. I climbed the steps to leave the garage. I was about to pop a Disparin when Jason opened the door to the map room and beckoned for me.

"I know a place where they have a tunnel," he said. "I've seen it. I don't know what you're doing, but if you mean to rescue Sheine… and… the others, maybe it will help."

We went to the map. Jason pointed to an area that was too far from where I wanted to go. "Any others?" I asked.

"Blackbird says she just found a weak spot. She hasn't explored it yet. It's across from the islands." He pointed.

"Okay, good to know."

"Do you know the sewer system?"

"Jason, don't try to follow me."

"I just want to show you your options." He dug into his pocket and pulled out something. "One more thing. I made these for me and my wife, for tonight. Just in case. I call it a vampulser. Take mine." In his hand was a tiny transparent disc that looked like a shirt collar button. "It sticks on your body. It's a repellant. For those… the monsters. Their vampires. It works. The cataphiles have tested them. It's the least I can do."

265

Jason trembled as he held it out to me. Clearly, he was terrified of having no resources. I folded the disc back into his hand. "No, no, you keep it."

Tears ran down his cheeks. "Please take it. I can use my wife's. It'll cover us both. Those things are in the tunnels. If that's where you're going, you'll need it. Or maybe the girls…"

I accepted and hugged him. I wanted to promise him the return of his daughter, but I couldn't lie. I really didn't know. At least I had some unique protection: poison, a shield and a repellant. In my pockets were a gun, the dossier, the suicide note, and one of the crystals. I felt like a warrior.

It was time to leave.

Chapter Sixty-Nine

I made it to the Place de la Fontaine St. Michel. The air was so moist I could hardly tell that the rain has stopped. I sensed *La Ville* holding her breath. Or maybe it was me. I looked up at the large bronze archangel in the act of slaying a writhing devil. Maybe someone from my new world had been the model. Maybe Mayon. Maybe Raydn.

Jack had taught me some undercover tricks, but I'd never used them. I didn't even know what I was dealing with. I repeated the prediction: *You will recover your property—unexpectedly.* This was the most specific—and optimistic—the *Oraculum* had ever been. But it had also warned me of an enemy.

I patted my pockets for reassurance. I did not feel invisible. Having half an hour for my shield had sounded longer than it now felt. I looked back and scanned the street. Nothing there. Nothing on the buildings above. I'd give anything to see those reddish-purple wings lit up again. Right now, I wished I were as predictable as Sitri had said. But even if he'd guessed my intent, he couldn't see me. To follow, he'd have to know where I was going. But in a way, he was with me. I was doing this for him.

Thick fog over the Seine blocked my view of Sainte-Chapelle. I hoped the *Lumé* had interrupted the *nejah* ceremony. Their mandate to protect the natural order would clash with any attempt at the *ma'limersion.* Ignis had failed for centuries. At best, they'd crammed some low-level *ma'lakhim* into human hosts, creating bloodthirsty monsters. No human had become a true immortal.

So far.

The *nejah* had taken down Teios with lightning speed. I hoped Sitri had solid shields. Whatever this tether thing was, I knew it was safe with Pascher. Yet, somehow they'd gotten past Handre, and Teios' absence gave their side advantages.

Near the foot of the statue, I saw a small shoe like those I wore. I recalled finding one of Sheine's in Glastonbury. Picking it up, I confirmed it as the other one. Sheine was close. Something rattled inside. I spilled it out and gasped. In my hand was the locket from Ender's cell! I ran my thumb over the edges and found the latch. But it wouldn't budge. I sniffed, but nothing suggested a strand of angel hair inside. I was sure this locket had once been mine. It had been left here for me. I was on the right track.

A red flash from an alley half a block away drew my attention. Walking over, I saw a set of blue double doors. One stood ajar. I was being led, but supposedly they couldn't see me. Except that I'd picked up the shoe. It must have tripped an alarm: *she's here*. I considered popping another Disparin. I discarded the shoe and slid the locket into my front jeans pocket.

Nudging the door, I listened. Nothing inside. It was dark. I wished I'd brought a flashlight. I thought I smelled blood.

A noise down the street drew me back out. I'd heard it before—the shambling gait and harsh breath of their vampires. The creature came fast around the corner. I pressed the tiny disc under my shirt. Maybe Jason's repellant worked, and maybe it didn't.

I took a step back toward the blue doors, heading for cover, but the vampire's shriek froze me in place. A thin shadowy thing jumped onto the vampire's back, grabbing its hair. I leaned against the brick wall. Another shadow leapt into the fray. Ratters! The vampire turned in a tight circle to fling them off, exuding the noxious stench of a rotting corpse. It struck me that the ratters were trying to free the trapped *ma'lakh* inside this vampire. I knew what to do.

Hugging the wall, I edged closer and withdrew Portia's dagger. I'd freed a *ma'lakh* in New York and Sitri had banished it. At the time, I hadn't understood, but now I did. To release it, I had to slit the host's throat and get out of the way.

Another ratter, aiming low, plowed into the vampire from behind and bit its leg. This set the monster into a frenzy as it swatted at its attackers. They were effective, avoiding its assault by flashing in and out of material form. Charmaine had warned that they were dangerous, but they were exciting to watch.

The vampire went to one knee, leaned down and flung a ratter off its back. It vanished, but another replaced it in a more strategic spot. I watched for them to bring this miscreant to the ground. Soon, I hoped. I didn't know how much longer the Disparin would work. If it wore off, it could alert the *diam*—and Sitri—to my location. I didn't want to distract him.

Gripping the knife hilt, I stepped closer. The vampire yelped again and I saw a rippling bulge the size of an orange beneath the strap on its neck. My target. Once the *ma'lakh* was free, the human would collapse. But I had to strike fast.

The vampire swung, bringing its arm around so fast it knocked me off my feet. I hit the pavement and rolled. I recovered, but my hand was empty. I'd lost the dagger! I looked over and saw the hilt. It was under the vampire's foot. *Putain!* I had just moments left. This wasn't going well. I had to act, *now!*

I looked for an opening, ready to spring. A ratter pushed the vampire and grabbed the dagger. Lifting it, the slinky creature plunged the blade into the vampire's throat and ripped. It grabbed at the gash and gave three sharp yelps. The oozy black substance gushed out. I looked for cover. The open door.

I ran as if the black mass were chasing me.

Inside, just past the door, I stumbled over something soft and went to the floor. From the size and the smell of blood, I knew it was a body. I scrambled away, bumping something else. A hand came over my nose and mouth with a cloth that smelled awful. I heard a familiar voice—"Gotcha!"—before my arms were pinned behind me. I fought until I went limp and things went dark.

Chapter Seventy

I heard a motor and felt padded leather. I was lying on a seat in a moving car that smelled like dirt and old sweat. I didn't know how long I'd been out, but I kept my eyes shut. I was cold. My jacket was gone and a sharp pain in my wrists told me they were bound in front. Obviously, I was visible. And I was in trouble. I should have taken that Disparin.

Two men were talking. I recognized Miegul's voice.

"...kill her first?"

"He wants her alive."

"Then we should cut her and take some blood."

"He'll know."

"He owes us."

"And he could kill us before we collect. We need him. We'll get her when he's done."

I opened my eyes a slit and saw a man with blondish hair. I couldn't believe it. Ender! I was confused. I'd expected them to be at their immortality portal. Instead, they sat across from me in a compact limo. Clearly, they hadn't yet achieved their goal. I suspected that this discussion was about me.

Ender looked in my direction. "She's awake." He moved and Miegul grabbed his arm. Ender shook him off. He came over, crouched and gripped my hair. This close, his blue eyes were startling. "Hello, bitch! Remember me? You almost killed me tonight. You've got heart." He leaned closer. "And I can't wait to eat it!"

I tried to push him away, but he forced me to sit up and knelt in front of me. I shot a look at Miegul and saw a slash across his right cheek—the result of our struggle in New York. I felt some small satisfaction.

"It won't be long now," Ender said. "We'll be meeting your father." He tapped his chest.

I seethed. "You won't succeed."

"You smug twit. You put yourself right into our hands. *You're* the bait. He'll come for you."

Miegul snorted. "She thinks she's untouchable."

I decided to bluff. He would certainly remember what had happened in New York. "Do you really think Sitri can't track me?"

"Do you really think we aren't ready?"

"You have a short memory."

Miegul leaned forward. "Home field advantage. We can fight fire with fire. So, let him come." He gestured with his head toward me. "You'll bring us one or the other. We don't care which. You just increased our odds."

My mouth went dry. I'd drastically miscalculated. If Sitri knew where I was he *would* come...right into a trap. And I had no way to warn him. "Where are you taking me?"

"To the portal, of course. Tonight's the night." I must have looked confused, because he added, "Oh, you thought it was Sainte-Chapelle? That's what we hoped with our little breadcrumbs. A nice bit of symbolism there. But we have bigger plans for Paris tonight. She will never be the same. And tomorrow we will rise from her ashes."

I looked around the car and saw crumpled leather on the seat next to Miegul. He dug into it and held up my Glock. "Looking for this?" Then he pulled out the dossier. "Or this?"

I'd been an idiot. I'd let them grab me. They'd used the vampire to herd me toward them. When I'd stumbled, they had me, despite the Disparin. And now they had all my weapons.

Ender reached for a button on my shirt and I brought my bound hands up hard into his jaw before I kicked him against the seat. He came back at me with a thin dagger, grabbing my hair to pin me. I tried to seize the dagger, but the cuffs were too tight. He leaned close to my face. "You've had one. I can smell him on you." He pulled aside my collar and found Sitri's puncture. His eyes lit up. He glanced at Miegul. "Looks fresh." Touching it, he said. "Maybe it will rub off on me, give me good luck."

He reached for the front of my jeans and pushed me into an awkward position. I tried shoving him away, but he was strong. The car hit something and jostled him off balance. I rolled away.

271

Miegul looked nervous. He pressed a button behind him and ordered, *"Aller plus vite."*

We picked up speed. I curled against the side of the car, ready to strike if Ender came at me again. I wished I could hit him with a bolt of fire.

Ender righted himself and turned to Miegul. "What now?"

Miegul leaned toward him, cupping his hand to whisper. Ender snapped out three words that I didn't understand.

"We're almost there," Miegul said. "Don't risk this."

Ender looked at me through dangerous eyes. "I'll have you later, as I'm cutting out your heart. Just deserts for the new world leader."

I lifted my chin to show him I wasn't scared. But I was. I now realized who'd torn apart Mary Kelly. I'd thought it was one of their vampires, but now I believed it was Ender. He'd done similar atrocities to women in the States before he'd been caught.

The car came to a stop and someone outside opened the door. Ender stepped out. Before Miegul followed, he looked at me and said, "You're in *our* camp now. No traitors here to help you."

He meant Alexandre, my father. He'd pretended to work with Miegul only to set him up and block his efforts. And it had worked, but Miegul had escaped.

He came at me with a black hood. I resisted, but he pinned me against the seat and got it on. Someone jerked me roughly from the car. I was led across a cold floor that felt like stone. I sensed from echoes and dampness that I was moving through a large underground space. I smelled a fragrance that reminded me of Pascher, but a dank odor smothered it. A hand pressed against my back to guide me. I repeated my mantra over and over. I *would* get what I was here for. But the thought that squeezed my heart was that the *Oraculum* had not assured me that I'd survive.

We stopped. I heard a door slide closed, then a motor. We went up. Doors opened. I was pulled for several minutes and then pushed. My right shoulder hit an obstruction, but I caught myself before I fell. Behind me, a door closed and locked. Feeling alone, I reached up to remove the hood.

Chapter Seventy-One

I wasn't locked in some rat-infested cell as I'd expected. Instead, I saw a spacious room with soft lighting, off-white walls and tall ceilings. Thick green drapes obscured windows and when I checked one for a potential escape route, I found it locked and painted over. Likewise, two others. The door was locked as well. I cursed myself for not asking Charmaine to teach me how to get past such barriers. She'd have escaped by now. I looked around for something to use to break a window, but a long table and three leather chairs too large to lift were the sole furnishings. Cupboards along the wall gave me hope, but their doors didn't budge.

From what I could tell, we'd left the city. Illuminated paintings that shimmered with gold leaf hung on the walls. I suspected I was in a country château. I tried to recall the four sites that Charmaine had mentioned to Bodin. One, I knew, was outside the city, but I couldn't remember what she'd said.

My aching wrists attested to the many mistakes I'd made this evening. I should have been more vigilant. I should have told Sitri what I'd seen on the map. I don't know why I'd thought I could do this alone. I'd learned the hard way what it meant to leave the shield. *Now* I was in the worst possible position: a weapon for Ignis...and bait for Mayon.

I estimated eight hours until the eclipse. Ender's threats to eat my heart chilled me. The legends depicted the *nejah* as ravenous cannibals. He might really do it. But they wanted me alive for now. Miegul's caution suggested that someone else was running this operation.

I went to the only window I hadn't checked and moved the heavy curtain. This one was different. I could see into an adjacent room, like a one-way mirror for interrogations. A middle-aged woman in tight jeans and a black tank top tended to three young girls who sat on a twin-size bed. Exactly the number of missing *noea* children. I peered at them and recognized Sheine, with her dark curls. She leaned against the wall, holding a doll. She wasn't bound. I wondered if Melanie was one of the other two. More importantly, I wondered why I was allowed to see this.

I thought of the Varian in my pocket. I needed to get one to Sheine. She and I were the only two with *Ser* blood that might be used to bait Mayon. But how could I connect? Despite my bonds, I felt my front pocket to determine if the capsules were still there. Miegul had taken my jacket, with the items in those pockets, but maybe not the pills. I felt a lump. The locket was still there. I thought I felt the shape of one of the red capsules. I breathed out. Now I just needed to get free of my bonds.

I thought Sheine glanced in my direction, but it was difficult to tell. She couldn't see me, anyway, through the glass. But when she pulled on her ear, I took it as a signal. She sensed I was here. The last time I'd seen her, she'd sent me an earring.

Ah! That's it. I knew what to do.

Struggling against the stiff cord around my wrists, I dug into my pocket and pulled out what felt like a tablet. It was Disparin. I tried again, but in the tight space the Varian tablet was hard to move upward against my body. I feared I might crush it into powder. I looked around for anything sharp to cut my bonds, but saw nothing obvious. I kept trying.

Finally, I maneuvered a tablet toward the top edge of my pocket. I pulled it out and held it up, with the Disparin, hoping she had some kind of ESP. But the woman who tended them moved toward her and blocked my view.

I had to get Sheine to understand. I had no idea what she'd been taught or if she even knew what these pills could do. One of the other girls looked in my direction. She resembled Jason, so I thought this must be Melanie. What had he said? She can see words in the air. I hoped this didn't require the *noea* language. I formed a mental image of what I had in mind: "Get Sheine to take what's in my hand." I held up my hand as best I could, although she couldn't actually see it. But I could. Maybe that would sharpen it for her. I imagined the pills lifting up and flying through the air. They remained in my hand.

Behind me, the door opened.

Chapter Seventy-Two

I closed the pills into my fist and turned around. A slender woman entered. She had long red hair, streaked with yellow, and wore mid-calf boots and a tight, thigh-length black dress. Her shoulders were bare and a single strap went up her bare chest to loop around her neck. Gold sparkled at her throat and ears. I knew who she was. Asha. Her face mirrored my mother's stunning perfection, but her eyes were bright blue, like mine. Presumably like our father's.

She seemed poised as she approached me, apparently unconcerned about what I might know. She was my height, although she felt taller. "*Bonsoir. S'il vous plaît, montrez-moi tes mains.*"

This was it. I'd missed my shot. She asked that I show her my hands. She would know what the Varian and Disparin were. For years, she'd been raised and trained like the others. Slowly, I raised my bound hands and opened my fingers. To my surprise, the pills were gone. I wondered if I'd dropped them but couldn't look at my feet to check.

Asha held up a small knife and cut the cord from my wrists. "Do you recognize me, Nisi?"

As I rubbed my wrists, I noticed my ring on her right hand. "I know you."

She smiled. "I'm so happy to see you alive! We looked for you everywhere."

I stared at her. This was not what I'd expected. "You abandoned me in a burning house."

Asha looked genuinely surprised. "This is the story you know? Of course I would not do this." She looked me over. "You look fine. I see no evidence of burns."

If she were telling the truth, the others were lying. If she were lying, I had to be careful. "So I'm not a prisoner? I can leave?" I pointed to the ring. "With my ring?"

She seemed surprised. "You have not seen me in years and you wish to leave?"

"I don't appreciate your thugs and rapists."

She narrowed her eyes. "You have been difficult to contact. But here you are now." She held up her hand with the ring. "And this is mine. It was made for me."

I recalled Sitri giving it to me when I was too scared to sleep. "Sitri had it. You wouldn't have given it to him."

I saw the brief flare in her eyes. "He stole it from me. But he has returned it for something he wants."

My stomach lurched. She'd seen him? I should have asked him why he'd let the ring go. It had nagged me. Now the hole in the story had put me at a disadvantage. I shook my head.

"Oh, he probably asked you to help him retrieve it." She walked around me to look through the window at the girls. "He's so persuasive, so alluring." She looked at me. "Isn't he?"

I stayed silent. A dangerous new narrative was unfolding in my blank spaces. Her voice was smooth and cultured. If she'd wanted me dead, she could have had Miegul kill me. I suspected she needed something.

Asha looked through the window at the kids. "You can see that they are fine. No one is hurt."

I flashed back to the scene in the cave. Children had died there. But did I really know who'd done it? "They'd rather be with their mothers."

She looked at me. "And that is in your hands."

There it was. I took a breath. "What do you want?"

"You will know soon." Asha swept her hand to gesture around the room at the paintings. "You recognize these? Our mother made them to embed the core sigils of the *Lumé* and *Ser*."

"Why are they here?"

Asha looked hurt. "She gave them to me, of course."

I nodded. "That's how you know Mayon's sigil. Did you show these *nejah* where Raydn was?"

She lifted her chin. "You fail to understand. The *nejah* wish only to protect themselves. They are not monsters. I am with them. No one has devoured me. It was Raydn who discovered that they did not all merit destruction. When he showed me, I agreed to help. Other *ma'lakhim* side with us. Handre was with us."

276

I couldn't mask my surprise. "But he…" Then it made sense. He'd been trying to stop me from removing Teios' trap. He'd been the traitor who'd steered the *nejah* to his *Lumé*.

Asha continued. "Handre was my mentor once, and my secret lover. For me, he won his place with the *Lumé*."

"So you could kill Teios?"

"We sought only to bring him here, to make him understand. You stopped this. And now Handre is gone. Sitri killed him."

I wanted to protest that she was wrong, but I didn't know for sure. "Raydn is here?"

"He is."

So, he was in charge. "I want to see him."

"First, you must understand the situation." Asha gestured for me to sit down. She remained standing, her hands clasped in front. I glanced at the floor near the window but didn't see either pill. I took a seat and crossed my arms.

She laughed. "So stubborn. As you always were."

"Just tell me what you want me to hear. I have other things to do."

"Maybe not after what I say."

I was sure my face showed her my doubt. I tried to look noncommittal.

"You are correct," she said, "that with our mother's codes I located Raydn. He was good to me. I wanted him back. The *nejah* helped me to free him."

I thought I saw the crack in her story. "Why didn't they just use *him* for their immortality plan?"

"Raydn is damaged. I am unable to heal him alone, so I sent you the dossier."

I sat forward. "*You* gave it back?"

"*Oui*. So you would come. Now you are here. And you know what the *noea* have hidden from you."

"No."

"You did not read it?"

I shook my head. She sat down. I kept my arms crossed. I recalled Sitri's warning to Kaitlyn that Asha had the same evil twist as the *nejah*. I'd accepted that they couldn't use her tainted blood to lure Mayon, but now I wondered.

"I was once intended to be Sitri's partner," she said. "And I loved him. Growing up, I spent so much time with him. But eventually I learned about him, about what he had done." She leaned toward me. "Do you know that he slaughtered his own children?"

She'd stabbed me. She didn't need a knife. Charmaine had hinted at secrets I didn't know.

"Of course, you don't believe me," Asha said. "You think he would not do this. If Kaitlyn were here, she would tell you, just as she told me. Or, perhaps you are not aware of *her* story?"

I leaned away, seeking solid ground. "I know enough."

Asha got up and sat in the chair next to me. A dark line around her azure irises gave her eyes a mesmerizing effect, as if she were pulling me into her pupils "I can see that you are loyal to Sitri. This can only mean you do not know. So let me tell you."

Chapter Seventy-Three

I wanted to block her words, but I was curious about my mother. I'd known for only a few days that for centuries she'd been the queen *noea*. She'd left me when I was four, but Asha had known her for far longer. This was too big a piece of my own puzzle to ignore.

Asha touched my hand. "You know that the *ma'lakhim* procreated with human women, yes? It all seemed cozy until the sons grew up and became fathers. Then the monsters arrived."

"I know all that," I interrupted. "The *ma'lakhim* wiped out their progeny, until Sitri saw Kaitlyn."

"It was worse. The *Lumé* decided to erase the entire episode, everyone who was aware of their illicit couplings. The *Ser* supported them. There was widespread slaughter."

I tried not to wince. I didn't want to think about Sitri's part.

"First, they killed their wives, and some had quite a few. This left the children vulnerable. The grown sons tried to defend themselves with alliances, but the females were helpless. There were several generations, scattered to many different places. The *ma'lakhim* hunted them down. Sitri killed his children himself. Then he helped to kill others. They called him the Slayer. No one survived him, until Kaitlyn. This was not her name then. It was Numinas."

I tried not to show a reaction. It had been another time, another moral universe. He wasn't like that now. I couldn't judge. But I was slipping over a cliff.

"I've seen the painting," I said. My mouth was dry.

"Of course you have. You were placed in front of it before you could walk. The myths have sweetened the story. But it is not sweet."

"In that painting," I said, "he looks sad."

"That is Kaitlyn's point of view. She was six. But he had come to annihilate her and everyone she loved."

"Then why didn't he?"

"Kaitlyn said she reminded him of one of his daughters. When he saw her standing there, this bold tiny girl, he could not kill her. He told her where to hide. After that, he slaughtered only the males. Some *ma'lakhim* allied with him. Raydn was one. But the *Ser* wanted to terminate all trace. They united against Sitri."

This helped redeem him a little. He'd had regrets. But, obviously, there was more. "So, that's it? Sitri let Kaitlyn go? They didn't have more contact?"

"Not for years. After Sitri got into a violent battle with a *Ser* scout, one of his wings was nearly severed. The injury froze him. He couldn't go into his human form or his energy form. He dragged himself into a cave. Two *noea* found him."

I could guess the next part. "One was Kaitlyn."

"Yes. At first, she intended to bind and disable him."

"Disable?"

"*Oui*, our mother was quite the *ma'lakh* hunter. She was brutal. Even barbaric. She made angel traps from their skin and hair. She knew how to get a trap on when the *ma'lakh* was most vulnerable. Then she'd pull him into solid form, kill him, scalp him, drain him, and cut him up."

I couldn't hide my horror. "What?"

"This is how she became a renowned healer. Angel blood is powerful. So is the meat, and especially the heart. Their hair makes amazing fabrics. She wore an angel-hair vest and belt, and made shoes from their skin."

I looked at my feet. Like these? I could hardly believe this. My mother, much beloved of the *ma'lakhim*, had once slaughtered them and used their parts? I couldn't imagine one of them cut up like a deer.

Asha continued. "So, she clamped a trap on Sitri. She knew she would have to wait to make him fully solid, because his damaged wing would make the transition too painful. She wanted him alive and strong to get the full power of his blood. She took care of him, like fattening an animal for the best meat. In the process, she realized that he was the *ma'lakh* who had spared her as a child. She owed him."

I snorted. "This sounds like a fairy tale."

Asha smiled. "I am certain it is more complicated. However this happened, they became allies."

"So, she healed him."

"And concealed him. The *Ser* were hunting him down. They knew he was injured. The *noea* did what they could, but Kaitlyn knew they required a better strategy. Invisible, she went looking for the scouts. You obviously know about this *noea* shield, since you are using it. She also poisoned her blood, in case she was caught. This is when she spotted Mayon."

I knew the rest. "She seduced him and they fell in love."

"So some stories tell us. But others diverge. If you read the dossier closely, you can see her regrets."

"About what?"

"Don't you see? Or, perhaps you *do*."

She held out her hand and I saw a small leather-bound book materialize. It was the dossier. When I looked at her in surprise, Asha said, "Sheine is not the only *noea* with this ability." She thumbed through the pages and opened it. Offering it to me, she showed me a page. "This is mine."

I glanced at it and saw a familiar image drawn in black ink. The peacock.

"I wrote down my observations," she said. "I believe that Sitri and Kaitlyn had planned Mayon's seduction together. Sitri taught her. Do you know this trick? Perhaps he has shown you?"

I sensed that Asha was fishing. I shook my head.

Asha set the dossier aside. "First, an intoxicant. Sitri taught Kaitlyn how to make it. Invisible, she could approach Mayon and trick him into drinking it. Then she would show herself to seduce him. She used a heat massage." Asha made a rubbing motion. "You float your hands over their back or the soles of their feet. It is quite sensual. Mayon could not resist. With her beauty and manipulation, she persuaded him to ally. The price was giving herself to him."

I frowned. "She didn't love him? But she stayed with him all this time."

Asha stood up. Only then did I see what I should have spotted at once. The shape of her dress formed an image. From its body to the single strap, it resembled the peacock from Ender's suicide note, with its beak pointed upward—the one I'd just seen in the dossier. There was even a cutout diamond on her chest where the eye would be. *Asha* was the peacock!

281

Chapter Seventy-Four

Asha opened her hands. A cup appeared. It contained some liquid. "Drink this," she said. "It will neutralize the Varian."

I blocked her. "No."

She set it on the chair beside me. "You still fail to understand." She leaned close. "I told you that Sitri wanted a trade. He loves Kaitlyn. He wants us to kill Mayon. What they will do tonight is *his* plan."

I felt the blood drain from my face. I looked at my hands. I couldn't listen. Sitri had said that Raydn wanted Kaitlyn. I searched for some anchor in his version.

"Raydn will show you proof, but you must be visible to him."

Asha reached for me, but I leaned away. Everything I thought I knew now felt like sand slipping through my fingers. I needed leverage. "Sitri's had access to Kaitlyn for centuries. Why now?"

"They needed a specific vehicle—one of her daughters with special skills. That was supposed to be me, but I guessed what they were planning and fled. This is why I joined Raydn's effort to stop Sitri's annihilation of the *nejah*. I tried to take you from them, for your protection, but they found you and took you back."

"No, you tricked Tariel—"

"Tariel?" Asha looked surprised. "Tricked? He is here with us, as Handre once was. You will see him."

A chill gripped me. No way! Now I was *really* lost. I fervently wished I'd stayed home in New York, that I'd never met any of these creatures, knew nothing of a sister. I wanted to be plucked out of this whole thing. I felt ill at the idea that Sitri had just been using me. Shifting everything in favor of Asha's account made me feel like a fool.

Asha walked around behind me and put her cool hands on my

shoulders. "When Sitri and Mayon imprisoned Raydn years ago, Sitri clipped his wings. To block Sitri tonight, Raydn must heal. He needs the *Lumé* blood source they used to make the ring." She held it so I could see it. "You have conduit abilities. You can help us to locate it. Raydn once knew, but they moved it."

"You have *Lumé* blood. I saw a speck of it on the peacock in the note."

"I used up what I had to move Raydn here. He needs more."

"Doesn't the ring show you?"

"It will, with your help."

Nettaline and Leith had urged me not to go to Raydn. He was dangerous. But maybe I'd been wrong. Maybe *Sitri* was the dangerous one. *Beware—an enemy is endeavoring to bring you to strife and misfortune.* Asha's tale explained why Sitri had left a hole in his security over the ring, as well as why he'd seemed annoyed that I'd burned off Teios' trap. If Sitri wanted Kaitlyn, I was of interest only as a means to that goal. Everything I thought I knew suddenly looked different, darker. Sitri had *purposely* let the ring come to Asha. He'd *wanted* Teios to be trapped. He'd killed Handre to keep him from sounding an alarm. And if he was doing this, his entire cohort was aligned with him, as well as Bodin. He'd know that Tariel was here. This also implicated Portia and Nettaline, and possibly Charmaine. Leith, too, was suspect.

I wanted to see Raydn for myself. I reached for the cup and drank the bitter liquid.

Asha seemed satisfied. "I will prepare." She slipped out of the room.

I went to the window. The room on the other side was empty. I wondered if I'd just made a supreme mistake. I felt dizzy.

Could this really be true? I reminded myself of what Alexandre had taught me: see past the surface. It's what had made me a good detective. I had to take this all in and sift through it before setting my base of operations. The right version would strip out the chaos and yield my course of action.

I searched for a memory, anything to affirm my commitment to Sitri. He'd said I'd get what I needed, and if ever I needed a solid sense of him, it was now. *Trust.* How many times had he flashed that signal to me? I sorted through what I knew. My aunt, who'd cared for me since I was four, had urged me to go with him. My father's last words were, "He found you." He'd given his life *for* Sitri's mission and my protection. He'd hidden the *Oraculum* and crystal to keep them out of *nejah* hands. Could Kaitlyn and Sitri have fooled them all?

I sat down and put my head in my hands. I'd had nightmares about fire. This supported Charmaine's story, as did my ability to endure Sitri's heat. Sitri had kissed me. He'd taken my blood. He'd given me his. He'd touched me intimately, had teased me. He'd worried when I took risks. He'd done little things for me. He'd bought me that jacket and given me a gun. He'd dressed for me. I felt that sense of his wings coming around me when I'd burned off Teios' trap. He'd done all of this just to get Kaitlyn?

No! No! No! It made no sense. I rocked against my confusion. I wanted to believe he cared for me and that others supported him for his goodness. The little *noea* girls adored him. The fox had come to him. Even Jack had begrudgingly liked him. An entire community radiated around him, putting themselves at grave risk for him. No way was Dorion duplicitous, or Pascher. Sitri hated Raydn, but I had no sense that he saw Mayon as anything but a brother. My instincts had either failed me or my sister was a supremely calculating liar.

If only I understood why he'd let the ring go. That was the stumbling block. He should have protected it. Now it was here. Why?

I looked over at the dossier. Sitri had wanted me not to read it, but I should have. I could have made my own deductions. I looked closer. A folded piece of paper stuck out about half an inch. I removed it and opened it. I stared in surprise. It was Ender's suicide note! Miegul must have given it to Asha when he found it in my pocket.

I laid it down on the chair seat and opened the dossier to Asha's writing, where I'd seen the peacock. I touched Sitri's mark on my throat. A warm sensation flowed through me. I compared the dossier to the note. There it was. I knew I'd seen it. The handwriting matched as well. This confirmed that Asha was the peacock, the symbol of immortality. She'd learned it from our mother's art. She hungered for the same thing the *nejah* wanted: power and immortality, like the angels. I looked at the flames around the peacock in the suicide note signature. Beautifully etched, they glowed red, with a yellow tint along the edges.

I sat up and put my hand to my mouth. "Oh my God!"

Stuffing the note into my pocket, I went to the door. I had to find the girls and get out. Asha wasn't just the peacock. With her red and yellow-streaked hair, *she* was the Black Torch. This whole elaborate Winternet plan was hers. A *noea* with the ravenous evil hunger of a *nejah* was orchestrating *Lights Out*. She'd used Raydn's blood to create the viral app, RIPT. I knew what the puzzling code word, "bloodshot," meant now. She would use *my* blood to lure and kill our father. *Tuer la lumiére.* Kill the light, and if she could eliminate Sitri in the bargain, so much the better. She had allied with Raydn to punish them all.

I touched my shoulder, sick at the memory of her contact. I had to get this information to Sitri. Trust meant believing in the other person, no matter how the evidence appeared. My heart said to trust. With my right hand, I made our signal.

My pocket felt warm. I rubbed my hand over it and remembered the locket. I pulled it out, shielded with my fingers so no camera could detect it. "You belong to me," I whispered. "You will open." It shimmered and appeared pliable. I imagined forcing it… No, no, not *forcing*. Nettaline had said to *pull* it. I took a breath. Then I invited whatever was inside to show itself. The locket sprang open. I stared at it. I couldn't believe I'd done it! I breathed the citrus fragrance. I didn't have to touch the strand of blond hair to know it was *Lumé*. It had to be Sitri's.

I caressed his mark on my neck and recalled that moment when we were alone. He'd run his finger over the puncture and said, "Keep this simmering." It had fresh blood. Maybe he knew where I was. Maybe he'd come.

Chapter Seventy-Five

The door was locked. I searched for Varian to reverse this potion, but my pocket was empty. No pills were on the floor. Sheine must have grabbed them all. At least the girls could get out. My fate lay in deeper penetration.

When Asha returned, Miegul was with her. On our way down, Miegul glowered at me while Asha chatted like a magician preparing a sleight-of-hand maneuver. I pretended to listen. I even smiled at Miegul, though it made me sick. If I had my way, he'd die tonight.

We returned to the underground area. This time I could see. It was not as impressive as Sitri's set-up, but the large space had a well-used appearance. I looked up at the illuminated lines of a thirty-foot diamond-shaped portal on a dark ceiling. Below it, a diamond on the stone floor mirrored it. Inside the portal was a flat-topped podium three feet wide with a red cloth across half of it. The other half supported a shoebox-size container—probably with Mary Kelly's heart.

About 30 yards away, Ender bent over a keyboard in an area with multiple screens, probably keeping track of his RIPT virus. Near him was a transparent glass cabinet that housed a set of hooks that appeared to hold collars. Angel traps! I longed to tell him that my sister was about to double-cross him. If anyone was getting a *ma'lakh* heart transplant tonight, it was she.

A set of wide double doors suggested an escape route, possibly into the tunnel that had led us here. I noted the locations of three other doors as well, and a long, wide hallway straight ahead. Behind me was the elevator that led outside. Near every door was a security camera.

Miegul left us while Asha led me into a room that felt warm enough to incubate chicks. Watching a wall-sized monitor that showed a bird's-eye-view of the city's lights was tall winged figure—a *ma'lakh*. One wing, in multiple shades of gold, was supported on a rack, where a young brunette worked on it. Barefoot and bare-chested, this *ma'lakh* covered his pale skin with only a pair of dark brown trousers. For being imprisoned for two decades, he had an impressive physique, although he lacked the *Lumé* fragrance and the bright layer that transitioned them into their incendiary form. Despite the dullness of his long bluish-gray hair, when he looked at me his eyes were full of fire.

I knew Raydn at once but didn't expect the wave of panic that hit me. I wanted to run at him and beat him with my fists. *He* had ignited the fire that had burned into my childhood trauma. He'd ripped apart my family and forced my mother away. He'd caused me endless pain and terror.

But I had to keep it together. I couldn't reveal my true intent.

My act nearly crumbled when another *ma'lakh* entered. I knew him as well, with his dark copper hair. Tariel. And he wore no trap. He *was* here by choice. When he glanced at me, I read a brief flash of surprise in his eyes. I tried to seem indifferent, as if I didn't know him.

To Tariel, Raydn said, "You see? Now we prepare." Tariel tilted his head in a half-bow, glanced at me again and left. I breathed out.

I peered at the screen and realized from lines snaking to all parts of the city just how extensive their cables were. I hoped our cataphiles had found them all. If Sitri's plan worked, this whole place would soon come down. I prayed that the girls had gotten out.

Raydn said something to the healer and she carefully lifted his wing off the rack. He drew himself up, arching both wings in a display of pride, but I sensed he was in pain. If his wings had been clipped, I knew he couldn't shift.

"Dianysus," he said with a slight bow, "we are pleased that you desire to assist." He looked me over in a way that felt invasive. I sensed that he was comparing me to my mother.

"Of course," I forced out. "Sitri lied to me. I want him to pay."

"And so he shall."

My crystal appeared in his hand. I suspected he was the *Lumé* that had betrayed his brothers by giving it to John Dee. It could pull the *Lumé* language and reveal secrets. It had shown us the location of

Mary Kelly's heart and drawn Asha's voice to me. Now Raydn wanted me to channel the location of the *Lumé* blood source that would restore his power.

Raydn held it up. "You know how to use this?"

"It got me here."

He peered at me, as if hoping for a better response. I searched for something. "I pulled *Lumé* language with it."

This got his interest. "You understood it?"

"Some of it."

Asha cut in. "She should just show us."

I glanced at her. "I'm ready."

Sitri had said that to defeat Raydn, we'd have to surprise him. What would happen, I wondered, if I ignored the safeguards? Bodin had cautioned me to hold the concave crystal with the rounded side up, to keep its energy contained. If I reversed it, I might pull a stronger force. It was a dangerous gamble, but the alternative was to play my cards with only Raydn's deck.

I had my plan. I'd draw as much force as possible into this space, maybe give Sitri a way to slide in. If nothing happened, I'd just say I was a novice. Win-win.

I reached for the crystal, but Raydn moved it away.

"I will hold it," he said. "You will do the rest."

Chapter Seventy-Six

Damn! I masked my disappointment. I had to pivot to plan B. But I had no plan B.

Raydn led us out to the room with the portal, his wings trailing behind him like a glittering cape. I noticed more activity near the computers. Two other males were over there, moving around. The glass cabinet was open. They were preparing the traps.

Asha took off the ring and placed it on the podium, near the box. She told me to stand three feet away but within the portal boundaries.

"If I can't touch anything," I said, "how do you expect me to help?"

"You shouldn't have to touch," she responded. "The location will come in the same way that you received my directions." She pointed to her head.

I suddenly realized that, once I delivered, my value would evaporate. They could kill me and still use my blood.

Tariel appeared again. I "heard" Raydn communicate but understood little. I did catch something familiar. It was Sitri's name in their language, the one he'd once told me. I now knew that this night's dark work wasn't just about Mayon. Raydn expected to kill Sitri as well. So, *he* must have disabled Teios. Of course he had. Sitri and Mayon together had crippled and caged him. He'd want revenge and a clear path to Kaitlyn. I recalled what Char had said about the connection to Sitri. If Tariel knew that code, Raydn had a dangerous advantage.

Tariel left and Raydn looked at me. "Are you ready?"

I nodded. I hoped I looked sincere, despite my racing heart.

Raydn's eyes narrowed. He reached for me. Before I could react, he placed his thumb under my collar. It hit Sitri's mark, sending sensual heat through me. I jerked back. Anger flashed in his eyes. He understood. "He has had your blood." He leaned toward me. "Have you tasted his?"

I couldn't think of a quick lie. He smiled. "You have." He laid the crystal on the podium. "This is unnecessary. We have a direct source. I can use *his* blood. How perfect."

I froze. He meant to force himself on me and take my blood. But he'd just given me plan B. I could use *myself* as a conduit for Sitri. I was inside a portal. I knew his sigil. I had his blood.

I stepped back, but Ender was there. He pulled my arms behind me. "In case you consider escape," he snarled. Miegul came into the circle. "Let's do this now. We have what we need." He pulled the cloth off the podium, exposing the three symbols that formed Mayon's sigil and awaited basting with *Ser* blood.

I looked at Raydn. "You can't break the seal." I recalled something about hemfidelity and death to violators. His angry frown confirmed it.

Asha stepped in. "He can't, but you can."

I shook my head.

Asha picked up my ring and placed it back on her finger before she looked at Miegul and said, "Bring her."

A woman entered from behind a door, leading a barefoot child with dark curls. It was Sheine. I couldn't believe it! I'd hoped she'd gotten out. Her eyes revealed nothing when she looked at me, but I was sure she was confused and scared.

Asha took her hand and brought her over to me. "Maybe this will persuade you. Break your seal or we use her." She slashed a finger across Sheine's throat.

They had me. I couldn't let them hurt this little girl, Dorion's child.

"I don't know how," I confessed.

Asha gestured toward Raydn. "Give him your blood. You know how to do *that*."

I saw the plan. He'd drink from me and use our mingled blood to pull Mayon through for Asha. This was no bumbling *nejah* design that produced vampires. This plan would merge *Lumé* and *Ser*. In a *noea* like Asha, the *ma'limersion* could actually work!

Miegul went to Asha and whispered something. She looked surprised and then pleased. "Get it."

He went to the computer area and picked up a small wooden box with a bronze latch. Dread flooded in. I'd seen it before. Miegul handed it to Asha and she opened it to show me. "Recognize it?"

A vial of blood with a purple stopper. Mine. I swallowed. Charmaine had warned me not to leave it. I wanted to grab it and smash it to the floor. I moved closer to look, but Asha stopped me. The vial lay in its red satin, exactly as Portia had placed it. Asha put the open box on the podium, next to the sigil.

I felt them watching me.

"You have no reason to honor the seal," Asha said. "Sitri did not protect this. He let you come here alone. He is not going to help you. He gave you to us."

I was cornered. "All right." I looked at Raydn. "Let Sheine go. Then I'll do what you want."

Ender relaxed his grip. It was time. I had to "unlock the door."

I shook Ender off and lunged toward the podium to grab the crystal. Asha tried to take it from me. I pulled it away, but Ender got it. He held it high and backed away. I reached for the box with my vial of blood, but Asha blocked me. Raydn grabbed for me, but I stepped on his wing and he jerked away. The crystal appeared in my hand. I turned the rounded side down and held the concave bowl toward the portal. Mentally, I pulled the three celestial symbols into Sitri's sigil.

Miegul shouted and Ender moved toward me. The crystal flew from my hand and slammed to the floor. It shattered into a hundred shards that transformed into pools of water. Pressing Sitri's puncture, I dodged Ender again, but Raydn grabbed me by the hair just as both portal outlines glowed red. The water ignited into flames.

Ender looked confused. Miegul backed away. I looked at Sheine and formed the word *run!* I touched my mouth, hoping she understood. She slipped from Asha's hand. Asha tried to catch her but stopped short of the portal's boundary. Ender, too, stayed in the hot zone. They both expected to become the host to whatever came through. I saw another man try to grab Sheine, but then he held up his hands and said, "She's gone." She'd understood me. She'd popped a Disparin and found a place to hide.

Raydn locked his arm around my throat and watched the ceiling portal. I was ready. But to my shock, it receded. No! Sitri had to come. I had no more moves. But the red lines faded into white. The flames around us sputtered.

Raydn ripped open my shirt to expose Sitri's mark. He was going to take my blood! And I'd said yes. I dug my fingers into his arm to get free. Ender pulled my hands away and wrapped a cord around one wrist. It ignited, making him jump back. I felt Raydn's dry tongue against my throat, ready to pierce. Desperate, I brought my entire weight down on his arm and jerked him off balance. I couldn't breathe, so I moved back up. His grip remained strong. I reached behind as far over his back as I could and grabbed the sensitive arch of his wing. With fingernails, I dug in, hard. His grip loosened enough for me to slip out and scramble away.

Raydn went to the podium and grabbed the vial of blood.

And then Sitri was there. Not as the warrior angel or the tornado of fire I'd seen in New York, but in human form, in his black leathers, facing Raydn.

I fervently hoped that my effort to draw him through hadn't backfired and stripped him of power. In this form, he was no match for a full-winged *Lumé*, no matter how damaged Raydn was.

Chapter Seventy-Seven

Ender backed into the shadows. Miegul had disappeared. Asha lifted her chin, looking pleased. Sitri ignored her. Even in human form, he was commanding as he addressed his foe. "She is sealed to me. If you drink that, you will die."

"There is no seal. She broke it. No consequences."

Sitri repeated his warning.

I saw Miegul stealthily approach with an angel trap. Ender was with him. I rose to my feet to warn Sitri, but he was focused on Raydn. I looked around. Where was Pascher? And the others?

Raydn gripped the vial. It gleamed with a reddish light. He popped off the stopper and held it over the sigil, slightly tipped. "Shall we let Mayon decide?"

"No!" I made a move, but Sitri held out his hand. This was *his* fight.

Raydn looked at me. "Second thoughts? Too late." He spilled some drops onto the sigil and then emptied the vial into his mouth. With a look of triumph, he smashed the glass tube on the floor. "Now she's mine. And Mayon *must* come. You lose." Then his expression changed to concern and he touched his throat. He began to gasp. Asha ran to him as he went to his knees, his wings thrashing.

Sitri shoved me back and transformed into the tall winged warrior. He shot a flaming rope that twisted around Raydn from head to toe. Asha's hair lit up. She screamed and jumped away. With a quick twist, Sitri flung Raydn to the ground, knocking over the podium, which ignited. Another rope of flames came from above. I saw red and black wings spread wide. Bodin!

Asha grabbed the unopened box and fled, beating at her yellow and red hair. *Now* she was the torch! I went after her. Tackling her to the floor, I was unprepared for her fierce resistance. She brought a stiletto around toward me, cutting into my upper arm. I punched her hard in the jaw, but my blow landed badly. She kicked me away, still trying to beat out flames. I wrenched her arm and she dropped the stiletto. We both scrambled for it. She nearly had it when it moved beyond her reach. It came to my hand.

Asha jumped to her feet, but I grabbed her right boot, tripping her. She dropped the box, which broke open. A red bag rolled out. I leapt onto her back and yanked her by the hair. The flames didn't burn me. Her right hand splayed out and I saw the ring. I brought the knife down, straight into her hand. Blood spurted and she screamed. I couldn't hold the knife and also grab the ring, so I twisted around. But when I reached for her hand, the ring was gone. I'd forgotten. She could apport things. Asha rolled, throwing me off. She was on her feet before I could stop her, and she ran down the hall.

I heard a shot, felt the *tcheyoo* of a bullet over my head and rolled to see Ender aiming at me. He fired again, missing me. I got to my feet and ran at him. He looked at his hand. The gun was gone. It was on the floor closer to me. We both dove for it. I felt it in my hand and pulled the trigger. I hit him square in the head. I breathed out, relieved. But he wasn't down. Right! He was *nejah*. Not easy to kill. I shot again and missed. He wrestled the gun from me, even as blood gushed from his wound. With Asha's stiletto, I swung hard, but he caught my hand. He pushed me onto my back and moved the blade toward my throat.

A blast of fire threw him off. Wings brushed over me as Sitri reached down, picked Ender up by his neck and slammed him against the wall. He struggled as flames emerged from his mouth. Sitri was cooking him! I got to my feet and looked for Miegul. He was *my* target. I saw him at the podium. I fired, missed, and that was it. No more bullets.

Sitri gripped my shoulder. "They've started the timer. You must leave now!"

"Sitri! Tariel is here. Be careful! I saw him! And Asha—"

I felt a tug on my arm. It was Dorion. I looked back at Sitri, but he was gone.

"Sheine's still here!" I yelled to Dorion. "We have to find her."

"She's out. And you must come, too!"

"Go after Asha! She could still pull Mayon through." I pointed toward where I'd seen her. "That way."

I looked around. Miegul had disappeared and Dorion was forcing me away. I tried to get loose. "I have to kill him!" Then I saw Miegul run through a door. He held a trap. I made a move and ran straight into Bodin. He turned me around.

The doublewide door burst into pieces as a black Escalade drove through it. The car skidded to a stop. "Get in!" It was Charmaine. "This place is going down!"

Suddenly I felt a choking sensation. Something was tight around my throat. I couldn't breathe. "Sitri!" I gasped. "Trapped!" The building began to shake and rumble. I grabbed my neck. I had to help Sitri. "Let me go!" I pointed to my neck and gasped, "Fire!" I grabbed Bodin's hand. A wall caved in and part of the ceiling crashed to the floor near us, raising a cloud of dust. I pointed again. "Fire!"

Bodin put his foot on mine and sent a bolt of heat through me. I grabbed his arms to stay steady. I was suffocating, but I gripped as hard as I could. I gestured for more. Another blast went up my arm. I felt hands behind me, supporting me while the heat burned its way to my throat. I gasped and shut my eyes. It hurt.

And then I could breathe. The tightness was gone. I went limp, coughing, feeling wings come around me as an earthquake shook the building. I could just see out, through the dust, that the ceiling had come down in the hallway where Sitri had gone. I went to my hands and knees, coughing to clear dust from my lungs. Someone lifted and carried me to the SUV. Everything hurt. I twisted around to see Bodin and Pascher on the other side of a pile of rubble. They pulled someone out. Sitri! His wing looked damaged. He wasn't getting up! More of the ceiling came down, blocking my view. I tried to scream but I had no voice.

Chapter Seventy-Eight

Charmaine sped down the tunnel. In a hoarse voice, I whispered, "Turn back! Turn back!" My ears rang so loud I could barely hear her voice. She wasn't turning around. Dust in my eyes blinded me. I held the bleeding wound on my arm. An explosion behind us brought debris down on the car. Char accelerated.

Sitri! I couldn't believe it. Miegul must have gone invisible and trapped him. I remembered Teios.

Each time I tried to speak, I coughed up dust. We finally made it out into fresh air. "Sitri!" I choked out. I thought I heard her say something but couldn't understand. She kept driving. Another explosion shook us.

I saw a dark shape ahead and made out a military-style helicopter, its lights on. Charmaine helped me out of the car and made me get on board. She climbed in after me. I took a seat and coughed violently. I rubbed my face, but grit from my hands hurt my skin.

Charmaine knelt in front of me with a first-aid kit. "Are you hit?"

I kept blinking. I pointed at my arm, where Asha had stabbed me. I rocked, unable to comprehend what had just happened. I saw Portia place a blanket over someone and tried to clear dust from my eyes to see. It was the girls. All three. They sat together on a bench. Dust coated their hair and they looked scared. But they were safe. Charmaine handed me a T-shirt the color of Sitri's eyes. "Yours is ripped. This should fit." I made a quick change.

My hands were raw from hitting the stone floor, so Charmaine helped me strap in while Portia climbed into the copilot seat. Leith was our pilot. Charmaine gave me a soft packet that smelled like fruit. "Drink this. It will cut the pain." I swallowed through fits of coughing, then closed my eyes while she wiped off my arm and applied a bandage. The ringing in my ears slowly subsided, but the chopper was loud. No point in trying to talk. Charmaine put a headset on me as we moved upward. She was talking to me, but I shook my head and pointed to my ear.

Then I heard her in my head. "He's out. They're taking him to Arren. That's all we know."

I nodded. My eyes welled up.

The side door remained open. As we lifted, I watched the ground below. Another explosion burst into a massive ball of fire and heat waves rippled through the air around us. The girls huddled together. Sheine looked at me. I tried to smile.

Charmaine went to the edge to watch. Over her shoulder, I saw illumination. "It's all going down," she said. "Their own explosives are ripping them apart." She pressed a button and the door closed. It felt like a door slamming on my quest. I'd lost Miegul, and Asha might have escaped. I'd lost the ring. This was not what I'd expected to happen.

"Okay?" Charmaine asked. I nodded. Leith looked back at me. She held up her thumb. I could barely respond. One of these women had betrayed me. Someone had given my blood to Ignis. I had to find out.

I thought about Sitri. *She is sealed to me.* He'd said he'd know when I was "all in." He'd affirmed it. I bit my lip.

Sheine got off the bench and came over to me. I removed the headset and reached to touch her face. "Thank you," I whispered. I had no doubt that she'd been my invisible assistant. She'd apported the crystal, the knife, and the gun. For a little girl, she was badass.

She held out her closed hand, as if she wanted to give me something, perhaps the leftover Varian. I opened mine to receive it. She gave me a small object. I blinked in surprise. There it was: my ring. I put my other hand to my mouth and started to laugh even as I cried. She'd apported it right off Asha's finger! *You will recover your property—unexpectedly.* I put it on and leaned as far as my seatbelt allowed to hug her.

"She also got this." Charmaine held up the red bag I'd seen roll out of the box that Asha had dropped.

I gasped. "The heart?"

Charmaine nodded. "And the dossier. Melanie brought it out." She sent Sheine back under her blanket. I leaned my head back. We'd achieved a lot this night, but at what cost? I touched Sitri's mark. There was no feeling from it now.

Chapter Seventy-Nine

I don't know how long we flew. I didn't even know what country we were in when I felt the chopper slow. I opened my eyes. The girls were asleep. Charmaine beckoned for me to look out a window to my right. It was still dark but dawn was near. We hovered over an expansive wooded property with multiple large buildings.

"Château de Porte," she said, "the doorway. A true portal. Kaitlyn designed the buildings and grounds when Mayon showed it to her. Her best art is here."

I cleared my throat and stared at the magnificent castle. "Who owns it?"

"It's in a trust. Arren set up a respite here for injured *ma'lakhim*. Below ground is a dead vault—where dead ones are preserved."

I looked at her. "What?"

"She uses them for healing."

I swallowed. "Will they bring Sitri here?"

"They just brought him in."

"Alive?"

"Yes, but badly injured. Pascher said the ceiling collapsed while he was still trapped. Damaged wing, broken bones, punctured lung. He and Bodin pulled Sitri out, but Sitri couldn't shift. They blasted through the floors to keep more from falling on him. He's in *somnotique* now. Arren is here, too. Bodin will bring the healing blood."

I sensed there was something she wasn't saying. I figured I would see for myself soon enough.

Nettaline helped us off the helicopter. The wound in my arm was killing me. In fact, everything ached, but I was pleased to see Sheine's reunion with her mother. Leith came in for hugs as well. Melanie scampered toward Jason, who rushed to meet her. I wished I were getting hugs from Sitri.

To Charmaine I said, "I have to see him. Where is he?"

"Follow me."

Jason joined us, breathless. He talked quickly as we walked toward the mansion. "Thank you so much for bringing Melanie back. You said you would and you did. I hope my vampulser helped. Are you all right? Oh, our reverse relays worked, all of them. Nothing happened in Paris. We found the cables and returned fire. The whole thing doubled back on them and crushed their operation. It was amazing to watch on the monitors! It all caved in. We're planting leads to the media that the Black Torch ended in a final mass suicide."

I stopped. "Were they all crushed out? If any survived, they could still orchestrate chaos."

"The force went out of the virus. It's just an app now that goes nowhere. Whatever fueled it is gone."

I looked at Charmaine. We both knew: Raydn was dead. I didn't know how, but something in my blood had taken him down. The assault had doubled back on him as well.

We moved toward the mansion and Jason kept talking. "The Whitechapel fire is doused and the NYPD announced the faked suicide and an extensive manhunt, so if Ender tries anything, he'll look like a fool. Nothing he set up will work. He's not immortal, he's got nothing. And there's gonna be a storm, so we won't even see the solar eclipse in Paris!"

"Ender's dead," I told him. "He's probably under all the rubble. So much for the immortal Ripper." I was still nervous about Asha and Miegul.

As soon as I walked into the great hall with its magnificent windows and chandeliers, I knew I'd been here before. I'd played here. I'd watched *ma'lakhim* come and go on a daily basis. I'd had a pet fox. But right now I had one thought only: Sitri.

Even after seeing Teios in this *somnotique* state, I wasn't prepared for Sitri's stillness. Coated in dust and fragments of concrete, he lay on a thick mattress as if he were dead. Both wings were racked and one looked broken.

I was relieved to see Arren busy with a small brush, singing in a low voice and carefully cleaning the red end feathers. "Arren?"

She looked up. "Hello, Dianysus. I'm Cypria."

"Arren's twin," Charmaine said.

"Arren will be back soon. She and Adria are evaluating the others."

I was surprised. "Others?"

Returning to her work, Cypria continued to talk. "The explosions exposed a vault where *Ignis* had imprisoned our *ma'lakhim*. We were able to save a dozen."

"Kihr?"

"Kihr, *oui*." She offered other names I didn't know.

Charmaine nodded. "Sitri suspected they would be wherever Raydn was, because he'd vamp off them to repair himself."

I went to Sitri's head and knelt, leaning over the mattress to touch his hair. His wonderful smell was gone. "Is he aware of us?"

"Probably not," Cypria said. "He went deep."

"Should he be this cold?" I recalled his concern about Teios "fading."

"In this state, they cannot generate heat. Do you know how to do this? We must first clean the feathers." To Charmaine, Cypria said, "Please bring anyone who can help. The cleaning will go faster. Then we can apply a heat blanket."

I couldn't bear to look at Sitri's crumpled left wing. Charmaine handed me a brush with soft three-inch bristles. "Just clean off the grime so they can evaluate what to do next." Then she left.

I brushed dust over Sitri's face and leaned down to kiss it. I'd give anything to have him wake up, even if it meant he'd be upset with me for going off on my own. I listened to Cypria sing. When she went to change the water, I touched my wound to get some blood and pushed it into Sitri's mouth. I didn't know if it would help but didn't think it would hurt. I shook the dust off strands of his long hair and brushed through it with my fingers before I pulled it away to clean his neck and upper back, between the wings. Leaning toward his ear, I whispered, "Now you *really* owe me and I won't let you off the hook. All in. That was the deal." I kissed him again and put my hand in his. "I love you. Come back to me." I thought his finger moved. It was so slight, I couldn't be sure, but I took it as a good sign.

I barely heard others come in. I shed my exhaustion as I worked on Sitri's wings. Both had rips and plenty of crevices for dust. Someone brought food and I ate a little. Cypria dressed my wound.

Adria suggested I get a shower, but I refused to leave. Arren returned and put a hot blanket over Sitri. I heard buckets of water being changed and women singing. Sitri never moved. Nettaline brought her instrument. Sheine was with her. Nettaline took a seat and began to play, while Sheine came over to Sitri's head. She leaned in to kiss his face. My eyes welled at the sweetness of this gesture. Returning to her mother, Sheine joined the singing.

Only when I felt the air change to announce the presence of *ma'lakhim* did I pause.

Bodin was here, with Dorion. Both were in human form. Dorion looked lost. I wondered where Pascher was. Then I realized I hadn't see Charmaine since she'd left.

Bodin felt along the back of Sitri's neck. The trap had been tight. I rubbed my own throat at the memory. He nodded to me in a reassuring way. Getting onto the mattress, he felt along the top part of the damaged wing. When he raised it higher, I saw a scar running along its base on Sitri's back. Asha had told me this story. I hadn't believed it, but the scar was proof. This wing had once nearly been torn off. Kaitlyn had healed it.

Bodin got down and looked at me. "Dianysus, you know that—"

I shook my head. "Don't say it. He's going to be fine." I sat on the mattress and put my hand on Sitri's head. "Just tell me what I need to do." I wouldn't look at Bodin, but I felt him watching me.

Teios entered with a blond male with the dark blue eyes of a *Lumé*. Teios put his hand on Sitri's head and said, "We will need space."

I got off the mattress. Bodin took me aside. "This will take some time. Will you go with me to remove the traps from the others?"

I didn't want to leave, but I saw the other *noea* exiting. Apparently this task was *Lumé* only. I suspected they had blood from their collective stash—what Raydn had tried to steal.

Sheine ran up and took my hand. She asked me in French whether she could come and then changed to English. Bodin picked her up and said, "You were such a brave girl. Of course you can join us."

We were given dark glasses, to prevent flashes of light or fire from blinding us. Sheine showed me what it must have been like for me here as a child. She was entirely comfortable with each *ma'lakh* we visited in the garden-like infirmary. She had bounced back well from the ordeal and they all enjoyed her childlike curiosity.

Arren joined us. The trapped *ma'lakhim* were mostly in near-human form, solid but winged. Some were naked. Most wore the sleeveless mantel I'd seen before, which covered them to their knees and accommodated wings. The fabric was gauzy but draped like silk, in colors that matched their wings. Arren saw me finger the fabric and said, "These *manteaux* dull their brightness, so they can be among us in this form." A dark gray one appeared on Bodin as he shifted into winged form to help me to burn off the traps. Arren applied salve to sore necks and directed a team to work on injuries. Those who could shift, did so, dissolving into a flash of light. It was exhilarating to free them.

I was so pleased to see Kihr. He seemed none-the-worse for wear and even had news. They'd kept him in a different area, so he'd seen more. He said that Asha had lost her hair and had fled into a tunnel. The *nejah* at the portal had been killed in the collapse. Bodin told him that when he was ready he would be with Teios, as *kunoui*. Kihr seemed pleased.

By the time we were finished, my hand was sore from all the fire. Yet I seemed to have lost my fear of it. When Bodin stayed to talk with the last *ma'lakh*, I took Arren aside. "Charmaine disappeared and I haven't seen Pascher. What's going on?"

She looked distressed. "You don't know?"

303

Chapter Eighty

A cold hand squeezed my heart. I had a bad feeling.

Arren glanced at Bodin before she told me. "Sitri was left vulnerable to a trap. Only his *kunoui* could have let it happen. The *Lumé* usually deal with this at once, but with Tariel—"

"Tariel? It was definitely him. I saw him."

"But Pascher was there as well. So, they are both detained, along with their *noea*, until it can be sorted out, in case there was collusion. Charmaine is in the blue wing. Go see her."

"But Sitri—"

"You can't go to him yet. You have time."

Charmaine was slumped in a chair, staring out the window. I went over to her. From her reddened eyes, I could tell she'd been crying. I pulled up a chair and sat in front of her. "What happened?"

Her face grew fierce. "Pascher did not do this!"

"I need to know what happened."

She shook her head.

I tried again. "Char, if Sitri doesn't… if he can't speak for himself, this could get very serious." I didn't need to remind her about Handre.

"I know. They will kill Pascher. And maybe me."

"Not if I can help it. Tell me whatever you can. Did Portia know Tariel was alive?"

Charmaine looked confused. "Tariel?"

"He was there, with Raydn. I saw him."

She shook her head. "She didn't. I would have known."

"I think he set up Sitri. But Portia's not in the clear for me. Someone also gave my blood to Ignis. Let's start with that. Who else had knowledge, opportunity and a motive?"

Charmaine pushed her hair back. "Potentially any of us. Maybe

Nettaline traded it for Sheine. Or Leith might have, for Nettie. Maybe Adria doesn't want you to change things. We all knew Asha before she left. And she knows our weaknesses."

"Would Portia have told anyone else about the blood, or put it where they could find it?"

Her defiance subsided but not the anger. "We're a family, and we've all trained together *against* Ignis. When you gave us the blood, we didn't think we had a mole. But when you told us you had the dossier, I knew we had trouble. Sitri didn't want you to have it because it made you vulnerable."

"How did Sitri get it from Asha? There had to be an intermediary."

Charmaine shrugged. "I don't know."

"Portia was in my room just before it appeared. So far, she's the common factor."

"She's loyal."

"That's what you said about Handre. It turns out that he was Asha's secret lover, and love can motivate treachery. How did Sitri find me? Who told him what I was doing? Again, Portia was the last one I saw and she knew I was going out alone."

Charmaine gave me a look that said I shouldn't be surprised. "Portia didn't tell him. Sitri knows you. He knew if he told you not to go on your own, you would anyway. He knew that Raydn was trying to get to you. So, he made sure he could track you. He put something on your fingers when you worked on Teios, and Orias had Jason make a GPS."

"Jason?" I touched my side. It was still in place. "The vampire repellant?"

"We told you, we don't let our sisters go solo. No one went to Sainte-Chapelle. The *ma'lakhim* stayed on you. Sitri saw your reaction to the map and knew you'd seen a location. They followed you, because they knew it would lead to Raydn and that crippling Raydn would collapse the Black Torch."

So much for being invisible.

I took her hands. "Look, Char. I guess they have to sort it out, but I'm sure that Pascher will be cleared. I don't know how much weight it will have, but I'll speak up for you both."

She wiped her eyes. "Why?"

"Because we've been through a lot together. Because you've

305

rescued me. Because Sitri needs Pascher. Because…because we don't let our sisters go solo. Good enough?"

Charmaine nodded. "Whatever you think, Portia was not a mole." Her phone chime sounded. She retrieved it and handed it to me. "Nolan has been texting."

Chapter Eighty-One

I told her I would be back when I had news. I left the room to call Jack. To my surprise, he said, "So, the eclipse got eclipsed."

"What do you mean?"

"We got Ender."

"What?"

"Apparently, he pulled the plug early."

"What are you talking about?" How could Jack possibly know?

"He wanted that big Ripper debut, but the fire—or should I say the *torch*—got him first. We think he was trying to blow up Whitechapel but got himself instead. He's in pieces. We'll run DNA to be sure, but Angel Ray Cinders ain't goin' back in handcuffs."

"Wow, that's...great!"

"Where are you?"

"France. We had some fireworks here as well but nothing like that!"

Down the hall, Arren beckoned for me.

Before I ended the call, I told Jack I wasn't going back to New York. He made a snarky comment. I said I'd keep in touch.

I was amazed how the *ma'lakhim* orchestrated these events. And Jack would get accolades, just as Sitri had said.

I strode toward Arren. "Has there been a change?"

"Bodin asks that you attend the council," she said.

"Council?"

"About Pascher and Tariel."

I stopped, surprised. "Shouldn't Sitri make this decision?"

"They want it done now."

I shook my head. "It was Tariel, and I don't want to see him."

Arren took my hand. "You have a position with the *noea*. You're Kaitlyn's daughter and…"

"And?"

"Bodin calls you Sitri's girl. You can stand in for him."

"Just kill Tariel, then. Eliminate him. I don't need to go. Tariel did this."

She squeezed my arm. "Is this what you think Sitri would do?"

I hugged myself, recalling the image of him roping Raydn with fire and frying Ender. But he hadn't actually killed Raydn. He'd even warned him. Technically, the only one responsible for Raydn's death was Raydn. I knew that Sitri had a history with Tariel. No matter how angry, he'd listen. "All right. Where are they?"

Just the idea of being near this disloyal *kunoui* made my stomach lurch. He could say nothing to change my mind. I desperately wished for Sitri's guidance. He'd be amused. *Finally*, I would accept his advice.

"They're gathering now in the courtyard. Take this." Arren placed something in my hand. It looked like a string of dark gray pearls, but they shone with so many colors I knew they were more exotic. "Kaitlyn gave it to me. I give it to you." She helped me to put them on. "May you have her wisdom."

On my way, I considered Kaitlyn's place among the *ma'lakhim*. She'd won their respect not so much for beauty as for her wit and cunning. She'd hunted and even killed them, wearing their woven hair as a chemise. She'd been formidable. And they'd respected her. I had to be direct and commanding, like her. I would do this for Sitri.

Bodin met me at the door, in his *manteau* and wings. "This is a *Lumé* council," he said. "They might dazzle you. Do not be intimidated. They are angry over this injury, but they will consider all sides."

"I don't want to do this."

He put a hand on my shoulder. "You have passed many tests. You will make the right decision. Sitri trusts you." Bodin offered his arm. I accepted and touched the necklace.

Chapter Eighty-Two

As I stepped into the flower-ringed courtyard, dimmed by thick gray clouds, I was glad that Bodin had warned me. In their natural state—the eight that were visible to me—they were very tall and slender. Each wore a *manteau* that matched his skin or wing color, and all had long hair. Relaxed, the multi-colored wings draped to the ground, but they were still startling. If this hadn't been such a solemn situation, I would have just stared in awe.

I tried to be regal, but I felt like a child. Most of these creatures had last seen me as a little girl. Their deferential bows suggested the respect they would have given to my mother. Those sitting on scattered stone benches stood. As Bodin introduced them, I tried to acknowledge each one. They moved to give me space. Multiple floral fragrances floated on the warm breeze, but the citrus scent stood out. For a moment, I wondered what Jack would say.

"Where is Sitri's cohort?" I asked Bodin.

"Not allowed."

I wanted to say they could be important witnesses, but this wasn't a human trial with human rules. The *Lumé* protocols seemed strict. If Asha were right, Sitri had processed Handre's betrayal in seconds and blasted him at once.

Bodin invited me to sit. He took the lead, addressing the others, who gathered in a circle. "Although we would usually conduct our business in our own language," he said, "we must include Dianysus. She may assist, but she may also decline. Our decision will be final and the consequences immediate. Sitri was left vulnerable. Only his *kunoui* can break the code, but two were present, so we will hear them."

The air pressure shifted as Pascher and Tariel were brought out. In human form, dressed in black, both were bound with a dark gray band that hugged their necks and ran down across their chests, pinning their upper arms. I felt anger from the *Lumé*. I understood. I had to clench my hands together to keep from rushing over to pummel Tariel. I glared at him. My heart beat so hard I couldn't breathe. Pascher looked at me briefly before staring forward. I wished I could reassure him. I was determined to see him go free.

Bodin faced them. "Sitri honored you both with his trust. I would destroy you myself, but he would want you to be heard." He looked at Tariel. "Who exposed the code?"

Tariel glanced toward me before he said, "I did, at Sitri's order."

A ripple ran through the council. I sensed consternation, even doubt. I stared at this copper-haired *ma'lakh*. He was lying. Sitri hadn't even seen him before the tunnel collapsed.

"You were with Ignis for years," shouted a chestnut-haired *Lumé*. His orange wings arched up and glowed. "You joined them! You betrayed him!"

Bodin made a gesture for quiet. I thought he was going to blast Tariel at once, but Teios, the mediator, stepped between them. He turned to Tariel. "Explain."

"Sitri has always told me to protect Dianysus first, even at cost to him."

I gripped my hands together, shaking my head.

Teios looked at Pascher. "Did you have the same mandate?"

"Yes," said Pascher. "We all did."

I put my hand to my mouth.

A *Lumé* with brilliant silver wings shouted, "He wouldn't have you break the link!"

Bodin glanced at me. To Tariel, he said, "Tell us."

I watched Tariel's quiet dignity as he related what had happened to him on the day Ignis took me. "When they trapped me, I went dark at once. I knew that Pascher would step in. They tried to turn me, but I resisted. I remained bound for a long time. Sitri tells us to stay active unless there is no other option."

I heard a collective murmur that felt like assent.

Tariel continued. "I knew that Raydn was imprisoned, but the *nejah* had recently brought him back. He freed me to obtain my help to kill Sitri." He looked at Teios. "Your *kunoui* was part of this. He made you vulnerable so they could subtract you. Then Raydn said he would use Dianysus to force me to give him access to Sitri. If I did not reveal the code, he would kill her. When I saw her there with him, I had to comply. I expected that Pascher would feel an attempted breach and shield Sitri, but with the chaos, I was able to warn Sitri myself. He ordered me to play it out. He wanted Miegul to approach him."

Pascher watched him and I could tell he agreed, but something was off. Teios noticed as well. He asked Pascher, "Is this what you saw?"

"I am the one who should be punished," Pascher said. "Tariel obeyed Sitri. I left the hole." He glanced at me as if to apologize.

"No." Tariel shook his head. "Sitri *made* the hole. He created a trap. He wanted Miegul to believe he was exposed, so he blocked us both and sent me away. When Miegul got close, Sitri attacked. But Miegul got the trap on, so Sitri could not shift when the building came down."

I stood. "Miegul's dead?"

Tariel looked at me. "Yes. Beheaded and burned."

Bodin nodded once. "I saw his body."

I put my hands to my face. I couldn't speak. My father's murder was avenged. I looked up at Tariel. The memory of that awful day when I was four washed over me. I was playing with the dossier, writing things I thought were pretty, letters and symbols that jumped out from the painting. I recalled Tariel's amusement as he watched me. Then my sister came in, distressed, and said she needed his help. She lured him away. *Disiono*. That's all it took for them to grab me. I'd *seen* Tariel trapped. The memory was so clear I was trembling.

I approached him. The fire in his cobalt eyes was present but dim. "My sister put the trap on you, didn't she? She was already with them."

He nodded. "Yes."

"But where were you when Sitri was crushed?"

"Near you. Their *ina* had followed you. Dorion and I shielded you."

Tearing up, I cleared my throat, but I could barely speak. "I came to this council hating you. I hoped to see them eliminate you." I felt Pascher's eyes on me. "But... I...believe you. Sitri would have done that. He'd have told you to take care of me first." A tear ran down my cheek.

I felt Bodin's hand on my shoulder. I turned to him. "You can't punish them. They both showed devotion to Sitri." I touched Kaitlyn's necklace. "Please don't."

Bodin bowed. "We will consider your wishes."

I sensed tension in the air, as if they were silently debating. I wanted to leave, just in case they decided against these two. Pascher's head was bowed, while Tariel held himself as if he knew he'd done the right thing, come what may. I wanted to believe the *Lumé* would be fair, but I knew they were warriors, with the mentality for swift justice. Then I saw the bindings melt off both *ma'lakhim*. Tariel, freed, put a hand on Pascher's shoulder. They looked at each other with affection, and Pascher nodded to me. I smiled through my tears.

Bodin gestured. "You will both come with me." He melted into the air. In an instant, the courtyard was empty, except for Teios. He bowed slightly, took my hand and said, "I am pleased to have you among us. Your mother would be proud." He followed the others into their alternate realm. I looked up. A storm was near. Jason was right. We wouldn't even see the eclipse. It would make no impact on any of us. The world would never know what had very nearly occurred.

When I felt the first drops, I went to the door to go back in. It was locked. I studied my palm. Waves of energy appeared to be moving toward it. *You will see differently*, Sitri had said. I put my hand on the doorknob, breathed in, and twisted. It turned easily in my hand.

Chapter Eighty-Three

Arren met me just inside with a warm hug. "That was difficult for one so young. It was the right decision. I sent word to release Charmaine and Portia. Sitri will be pleased."

"Thank you. I'm glad you advised me to go. Will Tariel replace Pascher now?"

"There might be realignments, but they are used to this. Dorion might step out to better protect and teach Sheine."

"He should. She's an asset. And I've made a decision as well."

"Yes?"

"I would like to stay here. I want to learn from you how to heal them."

Arren smiled. "It would be my honor." She touched the necklace. "Full circle, like this. Your mother taught me. I will teach you. I think you are quickly filling her shoes."

I shook my head. "I have a long way to go." We walked together down the hall. "Is Sitri better?"

"They have reset and fused his wing, but he is still cold."

"What does that mean?"

"Do you remember with Teios? We worked on him until he could push into another form?"

"Yes."

"Sitri must do this. But he still has not moved."

Her words scared me. I recalled Raydn going down. I knew from the legends that *Lumé* can die. "What if he doesn't?" I stopped and looked directly at her.

She lowered her eyes before she said, "If he does not soon ignite his own fire, we could lose him."

I shook my head as if I could erase this. "No! That can't happen."

Arren touched my arm. "The *Lumé* will try something else. We will prepare him."

When we entered the healing room, I saw that Sitri's damaged wing looked better and the grime was gone, but he was otherwise unchanged. My heart sank.

Dorion and Pehel were in human form, watching. Cypria and Nettaline were cleaning up. I took my spot by Sitri's head and smoothed back his hair to kiss him. I heard Arren tell Dorion that he and Pehel should leave the room. "Only those with *Lumé* blood can be in here now. Please ensure that no one else enters."

Arren gave me a dark blue apron that went over my head and covered me from throat to knees. "To protect your clothes from fire," she said. Nettaline smoothed my hair and braided it in back. Cypria gave me dark glasses and set out two white pottery bowls that held what looked like oil. "This will be good for your hands," she said, "for your scrapes."

Arren dipped her hands in one and let the oil drip. "This contains the heat." Cypria removed the blanket. Arren gestured to me. "You will work on his back. Only a lover should touch him there. It is sensitive, like foreskin."

"I'm not sure I qualify yet."

"You do."

Nettaline helped me to reposition the left wing to give me access. Up close, I could better see its stunning shades of purple and red feathers, even some blue. She held the bowl while I dipped my hands into the oil. It was warm and thin, like the finest olive oil. Nettaline watched me, her eyes wide, as if she could hardly believe she was allowed to be here.

"I don't know what I'm doing," I whispered, "but at least I get to touch him."

Arren and Cypria went to work on the right wing, painting it with brushes as they quietly sang in harmony. Nettaline joined in. I placed my palms in the center of Sitri's upper back. He didn't move. It was unnerving that he didn't even breathe, but I rubbed the oil onto his celestial skin. Despite its thick texture, I felt the contours of the firm muscles that anchored his wings. I massaged the scar before lightly rubbing between the wings. I imagined that he could feel it and that it brought him pleasure.

Dipping my hands again and again, I covered every inch of Sitri's back before moving to his firm buttocks. I recalled the first time I'd seen "Agent Brenner" from behind. Right then, his rounded little ass had spurred a sensual fantasy—the very one that had unlocked the *Oraculum*. I massaged the muscles and felt my way between his legs. I hoped this might wake him, but he remained still.

"Should we turn him over?" I asked. I wanted to.

"No, not with wings," Arren told me. "But cover his shoulders and as far down his chest as you can reach. Be careful. He has fractured ribs."

Nettaline held Sitri's hair out of the way as I rubbed oil into his shoulders and upper arms. When my mouth was near his ear, I whispered, "This is going on my list."

Nettaline cocked her head. "What list?"

"It's a joke. He said when I was a kid I kept a list of things he owed me."

She smiled. "You did! It was cute. Your *liste des dettes*. It amused him. He even told you to keep adding things because he liked to owe you. And you were very creative!"

I glanced at her. "Well, my *new* list is all grown up."

"We can give you ideas," Cypria said. "*S'envoyer en l'air!*"

"Yes," Arren added. "These we can teach you as well." The air sparkled with their laughter.

I hoped this mood could reach Sitri, wherever he was. I worked my way down his legs to the soles of his feet. I recalled that this, too, was a sensual zone. Despite the seriousness of this work, it aroused me. All I could think about was getting him ready for sex. Before, he'd been in human form. It had been hot, but I now imagined screwing with these fragrant wings wrapped around me. Would it be different in other ways? I worked the oil into his soles, wanting to lick the inner arches and drive him wild.

I stopped. "I feel something."

"Leave your hand there." Arren leaned toward me. "What does it feel like?"

I pressed the bottom of Sitri's right foot. "It's warm and kind of pulsing. Is that good?"

"You are sure it's not from the oil."

"It's deeper."

She pressed her hand on top of mine. "This is a good sign. He's responding to you." Placing her other hand on the back of my head, she whispered, "Love is the best healer." I blushed. Nettaline smiled.

315

She and Cypria cleared the empty bowls, while Arren touched several places on Sitri's foot. It gave me the opportunity to ask her something that had bothered me.

"You are with Bodin, right?"

She looked at me. "Yes. We are committed." She gestured toward Cypria. "We both are."

This surprised me. "They can be sealed to two?"

"If we decide, yes."

"Do you have children?"

"We do. Several generations of children and grandchildren."

"So, it didn't bother you that he—?"

She waited

I wasn't sure how to say it. "Asha told me that the *Lumé* had killed their children."

Arren's expression went dark. "She is a cruel woman."

"It's not true?"

"It is, but no doubt she made it something barbaric. The *nejah* were eating the children...alive! They would come, invisible, to take them. The *ma'lakhim* could not prevent it. Their wives begged them to end the suffering. They did, mercifully. Quickly. And it was terrible for them. They feel it still."

"Does Sitri have children? Or...?"

She shook her head. "Not since those days, except for a son who escaped the purge."

I did a double take. "One of the *nejah*...?"

"Yes."

I looked at Sitri. It now made sense that he'd spared Kaitlyn— Numinas, the child that had resembled his daughter. Her painting had captured his suffering.

Arren touched my hand. "Loving a *Lumé* is challenging. But I would not choose otherwise. They are exciting. And you have the temperament for it. Kaitlyn saw how you responded to him. She knew you could be his partner. But, she would caution you to decide with more than just your heart." She motioned with her head toward Sitri. "As would he. You are not fully sealed until you agree with the conditions."

I nodded. I didn't want to reveal that I'd broken the seal. I didn't know if it could be repaired. If only Raydn hadn't drank my blood from the vial. Whoever had brought it to him would pay a dear price.

Arren looked toward the door. "It is time."

Chapter Eighty-Four

Bodin entered, followed by Teios, with their wings and *manteaux*. Yet, they were bright. I recalled from the library chart that this was the form that transitioned into a burst of light. It suggested high energy. Their serious expressions scared me. Bodin gestured. "The *noea* must leave."

I shook my head, but Nettaline nudged me. "*Nous devons*. We have to."

"Why?"

"Dianysus, you must go," Bodin said. "This room must clear, now."

Arren took my hand.

I resisted. "What's happening?"

"This is *Lumé* business," Arren said. "Come!"

I reached down and touched Sitri's hair. He didn't stir. I was terrified that they were going to do something that would... I couldn't even think it. "We felt some heat! He's responding!"

Bodin lifted his wings and held his ground.

I shook my head. "Please, don't ..."

Arren pulled on my arm. Reluctantly, I let her guide me out. I kept my eyes on Sitri. This couldn't be my last sense of him, cold and lifeless. I thought of our encounters—his concern, his anger, his jokes, his flirting. *No!*

Just before the door shut, I spotted another *ma'lakh* in the room, on Sitri's far side. I'd seen him before—in a painting. I gasped and ran back in. Then I froze. I didn't know what to say. This was my father.

Mayon looked me over. His azure eyes, like Asha's, had a dark ring at the edges. He said something to Bodin, who looked at me. "You may stay. But you must stand away."

I backed away until I hit a wall. I kept my eyes on Mayon in his white *manteau*, although he was too bright to watch for very long. He was magnificent. I could see why my mother had been so struck. His black hair, lush and long, shone with reddish highlights, and his eyes had a fierce, fiery look. Talk about exciting! Behind him, rising high in a regal arch were the layered gray and white wings I'd seen in the painting of him, where he'd been in an ardent blood embrace with my mother. I couldn't believe I was this creature's child!

Mayon bent over Sitri, with his wings draped over his shoulders and down to the floor. He monitored the still form the way Sitri had done with Teios. Moving Sitri's hair, he worked his way down Sitri's back, between the wings, where I'd just rubbed oil.

Then I noticed two other *ma'lakhim*, nearly invisible. I guessed they were Mayon's cohorts. They obviously knew my mother, so they probably knew me. The one with transparent yellow wings and white hair handed Mayon a small bag, made from shiny fabric I couldn't identify. He glanced at me and seemed to communicate with Mayon, without words. Mayon gestured for me to come to him.

As I approached, I felt the air grow hot.

"Your hands," he said. His voice was deep. He showed me that he wanted my palms up. I did as he asked. My heart raced so fast I thought I might faint. I couldn't believe I was this close to my father. I had a thousand questions! He opened the bag and turned it. A viscous liquid came out onto my palms, much thicker than what we'd used on Sitri. It had a musky smell. Mayon rubbed it in and put some on his own hands.

"Your mother taught you this," he said. "You must be careful." Then he showed me how to hover my palms close to Sitri's skin, without contact. "Just here, between the wings. A layer of hot air will form."

I followed his lead, feeling as if every second I spent was a second more that would keep them from making a dire decision. I sensed that this was a last-ditch effort. Mayon seemed to read my thoughts. "He has come back from worse." My eyes welled up. I nodded.

It took several minutes to work up the layer of warmth he sought. When he was satisfied, I returned to the wall.

Mayon stood at Sitri's head. Teios and Bodin went to his feet.

Mayon placed his palms, fingers down, against the crown of Sitri's head. I recalled that *Ser* reflect *Lumé* fire. I'd done it myself when Sitri sent lightning at Miegul.

The *Lumé* placed their hands on the bottom of Sitri's feet. Mayon nodded once. A current shot through Sitri. Mayon tensed. Sparks flew like pyrotechnics, as the room grew even hotter. Sweat soaked my shirt under the apron.

I watched Sitri for a response. I saw none.

The white-haired *ma'lakh* pulled Mayon's hair out of the way. Mayon positioned himself for a second try. He nodded and the *Lumé* shot another a burst of fire through Sitri's inert form. Mayon reflected it, sending a wave of light through his wings that raised sparks.

Again, there was no response.

Their frowns scared me. They were losing hope.

"Once more," I begged. "Please try again. There's heat in him." I shot out from the wall and ran to Sitri. I grabbed his hair and whispered, "Don't leave me!"

Mayon watched me. Then he held out his hand. I stood and he positioned me in front of him, placing my palms against Sitri's head. He had the vanilla smell of a honeysuckle blossom. He brought his wings forward to form a sheltered space. The *Lumé* looked concerned.

"She has Kaitlyn's blood and my blood," Mayon said. "She has been in your water. She can do this."

Bodin stepped back. "If we kill her and Sitri survives, he will not forgive us."

"If you *don't* do this and he dies," I said, "*I* won't forgive you!"

I thought I saw a muscle tense in Sitri's shoulder.

Mayon pressed his hands on mine. I braced myself. When the fire shot through Sitri, I felt a painful shock in my palms that made me gasp. A bright spot appeared on his back and his left wing lifted slightly.

"Again," said Mayon. "More."

I held my breath. The next one hit harder, but Mayon kept me steady. The right wing arched up and Sitri breathed in. The left one twitched. Silently, I urged him, *get up!*

Bodin moved to Sitri's side. Brightness spread down Sitri's back as his right arm slid down to his side and his head turned to the right.

319

His other hand moved, gripping the mattress. Bodin lifted Sitri's left wing upward as Mayon gently urged me to step back. I hugged myself and held my breath. *This had to work.*

With Bodin's help, Sitri rose to his hands and knees. His head went down as his wings arched up together amid a flash of red sparks. He held still for a moment, then drew a knee forward for leverage. He reached toward me. Mayon gestured for me to approach. I grabbed Sitri's hand as tears rolled down my cheeks. He squeezed but didn't look at me. His wings fanned out as he rose to his knees and the three *Lumé* vanished.

Mayon's cohort dispersed, but he turned to me and wiped a tear off my face. "He goes now to Numinas. She will restore him." He leaned to kiss my forehead. Then he stepped away, lifted his wings and dissolved.

I went to the floor, shaking so hard I couldn't control it.

Chapter Eighty-Five

I had just taken the longest hot shower in my memory. I looked at the bed with longing, but I'd asked Charmaine to gather the *noea*. We still had loose ends—and a mole.

Rain tapped against the tall windows as I entered a spacious sitting room full of French antiques. It smelled of fresh coffee. Adria handed me a cup. I overheard Leith mention the *Lumé* council as she balanced on the arm of the gold-and-white brocade sofa on which Nettaline sat.

"*C'est incroyable!*" Nettaline said. "How amazing to have Tariel back."

"Is he here?" I asked.

Leith shook her head. "Not until Sitri allows it. And speaking of incredible, how about Mayon showing up! That must have been awesome!"

I nodded and took a seat. I couldn't yet put words to that experience.

Arren entered with a tray of pastries, followed by Portia and Charmaine. When Portia came over to me, I saw that she'd been crying. "Thank you for your kindness to Tariel."

"And for moving Pascher *out* of that precarious *kunoui* spot!" Charmaine added. She sat next to me and Nettaline threw a pillow at her.

I looked up at Portia. "Have you seen him?"

"No, but Dorion told us that the *Lumé* have cleared him. Sitri confirmed his account. He did risk himself. But he does that. Like you."

Arren asked Portia to take a seat. "As the eldest one here," she said, "I will direct this meeting. We—"

Leith waved a hand. "I mean no disrespect, but it should be me."

We all looked at her in surprise, except for Nettaline and Portia. I could tell they knew something.

Leith cleared her throat. "I wish Sitri were here to back me up, too, but we don't have a mole." She looked at me. "Well, not exactly how you're thinking. There were some clumsy moves, mostly by me, but no one betrayed us. This all started with Alexandre."

I sat up. "What?"

She held up a hand. "After you were kidnapped, Kaitlyn decided to leave, giving Alexandre custody of you." She pointed to me. I felt a stab in my stomach. I recalled the day my mother had left me behind. "She was worried that you weren't safe. She thought that if she left, Asha would think you'd died. She made the ring for you. So, that plan worked until Alexandre discovered Miegul's association with the Ripper, which led to Miegul's awareness of you and his intent to trap Sitri. Alexandre thought Asha was using Miegul to find you, and he said we should locate her. He wanted to reveal the existence of the ring and let Ignis steal it, because it would call to you." Again she pointed to me. "Then you would show us where Asha was."

I looked at the ring on my finger. "Asha said it was made for her."

"It wasn't. Your blood is in it, too. But not hers. Sitri rejected the plan, but Kaitlyn thought it could work. She knew you'd never be safe if Asha discovered you were alive."

"My father was still in touch with her?"

"Only through deeply layered codes. Then he disappeared and the intel suggested he was with Miegul. Sitri thought he might have turned. So, he went to New York. You know what happened there."

"Does she ever!" Nettaline said. I smiled and threw the pillow back at her.

Leith held up her hand. "Let me continue. As you discovered, Alexandre was still with us, but he helped stop only one part of the Black Torch operation."

"And by the way," I said, "*Asha* was the Black Torch, not Ender. She used Ender to create the network. But my father could have asked me for the ring and handed it over. Wouldn't that have been easier?"

"The Torch operation was already in motion. We think he wanted to handle it so you wouldn't start asking questions. But his associates got murdered and the FBI agent came after him, so he went undercover. No one expected Miegul to get the ring so fast, so we were off guard, but once he had it, Sitri moved forward with Alexandre's plan. We'd lost ground and they'd abducted our kids, but when they tried to grab you, you were on the plane, under shield. So, Asha called me to make a deal."

"*You?*"

Leith gestured around the room. "We all knew her. She told me she had Sheine and would trade her for you. All I had to do was put *Les Écrits*—the dossier—in your room so she could connect to you."

I crossed my arms, trying to be patient. Her behavior on the plane made sense now.

"I have no *affinité* that would network to Sitri," Leith continued, "so I was a safe choice. And I'm devoted to Sheine. Asha thought I'd be tempted. I agreed to the deal, and she told me where I could find it. But I was scared for our kids, so I told Portia to tell Sitri." She held up her hands. "He had the dossier in Montmartre. That's how he got it."

I nodded. "You made this deal while we were on the plane?"

"Yes. And when they rescued the kids that morning, Asha knew I hadn't followed through. So she upped the stakes. She sent a message that unless I complied, she would kill Sheine. I saw where Portia placed the dossier and I grabbed it to put in your room. I also left the pieces of your pages in that house near Glastonbury. But Sitri burned them before you read them. So now I was in over my head." She nodded toward Portia. "I didn't want Sitri to obliterate me, so I told Portia everything. She talked with Sitri. And, yes, he was pissed. But he decided to use it. He told me to keep Asha thinking that I was her mole. By this time, we'd tracked Ignis to Glastonbury and he'd discovered that they'd freed Raydn."

The "oh shit" moment in the cave. The memory chilled me.

"Sitri followed Miegul to London that night, and we figured he'd play off the Ripper stuff, so we had the big meeting there. But Sheine's location identified Paris. We got that, thanks to your buddy, Nick. Then our cataphiles found the explosives, so we pieced together their plan. But we couldn't locate their primary nest, where Raydn and Asha would be. And the ring. Sitri told us"—Leith gestured toward Portia—"that they'd send you a way to find it and that you'd respond, so we devised ways to track you. Personally, I doubted that you were that bold, so I goaded you, but you surprised me. And off you went."

"But who gave them the vial of my blood?"

Portia spoke up. "It was Sitri's idea."

I stared at her. "You told him about it?"

"He knew the minute we drew it. The *diam* conveyed it. And we didn't think it mattered that *he* knew. But he didn't send *your* blood to Ignis. He drank it when you took off so he could see and hear through you. Fortunately, you'd opened yourself back up to him, so it worked. Arren made something toxic to put in the vial and she left a trace of your blood on the rim and stopper, in case Raydn sniffed it. So, that was plan A, which would disable Raydn. But we didn't know if he would actually drink it."

Leith took over. "So we tried to make it enticing. When I told Asha I had it, I said we'd gotten it before Sitri gave you his, so there was no seal. Just a little lie. And I said it was pure, before you'd taken Varian."

Portia nodded. "We delayed the delivery because if Raydn had time to test it, he'd know it was a trick. It was tense! Sitri was monitoring you, and suddenly, he left. Then Bodin was gone. We were near their chateau, expecting to pull you out when Sitri signaled, but Jason told us the timers had started, so Charmaine drove in to get you."

I couldn't believe it. I shook my head. "This could all have gone so wrong!"

"Welcome to our world," said Charmaine. "You fit right in. And now your turn. Tell us what happened in there."

I gave them a brief version of the events inside, with praise for Sheine, but omitted that I'd agreed to break my seal. Now I realized that after I'd opened the way in for Sitri with the crystal, he'd spotted an opportunity to push Raydn toward the vial.

I crossed my arms. "So, that's why Mayon wasn't pulled through the portal. When Raydn poured blood on his sigil, it wasn't mine. Is he dead?"

Arren took this one. "Bodin confirmed that he is. They bound him but the poison killed him. And Bodin assured the *Lumé* council that Sitri had not done it. I made the poison and Leith delivered it."

Their teamwork impressed me. Miegul, Nick, Raydn and Angel Ray Ender had all been subtracted from the world. The Black Torch was crushed, the RIPT virus inert.

"What about Asha?" I asked. "She's still out there."

"Bald and short on allies," Portia said. "But if you are ready for another adventure…"

"No." I shook my head. "I'm ready for bed."

Nettaline stood up. "Before you go." She had a purple clipboard in her hand. I could tell that the others knew her intent. "To show our appreciation and to officially welcome you to our family—and we hope you stay—we wanted to do something special. We made you a list."

I cocked my head. "A list?"

She smiled. "To add to your *liste des dettes*—the things that Sitri owes you." She gave me the clipboard. I sensed suppressed giggles. Even Charmaine was smiling. I scanned the items but none was familiar.

Arren gestured around the room. "From our collective experience, we listed what our *ma'lakhim* can do in bed. This is your guide to celestial *faire l'amour*. Sitri will know what these items are."

Nettaline pointed at the top one. "This is my favorite. The one with lightning."

"And the floating one!" Portia added.

I laughed and thanked them. "I can't wait."

Secretly, however, I was scared that opening myself to Raydn by accepting his deal had closed off Sitri.

Chapter Eighty-Six

Over the past week, I'd settled in. I could have chosen a large apartment on an upper floor with a spectacular view, but I wanted the room my mother had used near her studio and gallery. Its French doors opened into a private garden with a bubbling fountain that soothed me. On left-behind clothing I picked up traces of Kaitlyn's rose perfume. Sometimes, I tried these items on. I'd even found a leather jacket to replace the one I'd lost.

With Arren, I'd tended the rescued *ma'lakhim*, often with Sheine's participation. It was gratifying to see them heal and move on. Pascher had come twice to report Sitri's progress and I'd sent him back with letters that included my new *liste des dettes*. Even Pascher, usually so serious, had found it amusing. I'd seen Tariel once with Portia before she'd returned with Jason and Adria to Paris. Tariel was *kunoui* again, with Pascher as Sitri's second. Pehel went to Bodin, Kihr and Tibreth to Teios. We'd burned Mary Kelly's heart to place the ashes in an urn near my father's, in the gallery. My aunt would be coming to spend time with me, and for now, the dossier, with its link to Asha, was locked away.

I'd spent hours among my mother's paintings, studying her vivid depictions of *ma'lakhim*, especially the *Ser* and *Lumé*. The colors of their wings were breathtaking. One of my favorites showed Mayon and Sitri in human form, in the garden, deep in conversation. As I'd witnessed, they had each other's backs. I'd looked at the many erotic depictions, with *noea* and their *ma'lakhim* lost in ecstasy—a *ma'lakhima sutra*. Some *noea* offered blood from their throat, a breast, or an inner thigh. *These* images were sizzling. Sitri had said that shared synthetry was the most intimate experience we could achieve. He now figured centrally into my many new fantasies.

I'd placed my favorite painting in this room. It featured me as a child, sitting on Sitri's shoulders, putting small braids into his long hair as he focused on other things. His wings were arched behind him, with morning sunlight igniting brilliant shades of red, magenta and purple.

I looked at it now by candlelight as I sat in the warm evening air near the open doors. I wore a nightgown from my mother's closet made from that silky *ma'lakhim* fabric. In the roses outside, the quick blink of a rare firefly mirrored flashes of heat lightning. *That* storm had put us behind it, but the air was still electric.

I rose to get another glass of *Vin Malique* but saw movement in the shadows at the far end of the garden. I held still. A fox sat there, watching me. I walked toward it and stopped. The fox lifted its nose, like the one in Glastonbury had done. I took another step, but it trotted away through the hedge. Behind me, I sensed a presence.

"You are a dangerous woman."

I turned around. Sitri leaned on the doorpost, framed in candlelight with his arms crossed. Barefoot, he wore snug jeans and a maroon shirt.

I strode toward him. "Yes I am! And don't you dare melt those clothes off and deprive me of the pleasure of undressing you!"

He raised his arms, ready.

I kissed him and he responded with equal ardor. His wonderful smell was restored, as if he'd just bathed in the lake, and his smooth tongue still tasted like honey. I unbuttoned his silky shirt to touch the warm skin over his chest muscles. His heartbeat reassured me. I pulled his shirt all the way off and kissed his chest. When I felt a breeze, I looked down. My nightgown had vanished. Sitri had a mischievous look. "You said nothing about *your* clothes."

I fingered his zipper, but he picked me up. As Sitri carried me to the bed, I hugged him around the neck, and he lowered me down. I rubbed his erection, still restrained in his jeans, pulling until the jeans gave way to his naked arousal. Now there were no barriers.

"Wings!" I said. "I want wings." I took his cock into my mouth and heard his appreciative moan, but he pulled away and turned around. As he walked toward the open doors, I leaned on my arm and watched his firm ass until his wings emerged and his hair grew long. He stepped outside and looked up, as if listening. I saw a bright flash. He reached up. A sizzling sound snapped through the air as his wings lifted, lit up and threw off red sparks. He'd caught the lightning!

I sat up to watch. A sparkling wave spread across his wings from the top to the tips, leaving a shimmer, before he came back inside, his body bright. *This* was my fantasy from the past few nights. My beautiful *Lumé*, naked and winged, approached me in full arousal. His eyes burned with that flickering flame I'd grown to love. I made room, opening my legs. He put a hand on my belly, which radiated a warm vibration down to my knees and up to my neck.

"First one on your list," Sitri said. "Ready?"

I reached for him. "Soooo ready!"

The buzz in my lips when he kissed me made me laugh, but he didn't let me pull away. As he probed with his tongue, a current darted from his lips to mine and down my neck to harden my nipples. I gasped. He kissed me along my neck to my breast, giving me access to his left wing. I touched the stiff bone in the arch and when I caressed the feathers, my fingertips tingled. And just as Arren had said, it made him "quite hard." He laid his head against my belly to let me experiment. While I felt my way into the soft layers, Sitri ran a finger around my vulva lips, eliciting an electrical charge that arched my back.

No wonder the *noea* had put this on the top of the list!

Sitri touched me again to spread the moisture. I felt static jump from his fingertips to my vulva. I grabbed his hair and pulled him closer. He pushed a finger into me and gave me another charge that tingled in my toes. Breathing hard, I thought I'd climax before we joined, but I remembered his lesson below Montmartre cemetery. I had to hold it and float. Synthetry! I evened my breathing and attuned myself to the vibrating currents.

As the electricity pulsed through me, I touched Sitri's wing and felt a connecting current that sent a pleasant shock. He moaned, flooding the room with his citrus scent. When I moved my fingertips on him I felt it, too. He was letting me in. I slid my hands up his back, which was the real foreskin on these creatures and he kissed my neck. Then Sitri rose to his knees and pulled me up against him. I felt buoyant, like when I'd jumped from the chopper. His wings came around me as he pushed between my legs to enter me. *All in!* I pressed down to get him in deeper.

Dropping my head back, I felt his lips caress his mark on my neck, as if preparing. He thrust in a slow rhythm that made me grip his arms. I felt the sting of his puncture as I opened to him. Hot currents zinged from my crotch and my blood moved toward his mouth. He grabbed my right breast, sending another pulse through my nipple as a delicious itch signaled the start of my climax. For a moment, I felt *his* pleasure as he took my blood. I had a wild thought of raking my fingernails over his chest, so I could draw his blood, but Sitri's hard thrusts quickened and brought a crescendo that melted my mind into my body.

He held me for several delicious minutes in his wings before he withdrew and lowered me to the bed. He lay down, his left wing covering me. I let my pleasure ripple until it receded. The fountain's tinkling water lulled me, but I fought to stay conscious. I needed to know something. I felt the wings disappear and looked at Sitri. In human form now, he watched me, the flames in his eyes at low flicker. I touched his face. "Do you know what I'm thinking?"

"I sense fear. Something bothers you."

He was right. I was afraid to ask. But I had to know. "Did I break the seal?"

Sitri looked at me for so long that I sat up in alarm. "Did I?"

"Do you want to?"

"No! I didn't...I—"

He pulled me back down and held me close. "Our *affinité* is unique. You completed the seal without knowing and you broke it under duress. But you sacrificed something dear to save a child. In this way"—he touched my heart—"we are bonded."

"So, I *did* sacrifice! I broke it!"

"Yes."

This was a blow. I felt tears welling. "Irreparably?"

"You let Raydn think he could take your blood, which assisted me. There should be no regret. And you are now in the best place to learn before you choose. A seal should be set on solid ground, in full agreement."

I swallowed and nodded. Bumping my crotch against him, I gestured between us. "What about this?"

Sitri gently turned me onto my back. "I have a long list to work through." He licked his mark, making me shudder. "Ready for another?"

I peered at him. "Another item from my list or another hot spot to extinguish?"

"Both."

About the Author

Dr. Katherine Ramsland, teaches forensic psychology at DeSales University and has published 64 books, including *Prism of the Night: A Biography of Anne Rice, The Vampire Companion, The Science of Vampires, The Mind of a Murderer, The Forensic Science of CSI, Inside the Minds of Serial Killers, The Human Predator: A Historical Chronicle of Serial Murder and Forensic Investigation, The Ivy League Killer*, and *The Murder Game*. Her book, *Psychopath*, was a #1 bestseller on the *Wall Street Journal*'s best-seller list. She has consulted for several television series, including *CSI* and *Bones,* and for numerous crime documentary production companies. She writes a regular blog for *Psychology Today* called "Shadow-boxing" and her most recent nonfiction book is *Confessions of a Serial Killer: The Untold Story of Dennis Rader, the BTK Killer.* Her first novel in the "Hearts of Darkness" series, *The Ripper Letter*, is a supernatural thriller based on Jack the Ripper lore.

Blog: **http://www.psychologytoday.com/blog/shadow-boxing**
https://www.facebook.com/Kath.ramsland/
https://twitter.com/KatRamsland

Other Mystery/Thriller Titles at Riverdale Avenue Books

Of White Snakes and Misshapen Owls:
The Charlotte Olmes Mystery Series
By Debra Hyde

The Tattered Heiress:
Book Two of the Charlotte Olmes Mystery Series
By Debra Hyde

Trashy Chic
Book One in the Bertie Mallowan Mystery Series
By Cathy Lubenski

Snarky Park
Book Two in the Bertie Mallowan Mystery Series
By Cathy Lubenski

Fifty Shades of Grey Fedora
By Robert J. Randisi

Sixers:
Volume One of the Macroglint Trilogy
By John Patrick Kavanagh

Weekend at Prism
Volume Two of the Macroglint Trilogy
By John Patrick Kavangh

Sanctuary Creek
Volume Three of the Macroglint Trilogy
By John Patrick Kavangh

Transition to Murder
By Renee James

www.ingramcontent.com/pod-product-compliance
Lightning Source LLC
Chambersburg PA
CBHW070844260626
47170CB00007B/2490